Commodore Junk

by

George Manville Fenn

Commodore Junk
by George Manville Fenn

ISBN: 978-93-59950-36-5

Published by

DOUBLE 9 BOOKS

2/13-B, Ansari Road
Daryaganj, New Delhi – 110002
info@double9books.com
www.double9books.com
Tel. 011-40042856

ABOUT THE AUTHOR

George Manville Fenn was a very productive author of novels, a writer, an editor, and an educator from England. He was born on January 3, 1831, in Pimlico, London. He mostly learned on his own; he taught himself Italian, French, and German. During the years 1851-1854, he went to Battersea Training College for Teachers and then became the head of a state school in Alford, Lincolnshire. In the early 1850s, Fenn started to write short stories and pieces for newspapers and magazines. The Old Forest Ranger, his first book, came out in 1856. Afterward, he wrote more than 100 books, many of them for teenagers and young adults. He was one of the most famous writers of his time, and his books were well-liked and read by many people. I also worked as a reporter and writer for Fenn. Among the newspapers and magazines, he worked for was The Boy's Own Paper, which he ran from 1866 to 1874. He worked hard to make children's books better and was a strong supporter of education and reading. The Englishman Fenn passed away on August 26, 1909, in Isleworth.

CONTENTS

Chapter One
Down in Devon

"Then you're a villain!"

"Nonsense, Mary; be reasonable."

"Reasonable, Captain Armstrong! I am reasonable, and I am telling you the truth. You are a villain!"

"Why, you foolish girl, what did you expect?"

"That you would be an officer and a gentleman. Once more, is it true that you are going to be married to that lady?"

"Well, you see—"

"Answer me, sir."

"Oh, well, then, yes, I suppose I am."

"Then I repeat it, James Armstrong, you are a villain!"

"What nonsense, you fierce-looking, handsome termagant! We have had our little pleasant chats and meetings, and now we'll say good-bye pleasantly. I can't help it. I have to marry; so you go and do the same, my dear, and I'll buy you a handsome wedding-dress."

"You cowardly, cold-blooded villain!"

"Come, come, my good girl; no more strong words, please don't spoil a pleasant little intimacy by a vulgar quarrel."

"Pleasant little intimacy!"

"Why, what did you expect?"

"That you were wooing me to be your wife."

"A captain in the King's Navy marry the daughter of an old wrecker, the sister of as utter a smuggling scoundrel as can be found about this port of Dartmouth!"

"When a girl gives her heart to the man who comes to her all soft words and smiles, do you think she remembers what he is? It in enough for her that she loves him, and she believes all he says. Oh, James, dear James! forgive me all I've said, and don't send me adrift like this. Tell me it isn't true."

"There, that's enough. You knew as well as I did that there was nothing serious meant, so now let's bring this meeting to an end."

"To an end?"

"Yes; you had no business to come here. But, as you have come, there are five guineas, Mary, to buy finery; and let's shake hands and say good-bye."

Captain Armstrong, a handsome man with a rather cruel-looking, thin-lipped mouth, took five golden pieces from his great, flapped, salt-box-pocketed waistcoat, gave the flowing curls of his wig a shake, and held out the money to the dark, black-eyed woman standing before him with her sun-browned cheeks lightly flushed, her full, red lips quivering, and a look of fierce passion distorting her handsome gipsy countenance, as she held out a well-shaped hand for the money.

"Come, that's right, Mary," said the captain. "You are going to be reasonable then. One, two, three, four, five—well, yes, I'll give you another guinea for being so good—six."

As he spoke he dropped the golden coins one by one into the woman's hand, smiled, glanced quickly at a door behind him, and caught her in his arms.

"There, one more kiss from those ripe red lips, and then—"

Spank!

As sharp a backhanded blow across the face as ever man received from an angry woman, and then, as the recipient involuntarily started back, Mary Dell flung the golden pieces at him, so that one struck him in the chest and the others flew tinkling across the room.

"Curse you!" cried the captain, in a low, savage voice, "this is too much. Leave this house, you low-bred shrew, and if you ever dare to come here again—"

"Dare!" cried the woman as fiercely. "I dare anything. I've not been a sailor's child for nothing. And so you think that a woman's love is to be bought and sold for a few paltry guineas, and that you can play with and throw me off as you please. Look here, James Armstrong, I wouldn't marry you now if you prayed me to be your wife—wife to such a cruel, mean coward! Faugh! I would sooner leap overboard some night and die in the deepest part of the harbour."

"Leave this house, you vixen."

"Not at your bidding, captain," cried the girl, scornfully. "Captain! Why, the commonest sailor in the king's ships would shame to behave to a woman as you have behaved to me. But I warn you," she continued, as in her excitement her luxuriant glossy black hair escaped from its comb and fell rippling down in masses—"I warn you, that if you go to church with that lady, who cannot know you as I do, I'll never forgive you, but have such a revenge as shall make you rue the day that you were born."

"Silence, woman; I've borne enough! Leave this house!"

"You thought because I was fatherless and motherless that I should be an easy prey; but you were wrong, Captain Armstrong; you were wrong. I am a woman, but not the weak, helpless thing you believed."

"Leave my house!"

"When I have told you all I think and feel, James Armstrong."

"Leave my house, woman!"

"Do you think you can frighten me by your loud voice and threatening looks?" said the girl, scornfully.

"Leave my house!" cried the Captain for the third time, furiously; and, glancing through the window as he spoke, he changed colour at the sight of a grey-haired gentleman approaching with a tall, graceful woman upon his arm.

"Ah!" cried Mary Dell, as she read his excitement aright; "so that is the woman! Then I'll stop and meet her face to face, and tell her what a contemptible creature she is going to wed."

"Curse you, leave this house!" cried the captain in a savage whisper; and catching his visitor roughly by the shoulder, he tried to pull her towards the door; but the girl resisted, and in the struggle a chair was overturned with a crash, the door was flung open, and a bluff, manly voice exclaimed—

"Why, hullo! what's the matter now?"

"What's that to you?" cried the captain, angrily, as he desisted from his efforts, and the girl stood dishevelled and panting, her eyes flashing vindictively, and a look of gratified malice crossing her face, as she saw the confusion and annoyance displayed by her ex-lover.

"What is it to me? Why, I thought there was trouble on, and I came to help."

"To intrude when you were not wanted, you mean. Now go," snarled the captain.

"No, don't go," cried the girl, spitefully. "I want you to protect me, sir, this man, this gentleman, who professed to love me, and who, now is going to be married, treats me as you see."   .

"It's a lie, woman," cried the captain, who noted that the couple whose coming had made him lower his voice had now passed after looking up at the window, and who now turned again fiercely upon the woman.

"No, it isn't a lie, Jem," said the new-comer. "I've seen you on the beach with her many a time, and thought what a blackguard you were."

"Lieutenant Armstrong, I am your superior officer," cried the captain. "How dare you speak to me like that! Sir, you go into arrest, for this speech."

"I was not addressing my superior officer," said the new-comer, flushing slightly, "but my cousin Jem. Put me in arrest, will you? Very well, my fine fellow; you're captain, I'm lieutenant, and I must obey; but if you do, next time we're ashore I'll thrash you within an inch of your life as sure as my name's Humphrey. Hang it, I'll do it now!"

He took a quick step forward; but the captain darted behind the table, and Mary caught the young man's arm.

"No, no, sir," she said in a deep voice; "don't get yourself into trouble for me. It's very true and gallant of you, sir, to take the part of a poor girl!; but I can fight my own battle against such a coward as that. Look at him, with his pale face and white lips, and tell me how I could ever have loved such a creature."

"Woman—"

"Yes, woman now," cried the girl. "A month ago no word was too sweet and tender for me. There, I'm going, James Armstrong, and I wish you joy of your new wife—the pale, thin creature I saw go by; but don't think you are done with me, or that this is to be forgotten. As for you, sir," she continued, holding out her hand, which her defender took, and smiled down frankly in the handsome dark face before him? "I sha'n't forget this."

"No," said Captain Armstrong with a sneer. "Lose one lover, pick up another. She's a nice girl, Humphrey, and it's your turn now."

Mary Dell did not loose the hand she had seized, but darted a bitterly contemptuous look upon her late lover, which made him grind his teeth as she turned from him again to the lieutenant.

"Was I not right, sir, to say he is a coward? I am only a poor-class girl, but I am a woman, and I can feel. Thank you, sir; good-bye, and if we never meet again, think that I shall always be grateful for what you have said."

At that minute there were voices heard without and the captain started and looked nervously at the door.

"I'm going, James Armstrong," said the girl; "and I might go like this; but for my own sake, not for yours, I'll not."

She gave her head a sidewise jerk which brought her magnificent black hair over her left shoulder, and then with a few rapid turns of her hands she twisted it into a coil and secured it at the back of her head.

Then turning to go, Humphrey took a step after her; but she looked up at him with a sharp, suspicious gaze.

"He told you to see me off the place?" she said quickly.

"No," cried Humphrey; "it was my own idea."

"Let me go alone," said the girl. "I want to think there is someone belonging to him who is not base. Good-bye, sir! Perhaps we may meet again."

"Meet again!" snarled the captain as the girl passed through the doorway. "Yes, I'll warrant me you will, and console yourself with your new lover, you jade."

"Look here, Jem," cried the lieutenant hotly; "officer or no officer, recollect that we're alone now, and that you are insulting me as well as that poor girl. Now, then, you say another word like that, and hang me if I don't nearly break your neck."

"You insolent—"

Captain Armstrong did not finish his sentence, for there was a something in the frank, handsome, manly face of his cousin that meant mischief, and he threw himself into a chair with an angry snarl, such as might be given by a dog who wanted to attack but did not dare.

Chapter Two
At the Cottage

"What's she a-doing of now?"

"Blubbering."

"Why, that's what you said yesterday. She ar'n't been a-blubbering ever since?"

"Yes, she have, Bart; and the day afore, and the day afore that. She's done nothing else."

"I hates to see a woman cry," said the first speaker in a low, surly growl, as he wrinkled his forehead all over and seated himself on the edge of a three-legged table in the low-ceiled cottage of old Dell, the smuggler, a roughly-built place at the head of one of the lonely coves on the South Devon coast. The place was rough, for it had been built at different times, of wreckwood which had come ashore; but the dwelling was picturesque outside, and quaint, nautical, and deliriously clean within, where Abel Dell, Mary's twin brother, a short, dark young fellow, singularly like his sister, sat upon an old sea-chest forming a netting-needle with a big clasp-knife, and his brow was also covered with the lines of trouble.

He was a good-looking, sun-browned little fellow; and as he sat there in his big fisher-boots thrust down nearly to the ankle, and a scarlet worsted cap upon his black, crisp curls, his canvas petticoat and blue shirt made him a study of which a modern artist would have been glad; but I the early days of King George the First gentlemen of the palette and brush did not set up white umbrellas in sheltered coves and turn the inhabitants into models, so Abel Dell had not been transferred to canvas, and went on carving his hardwood needle without looking up at the man he called Bart.

There was not much lost, for Bartholomew Wrigley, at the age of thirty—wrecker, smuggler, fisherman, sea-dog, anything by turn—was about as ugly an athletic specimen of humanity as ever stepped. Nature and his ancestors had been very unkind to him in the way of features, and accidents by flood and fight had marred what required no disfigurement, a fall of a spar having knocked his nose sidewise and broken the bridge, while a chop from a sword in a smuggling affray had given him a divided upper lip. In addition he always wore the appearance of being ashamed of his height, and went about with a slouch that was by no means an attraction to the fisher-girls of the place.

"Ay! If the old man had been alive—"

"'Stead o' drowned off Plymouth Hoo," growled Bart.

"In the big storm," continued Abel, "Polly would have had to swab them eyes of hern."

"Ay! And if the old man had been alive, that snapper dandy captain, with his boots and sword, would have had to sheer off, Abel, lad."

"'Stead o' coming jerry-sneaking about her when we was at sea, eh, Bart?"

"Them's true words," growled the big, ugly fellow.

Then, after a pause—

"I hate to see a woman cry."

"So do I, mate. Makes the place dull."

There was a pause, during which Abel carved away diligently, and Bart watched him intently, with his hands deep in his pockets.

"It's all off, ar'n't it, mate?" said Bart at last.

"Ay, it's all off," said Abel; and there was another pause.

"Think there'd be any chance for a man now?"

Abel looked up at his visitor, who took off the rough, flat, fur cap he wore, as if to show himself to better advantage; and after breathing on one rough, gnarled hand, he drew it down over his hair, smoothing it across his brow; but the result was not happy, and he seemed to feel it as the wood-carver shook his head and went on with his work.

"S'pose not," said the looker-on with a sigh. "You see, I'm such a hugly one, Abel, lad."

"You are, Bart. There's no denying of it, mate; you are."

"Ay! A reg'lar right-down hugly one. But I thought as p'r'aps now as her heart were soft and sore, she might feel a little torst a man whose heart also was very soft and sore."

"Try her, then, mate. I'll go and tell her you're here."

"Nay, nay, don't do that, man," whispered the big fellow, hoarsely. "I durstent ask her again. It'll have to come from her this time."

"Not it. Ask her, Bart. She likes you."

"Ay, she likes me, bless her, and she's allus got a kind word for a fellow as wishes a'most as he was her dog."

"What's the good o' that, lad? Better be her man."

"Ay, of course; but if you can't be her man, why not be her dog. She would pat your head and pull your ears; but I allus feels as she'll never pat my head or pull my ears, Abel, lad; you see, I'm such a hugly one. Blubbering, eh?"

"Does nothing else. She don't let me see it; but I know. She don't sleep of a night, and she looks wild and queer, as Sanderson's lass did who drowned herself."

"Then he has behaved very bad to her, Abel?"

"Ay, lad. I wish I had hold of him. I'd like to break his neck."

Bart put on his cap quickly, glanced toward the inner room, where there was a sound as of someone singing mournfully, and then in a quick, low whisper—

"Why not, lad?" said he; "why not?"

"Break his neck, Bart?"

The big fellow nodded.

"Will you join in and risk it?"

"Won't I?"

"Then we will," said Abel. "Curse him, he's most broke her heart."

"'Cause she loves him," growled Bart, thoughtfully.

"Yes, a silly soft thing. She might have known."

"Then we mustn't break his neck, Abel, lad," said Bart shaking his head. Then, as if a bright thought had suddenly flashed across his brain—

"Look here. We'll wait for him, and then—I ar'n't afeard of his sword—we'll make him marry her."

"You don't want him to marry her," said Abel, staring, and utilising the time by stropping his knife on his boot.

"Nay, I can do what she wants, I will as long as I live."

"Ah! you always was fond of her, Bart," said Abel, slowly.

"Ay, I always was, and always shall be, my lad. But look here," whispered Bart, leaning towards his companion; "if he says he won't marry her—"

"Ah! suppose he says he won't!" said Abel to fill up a pause, for Bart stood staring at him.

"If he says he won't, and goes and marries that fine madam—will you do it?"

"I'll do anything you'll do, mate," said Abel in a low voice.

"Then we'll make him, my lad."

"Hist!" whispered Abel, as the inner door opened, and Mary entered the room, looking haggard and wild, to gaze sharply from one to the other, as if she suspected that they had been making her the subject of their conversation.

"How do, Mary?" said Bart, in a consciously awkward fashion.

"Ah, Bart!" she said, coldly, as she gazed full in his eyes till he dropped his own and moved toward the door.

"I'm just going to have a look at my boat, Abel, lad," he said. "Coming down the shore?"

Abel nodded, and Bart shuffled out of the doorway, uttering a sigh of relief as soon as he was in the open air; and taking off his flat fur cap, he wiped the drops of perspiration from his brow.

"She's too much for me, somehow," he muttered, as he sauntered down towards the shore. "I allus thought as being in love with a gell would be very nice, but it ar'n't. She's too much for me."

"What were you and Bart Wrigley talking about?" said Mary Dell, as soon as she was alone with her brother.

"You," said Abel, going on scraping his netting-needle.

"What about me?"

"All sorts o' things."

"What do you mean?"

"What do I mean? Why, you know. About your being a fool—about the fine captain and his new sweetheart. Why, you might ha' knowed, Mary."

"Look here, Abel," cried Mary, catching him by the wrist, and dragging at it so that he started to his feet and they stood face to face, the stunted brother and the well-grown girl wonderfully equal in size, and extremely alike in physique and air; "if you dare to talk to me again like that, we shall quarrel."

"Well, let's quarrel, then."

"What?" cried Mary, staring, for this was a new phase in her brother's character.

"I say, let's quarrel, then," cried Abel, folding his arms. "Do you think I've been blind? Do you think I haven't seen what's been going on, and how that man has served you? Why, it has nearly broken poor old Bart's heart."

"Abel!"

"I don't care, Polly, I will speak now. You don't like Bart."

"I do. He is a good true fellow as ever stepped, but—"

"Yes, I know. It ar'n't nat'ral or you to like him as he likes you; but you've been a fool, Polly, to listen to that fine jack-a-dandy; and—curse him! I'll half-kill him next time we meet!"

Mary tried to speak, but her emotion choked her.

"You—you don't know what you are saying," she panted at last.

"Perhaps not," he said, in a low, muttering way; "but I know what I'm going to do!"

"Do!" she cried, recovering herself, and making an effort to regain her old ascendency over her brother. "I forbid you to do anything. You shall not interfere."

"Very well," said the young man, with a smile; and as his sister persisted he seemed to be subdued.

"Nothing, I say. Any quarrel I may have with Captain Armstrong is my affair, and I can fight my own battle. Do you hear?"

"Yes, I hear," said Abel, going toward the door.

"You understand! I forbid it. You shall not even speak to him."

"Yes, I understand," said Abel, tucking the netting-needle into his pocket, and thrusting his knife into its sheath; and then, before Mary could call up sufficient energy to speak again, the young man passed out of the cottage and hurried after Bart.

Mary went to the little casement and stood gazing after him thoughtfully for a few minutes, till he passed out of her sight among the rocks on his way to where the boat lay.

"No," she said, softly; "he would not dare!"

Then turning and taking the seat her brother had vacated, a desolate look of misery came over her handsome face, which drooped slowly into her hands, and she sat there weeping silently as she thought of the wedding that was to take place the next day.

Chapter Three
At the Church Door

Captain James Armstrong had a few more words with his cousin, Lieutenant Humphrey, anent his marriage.

"Perhaps you would like me to marry that girl off the beach," he said, "Mr Morality?"

"I don't profess to be a pattern of morality, cousin," replied the lieutenant, shortly.

"And don't like pretty girls, of course," sneered the captain. "Sailors never do."

"I suppose I'm a man, Jem," said Humphrey, "and like pretty girls; but I hope I should never be such a scoundrel as to make a girl miserable by professing to care for her, and then throwing her away like a broken toy."

"Scoundrel, eh?" said the captain, hotly.

"Yes. Scoundrel—confounded scoundrel!" retorted the lieutenant. "We're ashore now, and discipline's nowhere, my good cousin, so don't ruffle up your hackles and set up your comb and pretend you are going to peck, for you are as great a coward now, as you were when I was a little schoolboy and you were the big tyrant and sneak."

"You shall pay for this, sir," cried the captain.

"Pish! Now, my good cousin, you are not a fool. You know I am not in the least afraid of you."

"I'll make you some day," said the captain, bitterly. "You shall smart for all this."

"Not I. It is you who will smart. There, go and marry your rich wife, and much happiness may you get out of the match! I'm only troubled about one thing, and that is whether it is not my duty to tell the lady—poor creature!—what a blackguard she is going to wed."

Captain James Armstrong altered the sit of his cocked hat, brushed some imaginary specks off his new uniform, and turned his back upon his cousin, ignoring the extended hand. But he did as he was told—he went and was duly married, Lieutenant Humphrey being present and walking close behind, to see just outside the church door the flashing eyes and knitted brow of Mary Dell on one side; while beyond her, but unseen by Humphrey, were her brother Abel, and Bart, who stood with folded arms and a melodramatic scowl upon his ugly face.

"She's going to make a scene," thought Humphrey; and, pushing before the bride and bridegroom, he interposed, from a feeling of loyalty to the former, perhaps from a little of the same virtue toward a member of his family.

Mary looked up at him, at first in surprise, and then she smiled bitterly.

"Don't be alarmed, sir," she said coldly. "I only came to see the captain's wife."

"Poor lass!" muttered the lieutenant, as he saw Mary draw back among the people gathered together. "She seemed to read me like a book."

He caught one more sight of Mary Dell standing at a distance, holding her brother's arm, as the captain entered the heavy, lumbering coach at the church gate. Then she disappeared, the crowd melted away, and the bells rang a merry peal, the ringers' muscles having been loosened with ale; and as the bride and bridegroom went off to the lady's home at an old hall near Slapton Lea, Mary returned slowly to the cottage down in the little cove, and Humphrey went to the wedding breakfast, and afterwards to his ship.

Chapter Four
A Month Later

About a month after the marriage Captain James Armstrong was returning one night on horseback from Dartmouth to the home of his wife's family, where he was sojourning prior to setting off upon a long voyage, it having been decided that the young couple should not set up in housekeeping till his return from sea, so that the lady might have some companionship during his absence.

He had been to the principal inn to dine with some officers whose vessels had just touched there from Falmouth, and Humphrey, who had been present, had felt some doubt about letting him go home alone.

"You've had too much punch, Jem," he said. "Sleep here to-night, and don't let your young wife see you in that state."

"You're a fool," was the surly reply.

"You can get a good bed here, and ride home in the morning," said Humphrey, quietly. "You had better stay."

"Mind your own business, upstart," cried the captain; and ordering his horse he mounted and set off with a lurch, first on one side, and then on the other, each threatening to send him out of the saddle.

"He'll be all right, Armstrong," said a jovial-looking officer, watching. "Come, have another glass. By the time he is at the top of the long hill he will be sober as a judge."

"Perhaps so," said Humphrey aloud. Then to himself, "I don't half like it, though. The road's bad, and I shouldn't care for anything to happen to him, even if it is to make me heir to the estate. I wish I had not let him go."

He returned to the room where the officers had commenced a fresh bowl of punch, for they had no longer journey before them than upstairs to their rooms, and there were plenty of servants to see them safely into bed, as was the custom in dealing with the topers of that day.

"I've done wrong," said Humphrey Armstrong, after partaking of one glass of punch and smoking a single pipe of tobacco from a tiny bowl of Dutch ware. "He was not fit to go home alone."

He said this to himself as an officer was trolling forth an anacreontic song.

"It's a long walk, but I shall not feel comfortable unless I see whether he has got home safely; and it will clear away the fumes of the liquor. Here goes."

He slipped out of the room, and, taking a stout stick which was the companion of his hat, he started forth into the cool night air, and walked sturdily away in the direction of his cousin's home.

About half an hour later the drowsy groom, who was sitting up for the captain's return, rose with a sigh of satisfaction, for he heard the clattering of hoofs in the stable-yard.

"At last!" he cried; and, taking a lighted lantern, he hurried out, to stand in dismay staring at the empty saddle, which had been dragged round under the horse's belly, and at the trembling animal, breathing hard and shaking its head.

"Why, she's all of a muck," muttered the man; "and the captain ar'n't on her. He be fallen off, I'd zwear."

The man stood staring for a few minutes, while the horse pawed impatiently, as if asking to be admitted to its stable. Then he opened the door, the weary beast went in, and the man stood staring with true Devon stolidity before he bethought him of the necessity for removing the saddle from its awkard position.

This seen to, it suddenly occurred to him that something ought to be done about the captain, and he roused up the coachman to spread the alarm in the house.

"Nay, we'll only scare the poor ladies to death," said the Jehu of the establishment, grey hairs having brought him wisdom. "Let's zee virst, lad, if there be anything really bad. If he be droonk and valled off, he won't thank us for telling his wife. Zaddle the dwo coach-horses, Ridgard, and we'll ride to town and zee."

The horses were quickly saddled, and the two men-servants trotted along the Dartmouth road till about half-way, where, in one of the gloomiest parts, their horses began to snort and exhibit signs of fear, and as they drew up a voice shouted—

"Here! Who's that! Help!"

"Why, it be Mr Humphrey," said the old coachman; and dismounting he gave his rein to his companion, and ran forward. "What be wrong, zir?"

"The captain. Much hurt," was the reply.

"I thought zo, zir. His horse comed home without him. He's been throwed—or pulled off," he added to himself.

"It's something worse, I'm afraid. Here, help me, and let's get him home."

The old coachman lent his aid, and with some difficulty the captain was placed across one of the horses, the lieutenant mounting to hold him on and support him, while the two servants followed slowly behind.

"Pulled off?" whispered the groom.

"Mebbe," said the old coachman; and then to himself, "Looks bad for Mr Humphrey; and if he died, what should I zay to them as asked how I found 'em?"

The old man walked slowly on for half an hour before he answered his mental question, and his answer was—

"They'd make me tell 'em the truth, and it might bring Mr Humphrey to the gallows; and if it did, it would be all through me."

Chapter Five
A Keen Encounter

The prognostications of his fellow-officer did not prove true, for Captain Armstrong, instead of being sobered by the ride up the hill, grew more drunken. The fresh air blown straight from the ocean seemed to dizzy his muddled brain, and when he rode down the hill he was more drunken than ever, and rolled about in his saddle like his ship in a storm.

This seemed to amuse the captain, and he talked and chuckled to himself, sang snatches of songs, and woke the echoes of the little village street at the top of the next hill, where the tall, square church tower stood up wind-swept and dreary to show mariners the way to Dartmouth harbour.

Then came a long ride along a very shelf of a road, where it seemed as if a false step on the part of his horse would send both rolling down the declivity to the edge of the sheer rocks, where they would fall headlong to the fine shingle below.

But drunken men seem favourites with their horses, for when Captain Armstrong lurched to starboard his nag gave a hitch to keep him in the saddle, and when he gave another lurch to larboard the horse was ready for him again—all of which amused the captain more and more, and he chuckled aloud, and sang, and swore at his cousin for a cold, fishy, sneaking hound.

"He'd like to see me die, and get the estate," he said; "but I'll live to a hundred, and leave half a score of boys to inherit, and he sha'n't get a groat, a miserable, sanctified dog-fish. Steady, mare, steady! Bah, how thirsty I am! Wish I'd had another drop."

He kicked his horse's ribs, and the docile creature broke into a gentle amble, but only to be checked sharply.

"Wo-ho, mare!" cried the captain, shaking his head, for he was dizzy now, and the dimly-seen trees sailed slowly round. "Wind's changing," he said; "steady, old lass! Walk."

The mare walked, and the captain grew more confused in his intellect; while the night became darker, soft clouds rolling slowly over the star-spangled sky.

The ride was certainly not sobering James Armstrong, and he knew it, for he suddenly burst into a chuckling laugh.

"I know what she'll say," he said. "Ladyship will ride the high horse. Let her. I can ride the high horse, too—steady, mare! What's the matter with you?"

He had been descending into a narrow pass where the road had been cut down in the hill side, leaving a high, well-wooded bank on either hand, and here it was far more dark than out in the open, and the mare, after walking steadily on for some distance with her well-shod hoofs clinking upon the loose stones, suddenly shied, stopped short, and snorted.

"What's the matter with you, stupid? Can't you stand straight?" cried the captain, striking the beast angrily with his heels. "Go on."

The horse, however, backed and swerved from side to side, making as if to turn sharply and gallop back to Dartmouth; but just at that moment there was a rustling sound heard overhead, where the rough bushes fringed the bank, and directly after a rush and the sound of someone leaping down into the lane between the captain and the town.

This had the effect of startling the horse more and more, but instead of making now for the way by which they had come, it willingly obeyed the touch of the rider's spur, and continued its journey for half a dozen yards. Then it stopped short once again, for a dark figure leaped down into the lane just in front, and the captain found himself hemmed in.

And now, for the first time; he began to feel sobered as he took in the position. He had been attacked by highwaymen without a doubt, and unless he chose to do battle for his watch and money his only chance of escape was to force his horse to mount the precipitous side of the lane.

Without a moment's hesitation he dragged at the off rein, drove the spurs into the beast's flanks, and forced her to the leap; but it was poorly responded to. The half leap resulted in the mare gaining a footing a few feet up, and then scrambling back into the lane as the captain's two assailants closed in.

"Stand back, you scoundrels!" roared the captain. "Curse you! I'll blow your brains out."

A mocking laugh was the response, and as he dragged at the holster a smart blow from a cudgel fell upon his hand, making him utter a yell of pain. The next moment one of the men had leaped up behind him and clasped his arms to his side, and in the struggle which ensued both came down off the horse, which uttered a loud snort of fear and dashed off at a gallop down the hill for home, while, nerved to action now by his position and stung by the blows he had received from his assailant, the captain wrested himself free and dragged his sword from its sheath.

He had hardly raised it in the air when a tremendous blow fell upon the blade close to the hilt, the sword snapped in two, and the captain was defenceless.

This mishap took all the spirit-born courage out of him, and he threw down the broken weapon.

"I give in," he cried, backing away to the side of the lane and facing the two dimly-seen figures in the darkness; "what do you want?"

One of the men burst into a hoarse laugh.

"I've hardly any money," cried the captain; "a guinea or two. If I give you that will you go?"

"Curse your money, you cowardly hound!" cried the second man.

"How dare you, dog!" cried the captain. "Do you know who I am?"

"James Armstrong," said the same speaker. "Now, lad, quick!"

"You shall—"

The captain's words turned into a yell of agony as he received a violent blow from a stick across one arm, numbing it, and before its echo rose from the steep slope of the hill a second and a third blow fell, which were followed by a shower, the unfortunate man yelling, beseeching, and shrieking with agony and fear. He dropped upon his knees and begged piteously for mercy; but his tormentors laughed, and seized the opportunity he offered to apply their blows more satisfactorily. Back, arms, legs, all in turn, were belaboured as two men beat a carpet, till the victim's cries grew hoarse, then faint, and finally ceased, and he lay in the trampled road, crushed almost to a mummy, and unable to stir hand or foot; and then, and then only, did his assailants cease.

"Ain't killed him, have we, Abel, lad?" said the bigger of the two men.

"Killed? No. We never touched his head. It would take a deal to kill a thing like him. Captain!" he said, mockingly. "What a cowardly whelp to command men!"

"What shall we do now?" whispered the bigger man.

"Do! I'm going to make my mark upon him, and then go home."

"Well, you have, lad."

"Ay, with a stick, but I'm going to do it with my knife;" and, as he spoke, the lesser of the two men drew his knife from its dagger-like sheath.

"No, no, don't do that. Give him a good 'un on the head. No knife."

"Yes, knife," said the lesser of the two. "He's had no mercy, and I'll have none. He's stunned, and won't feel it."

"Don't do that, lad," whimpered the bigger man.

"Ay, but I will," said the other, hoarsely; and, dropping on his knees, he seized the prostrate man by the ear, when the trembling wretch uttered a shriek of agony, making his assailants start away.

"Did you do it, lad?"

"Yes; I done it. I'm satisfied now. Let's go."

"And leave him there?"

"Why not? What mercy did he show? He was only shamming. Let him call for help now till someone comes."

The bigger man uttered a grunt and followed his companion as he mounted the steep side of the lane, while, faint, exhausted, and bleeding now, Captain James Armstrong sank back and fainted away.

Chapter Six
Brought to Book

"You dare not deny it," cried Mary Dell, furiously, as she stood in the doorway of the cottage, facing her brother and Bart Wrigley, who attempted to escape, but were prevented by her barring the way of exit.

Neither spoke, but they stood looking sullen and frowning like a couple of detected schoolboys.

"No," she continued, "you dare not deny it. You cowards—lying in wait for an unarmed man!"

"Why, he'd got a sword and pistols," cried Bart.

"There!" shrieked Mary, triumphantly; "you have betrayed yourself, Bart. Now perhaps my brave brother will confess that he lay in wait in the dark for an unarmed man, and helped to beat him nearly to death."

"You're a nice fellow to trust, Bart," said Abel, looking at his companion. "Betrayed yourself directly."

"Couldn't help it," grumbled Bart. "She's so sharp upon a man."

"You cowards!" cried Mary again.

"Well, I don't know about being cowards," said Abel, sullenly. "He was mounted and had his weapons, and we had only two sticks."

"Then you confess it was you? Oh! what a villain to have for a brother!"

"Here, don't go on like that," cried Abel. "See how he has served you."

"What's that to you?" cried Mary, fiercely. "If he jilted me and I forgive him, how dare you interfere?"

"Phew!" whistled Bart to himself. "What a way she has!"

"Why, any one would think you cared for him, Polly," said Abel, staring, while Bart whistled softly again, and wiped the heavy dew from his forehead.

"Care for him!—I hate him!" cried Mary, passionately: "but do you think I wanted my own brother to go and take counsel with his big vagabond companion—"

"Phew!" whistled Bart again, softly, as he perspired now profusely, and wiped his forehead with his fur cap.

"And then go and beat one of the King's officers? But you'll both suffer for it. The constables will be here for you, and you'll both be punished."

"Not likely—eh, Bart?" said Abel, with a laugh.

"No, lad," growled that worthy. "Too dark."

"Don't you be too sure," cried Mary. "You cowards! and if he dies,"—there was a hysterical spasm here—"if he dies, you'll both go to the gibbet and swing in chains!"

Bart gave his whole body a writhe, as if he already felt the chains about him as he was being made into a scare-scamp.

"Didn't hit hard enough, and never touched his head," he growled.

"And as for you," cried Mary, turning upon him sharply, "never you look me in the face again. You are worse than Abel; and I believe it was your mad, insolent jealousy set you persuading my foolish brother to help in this cowardly attack."

Bart tried to screw up his lips and whistle; but his jaw seemed to drop, and he only stared and shuffled behind his companion in misfortune.

"Never mind what she says, Bart, lad," said the latter; "she'll thank us some day for half-killing as big a scamp as ever stepped."

"Thank you!" cried Mary, with her eyes flashing and her handsome face distorted, "I hope to see you both well punished, and—"

"Who's that coming?" said Abel, sharply, as steps were heard approaching quickly.

As Mary turned round to look, Abel caught sight of something over her shoulder in the evening light which made him catch his companion by the arm.

"Quick, Bart, lad!" he whispered; "through her room and squeeze out of the window. The constables!"

He opened the door of his sister's little room, thrust his mate in, followed, and shut and bolted the door; but as he turned then to the window, a little strongly-made frame which had once done duty in a vessel, Mary's voice was heard speaking loudly in conversation with the new arrivals in the outer room.

"Out with you, quickly and quietly," whispered Abel.

"Right, lad," replied Bart; and unfastening and opening the little window, he thrust his arms through and began to get out.

At that moment there was a loud knocking at the door.

"Open—in the king's name!"

"Open it yourself," muttered Abel, "when we're gone. Quick, Bart, lad!"

This remark was addressed to the big fellow's hind quarters, which were jerking and moving in a very peculiar way, and then Bart's voice was heard, sounding muffled and angry, warning somebody to keep off.

"Curse it all! too late!" cried Abel, grinding his teeth. "Here, Bart, lad, get through."

"Can't, lad," growled his companion. "I'm ketched just acrost the hips, and can't move."

"Come back, then."

"That's what I'm a-trying to do, but this son of a sea-cook has got hold of me."

"Open—in the King's name!" came from the outer room; and then, just as Abel had seized an old sea-chest and was about to drag it before the door, there was a tremendous kick, the bolt was driven off, the door swung open, and the Dartmouth constable and a couple of men rushed forwards, and, in spite of Abel's resistance, dragged him into the other room.

"Now, Dell, my lad," said the head man, "I've got you at last."

"So it seems," said Abel, who stared hard at his sister as he spoke; while she stood with her hands clasped before her and a peculiarly rigid look on her face, staring wildly back.

"Smuggling and wrecking weren't enough for you, eh?"

"What do you want here?" said Abel, giving his sister a final scowl and then facing the head constable.

"You, my lad—you," said that individual, with a grin.

"What for?"

"Attempted murder and robbery on the king's highway, my lad."

"It's a lie! Who says so?" cried Abel, setting his teeth and fixing his sister again with his dark eyes as she gave him an imploring look.

"Never mind who says so, my lad. Information's laid all regular against you and Master Bart Wrigley. You're both captured neatly. Here, how long are you going to be bringing forward the other?" cried the constable.

"We can't get him out," shouted a voice. "He's stuck in the little window."

"Pull him back, then, by his legs."

"Been trying ever so long," said another voice, "but he won't come."

"I'll soon see to that," said the constable, backing Abel into the little bedroom which was darkened by Bart's body filling up the window. "Here, lay hold of his legs, two of you, and give a good jerk."

Two men obeyed, but they did not give the jerk—Bart did that. Drawing in his legs like a grasshopper about to leap, he suddenly shot them out straight, when, though they did not alter his position where he was nipped in across the hips by the window-frame, they acted like catapults upon the two constables, who were driven backwards, the one into a chair, the other into a sitting position on the floor, to the great delight of those who looked on.

"Four of you," said the head constable stolidly; "and hold on this time."

The men obeyed, two going to each leg; and though Bart gave three or four vigorous kicks, his captors were not dislodged.

"Now," said the head constable, as the kicking legs became quiescent, "all together!"

There was a sharp jerk, and Bart's body was snatched out of the imprisoning frame so suddenly that five men went down on the floor together; while the first to rise was Bart, who kicked himself free, made for the door in spite of a pistol levelled by the head constable, and passed through.

"Come on, Abel!" he shouted as he went.

Abel made a dash to follow, but he only struck his face against the muzzle of a pistol, and the head constable held on.

There was a rush after Bart, but it was needless, for the great stolid fellow had seen the state of affairs, and come back.

"All right, Abel, lad," he growled; "I won't leave you in the lurch. What's it mean—lock-up!"

"Yes, my lad; charge of attempted murder and robbery," said the head constable.

"Took all the skin off my hips and ribs," growled Bart, rubbing himself softly.

"You'll have plenty of time to get well before your trial," said the constable, smiling. "Are you ready!"

This last to Abel, who was gazing fiercely at his sister, who met his angry eyes with an imploring look.

"And my own sister, too, Bart," he said, bitterly. "We fought for her, lad, and she gave information to the police."

"No, no, no, Abel!" cried Mary, running to him to fling her arms about his neck; but he gave her a rough thrust which sent her staggering back, and her countenance changed on the instant for her eyes flashed vindictively, and she stood before him with folded arms.

"Prisoner confessed in the presence of you all that he committed the act," said the constable; and his words were received with a mutter of assent in chorus.

"Here, I'm ready," said Abel. "Come along, mate."

"So'm I," growled Bart, laying a hand on Abel's shoulder. "I wouldn't ha' thought it on you, Mary, my lass," he said, and he gazed at her sadly as he shook his head.

Mary made no reply, but stood with her arms folded across her breast and her brow wrinkled while the party moved out of the cottage; but the next instant the scene which followed made her rush outside and gaze wildly with eyes dilated and breast heaving, and her hands now clasped as she watched the chase.

For as the little party stood outside, Bart still with his hand upon his companion's shoulder, Abel said quickly—

"The boat. Run!"

Bart was, as a rule, rather slow of comprehension; but at that moment the same idea was filling his mind. That is to say, it was already charged, and Abel's words were as so many sparks struck from steel to fire that charge. Consequently, as the young fellow struck the constable to the left, Bart did the same to the right, and they dashed off as one man towards where, just round the western point of rock which helped to form the little bay, they knew that their boat was lying, swinging with the tide to a grapnel lying on the sands.

As they dashed off, running swiftly over the hard sand, the head constable raised his old brass-mounted pistol and fired, when the shot might have been supposed to have struck Mary Dell, so sharp a start did she give as she clapped one hand to her side, and then peered at the rising smoke, and drew a long breath full of relief.

For, as the smoke rose, she could see the fugitives still running, and that quite a cloud of sea-birds had risen from the mew-stone, a hundred yards from shore, to fly circling round, screaming querulously, as they slowly flapped their black-tipped wings.

"They'll escape—they'll escape!" cried Mary, clapping her hands joyously. "The coward, to fire! And they're afraid to run hard and catch them now they are out in the open. Yes, they'll escape!" she cried again, as she saw the distance increasing between pursuer and pursued. "They'll get to the boat; the sail's in, and there's a good breeze. Oh, if I were only with them!"

A sudden thought struck her, and she caught up a sun-bonnet from where it lay on the open window-sill.

"I'll go," she thought. "They'll sail west. I could reach Mallow's Cove across the fields, and signal to them. They'd come in and pick me up, and we could escape together far, far from here."

All this with her cheeks flushing, her handsome eyes sparkling, and her breast rising and falling in the height of her emotion.

Then a change came over her. Her eyes looked heavy; her forehead wrinkled again.

"Escape! Where?" she said, half aloud. "I'd gladly go—away from all this torture; but they think I betrayed them, and would not come in."

The elasticity was gone out of her step, as she slowly climbed the face of the huge scarped rocks which towered above the cottage—a risky ascent, but one to which she was, as it were, born; and, with her eyes fixed upon the pursuers and the fugitives, she trusted to her hands and feet to take her safely to the top, passing spot after spot where one unused to climbing would have stopped and turned back, so giddy was the ascent. Higher and higher, past clinging ivy, fern, and clusters of yellow ragwort, with patches of purple heath and golden gorse, till the farther side of the rocky point was opened out, with the boat lying like a speck afloat beyond the line of foam.

Mary paused there with her sun-bonnet in her hand to watch the result; but there was no exultation in her eyes, only a look of stony despondency, for from where she stood she could see now that the effort of her brother and his companion was in vain.

They were still on ignorance as they ran on, for they were on the bay side of the point yet, toiling over the loose sand and shingle, where the washed up weed lay thick; but Mary had a bird's-eye view of what in the clear south air seemed to be close at her feet, as close almost as where the boat lay in shelter from the north and easterly wind.

The pursuers were now all together, and settled down to a steady trot, which pace they increased as Bart and Abel reached the rocks, and, instead of going right round, began to climb over some fifty yards from where the water washed the point.

"We're too many for him this time, Bart, my lad," cried Abel. "You weren't hit, were you?"

"Hit? No. Shot never went within a mile o' me."

"Then why are you dowsing your jib like that?"

"I were a-thinking about she, mate," said Bart, in a low growl.

"Curse her for a woman all over!" said Abel. "They take to a man, and the more he ill-uses 'em, they fight for him the more."

"Ay, lad; but to think of her putting them on to us! It don't seem like she."

"Curse them!" cried Abel, as he reached the other side of the point, and saw that which his sister had seen from the cliff behind the cottage.

"What for now?" said Bart, stolidly, as he reached his companion's side. "Hum, that's it, is it?"

He looked round him for a fresh way of escape.

There was the sea, if they liked to leap in and swim; but they could be easily overtaken. The rocks above them were too overhanging to climb, and there was no other way, unless they returned, and tried to rush through their pursuers; for beyond the point the tide beat upon the cliff.

"No good, Bart; we're trapped," said Abel, stolidly. "I'll never forgive her—never!"

"Yes, you will," said Bart, sitting down on a rock, and carefully taking off his fur cap to wipe his heated brow. "You will some day. Why, I could forgive her anything—I could. She's a wonderful gell; but, I say, my hips is werry sore."

He sat staring down at the boat beyond the point, the anchor having been taken on board, and the oars being out to keep her off the rocks, as she rose and fell with the coming tide.

"No!" said Abel, bitterly. "I'll never forgive her—never!"

"Nay, lad, don't say that," said Bart, rubbing one side. "Hey, lass! There she is. Top o' the cliff. Look at her, mate."

"No," said Abel; "let her look—at her cowardly work."

"Now, then!" shouted the head constable, as he came panting up. "Is it surrender, or fight?"

For answer, Abel climbed slowly down to the sands, followed by Bart; and the next minute they were surrounded, and stood with gyves upon their wrists.

"Warm work," said the constable, cheerfully; "but we've got you safe now."

"Ay, you've got us safe," growled Bart; "but it wouldn't ha' been easy if Abel here had showed fight."

"Been no use," said the constable. "I said to Billy Niggs here: 'Niggs,' I said, 'them two'll make for their boat, and get away.' 'Ay, zhure, that they 'ool,' he said. Didn't you, Billy?"

"Ay, zhure, sir, that's just what I did say," cried a constable, with a face like a fox-whelp cyder apple.

"So I sent on two men to be ready in the boat. Come on, my lads."

The boat was pulled ashore. The two constables in charge leaped out with the grapnel, and dropped it on the sand; and then in silence the party with their prisoners walked slowly back, and beneath the spot where Mary stood like a figure carved out of the rock, far above their heads, till they had gone out of sight, without once looking up or making a sign.

Then the poor girl sank down in the rocky niche where she had climbed first, and burst into an agonised fit of weeping.

"Father—mother—brother—all gone! Lover false! Alone—alone—alone!" she sobbed. "What have I done to deserve it all? Nothing!" she cried, fiercely, as she sprang to her feet and turned and shook her clenched fists landward. "Nothing but love a cold, cruel wretch. Yes, love; and now—oh, how I hate him—and all the world!"

She sank down again in the niche all of a heap, and sat there with the sun slowly sinking lower, and the sea-birds wheeling round and round above her head, and watching her with inquisitive eyes, as they each now and then uttered a mournful wail, which sounded sympathetic though probably it was the gullish expression of wonder whether the crouching object was good to eat.

And there she sat, hour after hour, till it was quite dark, when she began slowly to descend, asking herself what she should do to save her brother and his friend, both under a misconception, but suffering for her sake.

"And I stay here!" she said, passionately. "Let them think what they will, I'll try and save them, for they must be a prison now."

Mary was quite right; for as night fell Abel Dell and Bart his companion were partaking of a very frugal meal, and made uncomfortable by the fact that it was not good, and that they—men free to come and go on sea and land—were now safely caged behind a massive iron grill.

"Well," said Bart at last, "I'm only sorry for one thing now."

"What's that—Mary being so base?"

"Nay, I'm sorry for that," replied Bart; "but what I meant was that I didn't give the captain one hard un on the head."

Chapter Seven
Gathering Clouds

In spite of the declaration made by Captain Armstrong that he had identified his assailants by the heights, voices, and—dark as was the night—their features, Abel refused to be convinced. He had taken it into his head that Mary had denounced them to her former lover, and at each examination before the Old Devon magistrates he had sullenly turned away from the poor girl, who sat gazing imploringly at the dock, and hungering for a look in return.

The captain was not much hurt; that is to say, no bones were broken. Pain he had suffered to a little extent, for there was an ugly slit in one ear, but he was not in such a condition as to necessitate his limping into court, supported by a couple of servants, and generally "got up" to look like one who had been nearly beaten to death.

All this told against Abel and Bart, as well as the fact that the captain was of good birth, and one who had lately formed an alliance with a famous old county family. In addition, the prisoners were known to the bench. Both Abel and Bart had been in trouble before, and black marks were against them for wrecking and smuggling. They were no worse than their neighbours, but the law insists upon having scarecrows, and the constables did not hesitate to make every effort to hang the son of a notorious old wrecker and his boon companion.

There was not a dissentient voice. Abel Dell and Bartholomew Wrigley were both committed for trial; and Mary made quite a sensation by rising in the court as the prisoners were about to be removed, and forcing her way to where she could catch her brother's hand.

"Abe," she cried, passionately, "I didn't. I didn't, indeed. Say good-bye."

He turned upon her fiercely, and snatched his hand away.

"Go to your captain," he said, savagely. "I shall be out of the way now."

An ordinary woman would have shrunk away sobbing; but as Mary was flung off, she caught at Bart's wrist, and clung to that.

"Bart, I didn't! I didn't!" she whispered, hoarsely. "Tell him I wouldn't—I couldn't do such a thing. It isn't true!"

Bart's face puckered up, and he looked tenderly down in the agitated face before him.

"Well, lass," he said, softly, "I believe—"

"That you turned against us!" interposed Abel, savagely, for his temper, consequent upon the way matters had gone against him, was all on edge. "Come on, Bart; she'll have her own way now."

A constable's hand was on each of their shoulders, and they were hurried out of court, leaving Mary standing frowning alone, the observed of all.

Her handsome face flushed, and she drew herself up proudly, as she cast a haughtily defiant look at all around, and was about to walk away when her eyes lighted upon the captain, who was seated by the magisterial bench, side by side with his richly-dressed lady.

There was a vindictive glare in Mary Dell's eyes as she encountered the gaze of Mistress Armstrong, the lady looking upon her as a strange, dangerous kind of creature.

"Why should she not suffer as I suffer?" thought Mary. "Poor, weak, dressed-up doll that she is! I could sting her to the heart easy. How I hate her, for she has robbed me of a husband!"

But the next moment the lady withdrew her gaze with a shiver of dread from the eyes which had seemed to scorch her; and Mary's now lit upon those of Captain Armstrong, for he was watching her curiously, and with re-awakened interest.

Mary's face changed again its expression, as light seemed to enter her darkened soul.

"He used to love me a little. He would not be so cruel as that. I offended him, because I was so hard and—cruel he called it. He would listen to me now. I will, I will."

She gazed at him fixedly for a moment, and then hurried from the court.

"What a dreadful-looking woman, Jemmy!" whispered Mistress Armstrong. "She quite made me shudder. Will they hang her too?"

"No, no," he said, rising quickly and drawing a long breath. Then, recollecting himself, he sat down again as if in pain, and held out his hand to his wife, who supported him to the carriage, into which he ascended slowly.

"Sorry for you, Armstrong; deuced sorry, egad," said the senior magistrate, coming up to the carriage door. "Can't help feeling glad too."

"Oh, Sir Timothy!" cried Mistress Armstrong, who was a seventeenth cousin.

"But I am, my dear," said the old magistrate. "Glad, because it will rid us of a couple of dreadful rascals. Trial comes on in three weeks. I wouldn't get well too soon. Judge Bentham will hang them as sure as they're alive."

He nodded and walked off, with his cocked hat well balanced on his periwig. Then the heavy lumbering carriage drove out of the quaint old town, with the big dumpling horses perspiring up the hills; while, as soon as they were away from the houses, Mistress Armstrong leaned back on the cushions with a sigh of relief.

"I do hope the judge will hang them," she said. "A pair of wicked, bad, cruel ruffians, to beat and half-kill my own dear darling Jemmy as they did. Oh, the cruel, cruel creatures! I could hang them myself! Does it hurt you anywhere now, my own sweetest boy?" she added, softly, as she passed her arm caressingly round her liege lord, who gave such a savage start that she shrank into the other corner of the carriage, with the tears starting to her eyes.

"Don't be such a confounded fool!" her "sweetest" Jemmy roared; and then he sat back scowling, for she had interrupted a sort of day-dream in which he was indulging respecting Mary Dell, whose eyes still seemed to be fixed upon his; and as his wife's last words fell upon his ear they came just as he was wondering whether, if they met again, Mary would, in her unprotected state, prove more kind, and not so prudish as of yore.

The honeymoon had been over some time.

Chapter Eight
Mary Begins to Plan

Mary Dell was a girl of keen wits, but her education was of the sea-shore. Among her class people talked of the great folk, and men of wealth and their power—and not without excuse—for in those days bribery, corruption, and class clannishness often carried their way to the overruling of justice—the blind; and in her ignorance she thought that if she could win over Captain Armstrong to forgive her brother, the prosecution would be at an end, and all would be well.

Consequently she determined to go up to the big house by Slapton Lea, and beg Mistress Armstrong to intercede with her husband, and ask his forgiveness; so one morning soon after the committal she set off, but met the carriage with the young married couple inside—Mistress Armstrong looking piqued and pale, and the captain as if nothing were the matter.

The sight of the young wife side by side with the man who had professed to love her was too much for Mary, and she turned off the road and descended by the face of a dangerously steep cliff to the shingly shore; where, as she tramped homeward, with her feet sinking deeply in the small loose pebbles, her feeling of bitterness increased, and she felt that it would be impossible to ask that weak, foolish-looking woman with the doll's face to take her part.

No; she would go up to the house boldly and ask to see the captain himself; and then, with the memory of his old love for her to help her cause, he would listen to her prayer, and save her brother from the risk he ran.

Then a mental cloud came over her, and she felt that she could not go up to the big house. It was not the captain's, it was *her* mother's; and it would be like going to ask a favour of her. She could not do it; and there was no need.

Captain Armstrong would come down to the shore any evening if she sent him the old signal, a scrap of dry sea-weed wrapped in paper. Scores of times she had done this when Abel had gone to sea in his boat, with Bart for companion; and Mary's cheeks flushed at the recollection of those meetings.

Yes; she would send him the old signal by one of the fishermen's children.

No; only if all other means failed. He was better now, and would be about. She would watch for him, and, as she called it, meet him by accident, and then plead her cause.

And so a week glided away, and there was only about one more before the judge would arrive, and Abel and his companion be brought up in the assize court. Mary had haunted every road and lane leading toward the big house, and had met the captain riding and walking, but always with Mistress Armstrong, and she could not speak before her.

There was nothing for it but to take the bold step, and after long hesitation that step was taken; the piece of sea-weed was wrapped up in paper, entrusted to a little messenger, and that evening Mary Dell left the cottage and walked round the western point towards Torcross, her cheeks flushed, her eyes unusually bright, and her heart full of care.

She was not long in reaching the well-known spot—their old trysting-place, where the coarse sand was white, and the rocks which shut in the retired tiny cove rough with limpet, barnacle, and weed.

This was the first time she had been there since James Armstrong had wearied of the prude, as he called her, and jilted her for his wealthy wife; and now the question arose; Would he come?

The evening was glorious; but one thought filled Mary's breast—Abel shut up behind the prison bars, still obdurate, and believing her false to him, and his faithful friend.

The grey look on the face of the sea was reflected upon that of the watcher; and as the sky grew dark, so grew Mary Dell's eyes, only that there was a lurid light now and then glowing in their depths.

"He will not come," she said. "He hates me now as I hate him, and—"

She stopped short, for her well-trained ear caught the sound of a pebble falling as if from a height upon the strand below, and gazing fixedly above the direction of the sound, she made out something dark moving high up on the cliff track.

Mary's heart began to beat wildly, and she drew a long breath; but she would not let hope carry her away for a few moments till she could be certain, and then a faint cry of joy escaped her, but only to be succeeded by a chilling sensation, as something seemed to ask her why he had come.

"I'm late," cried a well-known voice directly after. "Why, Mary, just in the old spot. It's like old times. My darling!" He tried to clasp her in his arms, his manner displaying no trace of his injuries; but she thrust him sharply away, half surprised and yet not surprised, for she seemed now to read the man's character to the full.

"Captain Armstrong!" she cried, hoarsely.

"Why, my dear Mary, don't be so prudish. You are not going to carry on that old folly?"

"Captain Armstrong, don't mistake me."

"Mistake you! No. You are the dearest, loveliest woman I ever saw. There, don't be huffed because I was so long. I couldn't get away. You know—" and he again tried to seize her.

"Captain Armstrong—"

"Now, what nonsense! You sent for me, and I have come."

"Yes. I sent for you because there was no other way of speaking to you alone."

"Quite right, my darling; and what could be better than here alone? Mary, sweet, it will be dark directly."

"Sir, I sent for you here that I might beg of you to save my brother and poor Bart."

"Curse your brother and Bart!" said the captain, angrily. "It was not their fault that they did not kill me. They're better out of our way."

"Captain Armstrong—James—for our old love's sake will you save them?"

"No," he cried, savagely. "Yes," he added, catching Mary's wrist; "not for our old love's sake, but for our new love—the love that is to come. Mary, I love you; I always did love you, and now I find I cannot live without you."

"Captain Armstrong!"

"James—your lover. Mary, you are everything to me. Don't struggle. How can you be so foolish? There, yes, I will. I'll do everything. I'll refuse to appear against them if you wish me to. I'll get them set free; but you will not hold me off like this?"

"You will save my brother?"

"Yes."

"And his friend?"

"Yes."

"Then I will always be grateful to you, and pray for your happiness."

"And be mine, Mary, my love, my own?"

"You villain! you traitor!" hissed Mary, as, taking advantage of a momentary forgetfulness, he clasped her in his arms and showered kisses on her lips, her cheeks, her hair.

But Captain Armstrong had made a mistake. It was like caressing a Cornish wrestler. There was a sharp struggle, during which he found that Mary's thews and sinews were, softly rounded as she was, strong as those of a man. She had been accustomed to row a boat in a rough sea by the hour together, and there was additional strength given to her arm by the indignation that made her blood course hotly through her veins.

How dare he, a miserable traitor, insult her as he did?

The question made the girl's blood seem to boil; and ere he could place another kiss upon her lips Mary had forgotten brother, friend, the trial everything but the fact that James Armstrong, Mistress Armstrong's husband, had clasped her in his arms; and in return she clasped him tightly in hers.

They swayed here for a moment, then there, and the next the captain was lifted completely from the shingle and literally jerked sideways, to fall with a crash and strike his head against a piece of rock. Then a sickening sensation came over him and all seemed dark, while, when he recovered a few minutes later, his head was bleeding and he was alone, and afraid with his swimming head to clamber up the rough cliff path.

"The cursed jade!" he muttered, as he recovered after a time, and went cautiously back after tying up his head, "I wish I could lay her alongside her brother in the gaol."

"Yes; I'll save him," he said with a mocking laugh, as he reached the top of the cliff and looked down at the faint light seen in the old wrecker's cottage. "I'll save him; and, in spite of all, it'll be a strange thing if Mary Dell isn't lost.

"Curse her, how strong she is!" he said after a pause.

"What shall I say! Humph! a slip on the path and a fall. I'm weak yet after the assault. Some one will have to plaster her dearest Jemmy's head—a sickly fool!"

Chapter Nine
Behind Prison Bars

Mary Dell went again and again to the prison in the county town, tramping till she was footsore; but she did not see Abel, for she had to encounter double difficulties—to wit, the regulations of the authorities, and her brother's refusal to see her.

At last, though, she compassed an interview with Bart Wrigley, and the big fellow listened to her stolidly, as he enjoyed the sound of her voice, sighing heavily from time to time.

"But even you seem at times, Bart, as if you did not believe a word I say," she cried passionately.

"Who says I don't?" said Bart, in a low growl. "You told me you didn't, my lass, and of course you didn't. Why, I'd believe anything you told me; but as for Abel, he's dead-set on it that you told the captain, and there's no moving him."

"But tell him, Bart, tell him I was angry with him for what he did—"

"What *we* did," said Bart, who was too loyal to shirk his share.

"Well, what you both did, Bart; but that I would sooner have died than betray my own brother."

"Haw, haw! That's a wunner," said Bart, with a hoarse laugh. "That's just what I did tell him."

"You did, Bart?"

"Ay, my lass, I did; but he—"

Bart stopped.

"Yes, Bart, what did he say?"

"Said I was a blind, thick-headed fool."

"Oh, Bart, Bart, Bart! you are the best, and truest friend we ever had."

"Say that again, lass, will you?" said the rough fellow.

Mary said it again with greater emphasis, and big Bart rubbed the corner of one eye with the back of his hand.

"Tell him, dear Bart, that his sister was true to him all through, and that he must believe me."

"Ay, lass, I'll tell him; but don't call me 'dear Bart' again, 'cause I can't bear it."

"But you are our friend, and have always been like a brother to us."

"Ay, lass, I tried to be, and I'll speak to him again. Bah! you never went again us. You couldn't. Your tongue thrashed us a bit, as you allus did, but it was for our good. And now, look here, my lass, when we're gone—"

"When you're gone, Bart!" cried Mary, with her lip quivering.

"Ay, lass, when we're gone, for I daresay they'll hang us."

"Bart!"

"Oh, it won't hurt much. Not worse than being drownded, and much quicker."

"Oh, Bart, Bart!"

"Don't cry, my pretty one, only don't forget us. You won't forget Abel, of course; but—I never felt as if I could talk to you like this before—don't forget as Bart Wrigley was werry fond on you, and that, if he'd been a fine hansum chap, 'stead of such a rough un, with his figure-head all set o' one side, he'd ha' stuck up and said as no one else shouldn't have you."

"Oh, Bart, Bart!" sobbed Mary, piteously.

"Ay, lass, that he would; but he often says to himself, 'It wouldn't be kind to a girl like that to hang on to her.' So, good-bye, my pretty lady, and I'll tell Abel as he's the blind, thick-headed fool if he says it was you as got us into this hole."

Bart had to wind up his unwontedly long speech very quickly, for a couple of turnkeys had entered the stone-walled room, to conduct the big fellow back to his cell, and show Mary to the outside of the prison.

"Good bye, dear Bart, dear old friend!"

"Good bye, my pretty lady!" cried the big fellow? "You called me 'dear Bart' again."

"Yes, dear Bart, dear brother!" cried Mary, passionately, and, raising his big hand to her lips, she kissed it.

"Bah!" growled Bart to himself, "let 'em hang me. What do I care arter that? 'Dear Bart—dear Bart!' I wouldn't care a bit if I only knowed what she'd do when we're gone."

Then the time glided on, and Mary heard from one and another the popular belief that the authorities, rejoicing in having at last caught two notorious smugglers and wreckers red-handed in a serious offence, were determined to make an example by punishing them with the utmost rigour of the law.

The poor girl in her loneliness had racked her brains for means of helping her brother. She had sold everything of value they possessed to pay for legal assistance, and she had, with fertile imagination, plotted means for helping Abel to escape; but even if her plans had been possible, they had been crossed by her brother's obstinate disbelief in her truth. His last message was one which sent her to the cottage flushed and angry, for it was a cruel repetition of his old accusation, joined with a declaration that he disbelieved in her in other ways, and that this had been done in collusion with Captain Armstrong to get him and Bart out of her way.

"He'll be sorry some day," she said on the morning before the trial, as she sat low of spirit and alone in the little cottage.

"Poor Abel! he's very bitter and cruel; poor—Yes, do you want me?"

"Genlum give me this to give you," said a boy.

Mary excitedly caught at the letter the boy handed to her, and opening it with trembling hands, managed with no little difficulty to spell out its contents.

They were very short and laboriously written in a large schoolboy-like hand for her special benefit by one who knew her deficiencies of education.

"It is not too late yet. Abel will be tried to-morrow and condemned unless a piece of sea-weed is received to-night."

"And I used to love him and believe in him!" she cried at last passionately, as her hot indignation at last mastered her, and she tore the letter in pieces with her teeth, spat the fragments upon the ground, and stamped upon them with every mark of contempt and disgust.

Then a change came over her, and she sank sobbing upon a stool, to burst forth into a piteous wail.

"Oh, Abel!—brother!—it is all my doing. I have sent you to your death!"

Chapter Ten
A Daring Trick

The laws were tremendously stringent in those days when it was considered much easier to bring an offender's bad career to an end than to keep him at the nation's expense, and when the stealing of a sheep was considered a crime to be punished with death, an attack upon the sacred person of one of the king's officers by a couple of notorious law-breakers was not likely to be looked upon leniently by a judge well-known for stern sentences.

But a jury of Devon men was sitting upon the offence of Abel Dell and Bart Wrigley, and feeling disposed to deal easily with a couple of young fellows whose previous bad character was all in connection with smuggling, a crime with the said jury of a very light dye, certainly not black. Abel and Bart escaped the rope, and were sentenced to transportation to one of His Majesty's colonies in the West Indies, there to do convict work in connection with plantations, or the making of roads, as their taskmasters might think fit.

Time glided by, and Mary Dell found that her life at home had become insupportable.

She was not long in finding that, now that she was left alone and unprotected, she was not to be free from persecution. Her contemptuous rejection of Captain Armstrong's advances seemed to have the effect of increasing his persecution; and one evening at the end of a couple of months Mary Dell sat on one of the rocks outside the cottage door, gazing out to sea, and watching the ships sail westward, as she wondered whether those on board would ever see the brother who seemed to be all that was left to her in this world.

That particular night the thought which had been hatching in her brain ever since Abel had been sent away flew forth fully fledged and ready, and she rose from where she had been sitting in the evening sunshine, and walked into the cottage.

Mary Dell's proceedings would have excited a smile from an observer, but the cottage stood alone. She had heard that Captain Armstrong was from home and not expected back for a week, and there was no fear of prying eyes as the sturdy, well-built girl took down a looking-glass from where it hung to a nail, and, placing it upon the table, propped it with an old jar, and then seating herself before the glass, she folded her arms, rested them upon the table, and sat for quite an hour gazing at herself in the mirror.

Womanly vanity? Not a scrap of it, but firm, intense purpose: deep thought; calm, calculating observation before taking a step that was to influence her life.

She rose after a time and walked into her brother Abel's bed-room, where she stayed for some minutes, and then with a quick, resolute step she re-entered the cottage kitchen, thrust the few embers together that burned upon the hearth, took a pair of scissors from a box, and again seated herself before the glass.

The sun was setting, and filled the slate-floored kitchen with light which flashed back from the blurred looking-glass, and cast a curious glare in the girl's stern countenance, with its heavy dark brows, sun-browned ruddy cheeks, and gleaming eyes.

Snip!

The sharp scissors had passed through one lock of the massive black tresses which she had shaken over her shoulders, and which then rippled to the cottage floor.

Snip!

Another cut, and two locks had fallen. Then rapidly *snip, snip, snip*—a curious thick, sharp *snip*—and the great waves of glorious hair kept falling as the bare, sun-burned, ruddy arm played here and there, and the steel blades glittered and opened and closed, as if arm, hand, and scissors formed the neck, head, and angry bill of some fierce bird attacking that well-shaped head, and at every snap took off a thick tress of hair.

It was not a long task, and when the hair had all fallen, to lie around, one glorious ring of glossy black tresses, there were only a few snips to give here and there to finish off notches and too long, untidy spots, and then the girl rose, and with a cold, hard look upon her frowning face she stooped, and stooped, and stooped, and at each rising cast a great tress of hair to where the flames leaped, and seized it, torching the locks, which writhed, and curled, and flared, and crackled as if alive, while, as if to aid the idea that she was destroying something living, a peculiarly pungent odour arose, as of burning flesh, and filled the room.

An hour later, just as the red moon rose slowly above the surface of the sea, a sturdy-looking young man, with a stout stick in one hand—the very stick which had helped to belabour Captain Armstrong—and a bundle tied up in a handkerchief beneath his arm, stepped out of the cottage, changed the key from inside to outside, closed the old door, locked it, dragged out the key, and with a sudden jerk sent it flying far out into deep water beyond the rocks, where it fell with a dull *plash!* followed by a peculiar hissing sound, as the waves at high water rushed back over the fine shingle at the thrower's feet.

There was a sharp look round then; but no one was in sight; nothing to be heard but the hissing waters, and the splashing, gasping, and smacking sound, as the tide swayed in and out among the masses of stone. Then the figure turned once more to the cottage, gazed at it fixedly for a few moments, took a step or two away; but sprang back directly with an exceeding bitter cry, and kissed the rough, unpainted woodwork again and again with rapid action, and then dashed off to the foot of the cliff, and climbed rapidly to the sheep-track—the faintly-seen path that led towards Slapton Lea and the old hall, where the captain still stayed with his young wife, and then joined the west road which led to Plymouth town.

The risky part of the track was passed, and the open and down-like pastures beyond the cliffs were reached; and here, with the moon beginning to throw the shadow of the traveller far forward and in weird-looking length, the original of that shadow strode on manfully for another quarter of a mile, when all at once there was a stoppage, for another figure was seen coming from the direction of Torcross, and the moon shining full upon the face showed plainly who it was.

There was no question of identity, for that evening, after more than his customary modicum of wine, Captain James Armstrong—whose journey had been postponed—had snubbed his young wife cruelly, quarrelled with his cousin Humphrey, who had been there to dine, and then left the house, determined to go down to Mary Dell's solitary cottage.

"I'm a fool," he said; "I haven't been firm enough with the handsome cat. She scratched. Well, cats have claws, and when I have taught her how to purr nicely she'll keep them always sheathed. I'll bring her to her senses to-night, once and for all."

"Who the devil's this?" muttered the captain. "Humph! sailor on the tramp to Plymouth. Well, he won't know me. I won't turn back."

He strode on a dozen yards and then stopped short, as the figure before him had stopped a few moments before; and then a change came over the aspect of the captain. His knees shook, his face turned wet, and his throat grew dry.

It was horrible; but there could be no mistake.

"Abel Dell!" he cried, hoarsely, as he leaped at the idea that the brother had returned in spirit, to save his sister from all harm.

"Out of my path!" rang forth in answer, the voice being loud, imperious, and fierce; and then, in a tone of intense hatred and suppressed passion, the one word—"Dog!"

As the last word rang out there was a whistling as of a stick passing through the air, a tremendous thud, and the captain fell headlong upon the rocky ground.

Then there was utter silence as the young sailor placed one foot upon the prostrate man's chest, stamped upon it savagely, and strode on right away over the wild country bordering the sea.

The figure loomed up once in the moonlight, as the captain rose slowly upon one elbow, and gazed after it, to see that it seemed to be of supernatural proportions, and then he sank back again with a groan.

"It's a spirit," he said, "come back to her;" and then the poltroon fainted dead away.

Chapter Eleven
In the Plantation

Someone singing a West Country ditty.

"*His sloe-black eyes...*"

A pause in the singing, and the striking of several blows with a rough hoe, to the destruction of weeds in a coffee-plantation; while, as the chops of the hoe struck the clods of earth, the fetters worn by the striker gave forth faint clinks.

Then in a pleasant musical voice the singer went on with another line —

"*And his curly hair...*"

More chops with the hoe, and clinks of the fetters.

"*His pleasing voice...*"

A heavy thump with the back of the tool at an obstinate clod, which took several more strokes before it crumbled up; and all the time the fetters clinked and clanked loudly. Then the singer went on with the sweet old minor air with its childish words.

"*Did my heart ensnare...*"

Chop! chop! clink! clink! clank!

"*Genteel he was...*"

"But no rake like you."

"Oh, I say, Abel, mate; don't, lad, don't."

"Don't what?" said Abel Dell, resting upon his hoe, and looking up at big Bart Wrigley, clothed like himself, armed with a hoe, and also decorated with fetters, as he stood wiping the perspiration from his forehead.

"Don't sing that there old song. It do make me feel so unked."

"Unked, Bart! Well, what if it does? These are unked days."

"Ay; but each time you sings that I seem to see the rocks along by the shore at home, with the ivy hanging down, and the sheep feeding, and the sea rolling in, and the blue sky, with gulls a-flying; and it makes me feel like a boy again, and, big as I am, as if I should cry."

"Always were like a big boy, Bart. Hoe away, lad; the overseer's looking."

Bart went on chopping weeds, diligently following his friend's example, as a sour-looking, yellow-faced man came by, in company with a soldier loosely shouldering his musket. But they passed by without speaking, and Abel continued—

"There's sea here, and blue sky and sunshine."

"Ay," said Bart; "there's sunshine hot enough to fry a mack'rel. Place is right enough if you was free; but it ar'n't home, Abel, it ar'n't home."

"Home! no," said the young man, savagely. "But we have no home. She spoiled that."

There was an interval of weed-chopping and clod-breaking, the young men's chains clanking loudly as they worked now so energetically that the overseer noted their proceedings, and pointed them out as examples to an idle hand.

"Ah! you're a hard 'un, Abel," remarked Bart, after a time.

"Yes; and you're a soft 'un, Bart. She could always turn you round her little finger."

"Ay, bless her! and she didn't tell on us."

"Yes, she did," said Abel, sourly; and he turned his back upon his companion, and toiled away to hide the working of his face.

The sun shone down as hotly as it can shine in the West Indies, and the coarse shirts the young men wore showed patches of moisture where the perspiration came through, but they worked on, for the labour deadened the misery in their breasts.

And yet it was a very paradise, as far as nature was concerned. Man had spoiled it as far as he could, his cultivation being but a poor recompense for turning so lovely a spot into a plantation, worked by convicts—by men who fouled the ambient air each moment they opened their lips; while from time to time the earth was stained with blood.

In the distance shone the sea, and between the plantation and the silver coral sands lay patches of virgin forest, where the richest and most luxuriant of tropic growth revelled in the heat and moisture, while in the sunny patches brilliant flowers blossomed. Then came wild tangle, cane-brake, and in one place, where a creek indented the land, weird-looking mangroves spread their leafage over their muddy scaffolds of aërial roots.

"How long have we been here, mate?" said Bart, after a pause.

"Dunno," replied Abel, fiercely.

Here he began chopping more vigorously.

"How long will they keep us in this here place?" said Bart, after another interval, and he looked from the beautiful shore at the bottom of the slope on which they worked to the cluster of stone and wood-built buildings, which formed the prison and the station farm, with factory and mill, all worked by convict labour, while those in the neighbourhood were managed by blacks.

Abel did not answer, only scowled fiercely; and Bart sighed, and repeated his question.

"Till we die!" said Abel, savagely; "same as we've seen other fellows die—of fever, and hard work, and the lash. Curse the captain! Curse—"

Bart clapped one hand over his companion's lips, and he held the other behind his head, dropping his hoe to leave full liberty to act.

"I never quarrels with you, Abel, lad," he said, shortly; "but if you says words again that poor gell, I'm going to fight—and that won't do. Is it easy?"

Abel seemed disposed to struggle; but he gave in, nodded his head, and Bart loosed him and picked up his hoe, just as the overseer, who had come softly up behind, brought down the whip he carried with stinging violence across the shoulders of first one and then the other.

The young men sprang round savagely; but there was a sentry close behind, musket-armed and with bayonet fixed, and they knew that fifty soldiers were within call, and that if they struck their task-master down and made for the jungle they would be hunted out with dogs, be shot down like wild beasts, or die of starvation, as other unfortunates had died before them.

There was nothing for it but to resume their labour and hoe to the clanking of their fetters, while, after a promise of what was to follow, in the shape of tying up to the triangles, and the cat, if they quarrelled again, the overseer went on to see to the others of his flock.

"It's worse than a dog's life!" said Abel, bitterly. "A dog does get patted as well as kicked. Bart, lad, I'm sorry I got you that lash."

"Nay, lad, never mind," said Bart. "I'm sorry for you; but don't speak hard things of Mary."

"I'll try not," said Abel, as he hoed away excitedly; "but I hope this coffee we grow may poison those who drink it."

"What for? They can't help it," said Bart, smiling. "There, lad, take it coolly. Some day we may make a run for it."

"And be shot!" said Abel, bitterly. "There, you're down to the end of that row. I'll go this way. He's watching us."

Bart obeyed. He was one who always did obey; and by degrees the young men were working right away from each other, till they were a good two hundred yards apart.

Abel was at the end of his row first, and he stopped and turned to begin again and go down, so as to pass Bart at about the middle of the clearing; but Bart had another minute's chopping to do before turning.

He was close up to a dense patch of forest—one wild tangle of cane and creeper, which literally tied the tall trees together and made the forest impassable—when the shrieking of a kind of jay, which had been flitting about excitedly, stopped, and was followed by the melodious whistle of a white bird and the twittering of quite a flock of little fellows of a gorgeous scarlet-crimson. Then the shrieking of several parrots answering each other arose; while just above Bart's head, where clusters of trumpet-shaped blossoms hung down from the edge of the forest, scores of brilliantly-scaled humming-birds literally buzzed on almost transparent wing, and then suspended themselves in mid-air as they probed the nectaries of the flowers with their long bills.

"You're beauties, you are," said Bart, stopping to wipe his brow; "but I'd give the hull lot on you for a sight of one good old sarcy sparrer a-sitting on the cottage roof and saying *chisel chisel*. Ah! shall us ever see old Devonshire again?"

The parrots hung upside-down, and the tiny humming-birds flitted here and there, displaying, from time to time, the brilliancy of their scale-like feathers, and Bart glanced at his fellow-convict and was about to work back, when there came a sound from out of the dark forest which made him stare wildly, and then the sound arose again.

Bart changed colour, and did not stop to hoe, but walked rapidly across to Abel.

"What's the matter?" said the latter.

"Dunno, lad," said the other, rubbing his brow with his arm; "but there's something wrong."

"What is it?"

"That's what I dunno; but just now something said quite plain, 'Bart! Bart!'"

"Nonsense! You were dreaming."

"Nay. I was wide awake as I am now, and as I turned and stared it said it again."

"It said it?"

"Well, she said it."

"Poll parrot," said Abel, gruffly. "Go on with your work. Here's the overseer."

The young men worked away, and their supervisor passed them, and, apparently satisfied, continued his journey round.

"May have been a poll parrot," said Bart. "They do talk plain, Abel, lad; but this sounded like something else."

"What else could it be?"

"Sounded like a ghost."

Abel burst into a hearty laugh—so hearty that Bart's face was slowly overspread by a broad smile.

"Why, lud, that's better," he said, grimly. "I ar'n't seen you do that for months. Work away."

The hint was given because of the overseer glancing in their direction, and they now worked on together slowly, going down the row toward the jungle, at which Bart kept on darting uneasy glances.

"Enough to make a man laugh to hear you talk of ghosts, Bart," said Abel, after a time.

"What could it be, then?"

"Parrot some lady tamed," said Abel, shortly, as they worked on side by side, "escaped to the woods again. Some of these birds talk just like a Christian."

"Ay," said Bart, after a few moments' quiet thought, "I've heared 'em, lad; but there's no poll parrot out here as knows me."

"Knows you?"

"Well, didn't I tell you as it called to me 'Bart! Bart!'"

"Sounded like it," said Abel, laconically. "What does he want?"

For just then the overseer shouted, and signed to the gang-men to come to him.

"To begin another job—log-rolling, I think," growled Bart, shouldering his hoe.

At that moment, as Abel followed his example, there came in a low, eager tone of voice from out of the jungle, twenty yards away—

"Bart!—Abel!—Abel!"

"Don't look," whispered Abel, who reeled as if struck, and recovered himself to catch his companion by the arm. "All right!" he said aloud; "we'll be here to-morrow. We must go."

Chapter Twelve
In Deadly Peril

It was quite a week before the two young men were at work in the plantation of young trees again, and during all that time they had feverishly discussed the voice they had heard. Every time they had approached the borders of the plantation when it ran up to the virgin forest they had been on the *qui vive*, expecting to hear their names called again, but only to be disappointed; and, after due consideration, Abel placed a right interpretation upon the reason.

"It was someone who got ashore from a boat," he said, "and managed to crawl up there. It's the only place where anyone could get up."

"Being nigh that creek, lad, where the crocodiles is," said Bart. "Ay, you're right. Who could it be?"

"One of our old mates."

"Nay; no old mate would take all that trouble for us, lad. It's someone Mary's sent to bring us a letter and a bit of news."

It was at night in the prison lines that Bart said this, and then he listened wonderingly in the dark, for he heard something like a sob from close to his elbow.

"Abel, matey!" he whispered.

"Don't talk to me, old lad," came back hoarsely after a time. And then, after a long silence, "Yes, you're right. Poor lass—poor lass!"

"Say that again, Abel; say that again," whispered Bart, excitedly.

"Poor lass! I've been too hard on her. She didn't get us took."

"Thank God!"

These were Bart's hoarsely whispered words, choked with emotion; and directly after, as he lay there, Abel Dell felt a great, rough, trembling hand pass across his face and search about him till it reached his own, which it gripped and held with a strong, firm clasp, for there was beneath Bart's rough, husk-like exterior a great deal of the true, loyal, loving material of which English gentlemen are made; and when towards morning those two prisoners fell asleep in their chains, hand was still gripped in hand, while the dreams that brightened the remaining hours of their rest from penal labour were very similar, being of a rough home down beneath Devon's lovely cliffs, where the sea ran sparkling over the clean-washed pebbles, and the handsome face of Mary smiled upon each in turn.

"Abel, mate, I'm ready for anything now," said Bart, as they went that morning to their work. "Only say again as you forgive our lass."

"Bart, old lad," said Abel, hoarsely, "I've nought to forgive."

"Hah!" ejaculated Bart, and then he began to whistle softly as if in the highest of spirits, and looked longingly in the direction of the jungle beside the mud creek; but three days elapsed before they were set to hoe among the coffee bushes again.

Bart let his chin go down upon his chest on the morning when the order was given, and the overseer saw it and cracked his whip.

"You sulky ruffian!" he cried. "None of your sour looks with me. Get on with you!"

He cracked his whip again, and Bart shuffled off, clinking his fetters loudly.

"Do keep between us, Abel, lad," he whispered, "or I shall go off and he'll see. Oh, lor', how I do want to laugh!"

He restrained his mirth for a time, and they walked on to the end of the plantation and began their task at the opposite end to where they had left off, when the rate at which their hoes were plied was such that they were not long before they began to near the dense jungle, beyond which lay the mangrove swamp and the sea.

"I daren't hope, Bart," whispered Abel, so despondently that his companion, in a wildly excited manner, laughed in his face.

"What a lad you are!" he cried. "It's all right; he's waiting for us. It's some, sailor chap from Dartmouth, whose ship's put in at Kingston or Belize. Cheer up, mate!"

But it was all a mockery; and when they approached the jungle at last, hoeing more slowly for, much as they longed to go up at once, they knew that any unusual movement on their part, might be interpreted by watchful eyes into an attempt at escape, and bring down upon them a shot. Bart's voice trembled and sounded hoarsely as he said playfully—

"Now, Abel, my lad, I'm going to talk to that there poll parrot."

"Hush!" whispered Abel, agitatedly. "Keep on quietly with your work till we get close, and then call softly."

"Oh, it's all straight, lad," whispered back Bart, chopping away and breaking clods, as his fetters clanked more loudly than ever. "Now, then, Polly! Pretty Polly, are you there?"

"Yes, yes, Bart. Abel, dear brother, at last, at last!" came from the jungle.

"Mary—Polly, my girl!" cried Abel, hoarsely, as he threw down his hoe; and he was running toward the jungle, where a crashing sound was heard, when Bart flung his strong arms across his chest and dashed him to the ground.

"Are you mad!" he cried. "Mary, for God's sake keep back!"

The warning was needed, for from across the plantation the overseer and a couple of soldiers came running, every movement on the part of the prisoners being watched.

"Sham ill, lad; sham ill," whispered Bart, as a piteous sigh came from the depths of the jungle.

"Now, then, you two. Fighting again!" roared the overseer, as he came panting up.

"Fighting, sir!" growled Bart; "rum fighting. He nearly went down."

"He was trying to escape."

"Escape!" growled Bart. "Look at him. Sun's hot."

The overseer bent down over Abel, whose aspect helped the illusion, for he looked ghastly from his emotion; and he had presence of mind enough to open his eyes, look about, wildly from face to face, and then begin to struggle up, with one hand to his head.

"Is it the fayver, sor?" said one of the soldiers.

"No. Touch of the sun," said the overseer. "They're always getting it. There, you're all right, ar'n't you?"

"Yes, sir," said Abel, slowly, as he picked up his hoe.

"Sit down under the trees there for a few minutes," said the overseer. "Lend him your water bottle, soldier. And you stop with him till he's hotter. I'll come back soon."

This last was to Bart, playing, as it were, into the prisoners' hands, for Bart took the water bottle; and as the overseer went off with his guard, Abel was assisted to the edge of the jungle where a huge cotton-tree threw its shade; and here Bart placed him on an old stump, trembling the while, as he held the water to his companion's lips.

It was hard work to keep still while the others went out of hearing; but at last it seemed safe, and Abel panted out—

"Mary, dear, are you there?"

"Yes, yes, Abel. Oh, my dear brother, say one kind word to me!"

"Kind word? Oh, my lass, my lass, say that you forgive me!"

"Forgive you? Yes. But quick, dear, before those men come back."

"Tell me, then," said Abel, speaking with his back to the jungle, and his head bent down as if ill, while Bart leaned over him, trembling like a leaf, "tell me how you came to be here."

"I came over in a ship to Kingston. Then I went to New Orleans. Then to Honduras. And it was only a fortnight ago that I found you."

"But how did you come here?"

"I've got a small boat, dear. I asked and asked for months before I could find out where you were. I've been to other plantations, and people have thought me mad; but one day I stumbled across the sailors of a ship that comes here with stores from the station, and I heard them say that there were a number of prisoners working at this place; and at last, after waiting and watching for weeks and weeks, I caught sight of you two, and then it was a month before I could speak to you as I did the other day."

"And now you have come," said Abel, bitterly, "I can't even look at you."

"But you will escape, dear," said Mary.

"Escape!" cried Abel, excitedly.

"Steady, lad, steady. 'Member you're ill," growled Bart, glancing toward the nearest sentry, and then holding up the bottle as if to see how much was within.

"Yes, escape," said Mary. "I have the boat ready. Can you come now?"

"Impossible! We should be overtaken and shot before we had gone a mile."

"But you must escape," said Mary. "You must get down here by night."

"How?" said Bart, gruffly.

"You two must settle that," said Mary, quickly. "I am only a woman; but I have found means to get here with a boat, and I can come again and again till you join me."

"Yes," said Abel, decidedly; "we will contrive that."

"But is it safe, lass, where you are?"

"What do you mean?"

"They told us there was the crocodiles all along that creek, and sharks out beyond, if we tried to run."

"Yes," said Mary, calmly, "there are plenty of these creatures about."

"Listen," said Abel, quickly, and speaking as decidedly now as his sister. "Can you get here night after night?"

"Yes," said Mary. "I have been here every night since I spoke to you last."

"Then keep on coming."

"Yes," said Mary; "I will till you escape."

"You have the boat?"

"Yes."

"And provisions?"

"Yes; a little."

"But how do you manage?"

"I am fishing if any one sees me; but it is very lonely here. I see nothing but the birds," she added to herself, "and sharks and alligators;" and as she said this she smiled sadly.

"Be careful, then," said Abel. "Bart, old lad, we will escape."

There was a loud expiration of the breath from the jungle, and Abel continued —

"I must get up and go on work, or they will be back. Mary, once more, you have a boat?"

"Yes."

"And can come up here and wait?"

"Yes."

Quick, short, decided answers each time.

"Then be cautious. Only come by night."

"I know. Trust me. I will not be seen. I will do nothing rash. To-night as soon as it grows dark, I shall be here expecting you, for I shall not stir. At daybreak I shall go, and come again at night."

"And mind the sentries."

"Trust me, Abel. I shall not come now by day for six days. If at the end of six nights you have not been able to escape, I shall come for six days by day, hoping that you may be more successful in the daylight; for perhaps you will find that a bold dash will help you to get away."

"But the risk — the risk?" panted Abel — "the risk, girl, to you!"

"Abel, dear, I am here to risk everything. I have risked everything to join you."

"Yes," he said, hoarsely. "But afterwards. If we do escape?"

"Leave the plans to me," she said, with a little laugh. "I have boat and sail, and the world is very wide. Only escape. Take care; the men are coming back."

Mary's voice ceased; and Abel took hold of Bart's arm, rose, raised his hoe, and walked with him to where they had left off work, to begin again slowly, the two men trembling with excitement now; for, as the overseer neared them, a bird began flying to and fro over the edge of the jungle, screaming wildly, evidently from the fact that somebody was hidden there.

The excitement of the bird, whose nest was probably somewhere near, did not, however, take the attention of the overseer, who came up, followed by the Irish sentry, stared hard at Abel, gave a short nod as if satisfied that one of his beasts of burden was not going to permanently break down, and then, to the horror of the young men, took off his hat, began fanning himself, and went and sat down in the very spot where Abel had talked with his sister!

"Hot, Paddy, hot!" he said to the soldier.

"Dinny, sor, av you plaze. Thrue for you, sor, and a taste of dhrink would be very nice for ye; but I shouldn't sit there."

"Why not?" said the overseer.

"Because the place swarms with them ugly, four-futted, scaly divils. I've gone the rounds here of a night, sor, and heard them snapping their jaws and thumping the wet mud with their tails till I've shivered again."

"Yes, there's plenty of them in the creek, Dinny."

"Plinty, sor, 's nothing to it. There niver seems to have been a blessed Saint Pathrick here to get rid of the varmin. Why, I've seen frogs here as big as turtles, and sarpints that would go round the Hill of Howth."

"Well, look here, Dinny, cock your piece, and if you see anything stir, let drive at it at once."

"Oi will, sor," said the soldier, obeying orders; and, taking a step or two forward, he stood watchfully gazing into the dark jungle.

"Have you got your knife, Bart?" whispered Abel, whose face was of a peculiar muddy hue.

Bart nodded as he chopped away.

"Shall we make a rush at them, and stun them with the hoes?"

Bart shook his head.

"Mary's too clever," he whispered back. "She's well hidden, and will not stir."

"If that Irish beast raises his musket I must go at him," whispered Abel, who was trembling from head to foot.

"Hold up, man. She heer'd every word, and won't stir."

"Silence, there. No talking!" cried the overseer.

"Let the poor divils talk, sor," said the soldier. "Faix, it's bad enough to put chains on their legs; don't put anny on their tongues."

"If I get you down," thought Abel, "I won't kill you, for that."

"Against orders," said the overseer, good-humouredly. "Well, can you see anything stirring?"

"Not yet, sor; but I hope I shall. Bedad, I'd be glad of a bit o' sport, for it's dhry work always carrying a gun about widout having a shot."

"Yes; but when you do get a shot, it's at big game, Dinny."

"Yis, sor, but then it's very seldom," said the sentry, with a roguish twinkle of the eye.

"I can't bear this much longer, Bart," whispered Abel. "When I say *Now!* rush at them both with your hoe."

"Wait till he's going to shoot, then," growled Bart.

The overseer bent down, and, sheltering himself beneath the tree, placed his hands out in the sunshine, one holding a roughly rolled cigar, the other a burning-glass, with which he soon focussed the vivid white spot of heat which made the end of the cigar begin to smoke, the tiny spark being drawn into incandescence by application to the man's lips, while the pleasant odour of the burning leaf arose.

"Sure, an' that's an illigant way of getting a light, sor," said the sentry.

"Easy enough with such a hot sun," said the overseer, complacently.

"Hot sun, sor! Sure I never carry my mushket here widout feeling as if it will go off in my hands; the barl gets nearly red-hot!"

"Yah! Don't point it this way," said the overseer, smoking away coolly. "Well, can you see anything?"

"Divil a thing but that noisy little omadhaun of a bird. Sure, she'd be a purty thing to have in a cage."

Abel's face grew more ghastly as he gazed at Bart, who remained cool and controlled him.

"Bart," whispered Abel, with the sweat rolling off his face in beads, "what shall we do?"

"Wait," said the rough fellow shortly; and he hoed away, with his fetters clinking, and his eyes taking in every movement of the two men;

while involuntarily Abel followed his action in every respect, as they once more drew nearer to their task-master and his guard.

"There's a something yonder, sor," said the soldier at last.

"Alligator!" said the overseer, lazily; and Abel's heart rose so that he seemed as if he could not breathe.

"I can't see what it is, sor; but it's a something, for the little burrud kapes darting down at it and floying up again. I belayve it is one of they crockidills. Shall I shute the divil?"

"How can you shoot it if you can't see it, you fool?" said the overseer.

"Sure, sor, they say that every bullet has its billet, and if I let the little blue pill out of the mouth o' the mushket, faix, it's a strange thing if it don't find its way into that ugly scaly baste."

The overseer took his cigar from his lips and laughed; but to the intense relief of the young men, perhaps to the saving of his own life, he shook his head.

"No, Dinny," he said, "it would alarm the station. They'd think someone was escaping. Let it be."

Dinny sighed, the overseer smoked on, and the hot silence of the tropic clearing was only broken by the screaming and chattering of the excited bird, the hum of insects, and the clink-clink, thud-thud, of fetters and hoe as the convicts toiled on in the glowing sun.

They kept as near as they dared to their task-master, and he smiled superciliously as he put his own interpretation upon their acts.

"The artful scoundrels!" he said to himself; "they want me to believe that they always work like this. Well, it helps the plantation;" and he smoked placidly on, little dreaming that every time Abel reversed his hoe, so as to break a clod with the back, the young man glanced at him and measured the distance between them, while he calculated how long to hold the handle of the tool, and where would be the best place to strike the enemy so as to disable him at once.

"You take the soldier, Bart," said Abel, softly. "I'll manage the overseer."

"Right, lad! but not without we're obliged."

"No. Then, as soon as they're down, into the wood, find Mary, and make for her boat."

The heat was intense, the shade beneath the great cotton-tree grateful, and the aroma of the cigar so delicious that the overseer sank into a drowsy reverie; while the soldier gave the two convicts a half-laughing look and then turned to face the jungle, whose depths he pierced with his eyes.

Bart drew a long breath and gazed toward the dark part of the jungle, and there was an intense look of love and satisfaction in his eyes as he tried to make out the place where Mary lay, as he believed, hidden. The sight of the sentry on the watch with his gun ready had ceased to trouble him, for he had told himself that the clumsy fellow could not hit a barn-door, let alone a smaller mark; while Abel seemed to be less agitated, and to be resuming his normal state.

They were not twenty yards from the edge of the forest now, the sentry's back was toward them, and the overseer was getting to the end of his cigar, and watching the watcher with half-closed eyes, and an amused smile upon his yellow countenance.

"Every bullet finds its billet," he muttered to himself; and, stretching himself, he was in the act of rising, when the bird, which had been silent, uttered a shrill, chattering cry, as if freshly disturbed, and the soldier shouted excitedly— "Theer, sor, I can see it. A big one staling away among the threes. For the sake of all the saints give the wurrud!"

"Fire, then!" cried the overseer; and the sentry raised his piece to the "present."

Bart Wrigley had not been at sea from childhood without winning a sailor's eyes. Dark as the jungle was, and more distant as he stood, it was not so black that he could not make out the object which had oaken the sentry's notice, and at which he took aim.

One moment Bart raised his hoe to rush at the man; the next he had brought it down heavily on Abel's boulders, sending him forward upon his face, and uttering a cry of rage as he fell.

It was almost simultaneous. The cry uttered by Abel Dell and the report of the sentry's piece seemed to smite the air together; but Abel's cry was first, and disarranged the soldier's aim, his bullet cutting the leaves of the jungle far above the ground.

"Look at that now!" he cried, as he turned sharply to see Abel struggling on the ground, with Bart holding him, and the overseer drawing a pistol front his breast.

"Lie still!" whispered Bart. "It was not at Mary."

Then aloud—

"Quick, here! water! He's in a fit."

As Abel grasped his friend's thoughts he lay back, struggling faintly, and then half-closed his eyes and was quite still.

"It's the sun, sir," said Bart, as the overseer thrust back his pistol and came up. "Hadn't we better get him back to the lines?"

"Yes," said the overseer. "Poor devil! No, no! Back, back!" he roared, signalling with his hands as a sergeant's guard came along at the double. "Nothing wrong. Only a man sick, and Dinny Kelly here had a shot at an alligator."

"An' I should have hit him, sor, if he hadn't shouted. But think o' that, now! The sun lights gentleman's cigar one minute, and shtrikes a man down the next. But it's better than the yaller fayver, anyhow."

Five days had passed, and the prisoners were not sent again to the clearing, while, in spite of every effort, they found that their chances of eluding the guard set over them by night were small indeed.

Fettered by day, they were doubly chained by night. The building where they slept was strongly secured and guarded, and in spite of the newness of the settlement it was well chosen for its purpose, and stronger even than the prisoners thought.

"We shall never get away by night, Bart," said Abel, gloomily, "unless—"

He stopped and gazed meaningly at his companion.

"The knife?" responded Bart. "No, lad, we won't do that. I shouldn't like to go to Mary wet with blood."

Abel's countenance grew dark and deeply hard, for at that moment, in his despair and disappointment, he felt ready to go to any extremity, knowing, as he did, that his sister was waiting for him, holding out her hands and saying, "Come!"

Only another day, and then she would give up expecting them by night, and take to watching for them by day, when the attempt seemed hopeless.

And so it proved, for during the following week the prisoners were only once in the coffee-plantation, and so strictly watched that they felt that to attempt an evasion was only to bring destruction upon their hopes, perhaps cause Mary's imprisonment for attempting to assist prisoners to escape.

"It's of no use, Bart," said Abel at last, despondently. "Poor girl! Why did she come?"

"Help us away," said Bart, gruffly.

"Yes, but all in vain."

"Tchah! Wait a bit."

"Do you think she will still come and wait?" said Abel, dolefully.

"Do I think th' sun 'll shine agen?" growled Bart. "Here's a fellow! Born same time as that there lass, lived with her all his days, and then he knows so little about her that he says, 'Will she come agen?'"

"Enough to tire her out."

"Tchah!" cried Bart again, "when you know she'll keep on coming till she's an old grey-headed woman, or she gets us away."

Abel shook his head, for he was low-spirited and not convinced; but that night his heart leaped, for as he lay half asleep, listening to the thin buzzing hum of the mosquitoes which haunted the prisoners' quarters, and the slow, regular pace of the sentry on guard outside, there was the faint rattle of a chain, as if some prisoner had turned in his unquiet rest, and then all was silent again, till he started, for a rough hand was laid upon his mouth.

His first instinct was to seize the owner of that hand, to engage in a struggle for his life; but a mouth was placed directly at his ear, and a well-known voice whispered —

"Don't make a sound. Tie these bits of rag about your irons so as they don't rattle."

Abel caught at the pieces of cloth and canvas thrust into his hand, and, sitting up in the darkness, he softly bound the links and rings of his fetters together, hardly daring to breathe, and yet with his heart beating tumultuously in his anxiety to know his companion's plans.

For an attempt it must be, Abel felt, though up to the time of their going to rest after the day's work Bart had said nothing to him. He must have made a sudden discovery, and there was nothing for it but to obey in every way and trust to what was to come.

Abel felt this as he rapidly knotted the rag round his chains, and as he was tying the last knot he felt Bart's hand upon his shoulder, and his lips at his ear.

"Quiet, and creep after me. Keep touching my foot so's not to miss me in the dark."

Abel's heart thumped against his ribs as he obeyed, taking Bart's hand first in a firm grip, and then feeling a short iron bar thrust between his fingers.

Then he became conscious from his companion's movements that he had gone down upon his hands and knees, and was crawling toward the end of the long, low, stone-walled building that served as a dormitory for the white slaves whose task was to cultivate the rough plantation till they, as a rule, lay down and died from fever or some of the ills that haunted the tropic land.

Just then Bart stopped short, for there were steps outside, and a gleam of light appeared beneath the heavy door. Voices were heard, and the rattle of a soldier's musket.

"Changing guard," said Abel to himself; and he found himself wondering whether the sergeant and his men would enter the prison.

To add to the risk of discovery, there was a shuffling sound on the left, and a clink of chains, as one man seemed to rise upon his elbow; and his movement roused another, who also clinked his chains in the darkness and growled out an imprecation.

All this time Bart remained absolutely motionless, and Abel listened with the perspiration streaming from him in the intense heat.

Then there was a hoarsely uttered command; the light faded away, the steps died out upon the ear; there was a clink or two of chains, and a heavy sigh from some restless sleeper, and once more in the black silence and stilling heat there was nothing to be heard but the loud trumpeting buzz of the mosquitoes.

Softly, as some large cat, Bart resumed his crawling movement, after thrusting back his leg and touching Abel on the chest with his bare foot as a signal.

The building was quite a hundred feet long by about eighteen wide, a mere gallery in shape, which had been lengthened from time to time as the number of convicts increased, and the men had about two-thirds of the distance to traverse before they could reach the end, and at their excessively slow rate of progress the time seemed interminable before, after several painful halts, caused by movements of their fellow-prisoners and dread of discovery, the final halt was made.

"Now, then, what is it?" whispered Abel.

The answer he received was a hand laid across his mouth, and his heart began to beat more wildly than ever, for Bart caught his hand, drew it toward him, and as it was yielded, directed the fingers downward to the stone level with the floor.

Abel's heart gave another bound, for that stone was loose, and as he was pressed aside he heard a faint gritting, his companion's breath seemed to come more thickly, as if from exertion, and for the next hour—an hour that seemed like twelve—Abel lay, unable to help, but panting with anxiety, as the gritting noise went on, and he could mentally see that Bart was slowly drawing out rough pieces of badly-cemented stone—rough fragments really of coral and limestone from the nearest reef, of which the prison barrack was built.

Three times over Abel had tried to help, but the firm pressure of his companion's hand forcing him back spoke volume, and he subsided into his position in the utter darkness, listening with his pulses throbbing and subsiding, as the gritting sound was made or the reverse.

At last, after what seemed an age, a faint breath of comparatively cool air began to play upon his cheek, as Bart seemed to work steadily on. That breath grew broader and fuller, and there was a soft odour of the sea mingled with the damp coolness of a breeze which had passed over the dewy ground before it began to set steadily in at the opening at which Bart had so patiently worked, for that there was an opening was plain enough now, as Abel exultantly felt.

In his inaction the torture of the dread was intense, and he lay wondering whether, if they did get out, Mary would still be waiting, expecting them, or their efforts prove to have been in vain.

At last, just when he felt as if he could bear it no longer, Bart's hand gripped him by the shoulder, and pressed him tightly. Then in the darkness his hand was seized and guided where it hardly wanted guiding, for the young man's imagination had painted all—to a rough opening level with the floor, a hole little larger than might have been made for fowls to pass in and out of a poultry-yard.

This done, Bart gave him a thrust which Abel interpreted to mean, "Go on."

Abel responded with another, to indicate, "No; you go."

Bart gripped him savagely by the arm, and he yielded, crept slowly to the hole, went down upon his breast, and softly thrust his head through into the dank night air, to hear plainly the sighing and croaking of the reptiles in the swamp, and see before him the sparkling scintillations of the myriad fireflies darting from bush to bush.

He wormed himself on, and was about to draw forth one hand and arm, but always moving as silently as some nocturnal beast of prey, when it suddenly occurred to him that the glow of one of the fireflies was unusually large; and before he had well grasped this idea there was the regular tramp of feet, and he knew that it was the lantern of the guard moving across to the prison barrack, and that they must come right past where he lay.

He must creep back and wait; and as the steps steadily approached and the tramp grew plainer he began to wriggle himself through, getting his arm well in and his shoulders beginning to follow till only his head was outside, and the dull light of the lantern seeming to show it plainly, when to his horror he found that some portion of his garment had caught upon a rough projection and he was fast.

He made a tremendous effort, but could not drag it free, for his arms were pressed close to his sides and he was helpless. If Bart had known and passed a hand through, he might have freed him, but he could not explain his position; and all the time the guard was coming nearer and nearer, the lantern-light dancing upon the rough path, until it would be hardly possible for the nearest soldier to pass him without stumbling against his head.

Discovery, extra labour, the lash, more irons, and the chance of evasion gone; all those displayed, as it were, before Abel Dell's gaze as he thought of his sister waiting for them with that boat all plainly seen by the gleaming light of that lantern as the soldiers came steadily on.

It was absolutely impossible that the sergeant and his four men, whom the light had revealed quite plainly to Abel Dell, could pass him without something unusual occurred. The sergeant was carrying his lantern swinging at arm's length, on his left side, and the bottom as he passed would only be a few inches above the prisoner's head.

Abel knew all this as he pressed his teeth together to keep down the agonising feeling of despair he felt already as the men came on in regular pace, with the barrels of the muskets and their bayonets gleaming, and he expected to hear an exclamation of astonishment with the command "Halt!" — when something unusual did happen.

For all at once, just as the back of Abel's head must have loomed up like a black stone close by the sergeant's path, and the rays of light glistened on his short, crisp, black hair, there came a loud croaking bellow from down in the swamp by the crook, and Dinny exclaimed aloud:

"Hark at that now!"

"Silence in the ranks!" cried the sergeant fiercely; and then, as if the Irishman's words were contagious, he, turning his head as did his men towards the spot whence the sound proceeded, exclaimed, "What was it?"

"One of them lovely crockidills, sergeant dear—the swate craytures, with that plisant smile they have o' their own. Hark at him again!"

The same croaking roar arose, but more distant, as if it were the response to a challenge.

"Don't it carry you home again sergeant, dear?"

"Silence in the—How, Dinny?" said the sergeant, good-humouredly, for the men were laughing.

"Why, my mother had a cow—a Kerry cow, the darlint—and Farmer Magee, half a mile across the bog, had a bull, and you could hear him making love to her at toimes just like that, and moighty plisant it was."

"And used he to come across the bog," said the sergeant, "to court her?"

"And did he come across the bog to court her!" said Dinny, with a contemptuous tone in his voice. "And could you go across the bog courting if Farmer Magee had put a ring through your nose, and tied you up to a post, sergeant dear? Oh, no! The farmer was moighty particular about that bull's morals, and niver let him out of a night."

"Silence in the ranks! 'Tention!" said the serjeant. "Half left!"

Tramp! tramp! tramp! tramp, and the men passed round the end of the building just as the alligator bellowed again.

Abel drew a long breath and rapidly drew himself through the hole—no easy task and Bart began follow, but only to stick before he was half-way through.

"I'm at it again," he whispered. "Natur' made me crooked o' purpose to go wrong at times like this."

Abel seized his hands, as he recalled the incident at the cottage.

"Now," he whispered, "both together—hard!"

Bart gave himself a wrench as his companion tugged tremendously, and the resistance was overcome.

"Half my skin," growled Bart, as he struggled to his feet and stood by his companion. "Now, lad, this way."

"No, no; that's the way the soldiers have gone."

"It's the only way, lad. The dogs are yonder, and we couldn't get over the palisade. Now!"

They crept on in silence, seeing from time to time glints of the lantern, and in the midst of the still darkness matters seemed to be going so easily for them that Abel's heart grew more regular in its pulsation, and he was just asking himself why he had not had invention enough to contrive this evasion, when a clear and familiar voice cried, "Shtand!" and there was the click of a musket-lock.

What followed was almost momentary.

Bart struck aside the bayonet levelled at his breast, and leaped upon the sentry before him, driving him backward and clapping his hand upon his mouth as he knelt upon his chest; while, ably seconding him, his companion wrested the musket from the man's hand, twisted the bayonet from the end of the barrel, and, holding it daggerwise, pressed it against the man's throat.

"Hold aside, Bart," whispered Abel, savagely.

"No, no," growled Bart. "No blood, lad."

"'Tis for our lives and liberty!" whispered Abel, fiercely.

"Ay, but—" growled Bart. "Lie still, will you!" he muttered, as fiercely as his companion, for the sentry had given a violent heave and wrested his mouth free.

"Sure, an' ye won't kill a poor boy that how, gintlemen," he whispered, piteously.

"Another word, and it's your last!" hissed Abel.

"Sure, and I'll be as silent as Pater Mulloney's grave, sor," whispered the sentry; "but it's a mother I have over in the owld country, and ye'd break her heart if ye killed me."

"Hold your tongue!" whispered Bart.

"Sure, and I will, sor. It's not meself as would stop a couple of gintlemen from escaping. There's the gate, gintlemen. Ye've got my mushket, and I can't stop you."

"Yes, come along," whispered Bart.

"What! and leave him to give the alarm?" said Abel. "We're wasting time, man. 'Tis his life or ours."

"Not at all, sor," whispered the sentry, pleadingly. "I won't give the alarm, on my hanner; and you can't kill a boy widout letting him just say, 'How d'ye do?' and 'Which is the way yander?' to the praste."

"Shall we trust him?" said Bart, in a low growl.

"No!"

"Then take me wid ye, gintlemen. Faix, ye might force me to go, for the divil a bit do I want to shtay here."

"Look here," whispered Bart; "it's neck or nothing, my lad. If you give the alarm, it will be with that bayonet struck through you."

"And would a Kelly give the alarm, afther he said on his hanner? Sure, you might thrust me."

"Over with you, then, Bart," whispered Abel; "I'll stand over him here. Take the gun."

Bart obeyed, and Abel stood with one hand upon the sentry's shoulder, and the bayonet close to his throat.

"An' is that the way you thrust a gintleman?" said Dinny, contemptuously, as Bart, with all a sailor's and rock-climber's activity, drew himself up, and dropped from the top of the wall at the side.

"Now, you over," whispered Abel. "We shall take you with us till we're safe; but so sure as you give warning of our escape, you lose your life!"

"Ah! ye may thrust me," said the sentry, quickly. "Is it over wid me?"

"Yes; quick!"

The man scaled the gate as easily as Bart had done before him, and then Abel followed; but as he reached the top and shuffled sidewise to the wall, which he bestrode, there was the sound of a shot, followed by another, and another, and the fierce baying of dogs.

"Bedad, they've seen ye," said the sentry, as Abel dropped down.

"They've been in the barrack," whispered Bart.

"To be sure they have, sor; the sergeant was going round."

"Quick, take his hand!" said Bart.

"No!" whispered Abel, levelling the bayonet.

"No, no; for my mother's sake, sor!" cried the sentry, piteously. "She has only six of us, and I'm one."

"Put away that bagnet!" said Bart, hoarsely. "Take his hand, and run!"

"That's it, sor, at the double," said the sentry, rising from his knees, where he had flung himself. "I'm wid ye to the end of the world. It's a place I know, and—"

"Silence!" hissed Abel, as there was the loud clanging of a bell with the fierce yelping of dogs, and they dashed off, hand joined in hand, for the coffee-plantation, away down by the cane-brake and the swamp.

Chapter Thirteen
The Pursuit

The hue and cry rose louder and louder as the fugitives ran laboriously toward the jungle brake. Lights could be seen; a signal-gun was fired, and the little colony was up in arms, ready to hunt down the escaped criminals, lest they should take to the forest, from whence, after a time, they would issue forth as wild beasts. But in the darkness of that tropic night there would have been little danger of recapture but for those sounds which told the evading men that their greatest enemies were now afoot—those who could hunt them down without light or sight, but would track them by scent with the greatest ease.

"Hark at that, now!" said the Irishman, as he ran on, step by step with the escaping prisoners. "D'ye hear the dogs giving tongue? They haven't got the scent right yet, me boys; but they'll have it soon. G'long; ye don't half run."

He ceased speaking for a few moments, and then continued apologetically—

"Faix, and it's meself forgot. Ye've got the bilboes an, and they make it bad running. There, d'ye hear the dogs? It's like having the hounds back at home, before I 'listed for a soger, and got sent out here. Run, ye divils, run! But, I say: if we're tuk, and it comes to a thrial—court martial, ye know—be fair to a boy, now, won't ye?"

"What do you mean?" said Bart, gruffly.

"Remimber that it was you made me desart. I couldn't help meself, could I?"

Bart did not answer, but kept on with his steady, lumbering trot, which was the more laborious to him from the shortness of his fetters making it difficult to him to keep up with his companions.

"Bedad, they're well on the scent!" said the Irishman, gazing back as he ran; "and it'll not be long before they're up with us. What'll we do at all?"

"Do?" said Bart, gruffly; "leave you to tell that cursed brute that we sha'n't want his whip any more; for—"

"Hush!" cried Abel,

"Ay, I forgot," said Bart, nodding his head.

"We'll have to get up the trees before the dogs reach us, or it'll be awkward for the whole three. They'll forget to respect the king's uniform in the dark. It's no good, my lads; they'll take us, and ye've had all your throuble for nothing. Faix, and I'm sorry for ye, whativer ye did, for it's a dog's life ye lead."

"Silence, man," whispered Abel. "Do you want the dogs to be on us?"

"Divil a bit, sor; but they'll be down on us soon widout hearing us talk. Murther, but it's a powerful shensh of shmell they have. How they are coming on!"

It was quite true. The dogs were after them with unerring scent, and but for the fact that they were in leashes so that those who held them back might be able to keep up, they would have soon overtaken the fugitives. They were at no great distance as it was, and their baying, the encouraging shouts of their holders, and the sight of the lanterns rising and falling in the darkness, helped the Irishman's words to send despair into the fugitives' hearts.

"Sure, and we're in the coffee-tree gyarden!" said the sentry. "Oi know it by the little bits of bushes all in rows. Thin the wood isn't far, and we'll get up a tree before the bastes of dogs come up to us. Hark at the onnat'ral bastes; sure, it's supper they think they're going to have. Maybe they'd like to taste a Kelly."

"Now, Bart, lad, quick! Shall we let him go?" cried Abel.

"And is it let me go?" said the sentry, excitedly. "You'd niver be such cowards. Let the dogs have fair-play."

"Silence!" cried Abel, imperatively.

"Sure it's meself that's the most silent."

"Abel!—Bart! This way!"

"To the left, lad," cried Bart, for they had now reached the edge of the jungle; and just as despair was filling their breasts, for Mary made no sign, her voice proved her fidelity by its being heard some distance to their left.

"Thin it's all right," said Dinny, excitedly. "Ye've got friends waiting?"

"Silence, I say!" cried Abel.

"Sure, and I'll hold my pace, and good luck to ye, for I heard the boy's spache, and maybe he has a boat waiting down by the wather."

"Will you be silent, man?" cried Abel, fiercely, as the baying of the dogs increased. "Bart, we must not go on, for it would be bringing the dogs upon someone else."

"Not it," said Dinny; "ye've plenty of time yet, maybe. Go along, me boys, and bad luck to the dogs, for they'll be disappointed afther all!"

Abel gave a low, peculiar whistle like a sea-bird's cry, and it was answered not twenty yards away.

"Here, quick!" came in the well-known voice; "I'm here. Jump; never mind the mud!"

They all jumped together, to find themselves in a miry place where Mary was waiting.

"This way," she said. "I can guide you direct to the boat. Quick, or the dogs will be upon us!"

"Well done, boy!" cried Dinny. "That's good. I knew there was a boat."

"And now," cried Abel, turning upon him, "off with that pouch and belt."

"Certainly, sor," replied Dinny, slipping off and handing his cartridge-bag.

"Now, back to your friends, and tell them we're gone."

"My friends!" cried Dinny. "Sure, there isn't a friend among them."

"Stop back, then, whoever they are."

"But the dogs, sor!"

"Curse the dogs. Back, I say!"

"But, sor, they're the most savage of bastes. They won't listen to anny explanation, but pull a man down before he has time to say, Heaven presarve us!"

"Silence, and go!"

"Nay, sor, ye'll tak' me wid ye now? Quick! ye're losing time."

"Let him come, Abel," whispered Mary.

"That's well spoken, young sor. And if we're to have whole shkins, let's be getting on."

The advice was excellent, for the sounds of pursuit were close at hand, and the dogs were baying as if they heard as well as scented their prey.

"All's ready," whispered Mary. "I heard the shots, and knew you were coming. Abel, your hand. Join hands all."

Abel caught at that of his sister, at the same time extending his own, which was taken by Bart, and he in turn, almost involuntarily, held out his to Dinny.

In this order they passed rapidly through the jungle, along a beaten track formed by the animals which frequented the place, and one which during her long, patient watches had become perfectly familiar to Mary Dell, who threaded it with ease.

It was one wild excitement, for the dogs were now growing furious. The scent was hot for them, and ere the fleeing party had reached the creek the fierce brutes had gained the edge of the jungle, through which they dragged their keepers, who mingled words of encouragement with oaths and curses as they were brought into contact with the tangled growth.

But all the same the hunt was hot, and in spite of Mary's foresight and the manner in which she guided her friends, the dogs were nearly upon them as the boat was reached.

"In first," whispered Abel; but Mary protested and would have hung back had not Bart lifted her bodily in after wading into the mud, where he stood and held the side of the frail canoe.

"Now, Abe," he whispered.

"I can hear them," shouted a voice. "Loose the dogs. Seize 'em, boys, seize 'em!"

"Here, room for me?" whispered Dinny.

"No," cried Abel, fiercely. "Keep back!"

"I'm coming wid you," cried Dinny.

Bart caught him by the shoulder.

"No, no, my lad, we're escaping; this is no place for you."

"Be my sowl, this isn't," said Dinny, shaking himself free, and seizing the side of the boat he began to wade and thrust her from the shore. "In with you too."

Bart said no more, but followed the Irishman's example, and together they waded on into the muddy creek, only to get a few yards from the shore, as with a furious rush the dogs crushed through the canes and reeds, to stop, breast-deep, barking savagely.

"Purty creatures!" whispered Dinny. "Sure, and we musn't get in yet, or, if we do, it must be together. Push her out."

"Halt, there!" cried a loud voice, suddenly. "I have you. Down, dogs! Do you hear! Halt!"

"Kape on," whispered Dinny.

"Make ready!" cried the same voice. "Present! Will you surrender?"

"Lie down, me darlins," whispered Dinny. "Divil a bit can they see where to shoot."

"Fire!" cried the same voice, and a dozen flashes of light blazed out of the cane-brake. There was a roar that seemed deafening, and the darkness was once more opaque.

"Anybody hit?" whispered Dinny. "Silence gives consint," he added to himself. "Push along, and as soon as it's deep enough we'll get in. Ugh! bedad, it's up to me chin all at wanst," he muttered. "Can you give a boy a hand?"

A hand caught his wrist, and he was helped over the stern of the boat, dripping and panting, as Bart scrambled in simultaneously, and though the little vessel threatened to overset, it held firm.

Then another volley was fired, for the bullets to go bursting through the canes, but over the fugitives' heads, and once more darkness reigned over the hurried buzz of voices and the furious baying of the dogs.

Order after order came from the soft marshy land at the edge of the creek, mingled with shouts at the dogs, which were now loose, and barking and yelping as they ran here and there at the side of the water, where their splashing could be heard by those in the boat, which was being propelled slowly and cautiously by Mary, who knelt in the prow and thrust a pole she carried down in the mud.

The baying of the dogs as they kept making rushes through the canes gave the pursuers some clue as to where the fugitives would be; and from time to time, after a command given to the escaping men to surrender, a volley was fired, the bright flashes from the muskets cutting the darkness, and showing where their danger lay.

It was slow work for both parties, the pursuers having to force their way painfully through the tangled growth, while the heavily-laden boat had to be propelled through what was in places little more than liquid mud full of fibrous vegetation, and what had been but a light task to Mary when she was alone, proved to be almost beyond her strength with so heavy a load.

"Are you going right?" whispered Abel at last, for they were hardly moving, and it seemed to him that they were running right in among the growth that whispered and creaked against the boat.

"Yes; be patient," was the stern reply.

"I can see them. They're wading yonder in the mud up to their waists."

"There they are," came from apparently close at hand, and the dogs burst out more furiously than ever. "Now, then, you scoundrels, we can see you. Give up."

"Faith, and it's a cat he is," whispered Dinny. "What a foine senthry he'd make for night duty!"

"Surrender!" shouted the same voice, "or we'll blow you out of the water."

"The ugly, yellow-faced divil!" muttered Dinny.

"Now, then, come ashore, and I will not be so severe with you."

"Hark at that, now," whispered Dinny to Bart. "It's a baby he thinks ye, afther all."

"Curse them! Fire then, sergeant," cried the overseer. "No mercy now."

"Down, dogs!" roared the man again. "Quick, there—fire!"

A rattling volley from close at hand rang out, and it was followed by utter silence, as if those ashore were listening.

"Curse your stupid fellows, sergeant! Why don't you make them fire lower?"

"If they fired lower, we should have hit the dogs, sir."

"Hang the dogs! I wanted you to hit the men. Now, then, fire again."

There was the rattling noise of the ramrods in the barrels as the men loaded, and once more silence. The sinuous nature of the muddy creek had brought the fugitives terribly near to the dense brake; but Mary's pole remained perfectly motionless, and there was nothing to be done but wait till the party moved on, when there would be a chance to get lower down towards the open sea; while, after the next quarter of a mile, the creek opened out into quite a little estuary dotted by sandbanks and islets of bamboos and palms.

"Now I have them!" cried the overseer, suddenly. "Bring a gun, sergeant. I can pick off that fellow easily."

"Faith, and what a foine liar he would make wid a little training," whispered Dinny. "Why, I can't even see my hand before me face."

"Hush," whispered Bart, and then he half started up in the boat, for there was a sudden splashing, a shout, and the piteous yelping and baying of a dog, which was taken up in chorus by the others present.

Yelp—bark—howl, accompanied by the splashing and beating of water, and rustling of reeds and canes, and then a choking, suffocating sound, as of some animal being dragged under water, after which the dogs whined and seemed to be scuffling away.

"What's the matter with the dogs?" said the overseer.

"One of those beasts of alligators dragged the poor brute down," said the sergeant. "It struck me with its tail."

There was a rushing, scuffling noise here, and the heavy trampling of people among the tangled growth, growing more distant moment by moment, in the midst of which Mary began to use her pole, and the boat glided on through the thick, half-liquid mud.

"Sure, an' it's plisant," said Dinny, coolly; "the dogs on one side, and the crockidills on the other. It isn't at all a tempting spot for a bathe; but I've got to have a dip as soon as we get out of this into the sea."

"What for?" whispered Bart.

"Bekase I'm wet with fresh wather and mud, and I'm a man who likes a little salt outside as well at in. It kapes off the ugly fayvers of the place. Do you want me to catch a cowld?"

"Silence, there!" said Mary, gruffly, from her place in the prow; and for quite an hour she toiled on through the intense darkness, guiding the boat from the tangle of weedy growth and cane into winding canal-like portions of the lagoon, where every now and then they disturbed some great reptile, which plunged into deeper water with a loud splash, or wallowed farther among the half-liquid mud.

The sounds ashore grew distant, the firing had ceased; and, feeling safer, the little party began to converse in a low tone, all save Dinny, whose deep, regular breathing told that he had fallen fast asleep in happy carelessness of any risk that he might run.

"How came you out here?" said Bart from his seat, after another vain effort to take Mary's place.

"Ship," she said laconically, and with a hoarse laugh.

"But who gave you a passage?" said Abel.

"Gave? No one," she said, speaking in quite a rough tone of voice. "How could I find friends who would give! I worked my way out."

"Oh," said Bart; and he sat back, thinking and listening as the pole kept falling in the water with a rhythmic splash, and the brother and sister carried on a conversation in a low tone.

"I suppose we are safe now," said Mary. "They never saw the boat, and they would think you are hiding somewhere in the woods."

"Yes; and because they don't find us, they'll think the alligators have pulled us down," replied Abel. "Where are we going?"

"To get right down to the mouth of this creek, and round the shore. There are plenty of hiding-places along the coast. Inlets and islands, with the trees growing to the edge of the sea."

"And what then?" said Abel.

"What then?" said Mary, in a half wondering tone.

"Yes; where shall we go?"

There was an interval of silence, during which the boat glided on in the darkness, which seemed to be quite opaque.

"I had not thought of that," said Mary, in the same short, rough voice which she seemed to have adopted. "I only thought of finding you, Abel, and when I had found you, of helping you to escape."

"She never thought of me," muttered Bart, with a sigh.

"Good girl," said Abel, tenderly.

"Hush! Don't say that," she cried shortly. "Who is this man with you?" she whispered then.

"One of the sentries."

"Why did you bring him?"

"We were obliged to bring him, or—"

"Kill him?" said Mary, hoarsely, for her brother did not end his sentence.

"Yes."

"You must set him ashore, of course."

"Yes, of course. And then?"

"I don't know, Abel. I wanted to help you to escape, and you have escaped. You must do the rest."

"You're a brave, true girl," said Abel, enthusiastically; but he was again checked shortly.

"Don't say that," cried Mary, in an angry tone.

"What's she mean?" thought Bart; and he lay back wondering, while the boat glided on, and there was a long pause, for Abel ceased speaking, and when his deep breathing took Bart's attention and he leaned forward and touched him there was no response.

"Why, he's fallen asleep, Mary!" said Bart, in a whisper.

"Hush, Bart don't call me that!" came from the prow.

"All right, my lass!" said the rough fellow. "I'll do anything you tells me."

"Then don't say 'my lass' to me."

"I won't if you don't wish it," growled Bart. "Here, let me pole her along now."

"No; sit still. Is that man asleep?"

"Yes; can't you hear? He's fagged out like poor old Abel. But let me pole the boat."

"No; she'll drift now with the current and we shall be carried out to sea. If the people yonder saw us then they would not know who was in the boat. You have escaped, Bart?"

"Ay, we've escaped, my—"

"Hush, I say!" cried Mary, imperiously; and Bart, feeling puzzled, rubbed one ear and sat gazing straight before him into the darkness where he knew the girl to be, his imagination filing up the blanks, till he seemed to see her standing up in the boat, with a red worsted cap perched jauntily upon her raven-black hair, and a tight blue-knitted jacket above her linsey-woolsey skirt, just as he had seen her hundreds of times in her father's, and then in Abel's boat at home on the Devon shore.

All at once Bart Wrigley opened his eyes and stared. Had he been asleep and dreamed that he and Abel had escaped, and then that he was in the Dell's boat, with Mary poling it along?

What could it all mean? He was in a boat, and behind him lay back the soldier with his mouth open, sleeping heavily. On his left was Abel Dell, also sleeping as a man sleeps who is utterly exhausted by some terrible exertion. But that was not the Devon coast upon which the sun was shedding its early morning rays. Dense belts of mangrove did not spread their muddy roots like intricate rustic scaffoldings on southern English shores, and there were no clusters of alligators lying here and there among the mud and ooze.

It was true enough. They did escape in the night, and Mary had been there ready to help them with a boat; but where was she now? and who was this sturdy youth in loose petticoat-canvas trousers, and heavy fisherman's boots?

Bart stared till his eyes showed a ring of white about their pupils, and his mouth opened roundly in unison for a time. Then eyes and mouth closed tightly, and wrinkles appeared all over his face, as he softly shook all over, and then, after glancing at Abel and the Irish soldier, he uttered a low—

"Haw, haw!"

The figure in the boat swung round and faced him sharply, glancing at the two sleeping men, and holding up a roughened brown hand to command silence.

"All right," said Bart, half-choking with mirth; and then, "Oh, I say, my lass, you do look rum in them big boots!"

"Silence, idiot!" she whispered, sharply. "Do you want that strange man to know?"

"Nay, not I," said Bart, shortly, as he too glanced at Dinny. "But I say, you do look rum."

"Bart," whispered Mary, fiercely, and her eyes flashed with indignant anger, "is this a time to fool?"

"Nay, my lass, nay," he said, becoming sober on the instant, "But you do look so rum. I say, though," he cried, sharply, "what's gone of all your beautiful long hair?"

"Fire," said Mary, coldly.

"Fire! what!--you've cut it off and burnt it?" Mary nodded.

"Oh!" ejaculated Bart, and it sounded a groan.

"Could girl with long hair have worked her passage out here as a sailor-boy, and have come into that cane-brake and saved you two?" said Mary, sharply; and as Bart sat staring at her with dilated eyes once more, she bent down after gazing at Dinny, still soundly sleeping, and laid her hand with a firm grip on her brother's shoulder.

He started into wakefulness on the instant, and gazed without recognition in the face leaning over him.

"Don't you know me, Abel?" said Mary, sadly.

"You, Mary?—dressed like this!"

He started up angrily, his face flushing as hers had flushed, and his look darkened into a scowl.

"What else could I do?" she said, repeating her defence as she had pleaded to Bart. Then, as if her spirit rebelled against his anger, her eyes flashed with indignation, and she exclaimed hoarsely, "Well, I have saved you, and if you have done with me—there is the sea!"

"But you—dressed as a boy!" said Abel.

"Hush! Do you want that man to know?" whispered Mary, hoarsely. "My brother was unjustly punished and sent out here to die in prison, while I, a helpless girl, might have starved at home, or been hunted down by that devil who called himself a man? What could I do?"

"But you worked your passage out here as a sailor?" whispered Abel.

"Ay, and she could do it, too—as good a sailor as ever took in sail; and, Mary, lass, I asks your pardon for laughing; and if I wasn't such a big ugly chap, I could lie down there and cry."

He held out his great coarse hand, in which Mary placed hers to return his honest clasp, and her eyes smiled for a moment into his, while Abel sat frowning and biting his lips as he glanced at Dinny.

"I don't know what to do," he said, hesitatingly. "It seems—"

"Heigh—ho—ho! Oh, dear me!" cried Dinny, opening his eyes suddenly, making Mary start and Abel mutter a curse.

There was only one of the two equal to the emergency, and that was Bart, who gave his knee a sounding slap and cried aloud—

"Jack Dell, my lad, you've behaved like a trump, and got us away splendid. I on'y wish, Abel, I had such a brother. Hallo, soger, where shall we set you ashore?"

"Set me ashore?" said the Irishman, nodding at Mary; "what for?"

"What for?" cried Bart. "To go back."

"I'm not going back," said the Irishman, laughing. "Sure, I want a change."

"Change!" cried Abel. "You can't go with us."

"Sure, and you forced me to come, and ye wouldn't behave so dirthily as to send me back?"

"But we're escaping," said Bart.

"Sure, and I'll escape too," said Dinny, smiling. "It's moighty dull work stopping there."

"But you're a soldier," said Abel.

"To be sure I am—a sowldier of fortune."

"You'll be a deserter if you stop with us," growled Bart.

"The divil a bit! Ye made me a prishner, and I couldn't help meself."

"Why, I wanted you to go back last night!" growled Bart.

"To be ate up entoirely by the ugly bastes of dogs! Thank ye kindly, sor, I'd rather not."

Dinny looked at Mary and gave her a droll cock of the eye, which made her frown and look uneasy.

"Sure, Misther Jack," he said, coolly, "don't you think they're a bit hard on a boy?"

"Hard?" said Mary, shortly.

"Av coorse. They knocked me down and took away me mushket and bagnet, and there they are in the bottom of the boat. Then they made me get over the gate and eshcape wid 'em; and, now they're safe, they want to put me ashore."

"We can't take you with us," said Abel, shortly.

"Aisy, now! Think about it, sor. Ye're going for a holiday, sure; and under the circumstances I'd like one too. There! I see what ye're a-thinking— that I'd bethray ye. Sure, and I'm a Kelly, and ye never knew a Kelly do a dirthy thrick to anyone. Did I shout for help last night when you towld me not?"

"You were afraid," growled Bart.

"Afraid!—me afraid! Did ye ever hear of a Kelly who was afraid? No, sor; I said to meself, 'The poor boys are making a run for it, and I'll let them go.' Sure, and I did, and here ye are."

"It would not be wise to go near the shore now," said Mary, in a whisper to her brother. "You have nothing to fear from him."

Abel glanced at the happy, contented face before him, and then turned to Bart.

"What do you say?" he asked.

"There's no harm in him," said Bart, with a suspicious look at the Irishman.

"Sure, an' ye'll find me very useful," said Dinny. "I was at say before I 'listed, so I can steer and haul a rope."

"Can you keep faith with those who trust you?" said Mary, quickly.

"An' is it a Kelly who can keep faith, me lad? Sure, an' we're the faithfullest people there is anny where. And, bedad! but you're a handsome boy, and have a way wid you as'll make some hearts ache before ye've done."

Mary started, and turned of a deep dark red, which showed through her sun-browned skin, as she flashed an angry look upon the speaker.

Dinny burst into a hearty laugh.

"Look at him," he said, "colouring up like a girl. There, don't look at me, boy, as if ye were going to bite. I like to see it in a lad. It shows his heart's in the right place, and that he's honest and true. There, take a grip o' me hand, for I like you as much for your handsome face as for the way you've stood thrue to your brother and his mate. And did ye come all the way from your own counthry to thry and save them?"

Mary nodded.

"Did ye, now? Then ye're a brave lad; and there ar'n't many men who would have watched night after night in that ugly bit o' wood among the shnakes and reptiles. I wouldn't for the best brother I iver had, and there's five of 'em, and all sisters."

Mary smilingly laid her hand on Dinny's, and gazed in the merry, frank face before her.

"I'll trust you," she said.

"And ye sha'n't repent it, me lad, for you've done no harm, and were niver a prishner. And now, as we are talking, I'd like to know what yer brother and number noinety-sivin did to be sint out of the counthry. It wasn't murther, or they'd have hung 'em. Was it—helping yerselves?"

"My brother and his old friend Bart Wrigley were transported to the plantations for beating and half-killing, they said, the scoundrel who had insulted and ill-used his sister!" cried Mary, with flashing eyes and flaming cheeks, as she stood up proudly in the boat, and looked from one to the other.

"Wid a shtick?" said Dinny, rubbing his cheek as he peered eagerly into Mary's face.

"Yes, with sticks."

"And was that all?"

"Yes."

"They transported thim two boys to this baste of a place, and put chains on their legs, for giving a spalpeen like that a big bating wid a shtick?"

"Yes," said Mary, smiling in the eager face before her; "that was the reason."

"Holy Moses!" ejaculated Dinny. "For just handling a shtick like that. Think o' that, now! Why, I sent Larry Higgins to the hospital for sivin weeks wance for just such a thing. An' it was a contimptibly thin shkull he'd got, just like a bad egg, and it cracked directly I felt it wid the shtick. And what did you do?" he added sharply, as he turned to Mary. "Where was your shtick?"

"I struck him with my hand," said Mary, proudly.

"More sorrow to it that it hadn't a shtick in it at the time. Sint ye both out here for a thing like that! Gintlemen, I'm proud of ye. Why didn't ye tell me before?"

He held out his hands to both, and, intruder as he was, it seemed impossible to resist his frank, friendly way, and the escaped prisoners shook hands with him again.

"And now what are ye going to do?" said Dinny, eagerly.

"We don't know yet," said Abel, rather distantly.

"That's jist me case," said Dinny. "I'm tired of sogering and walking up and down wid a mushket kaping guard over a lot of poor divils chained like wild bastes. I tuk the shilling bekase I'd been in a skrimmage, and the bowld sergeant said there'd be plinty of foighting; and the divil a bit there's been but setting us to shoot prishners, and I didn't want that. Now, ye'll tak me wid ye, only I must get rid o' these soger clothes, and—look here, what are ye going to do wid thim chains?"

"Get rid of them," said Abel, "when we can find a file."

"I did not think of a file," said Mary, with a disappointed look.

"There's plinty of strange plants out in these parts," said Dinny, laughing, "but I never see one that grew files. Only there's more ways of killing a cat than hanging him, as the praste said when he minded his owld brogues wid a glue-pot. Come here."

He took off his flannel jacket, folded it, and laid it in the bottom of the boat, but looked up directly.

"Ye've got a bit o' sail," he said, "and there's a nice wind. Where are you going first?"

Mary looked at her brother, and Abel glanced at Bart.

"Ye haven't made up yer minds," said Dinny, "so look here. About twenty miles out yander to the west there's a bit of an island where the overseer and two officers wint one day to shute wild pig and birds, and I went wid 'em. Why not go there till ye make up yer minds? It's a moighty purty place, and ye're not overlooked by the neighbours' cabins, for there's nobody lives there at all, at all, and we can have it our own way."

"Wild pig there?" said Abel, eagerly.

"Bedad, yis, sor; nice swate bacon running about on four legs all over the place, and fruit on the trees, and fish in the say for the catching. Oh, an' it's a moighty purty little estate!"

"And how could we find it?" cried Mary.

"By jist setting a sail, and kaping about four miles from the shore till ye see it lying like a bit o' cloud off to the south. Sure, and we could hang our hammocks there before night, and the mushket here all ready to shoot a pig."

"Yes," said Mary, in response to a glance from her brother.

"Then I'll hoist the sail," said Bart.

"Nay, let the boy do it," said Dinny, "and you come and sit down here. I'll soon show you a thing as would make the sergeant stare."

Dinny drew a large knife from his pocket, and a flint and steel. The latter he returned, and, taking the flint, he laid his open knife on the thwart of the boat, and with the flint jagged the edge of the blade all along into a rough kind of saw.

"There!" he said; "that will do. That iron's as soft as cheese."

This last was a slight Hibernian exaggeration; but as Mary hoisted sail, and Abel put out an oar to steer, while the little vessel glided swiftly over the sunlit sea, Dinny began to operate upon the ring round one of Bart's ankles, sawing away steadily, and with such good effect that at the end of an hour he had cut half through, when, by hammering the ring together with the butt of the musket, the half-severed iron gave way, and one leg was free.

"Look at that, now!" said Dinny, triumphantly, and with an air of satisfaction that took away the last doubts of his companions. "Now, thin, up wid that other purty foot!" he cried; and, as the boat glided rapidly toward the west, he sawed away again, with intervals of re-jagging at the knife edge, and soon made a cut in the second ring.

"Keep her a little farther from the shore, Abel," said Mary, in a warning tone, as the boat sped westward.

"Ye needn't mind," said Dinny, sawing away; "the inhabitants all along here are a moighty dacent sort of folk, and won't tell where we're gone. They're not handsome, and they've got into a bad habit o' wearing little tails wid a moighty convanient crook in 'em to take howld of a tree."

"Monkeys?" said Mary, eagerly.

"Yes, Masther Jack, monkeys; and then there's the shmiling crockidills, and a few shnakes like ships' masts, and some shpotted cats. There's nobody else lives here for hundreds o' miles."

"Then you are safe, Abel," said Mary, with the tears standing in her eyes.

"Yes, Ma— yes, Jack," cried Abel, checking himself; and then meaningly, as he glanced at Bart, "you're a brother of whom a man may well be proud."

"Ay," cried Bart, excitedly, "a brother of whom a man may well be proud."

"Hurroo!" cried Dinny. "Howlt still, my lad, and I'll soon be through."

And the boat sped onward toward the west.

The island was found just as the Irishman had foretold, and as evening approached, without having even sighted a sail on their way, the little boat began coasting along, its occupants eagerly scanning the low, rock-reefed shore, above which waved a luxuriant tropic growth, but for some time no landing-place was found, while, though the sea was calm, there was a heavy swell to curl up and break upon the various reefs in a way that would have swamped their craft had they attempted to land.

The last fetter had been laboriously sawn through, Dinny having persisted in continuing the task, and he now sat resting and watching the shore with a critical eye.

All at once, upon sailing round a jagged point to which they had to give a wide berth on account of the fierce race which swept and eddied among the rocks, a pleasantly-wooded little bay opened out before them with a smooth sandy shore where the waves just creamed and glistened in the sun.

"Look at that, now," said Dinny. "That's where we landed; but I was ashleep after pulling a long time at the oar, and I disremembered all about where we went ashore."

"How beautiful!" said Jack, gazing thoughtfully at the glorious scene, and asking herself whether that was to be her future home.

"An' d'yer caal that beautiful?" said Dinny, contemptuously. "Young man, did ye iver see Dublin Bay?"

"No," said Jack, smiling in the earnest face before him.

"Nor the Hill of Howth?"

Jack shook his head.

"Then don't call that beautiful again in me presence," said Dinny.

"Puts me in mind of Black Pool," said Bart, thoughtfully.

Further conversation was checked by the interest of landing, the boat being run up on the shore and hidden among the rocks, not that it was likely that it would be seen, but the position of the fugitives and the dread of being retaken made them doubly cautious, Bart even going so far as to obliterate their footprints on the sand.

"Now, then," said Dinny, "you've got the mushket and the bagnet, and those two make one; but if I was you I'd cut down one of them bamboos and shtick the bagnet an that, which would make two of it, and it would be a mighty purty tool to kill a pig."

The hint was taken, Bart soon cutting down a long, straight lance shaft and forcing it into the socket of the bayonet.

"Then next," said Dinny, "if I was captain I should say let's see about something to ate."

"Hear that, Abel?" said Bart.

"Yes. I was thinking of how we could get down some cocoa-nuts. There are plenty of bananas."

"Hapes," put in Dinny; "and there's a cabbage growing in the heart of every one of thim bundles of leaves on the top of a shtick as they call palms; but them's only vegetables, captain, dear, and me shtomach is asking for mate."

"Can we easily shoot a pig—you say there are some," said Abel.

"And is it aisily shoot a pig?" said Dinny. "Here, give me the mushket."

He held out his hand for the piece, and Abel, who bore it, hesitated for a moment or two, and glanced at Jack, who nodded shortly, and the loaded weapon was passed to the Irishman.

"Ye doubted me," he said, laughing; "but niver mind, it's quite nat'ral. Come along; I won't shoot anny of ye unless I'm very hungry and can't get a pig."

He led the way through an opening in the rough el if, and they climbed along a narrow ravine for some few hundred yards, the roar of the sea being hushed and the overhanging trees which held on among the rifts of the rocks shutting out the evening light, so that at times it was quite dusk. But the rocky barrier was soon passed, and an open natural park spread before them, in a depression of which lay a little lake, whose smooth grassy shores were literally ploughed in every direction with shallow scorings of the soil.

"Look at that now," said Dinny in a whisper, as he pointed down at some of the more recent turnings of the soft earth. "The purty creatures have all been as busy as Pat Mulcahy's pig which nobody could ring. Whisht! lie down, ye divils," he whispered, setting the example, and crouching behind a piece of rock.

The others hid at once, and a low grunting and squeaking which had suddenly been heard in the distance increased loudly; and directly after a herd of quite two hundred pigs came tearing down through a narrow opening in the rocky jungle and made straight for the lake.

They were of all sizes, from little plump fellows, half the weight of ordinary porkers, to their seniors—the largest of which was not more than half the dimensions of an English pig.

They trotted down to the water side, where they drank and rolled and wallowed at the edge for a few moments, and then came back in happy unconsciousness of the fate which awaited one of their number, and passing so near the hidden group that Dinny had an easy shot at a well fed specimen which rolled over, the rest dashing on through the trees squealing as if every one had been injured by the shot.

"We sha'n't starve here," said Dinny, with a grin of satisfaction, and before many minutes had passed a fire was kindled in a sheltered nook, where the flame was not likely to be seen from the sea, and as soon as it was glowing, pieces of the pig, cut in a manner which would have disgusted a butcher, were frizzling in the embers.

Chapter Fourteen
"Master Jack"

They had been a month on the island, leading a dreamy kind of existence, and had begun to sleep of a night deeply and well without starting up half a dozen times bathed in sweat, and believing that the authorities from Plantation Settlement were on their track and about to take them by surprise. The question had been debated over and over again—What were they to do? but Dinny generally had the last word.

"Why, who wants to do anything? Unless a man was in Ireland, where could he be better than he is here, with iverything a man could wish for but some more powder and a wife. Eh! Master Jack, ye handsome young rascal, that's what ye're always thinking about."

"Jack" gave him an angry look, and coloured.

"Look at him!" cried Dinny. "There's tell-tales. Niver mind, lad, it's human nature, and we're all full of it, and a good thing, too. Now come and get some cocoa-nuts, for the powder's growing very low and we shall have to take to pig hunting instead of shooting when its done."

"Jack" hesitated, and then, as if suddenly making up his mind, accompanied the Irishman to the nearest grove where the cocoa palms grew close down to the sea.

Here Dinny rolled up the sleeves of his coarse and ragged shirt, and climbed one tree as a lad does a pole; but the fruit when he reached it was immature, and he threw only one of the great husks down.

"We don't want dhrink, but mate," said Dinny, selecting another tree, and beginning to climb; but the day was hot, there was a languid feeling induced by the moist atmosphere, and Dinny failed three times to reach the glorious green crown of leaves where the nuts nestled, and slid down again, sore in body and in temper.

"A failure, Dinny!" said Jack.

"Failure! yes. Can't ye see it is?" said the Irishman sourly, as he bent down and softly rubbed the inner sides of his knees. "Here, I'm not going to do all the climbing. You have a turn."

"Jack" shook his head.

"No skulking!" cried Dinny; "fair-play's a jool, me lad, so up you go. Ye're younger and cleverer wid yer arms and legs than I am. Why, ye ought to go up that tree like a monkey."

"Jack" shook his head and frowned.

"No," he said, "I'm no climber. Let's go back."

"Widout a nut, and ready to be laughed at? Not I, me lad. Now, then, I shall have to tak ye in hand and mak a man of ye. Up wid ye."

He caught the youth by the arm, and drew him, half-resisting, toward the tree.

"No, no, Dinny. Nonsense! I could not climb the tree."

"Bedad, an' ye've got to climb it!" cried Dinny. "Now, thin, take howld tightly, and up you go."

"Loose my arm," said Jack, speaking in a low voice, full of suppressed anger.

"Divil a bit. Ye've got to climb that three."

"Loose my arm, Dinny," said Jack again.

"Ye've got to climb that three, I tell ye, boy. Now, thin, no skulking. Up wid ye."

"Jack" hung back, with the colour deepening in his cheeks, and a dark look in his eyes, which Dinny could not interpret and, half in anger at the lad's opposition, half in playful determination, he grasped the youth firmly, and forced him toward the tree.

In an instant Jack flung himself round, with his eyes flashing, and before the Irishman could realise what was coming he went staggering back from the fierce blow he received in his chest, caught his heels against the husk of an overgrown nut, and came down heavily on the sand.

Dinny was an Irishman, and he had received a blow.

"Bad luck to ye, ye arbitrary young divil!" he cried, springing up. "It's a big bating ye want, is it, to tache ye manners! thin ye shall have it."

Jack trembled with indignation and excitement, but not with fear, for his cheeks were scarlet instead of pale. A blow had been struck, and he knew that no Irishman would receive one without giving it back with interest, and the only way out of the difficulty was to run, and he scorned to do that.

Quick as lighting he snatched a knife from his pocket, threw open the blade, and held it across his chest, half turning from his assailant, but with the point so directed that, if Dinny had closed, it could only have been at the expense of an ugly wound.

"Look at that now!" cried Dinny, pausing with hands raised to grip his adversary; "and me widout a bit o' shtick in me fist. Ye'd shting, would ye, ye little varmint! Put down yer knoife and fight like a man. Bah!" he cried contemptuously, as his anger evaporated as rapidly as it had flashed up, "ye're only a boy, and it's no dishgrace to have been hit by one o' yer size. I could nearly blow ye away. There, put away yer knoife and shake hands."

A hail from the cluster of trees which they made their camp, and Bart and Abel came into sight.

Jack closed his knife with a sigh of relief, and dropped it into his pocket.

"An' ye won't shake hands?" said Dinny, reproachfully.

"Yes, I will, Dinny," cried Jack, warmly, holding out his hand; "and I'm sorry I struck you."

"That's handsome, me lad," cried the Irishman, gripping it tightly. "I'm not sorry, for it don't hurt now, and I'm glad ye've got so much fight in ye. Ye're a brave lad, and there's Irish blood in ye somewhere, though ye're ignorant of the fact. Hallo, captain! what ye're going to do?"

Abel strode up with Bart at his side, looking curiously from one to the other.

"I want to have a talk with you two," said Abel, throwing himself on the sand. "Sit down."

"Did he see?" said Jack to himself, as he took his place a little on one side.

"A talk, and widout a bit o' tobacky!" said Dinny, with a sigh. "What is it, captain, dear?"

"Bart and I have been thinking over our position here," said Abel, "and we have determined to go."

"To go!" said Dinny. "Why, where would ye foind a bether place?"

"That has to be seen," said Abel; "but we can't stay here, and we want to know where the nearest port to which we could sail and then get ship for home."

"Get ship for the prison, ye mane!" cried Dinny, indignantly. "They'd send the lot of us back, and in less than a month you and Bart there would be hoeing among the bushes, young Jack here would be thried and punished for helping ye to escape, and as for me—well," he added, with a comical grin, "I don't, know what they'd do with me, but I'm sure they wouldn't give me my promotion."   ·

"But we shall starve if we stay here," said Abel, sternly.

"And is it shtarve wid you two such fishermen? Get out wid ye! Let's build a hut before the rainy time comes, and settle down. Here's as foine an estate as a gentleman need wish to have; and some day wan of us 'll go for a holiday to Oireland or Shcotland, and persuade four illigant ladies to come wid us and be married; and what more could a boy wish for then, eh, Masther Jack? What do you say, Bart?"

"That we must go," said Bart, gruffly.

"Let's think it over first," said Dinny. "At all events ye can't go for months to come; for ye'd be taken for eshcaped prisoners at wanst; so, as we've got no vittles, let's tak the boat and go out and catch some fish."

Abel frowned, and seemed disposed to continue the discussion; but everyone else was silent, and he rose slowly, ready enough, from old associations, to obey a command. So the little party walked slowly down toward where the boat lay hidden, ready to row it out to the edge of one of the weed-hung reefs, where fish were plentiful; and in spite of the roughness of their hooks and lines a pretty good dish could always be secured.

They had reached the end of the ravine, where the trees and bushes grew thickly, and Jack, who was first, was in the act of passing out on to the sands of the little bay, when a great hand seized him by the shoulder, and he was dragged back.

His hand went to his pocket again in the instinct of self-defence, for it seemed to be a repetition of Dinny's attack; but, turning sharply, he found that it was Bart who had dragged him back among the trees, and stood pointing seaward, where the solution of their difficulty appeared in, as it were, a warning to escape; for at about half a mile from the shore a white-winged cutter was coming rapidly toward the little bay; and as she careened over they could see that she was occupied by at least a dozen men.

"Quick, the boat!" cried Abel, excitedly.

"Are ye mad!" cried Dinny. "They could see us, and would be here before we could got round the point."

"Right," growled Bart.

"It's the cutter from the settlement," said Dinny, watching the coming vessel. "She sails like the wind, and, bedad, it's wind they've got of where we are, and they've come to fetch us. Now, thin, boys, the divil a bit will I go back, so who's for a foight?"

The sight of the cutter seemed to chase away all discontent with their position, bringing up, as it did, the recollection on the part of one of months of longing to give freedom to brother and friend; on the part of the other three, of long periods of toilsome labour in chains, and of wearisome keeping guard over the wretched convicts, sickening in the tropic sun. The island suddenly assumed the aspect of a paradise, from which they were to be banished for ever; and stealing silently back to their little camp, the fugitives hastily did what they could to destroy traces of their presence, and then turned to Abel to ask what next.

"The woods," he said. "We must hide while we can, and when they hunt us to bay we must fight for it."

"No," said Jack, quickly. "They will think we are in the woods, as being the most likely place for us to hide. We should be safer among the rocks in the cliff side, and should be able to watch the cutter as well."

"It's a born gin'ral ye are," said Dinny, enthusiastically.

"Right, Abel, lad; Jack's right," growled Bart; and Abel acceded with a nod of his head.

"You are lightest," he said. "Go first, Jack. Steal down by the side of the cliff, and get a good way round."

"No," said Jack, "there is neither time nor need. We must stay where we are, and wait and see which way they go. It will be time then to retreat."

"Hark at him! Sure, and if I wasn't certain that there's Oirish blood in his veins, I'd say his grandfather was the Juke o' Marlbrook."

"Right," growled Bart; and they drew back among the rocks and waited, lying down so as to be well hidden, Jack climbing a little way up the slope above them, and getting into a position which commanded the ravine leading down to the bay.

They had not long to wait before voices were heard coming up from the shore, and soon after the overseer made his appearance, in company with a young officer, both carrying pieces over their shoulders, and followed by half a dozen soldiers in their flannel undress.

They were chatting and smoking, and quite off their guard, taking matters so leisurely that the watcher felt doubtful as to their intentions, and lay trying to catch the bent of their conversation, as they went on toward the interior of the little island, their voices dying out in the distance, before he attempted to stir.

When he drew himself slowly back and crept through the bushes till he rejoined his companions, every mouth parted to ask for news; and anxiety, mingled with the stern determination painted in their faces, told of the stubborn resistance that their pursuers might expect before they had achieved their ends.

"They have gone right on into the woody part."

"Yes, the gin'ral's right," said Dinny.

"But I have my doubts of their intentions," said Jack.

"And so have I—big doubts," said Dinny; "so I won't thrust them."

"I don't think they've come in search of you," continued Jack.

"Not come in search of us?" said Abel, excitedly.

A shot rang out from the distance, followed immediately by another.

"That proves it," said Jack. "It is a shooting party."

"Av course it is," cried Dinny, laughing. "I could have told ye that, only I didn't think of it. It's the pigs they're after, and they're making free wid our flocks and herds."

"What a relief!" said Abel, wiping the sweat from his brow. "What shall we do next?"

"Keep in hiding; but I'll climb up till I can see their cutter. It may be near our boat."

"A born gin'ral," said Dinny, giving his head a roll and gazing approvingly at Jack. "There'll be two or three left in charge of their boat, and—what would you do next?"

Jack held up his hand, and softly retraced his course up the steep slope; and they could trace him from time to time by the waving of the leaves, but he went so cautiously that he was not seen once; and while they kept their eyes fixed upon one spot the bushes and leaves were seen to rustle softly some distance higher up.

Then they saw no more, but lay listening to the distant shouts and firing which reached their ears again and again, till, to the surprise of all three, Jack suddenly came upon them from behind.

"Well?" said Abel, eagerly.

Jack could not speak for a few moments, being breathless with exertion.

"Three men left with the cutter and they are ashore, lying upon the sands."

"Abel," said Jack, after a long, thoughtful silence, "we shall never be safe here with these people coming from time to time."

"No; that settles our plans. We must take the boat and go."

"Why not take our enemy's vessel? We could sail where we liked then."

"Didn't I say he was a born gin'ral?" cried Dinny, enthusiastically.

"Take their boat!" said Abel.

"They're three men, and we're three," said Bart, in a low growl.

"Four!" cried Dinny, excitedly. "Ye never see how Masther Jack can foight."

"Hush!" said the latter, sternly. "The men are lying about half asleep. If we waited, we might get on board, cut the anchor rope, and drift out with the tide perhaps without rousing them."

"And if it came to the worst we could fight," said Abel.

"Are ye ready?" whispered Dinny. "See that your piece is well primed. My shtick's loaded, and I'm ready to fire it off."

"Hush!" said Jack, sternly. "I will climb up to where I can watch the men, and if they go to sleep I will wave a branch. Then creep up to me, and we may succeed without trouble."

The proposal was agreed to at once, and a long, tedious time of waiting ensued, at the end of which Bart bared his arm.

"We're strong enough for 'em," he whispered. "Let's go at once and fight it out."

At that moment, high above their heads, a branch was seen waving just as a shot rang out at no great distance, shouts were heard, and the grunting of a herd of the wild pigs rose from the wooded part on their left.

"Too late!" whispered Abel.

"Right!" growled Bart.

"Then we'll foight for it," whispered Dinny. "Bedad, I believe they'll run as soon as they find us here, and small blame to 'em."

Chapter Fifteen
Another Escape

The excitement seemed to bring Jack more and more to the front, and those who followed read in his actions why it was that he had been successful in freeing them from their pursuers at the time of the escape.

For, active as a goat, he crept from rock to rock, lowering himself down here, dropping there, and having from time to time to wait to give the rest an opportunity for keeping up. And all the while the parts of the cliff side that were the most wooded, and which offered the best shelter, were selected, and discovery by the sleeping men avoided.

It was an arduous task; but the guide was equal to the emergency, and continuously and silently proceeding succeeded at length in dropping down to the sandy shore about fifty yards from where the men lay apparently asleep and sheltered by a huge mass of weed-grown stone, while the cutter swung by its anchor a hundred yards further on beyond the sailors, and she rose and fell easily as the slight tide ran softly down.

Jack grasped the situation clearly, and felt how little time there was to lose. At any moment the heads of the hunting party might appear as they came down the ravine to the bay, while, supposing these to be really asleep, the first shout would bring them to their feet, and then all chance of escape would be gone.

The men had laid down close up under the cliff so as to be sheltered from the sun and from an instinctive desire to be beyond the reach of any venturesome wave, so that to reach the cutter the fugitives would have to pass her guardians between them and the sea.

This brought the escaping party nearer to the cutter, but placed them full in the view of those who might be coming down the ravine at the head of the bay, and also shut them off from shelter and concealment should an emergency arise.

Jack had played so prominent a part hitherto that the eyes of all were directed to him for further instructions, and for a moment he hesitated and pointed to Abel.

"No," whispered the latter, "you have done so well; go on."

Jack hesitated for a moment or two more, and then said in a low voice —

"All follow quickly and go to the far side of the bay, seize the boat, and we are safe."

"But there is no boat," said Bart.

Jack pointed to a mass of rock, some fifty yards away, where a few inches of the stern of a boat were visible, but which had not been seen by the others.

"Lead on," said Abel, abruptly; "and if the men wake up Bart and I will tackle them while you and Dinny here get into the boat and row out. We'll swim to you, and you can take us in."

"And d'ye think I'm going to run away like that?" whispered Dinny. "I'll shtay."

"Dinny!" whispered Jack, fiercely.

"Ah, well, I forgot I was a soldier, my lad. I'll obey orders."

Whereupon Abel examined the priming of his musket, and Bart tried the bayonet at the end of the bamboo shaft to see if it was firm, while Dinny whispered —

"Howld her tight to yer shoulther, lad, when ye fire, for she's a divil to kick."

Jack gave a glance round once more, and then, holding up a hand to command silence, he listened, but all was still save the lapping of the waves as the tide retired and then returned.

His next proceeding was to steal out to where he could get a good look at the three sailors left in charge.

One lay on his breast, with his arms folded and his brow resting upon them. The second lay upon his back, with his hands beneath him, and his cap tilted over his eyes. The third was upon his side with his back to them, and all apparently fast asleep, for neither stirred.

Jack would have gladly waited till dark; but to have done this might have meant losing their means of escape, for they were not certain that the party would stay all night.

So, feeling this, and that their only chance lay in a bold attempt, he glanced back once, and after seeing that his companions were quite ready to follow, he stepped out quietly on to the yielding sand and made for the spot where the small boat lay.

To reach this boat the party had to pass within some fifty feet or so of the sleepers, and the crucial moments would be when they had passed within ken of the man lying upon his side with his back to them. Even if the others were awake it would be possible to pass them unseen; but it was otherwise with the third man, whose position would enable him to see whoever crossed the sands of the little bay, while, for aught they knew, he might be a faithful guardian, keeping strict watch over both boat and cutter while his companions slept.

Jack walked softly on, the sand deadening his tread, so that he was soon abreast of the guardians of the boat, and another five minutes would suffice for him and his party to reach the boat and push her off, when, armed as they were, they could have laughed at pursuit.

Another few yards and no one stirred. Jack gazed over his left shoulder at the dangerous reclining figure, but its position remain unchanged.

Another few yards, and still there was no sign, nor likely to be, for there could be no doubt of the fact—the man was fast asleep, and the agitation and anxiety of the fugitives was apparently wasted.

Jack glanced back to see that his companions were following in Indian file, walking upon the tips of their feet, and casting glances from time to time at the spot from which danger would arise.

Another dozen yards and the leader of the little party felt safe, when a sharp report came from the ravine above, the shot echoing and reverberating along the sides of the cliffs till it sounded like a peal of thunder which drowned the shout that followed, a shout meant as a warning to the guardians of the boat that their party was close at hand.

The man lying upon his side sprang to his feet, and the other two woke up, to stare stupidly about them before they realised the state of affairs, and that their companion had seized his musket, from where it lay with those of his fellows against the foot of the cliff which towered above their heads; for in accordance with their plans, Jack and Dinny had run on and seized the boat, while Abel and Bart had faced round with their weapons ready, retreating slowly toward the sea.

For a few moments no word was spoken, and then it was the first of the three sailors who realised their position.

"It's cat or a bullet in us, mates," he cried, desperately. "I says bullet; so come on."

The other two were Englishmen like himself, and evidently entertained their comrade's preference for a chance bullet or a stab to being tried by court martial and sentenced to a flogging, so they also snatched up their muskets and belts, hastily threw the latter over their shoulders, and, taught by training, brought their pieces to bear, shouting to the prisoners to surrender.

"Give up, you lubbers!" cried the first sailor. "It's of no good."

For answer Abel glanced over his shoulder, and seeing that Jack and Dinny had reached the boat, slowly continued the retreat.

"Will you surrender?" roared the sailor, as another shout came from the ravine.

"Surrender yourselves," cried Bart, fiercely. "Lay down them guns."

"Surrender, or we fire," cried the sailor again, as the two men slowly backed toward the boat, watchful of a rush being made.

Bart uttered a low, defiant growl, and the bamboo he held quivered in his knotted hands.

"All together, then, mates," shouted the sailor, "*fire!*"

Jack uttered a groan as he stood knee deep in water, running the boat as near as it could be got to his friend, and a mist swam before his eyes.

Click click click! — and as many tiny showers of sparks were struck in the pans of the pieces.

"Why, you stupid lubbers, you didn't load!" roared the sailor. "Now, then, ground arms — load!"

A shout of derision arose from Abel and Bart, and the former took up the tone of menace now.

"Throw down your muskets, or I fire," he cried.

"P'raps you're not loaded neither, mate," cried the sailor, laughing. "Now, lads. Bagnets: charge."

His companions hesitated for a moment, and then, lowering their pieces, they made a rush for those who barred their way to the boat.

Bang!

One sharp report. The right-hand sailor span round, dropped his musket, stooped down and seized his leg beneath the knee, and dropped into a sitting position upon the sand.

"Hurt, mate?" cried the first sailor, halting.

"Leg," was the laconic reply.

"Never mind," cried the first sailor. "Come, on, mate."

He lowered his piece again, and the two rushed upon Bart and Abel, as brave as lions now in the excitement.

These two had taken advantage of the man being wounded to back rapidly toward the boat, lying in the shallow water; but the sand was heavy, and they had to face the enemy all the time. For the latter came at them with stubborn determination, reached them while they were a good twenty yards from the water, and a fierce fight ensued.

It was as brief as it was hot and determined, for, after a few moments' fencing, the second sailor delivered a deadly thrust, at Abel; while the principal man, a sturdy, tall fellow, crossed weapons with Bart, whose slight bamboo lance was a feeble defence against the bayonet at the end of the musket. Moreover, the fugitives were fighting with the disadvantage of being seen now by the well-armed party returning from the hunt. These had received warning that something was wrong by hearing the shots, and were now running rapidly down toward the sandy shore.

"Now," said the second sailor, presenting his piece, which was opposed to one minus the bayonet blade—"now I have you. Surrender!"

For answer Abel stepped back, clubbed his weapon, swung it round, and brought it down with such violence that the butt struck the other musket full upon the stock, and dashed it from its holder's hand.

Before Abel could get another blow round, the man had dashed in, closed with him, and, to Jack's agony, capture seemed certain.

Meantime the first sailor had made several fierce passes at Bart, who was scratched once upon the wrist, and had drawn blood on the other side, when his bamboo lance broke, and he seemed at the mercy of his antagonist.

Heavy as he was, Bart was activity itself, and reversing the encounter going on between the other two, he avoided a thrust by striking the bayonet aside with his arm, and closed with his adversary.

The two locked together in a desperate struggle directly, for the sailor abandoned his musket as soon as Bart was at close quarters, and gripped him round the waist.

"I'll have you, anyhow," he panted, as he lifted Bart from the ground.

"Let go, or I'll crush in your ribs," growled Bart, savagely.

"Do it, mate," retorted the sailor, swinging Bart round, and trying to throw him; but he might as well have tried to throw off his arms. Then by a desperate wrench Bart loosened the other's grip, so that he could touch ground once more, and the struggle went on like some desperate bout in wrestling.

These encounters were matters of a minute or so; but to Jack and Dinny, standing knee deep in the water holding the boat ready for the escape, and the oars where they could be seized in an instant, the minute seemed an hour. They would have gone to the help of their comrades, but it seemed to them that they would be cutting off the means of escape; and in addition, the various phases of the fight succeeded each other so rapidly that there was hardly time to think.

"Give me that shtick," cried Dinny at last; and he snatched one from where it lay upon the thwarts of the boat, just as Abel sent his adversary down half-stunned and turned to help Bart.

"Quick, lad! Hold still a moment!" cried Abel, as the overseer came running down from the head of the bay, in company with the officer and half a dozen men.

The words were wasted, for Bart and the first sailor were writhing and twining on the sands like two wild beasts. Bart strove hard to shake himself free; but the effort was vain, for the sailor had fastened on him like a bull-dog, and held on with a tenacity that could not be mastered.

"It's of no use," panted Bart, as Dinny ran up. For the enemy were not two hundred yards away, and running fast. "Escape, my lads! Never mind me!"

"Let me get one hit at him," cried Dinny.

"Ah, would you, Paddy!" roared the sailor, wresting Bart round as a shield. "I know you."

"Now, you!" cried Dinny to Abel.

But it was like striving to hit a twining serpent upon the head, and strive how they would, Bart's friends could do nothing till the pair had struggled together to the very edge of the water, and then went splashing in.

"Get his head down, Bart, and he'll soon let go."

Easier said than done. The sailor had his arms well about his adversary, and Bart's effort was vain.

"Surrender, there!" shouted the overseer. "Give up, or we'll fire!"

"Let go, or I'll smash you," growled Bart, as he caught sight of the enemy coming on.

For answer the sailor clung the more tightly; and as Bart rose to his knee after a fall, the water was now well up to their middles.

"Here, boat, Jack, lad!" cried Dinny. "Now, captain, lay howlt!"

Abel grasped his meaning, and seized one side of the human knot, composed of two bodies and the customary complement of arms and legs, while Dinny caught the other, and together they trailed it through the shallow water to meet the boat.

"Now, Master Jack," cried Dinny, "take a howlt!"

Jack seized Bart by the waist as the boat's gunwale touched him. Abel and Dinny lifted together, and the result was that a certain amount of water went in over the side; but with it, heaving and struggling still, the knotted together bodies of Bart and his adversary, to lie in the bottom of the little craft, the sailor, fortunately for the escaping party, undermost.

"Sit down and row!" roared Abel; but his order was needless, for Jack had seated himself on the thwart, thrust out the oars at once, and began to pull; while on opposite sides, Dinny and Abel ran the boat out till they were breast-high in the water, when they gave it a final thrust and began to climb in.

By this time they were thirty or forty yards from the dry sand, down which the overseer and his party came running, and stopped at the edge.

"Halt! Surrender!" roared the overseer, savagely.

There was no reply, but the oars were plied swiftly, and the boat glided over the glassy swell.

"Fire!" roared the overseer, raising his piece; and a shower of buckshot came whistling and pattering by them, several of the little bullets striking the boat.

"Fire!" roared the overseer again. "Curse you! Why don't you fire!"

A scattered volley from half a dozen pieces answered his furious order, and as the little party glanced back, it was to see that those on shore were reloading rapidly, the peculiar noise made by the ramming down of the wads being plainly heard, mingled with the thudding of the ramrods as the charges were driven home.

No one spoke in the boat, but Abel and Dinny rapidly got oars over the side and began to pull, the latter having the harder work from the heaving bodies of the two combatants occupying the bottom of the boat, a fact which necessitated his standing up; but all the same he helped the boat vigorously along.

"Are ye going to lie down?" said Dinny, as he saw the enemy wade out as far as they could and prepare to fire.

"No!" said Abel. "You can."

"Divil a bit will I, if you don't," said Dinny, "and good luck to 'em! They've only got big pellets for shooting the pigs, and they won't kill except at close quarters."

Another scattered volley rang echoing out, and thundered along the cliffs, the smoke hiding the enemy from the gaze of those in the boat.

"Murther!" yelled Dinny, dropping his oar, but stooping to pick it up again as he shook his hand. "It's gone right through," he continued, as he gazed at a bead of blood oozing from the back of his hand, and another on the other side in the centre of his palm. "I wish I knew the divil who fired that. It feels like one of the overseer's games."

"Anyone else hit?" said Abel. "Jack!"

"It's nothing—a scratch," said Jack, rowing away with all his might, as the blood began to trickle down from a scored place upon his forehead. "Go on rowing."

"Bad luck to 'em! There's so many shot in a charge; it gives 'em such a chance," grumbled Dinny. "But niver mind, Masther Jack. It'll be a bit of a shmart; but losing a dhrop o' blood won't hurt ye."

Jack nodded, and tugged away rapidly, reducing the distance between them and the cutter; but they could not get farther from the firing party, who kept up a furious fusillade as they followed along round the side of the little bay, the pellets whistling by the fugitives, and more than one finding a home.

"Faix, and ye've got the best place there, Bart, me lad," cried Dinny, merrily. "Shall I come and howlt him while you take a change?"

"Look here!" growled Bart, as another volley was fired at them, and the shot came hurtling round; "it's no good now. Are you going to give in?"

The sailor looked from one to the other as he lay, with his head in the water at the bottom of the boat.

"Well, this here ar'nt cheerful," he said.

"You're beat. Why don't you give in?"

"Is it weazand slitting?" he said. "Snickersnee!"

"Get out!" cried Dinny. "Did they cut mine?"

"Yours, you deserter!" said the sailor, contemptuously.

"As much a deserter as you are, Dick Dullock. Sure, and they tuck me prishner, wid a musket to me ear and a bagnet to my chist."

"You look like one," said the sailor, sourly.

"Will you surrender?" growled Bart.

"Yes. Can't do no more, can I? Only bear witness, all on you, as I did my dooty. Didn't I, youngster?"

"You fought like a brave man," said Jack, gravely; "but it is of no use to struggle now, so give up."

"Ay, I'll give in," said the sailor; "but I'm a-going to lie here till the firing's done. I'll stand fire when there's fighting o' both sides; but I'm a prisoner now, and out of it, so here I stays."

Bart rose from where he had been kneeling on the man's chest, and straightened himself slowly, but only to start as a fresh volley was fired and a pellet grazed his chin; but he only uttered a savage growl like an angry beast, and made way for Dinny to sit down and row with all his strength.

Suddenly a shout from the bay shore took the attention of those in the boat, and the firing ceased.

"What's that mean?" cried Abel.

"They've found our boat," said Jack, excitedly.

It was true enough; and the fugitives redoubled their efforts to reach the cutter, while the overseer continued the firing, so as to disable some of the party before they could attain the shelter the vessel would give.

Abel was hit twice, and Bart received another shot, but the distance was great now, and the pellets too small to do serious mischief; but as they rowed round behind the cutter, anxiously watching to see that no one was aboard, its hull sheltering them from the firing, the noise and the buzz of voices ashore drew their attention to the fact that the overseer, the officer, and four more had entered the boat, which started with a cheer from those left behind, and pulled rapidly in pursuit.

"Quick, Bart, run up the jib while I cut the rope."

"Nay, haul up to it, you and Dinny," cried Bart, as he ran forward. "It's only a grapnel."

The firing recommenced now so viciously that every act on board the cutter was performed with great risk, the overseer and the officer taking it in turns to send a hail of buckshot at everyone who showed a head above the low side of the vessel.

But in spite of this the party worked well, and the sailor having surrendered, contented himself, as soon as he was aboard, by lying down upon the deck and beginning to chew.

The grapnel was hauled in, the jib hoisted, and Jack stationed at the tiller; but the sail slowly flapped to and fro, refusing to fill, and the only way on the cutter was that given by the falling tide.

"She'll be aboard of us, Bart, long before we get out of the bay," said Abel, with a groan of despair.

"Niver say die," cried Dinny, who had just given a turn to the painter which held the cutter's boat.

"Are there any arms aboard?" growled Bart. "Cuss it! look there!"

This last was consequent upon a shot ploughing a little channel along his neck. "D'yer hear what I say—you?" he said again to their prisoner. "Are there any arms aboard?"

"Yes, in the cabin—muskets," said the sailor; "but you leave 'em alone, my lad. This here as you've done's piracy, and if you kill anybody it's murder."

"Then let 'em keep off," said Bart, with a fierce growl as he followed Abel into the cabin, both reappearing again directly with muskets and ammunition.

"I tell you it's piracy," said the sailor from where he lay. "Isn't it, Dennis Kelly?"

"Faix, I s'pose it is," said Dinny, smiling. "There's so much in a name."

"Here you, Dinny, get up a musket," cried Abel. "You can shoot."

"Don't you, Dinny!" said the sailor. "It's hanging business."

"But I'm a prishner," said Dinny, grinning, "and obliged."

"It'll be a hanging matter, Dinny," cried the sailor, as the Irishman reappeared with a musket in his hand.

"It'll be a flogging sure if I'm took," said Dinny, "for they'll niver belave I'm acting against my will. Now, Captain Abel," he continued, as he loaded his piece, and laid it so that he could command the boat, "whin you ordher me to fire, why, av coorse I shall, but you must take the credit of the shot."

"Keep off!" roared Abel, as the boat now neared them fast. "You'll get bullets instead of buckshot: you come nearer."

"Surrender, you piratical scoundrel!" roared the overseer. "Put down that musket. Row hard, my lads!"

Whatever may have been the overseer's weakness, want of courage was not one; and this he proved by discharging his piece, and standing up in the boat to watch the effect.

The distance was short, but there was a faint puff of air now which filled the sail, and there was a feeling of intense relief as the cutter rapidly left the coming boat behind.

Jack's cheeks flushed, and his eyes sparkled as, with a touch of the tiller, he seemed to send the cutter rushing through the water; while an angry yell rose from behind as the boat dropped back.

But their despondency in the boat was only of a minute's duration, for the wind dropped as suddenly as it had risen, the cutter ceased to glide onward with the water rattling and splashing beneath her bows, the jib shivered and hung motionless, and a cheer arose from the pursuers as the firing recommenced.

"Be ready, Bart," said Abel, with a lurid look in his eyes, as he once more levelled his piece. "You, Dinny, are you going to help?"

"No," said the sailor. "It's piracy and murder if you shoot them, Dinny Kelly, and it's fair-play if they shoot you."

"Yis, it is awkward," said Dinny; "but Oi'm thinking I don't want to go back and be on senthry again, and there, Oi'll make a compromise of it. I won't shoot, but I'm mak' believe, and frecken 'em."

As he spoke he lay down on the deck and took aim at the occupants of the coming boat, whose position was extremely perilous, while the sides of the cutter sheltered those on board.

"Keep back!" roared Abel, as the boat neared them fast. "We're loaded with ball, not shot."

There was a momentary indecision on the part of the overseer, and it was instantly communicated to the men, for they ceased to paddle, while the two principals bent forward and spoke earnestly.

"No, they will not dare," said the overseer, loudly. "Go on, my lads! Surrender, you dogs, or you shall all be hung."

The boat was urged through the water again, and the overseer raised his fowling-piece, took aim, and was about to fire, when the officer with him laid his hand upon his arm.

"Wait," he said. "Then both fire together, close in, and board."

"We'll do that afterwards," cried the overseer, discharging his piece and rapidly reloading as the boat glided on till it was only about twenty yards away, and, in spite of a fierce threat or two, the repugnance to shed blood and the natural desire not to fight against the law had kept Abel and Bart from returning the fire.

Their case seemed hopeless now, unless in the struggle to come they repelled the boarders, for the wind which dotted the sea a hundred yards away with ripples refused to kiss their sail, and in another minute the overseer and his party would have been alongside, when, just as he covered Jack's arm, which could be seen lying upon the tiller, and when a shot at such short range would have been almost as bad as one from a bullet, there was a puff of smoke, a sharp report, and the overseer started up in the boat, dropped his fowling-piece, which fell into the sea with a splash, and then, before the officer could save him, he pitched head foremost over the side.

"Look at that now," said Dinny, who had risen into a sitting position on the deck, with his musket across his lap.

"Yes; you've done it now, Dinny Kelly," said the sailor, gruffly. "Desarted from the station, and shot the superintendent."

"Sorra a bit," said Dinny, as the wind suddenly struck the cutter, which heeled over and began to forge rapidly through the water. "Sorra a bit, man. It was this awkward baste of a mushket. I just closed my finger for a moment on the thrigger, and whoo! off she went, kicking up her heels like a nigger's mule. D'yer think the overseer's hurt?"

"I think you've killed him."

"Not I, bedad. It was me mushket," said Dinny. "Divil a bit will I have any more to do wid it. I'll have another with a thrigger which isn't wake."

"You've saved us, Dinny," said Jack, excitedly, as the boat was being left far behind.

"Not I, my lad. Shure, it's between the wind and this worn-out old mushket. It's a baste of a thing. Why, it moight have killed the poor man. I say, lad; d'yer think he's much hurt?"

"A broken arm, that's all, Dinny," said Jack, smiling.

"Ah, well!" said Dinny, reloading the piece; "that'll do him good, and give the poor divils at the plantation a bit of a rest."

He paused in the act of reloading, drew the charge with a dry look upon his countenance, and laid the musket down upon the deck.

"No, thank ye," he said, shaking his head at the piece. "It's a murdhering baste ye are, and ye'll be getting some poor fellow into throuble wan of these days. Don't you think so, Dick?"

The prisoner screwed up his countenance, and then relaxed it as he looked hard at Dinny.

"Well, it's pretty nigh a hanging matter for you, Dinny," he said.

"What! for an accident, man?"

"Accident! you've gone and committed a rank act of piracy! But, I say, what'll they do with me?"

"Hang ye, I should say," replied Dinny, with a droll look in his eye. "Hang ye as soon as they've got toime to think about ye; or no: maybe they'll save themselves the throuble, and hand ye over to thim ruffians there."

He pointed over the side, and the sailor gave a start and changed colour as he caught sight of the back-fins of a couple of huge sharks gliding along through the water a little way astern.

"Oh, they're a bad lot with their prisoners, Dick. Look at me."

"But what are they going to do?" said the sailor, eagerly. "They can't put in anywhere, and as soon as this day's work's known, they'll have a man-o'-war sent after 'em."

"Sorra a wan o' me knows," said Dinny; "but it's moighty plisant out here. I'm toired o' pipe-claying me belts and marching and being senthry, and they may make me prishner as long as they like."

"You didn't half-kill one of them, and they don't bear malice against you," said the sailor, thoughtfully.

"An' is it malice? Why, didn't I thry to run wan of 'em through wid me bagnet, and attimpt to shoot the other! Malice! I belave they liked it, for we've been the best o' friends iver since. Here, Bart, me lad; Dick here wants to shake hands with yez."

"I don't," said the sailor, sternly; but as Bart came from where he had been taking a pull at one of the ropes, smiling and open-handed, Dick's face relaxed.

"That was a pretty good wrastle," said Bart, running his eye approvingly over the physique of his late opponent, and gripping Dick's hand heartily; "but I got the best of you."

Dick did not answer, but he returned the grip, and Bart went aft directly to relieve Jack at the tiller, while the darkness came on rapidly, and with it the breeze increased in force till the cutter careened over and rapidly left the island behind.

"Well, Dennis Kelly," said the sailor, as they sat together on board later, with the stars gathering overhead, and faint sounds wafted to them from time to time as they glided rapidly along a few miles from land, "you can only make one thing of it, my boy, and that's piracy; and piracy's yard-arm, and a swing at the end of the rope."

"Ah! get along wid ye," said Dinny, contemptuously, "and don't call things by bad names. They're three very plisant fellows, and they've borried the boat and taken us prishners to help them in the cruise; or, if ye like it better, we're pressed men."

"But what are they going to do next?"

"Divil a bit do I know, and the divil a bit do I care. I've no belts to pipe-clay, and you've no deck to holy-stone. What there is to ate they share wid ye, and they take their turn at the watch. Sure, it's a gintleman's life, and what more would ye have?"

"But it's piracy—rank piracy!" said Dick, stubbornly; "and I want to know what we're going to do next."

"Well, thin, I'll tell ye," said Dinny; "but it's a saycret, moind."

"Well, what?"

"It's a saycret, moind," said Dinny, "and ye won't tell?"

"Tell! Who is there to tell here?"

"Nobody yet; but ye'll keep the saycret?"

"Yes," said Dick, earnestly. "What are they going to do?"

"Didn't I say I'd tell ye," said Dinny, "as soon as I know?"

"Yah!" snarled Dick.

"Well," cried Dinny, "how can I tell ye till I know? Why, it's my belief, Dick, me lad, that they don't know themselves."

"Where do you mean to go, Abel?" said Jack at last.

"Go, my lass—my lad!" he said, correcting himself. "Anywhere. We can't touch port, but we've got a tidy little vessel, not too big to manage, and we must sail somewhere to be safe."

"Well, I don't care," came from forward, as Dick raised his voice in stubborn reiteration with Dinny. "I says it's piracy, and if they're ketched, they'll all be hanged."

A dead silence fell upon the little group, and at last it was Bart who spoke, as if to himself.

"If you helps yourself to a bit o' anything that comes ashore, they says it's wrecking; and if you want a drop o' brandy or a bit o' lace from a furrin boat, it's smuggling; and now, if a man wants to get away, and fights for his liberty, he's a pirate."

"For seizing a vessel, Bart," said Jack.

"Yes, lad, I know. Well, they may call me what they like. Here we are, and we've got to live."

"Where d'ye think they'll sail?" said Dick again, raising his voice, but in ignorance that the words could reach the group by the tiller.

"Where shall we sail?" said Jack, who was steering. "I don't know, for all before us seems black; but I've saved my brother and his true old friend, so let fate guide us: the world is very wide."

"Yes, Dinny, I don't mind for a change; but it's piracy, and I hope as we sha'n't all be hung."

"The same to you," said Dinny, giving the sailor's shoulder a sounding slap.

"Piracy!" said Jack, softly, as the boat glided on. "Well, it was not our choice, and, at all events, we're free."

Chapter Sixteen
After a Lapse

"Then we'll die for it, Bart," said Jack, fiercely.

"If so be as you says die for it now, or to-morrow, or next day, or next week, die it is, my lad," said Bart, despondently; "but luck's agen us, and we're beat. Why not give up?"

"Give up?" cried Jack, whose appearance was somewhat altered by his two years of hard sea-life in the tropics since the night when the cutter sailed away into the darkness of what seemed to be their future. "Give up?"

"Yes; and back out of it all. Why not take passage somewhere, not as Jack, Commodore Junk's brother, but as bonny Mary Dell o' Devonshire, going back home along o' Bart Wrigley, as is Bartholomew by rights?"

"Well?" said Jack, sternly.

"Don't look black at me, my lad. I'm tired o' boarding ships and sending people adrift."

"Growing afraid, Bart?"

"Yes, my lad; but not for Bart Wrigley. For someone else."

"You are preaching to-night, Bart."

"Maybe, my lad, for it's solemn times; and something keeps a-saying to me: 'Don't run no more risks! There's old Devon a-waiting for you, and there's the old cottage and the bay, and you've got the money to buy a decent lugger, and there's plenty o' fish in the sea.'"

"Go, on," said Jack, mockingly.

"Ay, lad, I will," said Bart. "And you might settle down there, and live happy with a man there to wait on you and be your sarvent—ay, your dog if you liked; and some day, if you thought better of it, and was ready to say, 'Bart, my lad, you've been a true chap to me, and I know as you've loved me ever since you was a boy, so now I'll be your wife,' why, then—"

Bart stopped with his lips apart, gazing wonderingly at the angry countenance before him.

"You madman! What are you saying?" was hissed into his ears. "Mary Dell died when she left her home, driven away by man's tyranny—when she sought out her brother and his friend, to find them working like slaves in that plantation. It was John Dell who became your companion: Mary Dell's dead."

"No," said Bart, speaking softly and with a homely pathos, full of a poetical sentiment that could not have been expected from his rough exterior as he sat on the deck of a long, low, heavily-sparred schooner. "No, my lad, Mary Dell isn't dead. She's hidden here in my breast, where I can look inwards and see the bonny lass with the dark eyes and long black hair as I knowed I loved as soon as I knowed what love meant, and as long as I've that lass will never die."

"Hush, Bart, old friend!" said Jack, softly. "Let her live, then, there; but to me she is dead, and I live to think of her persecutions, and how for two years man has pursued us with his bitter hatred, and hunted us down as if we were savage beasts."

"Ay," said Bart, softly; "but isn't it time to take the other road, and get away?"

"No," said Jack, fiercely. "Bart, old friend—you are my friend."

"Friend!" said Bart, in a reproachful tone.

"Yes. I know you are; but once more, if you value my friendship, never speak to me again as you have spoken now."

"You're captain, my lad. I'll do what you like."

"I know you will. Well, then, do you think I can forgive the treatment we have received? It has been a dog's life, I tell you—the life of a savage dog."

"Ay, but we've bit pretty sharp sometimes," said Bart, smiling. "See how we've growed, too. First it was the bit of a canoe thing as you came in up the creek."

Jack nodded.

"Then we took the cutter."

"Yes, Bart."

"And with that cutter we took first one ship, and then with that another, always masters, and getting, bit by bit, stout, staunch men."

"And savages," said Jack, bitterly.

"Well, yes, some on 'em is savage like, specially Mazzard."

"Black Mazzard is a ruffianly wretch!"

"True, lad; but we've gone on and got better and stronger, till we have under our feet the swiftest schooner as swims the sea, and Commodore Junk's name's known all along the coast."

"And hated, and a price set upon his head; and now that he is a prisoner his people turn against him, and his most faithful follower wants to go and leave him in the lurch."

"Nay, don't say that, my lad," cried Bart. "We was overmatched, and he was took."

"Yes, by his men's cowardice."

"Nay; you're cross, my lad," said Bart, unconsciously raising one arm and drawing back the sleeve to readjust a bandage. "Month to-night and the deck was running into the scuppers with blood, half the lads was killed, and t'other half all got a wound. We was obliged to sheer off."

"Yes, you coward! you left your captain to his fate."

"But I saved the captain's—brother," said Bart, slowly, "or he'd have been shut up in prison along with poor Abel now."

"Better so," said the other, fiercely; "and then there'd be an end of a persecuted life."

"Better as it is," said Bart, quietly; "but I did save you."

"Bart, old lad, don't take any notice of what I say," whispered Jack.

"I don't, lad, when you're put out. I never do."

"Don't speak to me like that. It maddens me more."

"No, it don't, lad. It's only me speaking, and you may hammer me with words all night if it does you good. I don't mind, I'm only Bart."

"My true old friend," whispered the other, quickly; "but it's time they were back."

"Nay, not yet," said Bart, as the other stood gazing over the side of the schooner toward where a long, low bank of mist seemed to shut out everything beyond.

"They've been gone two hours, and it's now four bells."

"Ay, and it'll be six bells before they get back, and it's a long way to row. Do you mean to try it, then?"

"Try it? Yes, if I die in the attempt. Did I hesitate when you two were on the plantation, and I was alone and—a boy?"

"Not you," said Bart.

"Then, do you think I shall hesitate now that I have a ship and followers to back me up?"

Bart shook his head.

"Abel must be saved; and the men agree."

"Ay; they say they'll have the skipper out of the prison or they'll die first."

"Brave fellows!" cried Jack, enthusiastically.

"But I don't see how a schooner's to attack forts and cannon and stone walls. My lad, it can't be done."

"It shall be done!" cried Jack. "How's Dinny?"

"Bit weak still; but he says he can fight, and he shall go."

"Brave, true-hearted fellow! And Dick?"

"Says he shall be well enough to go; but he won't—he's weak as a rat."

Jack drew a deep breath, and a fiercely vindictive look flashed from the dark eyes which glared at Bart.

"They shall suffer for all this. Abel will pay them their due."

"Ay," said Bart; and then to himself—"when he gets away."

"It was a cruel, cowardly fight—four to one."

"He would attack," said Bart, heavily. "He'd had such luck that he wouldn't believe he could be beat."

"He was right," said the other, fiercely. "He is not beaten, for we will fetch him out, and he shall pay them bitterly for all this."

The speaker strode forward, and went below into the cabin, while Bart drew his breath hard as he rose from where he had been seated and limped, slightly bending down once to press his leg where a severe flesh-wound was received on the night of the engagement when Abel Dell—whose name had begun to be well-known for freebooting enterprise as Commodore Junk—had been taken prisoner.

Bart walked to the forecastle, where, on descending, he found Dinny and Dick Dullock playing cards, the life they had led with their three companions being one to which they had settled down without a hint of change.

"Well!" asked Dinny, looking up from his dirty cards; "what does he say?"

Dick the sailor gazed inquiringly at both in turn.

"Says he shall fetch the captain out."

Dinny whistled.

"And what does Black Mazzard say?" asked Dick.

"Don't know. Hasn't been asked."

"Look here," said Dick, in a low voice. "There's going to be trouble over this. Black Mazzard's captain now, he says, and he's got to be asked. He was down here swearing about that boat being sent off, and he's been drunk and savage ever since."

"Hist! What's that?" said Dinny, starting up, and then catching at Bart's shoulder to save himself from falling. "Head swims," he said, apologetically.

"Ay, you're weak, lad," said Bart, helping him back to his seat. "Why, the boat's back!"

He hurried on deck, to find a boat alongside, out of which four men climbed on deck, while Jack Dell, who had just heard the hail, came hurrying up.

"Well?" he said. "What news?"

The one spoken to turned away and did not answer.

"Do you hear?" cried Jack, catching him by the shoulder as a heavy-looking man came on deck, lurched slightly, recovered himself, and then walked fiercely and steadily up to the group.

"Bad news, captain," said another of the men, who had just come aboard.

"Bad—news?" said Jack, heavily.

"Bad news of the Commodore!" said the heavy-looking fellow, who was now swaying himself to and fro, evidently drunk in body but sober in mind.

"Yes," said the man who had first spoken, "bad news."

"Tell me," cried Jack, hoarsely, as he pressed forward to gaze full in the speaker's face, "what is it? They have not sent him away?"

The man was silent; and as the rest of the crew, attracted by the return of the boat, clustered round, Jack reeled.

"Stand by, my lad," whispered Bart at his ear. "Don't forget."

The words seemed to give nerve to the sturdy, broad-shouldered young man, who spoke hoarsely.

"Tried and condemned," he said, in a hoarse, strange voice.

"They've hung him—"

"What!"

"In chains on a gibbet."

A hoarse, guttural sound escaped from Jack's throat as he clung tightly to Bart's arm.

"The gibbet's on the low point by the mangrove swamp," said the man. "They've cut down two palms about a dozen feet and nailed another across, and the captain's swinging there."

"A lie!" yelled Jack; "not my brother!"

There was a dead pause of utter silence for a few moments, and then the man said slowly:

"Yes, we all saw it and made sure;" and a murmur of acquiescence arose from his three companions, who had been in the boat in search of far different information to that which they had brought.

"But not my brother?" groaned Jack.

"Yes," said the man. "It was Commodore Junk."

As a dead silence once more fell upon the poop, the dark, heavy-looking man stood swaying to and fro for a few minutes, gazing down at Jack, who had dropped into a sitting position upon a water-keg, his arms resting upon his knees, his hands hanging, and his head drooped; while Bart stood by his shoulder with his face wrinkled and a pained expression upon his brow, just illumined by the bright glint of the stars.

The heavy man nodded and seemed about to speak, but remained silent for a time. Then patting Jack on the shoulder:

"Brave lad! Good captain! For time of war!" he said. "But never mind, my lads. We'll pay them for it, yet."

He lurched slightly and walked slowly toward the captain's cabin, unnoticed by Jack and Bart; but Dinny's eyes were sharp enough to read what all this meant, and he turned to his comrade Dick.

"Look at that, now!" he whispered.

"Ay, I was looking. What does it mean?"

"Mane!" said Dinny, scornfully. "It manes that Black Mazzard thinks he's captain now."

"Then if the throat-cutting scoundrel is, I'm off first chance."

"An' I'm wid ye," said Dinny, earnestly. "I'll go and lade a virtuous life."

"And leave the skipper's brother and Bart?"

Dinny pulled off his cap and rubbed his head viciously.

"Now, why did ye want to go and say that?" he cried. "Iverything was as aisy as could be, and you go and upset it all."

"Poor Abel!" said Jack at last, softly.

"Ay, poor old Abel!" said Bart, with a groan.

"You here?" said Jack, starting up and catching the rough fellow by the arm.

"Here?—ay!" growled Bart, slowly. "Where did you think I was, lad?"

"I didn't think, Bart, or I shouldn't have said that," cried Jack, earnestly. "Where would you be but at my elbow if I was in trouble, ready to be of help?"

"Ay, but there's no helping you here, lad," said Bart with a groan.

"No helping me! But you can, Bart. Do you wonder that I hate the world?—that I see it all as one crowd of enemies fighting against me and trying to crush me down? Not help me! Oh, but you shall! My poor brother! They shall pay heavily for this!"

"What'll you do, lad?" said Bart, despondently.

"Do!" cried Jack, with a savage laugh—"do what poor Abel always hung back from doing, and stopped Black Mazzard from many a time. I don't read my Bible now, Bart; but doesn't it say that there shall be blood for blood; and my poor brother's cries aloud for vengeance, as they shall see!"

"No, no, my lad," whispered Bart, hoarsely; "let it stop here. It seems to me as if something said: 'This here's the end on it. Now get her to go back home.'"

"Home!" said Jack, with a fierce laugh. "Where is home?"

"Yonder," said Bart, stolidly.

"No! Here—at sea. Bart, there is no other home for me; no other hope but to have revenge!"

"Revenge, lad?"

"Ay, a bitter, cruel revenge. I could have been different. I was once full of love and hope before I knew what the world was like, but that's all past and dead—yes, dead; and the dead yonder is looking toward me and asking me to remember what we have suffered."

"But think."

"Think, Bart? I have thought till my brain has seemed to burn; and everything points to revenge, and revenge I'll have!"

"It's the end of it all now," said Bart, solemnly. "Let's go back."

"The way is open, Bart Wrigley. I have no hold upon you, and I can work alone. Go!"

"You wouldn't talk like that," said Bart, huskily, "if you was cool."

"What do you mean, man?"

"'Bout me going," said Bart, in a low, husky voice. "There's only one way for me, and that's where you go, lad. It allus has been, and it allus will be till I'm took. What are you going to do?"

The question was asked in a quick, decisive way, very different to the despondent air that had pervaded his words before, and the manner was so marked that Jack laid his hands on his companion's shoulders.

"It's my fate to be always saying bitter things to you, Bart, and wounding you."

"Never mind about that," said Bart, huskily. "Long as I'm the one as you trusts, that's enough for me. What are you going to do next?"

There was no answer for a few minutes, and then the words whispered were very short and decisive.

"And let 'em think it's scared us, and we've gone right away?" said Bart.

"Yes."

Bart gave a short, quick nod of the head, walked sharply to the forecastle and yelled to the men to tumble up. The result was that in a very short time sail after sail was spread till a dusky cloud seemed to hover over the deck of the schooner, which heeled over in the light breeze and began skimming as lightly as a yacht eastward, as if to leave the scene of the Commodore's execution far behind.

Chapter Seventeen
The Gibbet Spit

It had been a baking day in the town of Saint George, British Honduras, and the only lively things about the place had been the lizards. The sky had seemed to be of burnished brass, and the sea of molten silver, so dazzling that the eye was pained which fell upon its sheen. The natives were not troubled by the heat, for they sought out shady places, and went to sleep, but the British occupants of the port kept about their houses, and looked as if they wished they were dogs, and could hang out their tongues and pant.

Saint George, always a dead-and-alive tropic town, now seemed to be the dead alone; and as if to prove that it was so, the last inhabitant seemed to have gone to the end of the spit by the marsh beyond the port, where every one who landed or left could see, and there hung himself up as a sign of the desolation and want of animation in the place.

For there, pendent from the palm-tree gibbet, alone in the most desolate spot near the port, was the buccaneering captain, whose name had become a by-word all along the coast, whose swift-sailing schooner had captured vessels by the score, and robbed and burnt till Commodore Junk's was a name to speak of with bated breath; and the captains of ships, whether British or visitors from foreign lands, made cautious inquiries as to whether he had been heard of in the neighbourhood before they ventured to sea, and then generally found that they had been misled. For that swift schooner was pretty certain to appear right in their path, with the result that their vessels would be boarded, the captain and crew sent afloat in their boat not far from land, and the ship would be plundered, and then scuttled after all that attracted the buccaneers had been secured.

There had been rejoicings when the king's ship, sent over expressly to put an end to piracy, found and had an engagement with the schooner — one of so successful a nature that after the bloody fight was over, and the furious attack by boarding baffled, three prisoners remained in the hands of the naval captain, two of whom were wounded unto death, and the other uninjured, and who proved to be the captain who had headed the boarders.

Abel Dell's shrift had been a short one. Fortune had been against him, after a long career of success. He saw his ship escape crippled, and he ground his teeth as he called her occupants cowards for leaving him in the lurch, being, of course, unaware that the retreat was due to his lieutenant, Abram Mazzard, while when she returned through the determined action of Jack, it came too late, for Abel Dell, otherwise Commodore Junk, was acting as warning to pirates, his last voyage being over.

The heat seemed to increase on that torrid day till nightfall, when clouds gathered, and the flickering lightning flashed out and illumined the long banks of vapour, displaying their fantastic shapes, to be directly after reflected from the surface of the barely rippled sea.

"Hadn't we better give up for a bit? Storm may pass before morning," whispered the thick-set figure standing close by the wheel.

"No, Bart; we must go to-night," was the reply. "Is all ready?"

"Ay, ready enough; but I don't like the job."

"Give up, then, and let Dinny come."

"Did you ever know me give up?" growled Bart.

"'Tain't that: it's leaving the ship. Black Mazzard ar'n't to be trusted."

"What! Pish! he dare do nothing."

"Not while you're here, my lad. It's when you're gone that I feel scared."

"You think—"

"I think he's trying to get the men over to his side, and some on 'em hold with him."

Jack remained thoughtful for a few minutes.

"It is only lightning, Bart. There'll be no storm. We can get what we want done in six hours at the longest, and he can do nothing in that time— he will do nothing in that time if you put a couple of bottles of rum within his reach."

Bart uttered a low, chuckling laugh.

"That's what I have done," he said.

"Then we're safe enough. Where's Dinny?"

"Forward, along of Dick."

"Tell them to keep a sharp look-out while we're gone, and to be on the watch for the boat."

Half an hour later, when the schooner was deemed to be near enough for the purpose, an anchor was lowered down, to take fast hold directly in the shallow bottom, a boat was lowered, into which Jack and Bart stepped, the former shipping the little rudder, and Bart stepping a short mast and hauling up a big sail, when the soft sea-breeze sent them gliding swiftly along.

"He was asleep in the cabin," said Bart. "Soon be yonder if it holds like this. Do you feel up to it, my lad, as if you could venter?"

"Yes," said Jack, sternly.

"But it's a wicked job, my lad, and more fit for men."

"I've thought all that out, Bart," was the reply. "I know. It is my duty, and I shall do it. Are the pistols loaded?"

"Trust me for that," growled Bart. "They're loaded enough, and the cutlashes has edges like razors. So has my axe."

"Have you the tools?"

"Everything, my lad. Trust me for that."

"I do trust you, Bart, always."

"And how are we to find our way back to the schooner in the dark?"

"We shall not find our way back in the dark, Bart, but sail right out here as near as we can guess, and then lie-to till daybreak."

Bart kept his eyes fixed upon one particular light, and tried to calculate their bearings from its relation to another behind; but all the same, he felt in doubt, and shook his head again and again, when some blinding flash of lightning gave him a momentary glance of the shore.

But Jack did not hesitate for a moment, keeping the boat's head in one direction with unerring instinct, till the waves were close upon their left, and it seemed that in another minute they must be swamped.

Bart half rose, ready to swim for his life, as the boat leapt high, then seemed to dive down headlong, rose again, dived, and then danced lightly up and down for a few minutes before gliding slowly on again.

"Was that the bar?" he whispered eagerly.

"Yes. It is rough at this time of the tide," was the answer, given in the calmest manner, for Jack had not stirred.

Bart drew a breath full of relief.

"Be ready."

"Ready it is."

"Down sail."

The little yard struck, the sail collapsed, and, acting by the impetus already given, the boat glided forward some distance and then grated upon a bed of sand.

Bart shuddered slightly, but he was busy all the while arranging the sail ready for rapid hoisting; and this done, he carried the grapnel out some fifteen or twenty yards from the bows and fixed it cautiously in the shore.— He was about to return when a hand was laid upon his shoulder—a hand which seemed to come out of the black darkness.

Bart snatched a pistol from his belt, and put it back with a grunt.

"I didn't know it was you," he said, in a hoarse whisper. "Lightning seems to make it darker. Where away?"

"Fifty yards south," said Jack, quietly.

"Then look here, my lad. I don't want to disobey orders; but I'm a man and you're only a—"

"Man," said Jack, quietly.

"Then you stop by the boat and—"

"Bart!"

"Nay, nay, let me speak, my lad. Let me say all I want. You can trust me. If Bart Wrigley says he'll do a thing for you, he'll do it if he's got the strength and life in him. So let me do this, while you wait for me. Come, now, you will!"

"No! Come with me. I must be there."

Bart drew in a deep breath, and muttered to himself as he listened to the peculiarly changed voice in which his companion spoke.

"You're master," he said; "and I'm ready."

"Yes. Take my hand, and speak lower. There may be watchers about."

For answer Bart gripped his companion's hand, and together they walked for some distance along the hard sand, where the spray from the rollers swept up. Then turning inland suddenly, they had taken about twenty steps to the west when a vivid flash of lightning showed them that their calculations had been exact, for there before them in all its horror, and not a dozen yards away, stood the rough gibbet with the body of a man pendent from the cross-beam, the ghastly object having stood out for a moment like a huge cameo cut in bold relief upon some mass of marble of a solid black.

"Abel! Brother!" moaned Jack, running forward to sink kneeling in the sand, and for a few moments, as Bart stood there in the black darkness with his head instinctively uncovered, there arose from before him the wild hysterical sobbings of a woman, at first in piteous appeal to the dead, then in fierce denunciation of his murderers; but as the last cry rang out there was a flickering in the sky, as if the *avant garde* of another vivid flash—

the half-blinding sheet of flame which lit up the gibbet once again; and it seemed strange to Bart that no woman was there, only the figure of a short, well-built man, who stood looking toward him, and said in a hoarse, firm voice—

"We are not likely to be interrupted; but to work, quick!"

"Right!" said Bart, hoarsely; and directly after, a rustling sound, accompanied by a heavy breathing, was heard in the black darkness, followed soon after by the clinking of iron against iron.

There was a faint flicker in the sky again, but no following flash, and the darkness seemed to have grown more intense, as the panting of some one engaged in a work requiring great exertion came from high up out of the ebon darkness.

"The file, man, the file."

"Nay, I'll wrench it off," came from where the panting was heard. Then there was more grating of iron against iron, repeated again and again, when, just as an impatient ejaculation was heard, there was a loud snap, as if a link had been broken, a dull thud of a bar falling, and the panting noise increased.

"Now, lad, quick! Can you reach? That's right. Steady! I can lower a little more. Easy. A little more away. You have all the weight now. May I let go?"

"Yes."

There was the clank of a chain. Then a heavy thud as if someone had dropped to the ground, and then the chain clanked again.

"No, no; wait a moment, my lad. Lower down. That's it. Let's leave these cursed irons behind."

The rough grating of iron sounded again, the heavy panting was resumed, and another sharp crack or two arose, followed by the fall of pieces on the sand.

"That's it!" muttered Bart, as a dull clang arose from the earth. "We needn't have been afraid of any one watching here."

"I'll help."

"Nay; I want no help," panted Bart, as he seemed to be lifting some weight. "You lead on, my lad. Pity we couldn't have landed here."

The reason was obvious; for seaward the waves could be heard rushing in and out of a reef with many a strange whisper and gasping sound, giving plain intimation that a boat would have been broken up by the heavy waves.

"Shall I go first?"

"Ay; go first, lad. Keep close to the water's edge; and you must kick against the rope."

There proved to be no need to trust to this, for, as they reached the water's edge, where the sand, instead of being ankle deep, was once more smooth and hard, a phosphorescent gleam rose from the breaking waves, and the wet shore glistened with tiny points of light, which were eclipsed from time to time as the two dark, shadowy figures passed slowly along, the first accommodating its pace to that of the heavily-burdened second, till the first stopped short, close to where the boat was moored.

It was plain to see, for the rope shone through the shallow water, as if gilded with pale, lambent gold; while, when it was seized and drawn rapidly, the boat came skimming in, driving from each side of its bows a film as of liquid moonlight spread thinly over the water beyond, where the waves broke upon the sand.

There was the sound of a voice as the figures waded in, one holding the boat, and the other depositing his burden there.

"What's that?" whispered Bart. "Did you speak?"

"No."

"Quick! Get hold of the grapnel. No. On board, lad, quick!"

"Halt! Who goes there?" cried a voice close by from where the darkness was thickest.

For answer Bart cut the grapnel line, made sure that his companion was in the boat, and then, exerting his great strength, he ran out with it through the shallow water, just as there was a vivid flash of lightning, revealing, about twenty yards away, a group of soldiers standing on the rough shore, just beyond the reach of the tide.

"Halt!" was shouted again, followed by a warning. And then followed a series of rapid orders; four bright flashes darted from as many muskets, and the bullets whistled overhead, the intense darkness which had followed the lightning disturbing the soldiers' aim.

Orders to re-load were heard; but the boat was well afloat by now, and Bart had crawled in, the tiller had been seized, and the sail was rapidly hoisted, the wind caught it at once, and by the time another flash of lightning enabled the patrol to make out where the boat lay, it was a hundred yards from shore, and running rapidly along the coast.

A volley was fired as vainly as the first, and as the bullets splashed up the water, Bart laughed.

"They may fire now," he said. "We shall be a hundred yards farther before they're ready again."

They sailed on into the darkness for quite two hours, during which the lightning ceased, and the mutterings of the thunder were heard no more. But though a careful look-out was kept—and Bart felt that they had pretty well calculated the position of the schooner—they could not find her, and the sail was lowered down.

"We've gone quite far enough," growled Bart. "Where's that light that Dinny was to show?"

There was no answer, and no light visible from where they lay for the next three hours, waiting patiently till the first faint streak of dawn should show them the waiting vessel, and their ghastly burden could be carried aboard ready for a sailor's grave.

"It is a trick, Bart," said Jack at last, as he glanced at their freight lying forward beneath a spare sail.

"Ay, I felt it, my lad," said Bart, frowning. "I felt it last night. Black Mazzard hain't the man to leave alone; and what's a couple o' bottles o' rum to such as he?"

"The villain—the coward!" cried Jack, bitterly. "At a time like this!"

"Ay, it's a bad time, my lad," said Bart, "but we've done our work, poor chap; and the sea's the sea, whether it's off a boat or a schooner. You mean that, don't you, now?"

"No," said Jack, fiercely, as he pointed to the back-fins of a couple of sharks.

"Ugh!" ejaculated Bart. "What, then, my lad?"

"To find the schooner first, and if not, to make for one of the little islands, where we'll land."

"Little more to the west, my lad," said Bart, after they had been sailing in silence for some time. "You'll land at the Sandy Key, won't you?"

"Yes," said Jack, shortly, as he sat there with eyes fixed and frowning brow.

"Poor old Abe!" said Bart to himself, as he gazed in turn at the ghastly object in the bottom of the boat. "One never used to think much of dying in the old days; but if one did, it was of being drowned at sea, washed ashore, and buried decently in the old church-yard atop of the hill. And now, old mate, after being a captain out here, we're a-going to lie you over yonder in the warm, dry sand, where the sun always shines and the cocoa-nuts grow;

but you'll have no tombstone, lad, and no words writ, only such as is writ in her heart, for she loved you, Abe, old mate, more than she'll ever love me."

A sharp look-out was kept for the schooner; but though the horizon was swept again and again, she was not in sight.

"It's one o' Black Mazzard's games, lad," Bart said at last, as a faint, cloudy appearance was visible on their bow; "but we shall find him yonder."

Jack bowed his head in acquiescence, and the boat skimmed rapidly on, till the cloudy appearance began to take the form of a low island, from whose sandy shore cocoa-nut palms waved their great pinnate leaves, looking lace-like against the clear blue sky.

In a couple of hours they were close in, and the boat was run up in a sandy cove sheltered by a point, with the result that, instead of the tide setting in heavy rollers, there was just a soft curl over the waves, and a sparkling foam to wash the fine pebble sand.

"No," said Bart, speaking as if in answer to his companion.

"Never mind," said Jack, quietly. "We shall find the schooner by-and-by. Let's land."

Bart assisted to draw the boat well ashore, waiting till a good-sized wave came, and then running the boat on its crest some yards farther up the sand.

He looked up then at Jack, who nodded his head, and the canvas-draped figure was lifted out and borne up to where the sand lay soft and thick, as it had been drifted by the gales of the stormy season.

As Bart bent beneath his burden he nearly trod upon one of the great land-crabs, with which the place seemed to swarm, the hideous creatures scuffling awkwardly out of his way, snapping their claws menacingly, and rolling their horrible eyes, which stood out on foot-stalks far from their shelly orbits, and gave them a weird look as they seemed to be inspecting the canvas-wrapped bag.

"Here?" said Bart, as they reached a smooth spot, where a clump of palms made a slight shade.

"Yes," was the laconic reply.

"No tools," said Bart, half to himself; "but it don't matter, Abe, old lad. I can scratch a grave for you, and cut your name arter with my knife on one o' them trees."

He laid his load tenderly down upon the sand, in the shadiest spot, and then, stripping off his jacket and rolling up his sleeves over his muscle-knotted arms, he began to scrape the sand away rapidly, and soon made a long, narrow trench, though it was not easy work, for the soft, fine, dry sand flowed slowly, as if it were a liquid, back into the trench.

"That will do," said Jack, suddenly rising from where he had been kneeling by Abel's side.

Bart ceased his task without another word, and at a sign from his companion reverently went to the foot of the canvas-covered figure, while Jack went to the head, and they lifted it into the shallow trench.

"And never said so much as a prayer over it!" muttered Bart to himself, as he rapidly scooped back the sand with his hands, till the lower part of his old mate's body was covered, leaving the head instinctively to the last.

He was then about to heap the sand over gravewise, but Jack stopped him, and, taking a piece of wreck wood, drew it along the place so as to leave the sand level.

"What are you going to do?" he said, sternly, as Bart drew his knife.

"Cut a hay and a dee on that there tree," said the man, shortly.

"No."

"Not cut his letters there?" cried Bart, in a wondering tone.

"No, man, no. Do you suppose I am going to leave him here?"

Bart closed his knife with a click, and screwed up his face.

"You're captain," he said, quietly; "what next?"

"Back to the boat."

Bart obeyed without another word, and as they walked down over the hot sand, it was to pass several of the land-crabs, which rolled their eyes and leered at them in a goblin way till the boat was launched, the sail hoisted, and they coasted the side of the island to get round to its back, and make sure that the schooner had not cast anchor off this—one of the rendezvous for boats which had missed the schooner after being sent away upon some expedition.

But their sail availed them nothing. The schooner was not off the island, and Bart looked at his companion for orders.

"It would take three days to reach the shelter," he said at last.

"With this wind—yes," replied Bart. "No food, no water. Shall us get some nuts?"

There was no reply. Jack sat with his arms resting upon his knees, holding the tiller and gazing right before him, seeing nothing, but trying to pierce the future.

"A-wondering what to do next," muttered Bart, watching his companion furtively. "If the poor thing could see the old cottage now, and the bay, and a decent lugger lying off the point with her sails shivering, would it still be no?"

"Still be no," he said to himself softly; "and yet I wouldn't ask to be different to what I am."

"Mazzard has taken command, Bart," said Jack at last, "and we must make a fresh start, my lad."

"Ay, ay, sir," cried Bart, sharply.

"We must get sufficient provisions somehow, and run across to the shelter. If the schooner is not there we must wait till she comes in."

"And you won't give up without a struggle?"

"Give up?"

"Hurrah!" cried Bart, joyously. "Let's run up the Usa river to one of the Indian places, and get some food and nuts, and then be off. Hard down!"

Instead of obeying and changing the boat's direction, Jack suddenly pointed right away into the distance.

"What's that?"

Bart stood up and sheltered his eyes with his hand, so as to get a good view of a triangular piece of sail glistening white in the sunshine, far away, about the horizon line.

"There ain't another vessel with a raking sail like that!" he cried. "I shaped that sail. Why, it is she!"

"Yes," said Jack, after a long look across the dazzling blue sea, "it's the schooner, Bart; and she's coming here."

The boat danced over the sparkling waves, and three hours after she was alongside the schooner, which was hove to—the wind being contrary—as soon as the boat was descried by those on board. Dinny was the foremost in the group waiting to lower down the falls, and in a few minutes the boat hung from the davits, and Jack gave a sharp look round as he stepped upon the deck.

"Why was the schooner not waiting?"

"Faix, the captain gave orders for sail to be made," said Dinny, in a meaning tone; "and away we wint."

"The captain!" said Jack, with a angry look in his eyes. "Where is the captain, then?"

"Sure," cried Dinny, as a murmur ran through the group gathered on the deck; "sure, he's in his cabin, having a slape."

"It's all over, Bart, my lad," said Jack, bitterly. "What will you do—stop and serve under Captain Mazzard, or shall we go?"

"Do!" cried Bart, angrily, as he turned toward the men, who seemed to be divided into two parties. "Look here; I can't parley; but is it going to be fair-play or no?"

"Yes!" rose with a shout; but it was met by a menacing growl; and one man ran to the cabin, to return directly, half dragging, half leading Mazzard, who stared round wildly in a drink-stupefied manner, and faltered out, as if in answer to a question—

"No more, now! Who's altered her course?"

There was a few moments' silence, during which the self-elected captain stared about him, and tried to comprehend what was going on, for he had just been roused suddenly from a rum-engendered sleep, and seemed like one in a dream.

"What, isn't annybody going to spake?" cried Dinny; "thin I will. Who althered the ship's course! Why, I did. D'yer think I was going to stand by and see a messmate left in the lurch? Look here, my lads; I am not going to make a spache, but the captain's dead, and you've got to choose a new one."

"Hurrah for Dinny Kelly; he's the man!" shouted one of the sailors.

"If I didn't know ye can't help it, Sam Marlow, I'd say don't be a fool!" cried Dinny, scornfully. "Now, do I look like a captain! Bad luck to ye for an omadhaun. I'm a foighting man, and not a sailor at all; but ye've got to choose bechuckst two. Who is it to be—Black Mazzard there, or the old captain's brave little brother, Master Jack here, the best sailor, steersman, and bravest little chap that ever stepped on a plank? What do you say, Dick?"

"Three cheers for Captain Jack!" cried Dick Dullock.

"Nay, nay, Commodore Junk!" cried Dinny; "that name's a power, me boys. Now, then, who among ye says it isn't to be the captain's brother?"

"I do!" cried Mazzard, who was growing sobered by the excitement of the scene. "I do. I'm captain of the schooner now; and if any man dares—"

He dragged a pistol from his belt and cocked it.

"Do you hear?" cried Mazzard again. "I'm captain now, and if any man dares to say I'm not, let him—Well, no, I won't give him time to say his prayers!"

He stared round the ring of people, of which he now formed the centre, the pistol barrel pointing all round, as if its holder were in search of a mark.

Just then Bart stepped forward, but Jack drew him aside.

"No; let me speak," he said.

"Oh, it's you, is it, my whipper-snapper!" cried Mazzard, scornfully. "There, we had enough of your little baby of a brother, and he's dead; so now, if you want to keep your skin whole, go back to your place, and if you behave yourself I'll make you my cabin-boy."

Jack continued to advance, looking round at the crew, who, some fifty strong, had now hurried upon deck.

"D'yer hear?" roared Mazzard, who seemed brutally sober now. "Go back, or—"

He took aim at Jack with the pistol, and a murmur ran round the crew once more—a murmur which was turned to a shout of applause, for, gazing full at the drink inflamed countenance before him, Jack stepped right up to Mazzard and seized the pistol, which exploded in the air.

The next moment it was wrenched out of the ruffian's hand, and sent flying over the side, to fall with a splash in the sea.

"Look here, my lads," cried Jack, turning his back to Mazzard, and ignoring the threatening gesture he made with a knife; "look here, my lads; it is not for any man to say he will be your captain. My brave brother is dead—"

"God rest him!" cried Dinny.

"And it is for you to choose someone in his place. Do you select Black Mazzard?"

"No," roared Dinny, "the divil a bit! Three cheers, me boys, for the bowld little Commodore Junk!"

The crew burst into a roar, even those who had favoured Mazzard being carried away.

"A lad who was niver afraid of anny man's pishtle," cried Dinny, leaping on a cask and waving his cap.

"Hurrah!" shouted the men, enthusiastically.

"A lad who has only wan failing in him."

"Hurrah!" came in chorus, and a voice cried: "What's that, Dinny?"

"Faix, his mother made a mistake and let him be born out of Oireland."

There was another roar, and the crew pressed round Jack, whose face flushed as he hold up his hand.

"Stop a minute, my lads!" he cried. "Don't decide in haste, for I shall be a hard officer."

"And a brave one," shouted Dinny.

"Hurrah!"

"Am I to understand," continued Jack, "that you select me for your captain?"

"Yes, yes," came in a roar.

"Then I have a request to make," cried Jack; "and that is, that you support and obey my first lieutenant."

"Hurrah for owld Bart Wrigley!" roared Dinny.

"No, no; stop!" cried Jack. "I choose my own lieutenant. Mazzard, will you serve under me faithfully as a man?"

Black Mazzard stood scowling for a few moments, and then held out his hand.

"I will," he said. "There's no jealousy in me."

"Hurrah!" shouted the crew again; and directly after the new captain gave orders for the schooner's head to be laid for Sandy Key, towards which she was soon tacking to and fro.

Chapter Eighteen
A Horrible Task

Two days elapsed before the schooner was again well under the lee of Sandy Key, and preparations were made to land as soon as it grew dusk.

It was a soft, calm evening, and the sea looked solemn and desolate as the sun went down in a bank of clouds. A good look-out had been kept, but there was no sign of sail upon the wide spread sea, while the solemnity of the hour seemed to have influenced the men, who had gathered some inkling of their commander's intentions.

"Whisht! Don't talk about it," said Dinny to one questioner. "Sure, it's a whim of the skipper's, and if he likes to take his brother and bury him a bit more dacently at the shelter, who has a better right?"

"Are you going?"

"And is it me? They wouldn't ask me."

Just at the same time a conversation was going on in the fore-part of the vessel, where the captain had been standing for some time with Bart.

"Nay, nay, my lad," the latter whispered; "not this time."

"Have you got all ready?"

"Ay. Just as you said."

"Then, an hour after sundown, we'll go."

Bart tightened up his lips and looked more obstinate than he had ever before looked in his life.

"What is it?" said the captain, sharply.

"I was a-thinking," said Bart, shortly.

"Well—of what?"

"I was a-thinking that you've just been made captain, and that the crew's with you, and that you're going to chuck it away."

"What do you mean, Bart?"

"I mean captain, as so sure as you give the lieutenant another chance he'll take it, and the lads, like Dinny and Dick, mayn't have the chance to get Mazzard drunk and come to your help."

"You do nothing but doubt your officer," said the captain, angrily.

"More do you," retorted Bart.

The captain started, and then turned angrily away; but Bart followed him.

"You're skipper, and I'll do aught you like; but so sure as you leave this here ship there'll be a row, and you won't be able to go again, for you won't come back."

The captain took a turn up and down, and then stopped opposite Bart.

"I'll take your advice, Bart," he said, "though it goes very much against the grain. Take Dinny with you, and do this for me as if I were helping you all the time."

"Ay; you may trust me."

"I do trust you, Bart, heartily. Remember this: Abel and I were always together as children and companions; to the last I loved my brother, Bart."

Bart listened to the simply-uttered words, to which their tone and the solemn time gave a peculiar pathos; and for a few moments there was silence.

"I know," he said, softly. "And in my rough way I loved Abel Dell as a brother. Don't you think because I say nought that I don't feel it."

"I know you too well, Bart. Go and do this for me; I will stay aboard. I'm captain now, since fate so wills it, and the men shall find that I am their head."

"Hah!" ejaculated Bart, raising his hand, but dropping it again and drawing back. "That's how I like to hear you speak, captain. Trust me, it shall be done."

An hour later the men stood aloof as Bart and Dinny lowered a long deal case into the boat and, as soon as the rope was cast off, hoisted the little sail and ran for the sandy cove where the boat had landed before.

They were provided with a lantern, and this they kept shrouded in a boat-cloak originally the property of the Spanish captain of a vessel that had been taken.

The precaution was needless, for nothing was within sight; and they landed and drew up the boat upon the sand, where the phosphorescent water rippled softly, and then the long chest was lifted out, and Bart bore it toward the cocoa-nut grove.

"Well," said Dinny, following close behind, "I did say that I wouldn't do such work as this; but it's for the captain, and maybe some day I shall be wanting such a job done for me."

Bart set down the case and Dinny the lantern beneath the cocoa-nut trees close by the levelled patch of shore; and then, with the dull light shining through the horn panes upon the sand, the two men stood in the midst of the faint halo listening to the soft whispering of the tide among the shingle, and the more distant boom of the surf.

"It's an unked job," said Bart at last. "But, poor lad, it's the skipper's wish. A lovely spot for a man to be put to rest."

Dinny did not speak for a few moments. Then with an effort—

"Let's get it done, me lad. I niver belaved in annything worse than the good people, and the phooka, and the banshee, of coorse; but it makes a man's flesh seem to crape over his bones to come body-snatching, as ye may call it, on a dark night like this."

They both stood hesitating and shrinking from their task for a few minutes longer, and then Bart stooped down and began to sweep back the sand.

"It's laid light over him, Dinny, my lad," he said. "Just sweep it away, and we can lift him into his coffin."

"But—"

"He's wrapped in a canvas for his winding sheet, lad. Sweep away the sand there from his feet."

Dinny bent down and was in the act of scooping away the dry sand when he uttered a yell and darted away, followed by Bart, who was somewhat unnerved by his weird task, and who did not recover himself till they reached the boat.

"Here, what is it?" cried Bart, recovering himself, and grasping Dinny by the arm, feeling indignant now at his own cowardice. "Are you afraid of a dead man?"

"No; but he isn't dead!" panted Dinny.

"What?"

"As soon as I touched him I felt him move!"

"Dinny, you're a fool!" cried Bart, in an exasperated tone of voice. "I wish he was alive, poor lad!"

"I tell you," cried Dinny, catching his arm, "he moved in his grave—I felt it plain!"

"Come back!" said Bart, fiercely.

"Divil a bit!"

"Come back!"

"Divil a bit, I say!"

"You coward!" cried Bart. "Am I to go and do it alone?"

"No, no, Bart, me lad, don't thry it. There's something quare about the owld business."

"Yes," said Bart, savagely. "You turned coward and upset me. I don't know whether I'm most ashamed of you or of myself."

He walked straight back toward where the soft yellow light of the lantern could be seen under the trees, leaving Dinny staring, trembling, and scratching his head.

"He's gone and left me alone," muttered Dinny. "Sure, and is it a Kelly as is a coward? If it was to face a man—or two men—or tin men—I'd do it if I had me shtick. But a dead body as begins to move in its grave as soon as ye thry to lift it out, and says quite plain, wid a kick of its legs, 'Lave me alone, ye spalpeen!' why, it's too much for a boy."

"Are you coming, Dinny?" cried Bart, as he approached the lantern.

"Bedad, and he'll think me a coward if I don't go," said Dinny, panting. "Sure, and what are ye thrimbling about? D'ye call yourselves legs, and go shakking undher a boy like that? Faix, I'm ashamed of ye! Go along, do; and it isn't me that's freckened, but me legs!"

He mastered his dread and ran swiftly after Bart, who had once more reached the sandy trench.

"I thought you'd come, Dinny," said Bart. "You're not the lad to leave a mate in the lurch."

"Thrue for ye, me boy; but are we to tak' him back in the boat?"

"Yes, it's the captain's orders."

"Howly Pater, but it's dreadful work!" said Dinny.

"Then let's get it done," said Bart, stolidly; and he drew off the lid of the rough case. "Come, lad, let's lift the poor fellow quickly into his coffin and act like men."

"But didn't ye fale him move, Bart, lad?" whispered Dinny.

"No. What foolery!" growled Bart. "Fancy!"

"Divil a bit, sor! I just touched him," whispered Dinny; "and he worked his toes about, and thin give quite a kick."

"Bah!" ejaculated Bart.

"Bedad, but he did!" whispered Dinny. "Wait a minute. The poor boy don't like it, perhaps. If we only had Father McFadden here!"

"What are you going to do?"

"Shpake to him," said Dinny, trembling; "and the blessed saints stand bechuckst me and harm!" he muttered, fervently. "Abel, me lad—captin, don't ye want to go?"

There was a dead silence.

"Shpake to us, me lad, and say *no* if you don't; and we'll respect your wishes."

The silence that followed Dinny's address to the dead was broken by an impatient ejaculation from Bart.

"Come on!" he said. "Do you take me for a fool? Lift, man, or I'll do it myself!"

Thus adjured, Dinny went once more to the foot of the shallow trench, and stooped down.

"Now, then, together!" said Bart. "The dead can't hurt the quick."

Dinny thrust his hands down in the sand on either side of the rolled-up canvas, made as if to lift, and then, as his hands met, he uttered another yell and fell upon his knees.

Bart started away as well, and stood in the dim light, trembling.

"There! Didn't you fale him move?" whispered Dinny, who was shaking violently. "Captin darlin', we were only obeying ordhers. Sure, and we wouldn't disthurb ye for all the world if ye didn't want to come. Don't be angry wid us—it was ordhers, ye know; and av coorse ye know what ordhers is."

"Did—did you feel it too, Dinny?" said Bart, hoarsely.

"Did I fale it! Sure, and he worked his toes again, and then give a bigger kick than ever!"

"Dinny," cried Bart, passionately, "the poor fellow has been buried alive!"

"Buried aloive!" said Dinny.

"Yes; he has come to. Quick, uncover him!"

"Buried aloive! And it isn't a did man kicking again' being disthurbed in his grave!" cried Dinny, changing his tone and springing up. "Howly Pater! why didn't ye say so before? Here, have him out at wanst!—the poor boy will be smothered wid the sand! Quick, me boy! quick!"

He dashed at the trench again, and Bart seized the head, both lifting together; and then, as the sand streamed away from the canvas cover in which the remains of poor Abel had been wrapped, they both uttered a hoarse cry of horror and stood holding up their ghastly burden as if in a nightmare, terror paralysing them. For they felt that the long wrapper was alive; and from out of holes eaten in it, and dimly-seen in the lantern's yellow light, dozens of the loathsome land-crabs scuffled quickly out, to keep falling with a heavy pat upon the sand and crawl away; while as their shells rattled and scratched and their claws clinked together, the burden grew rapidly lighter, the movement gradually ceased, and the two men stood at last, icily cold, but with the sweat streaming from them, holding up the old sail containing nothing but the skeleton of the poor fellow they sought.

"Oh, murther!" gasped Dinny at last. "Bart, lad, think o' that!"

Bart uttered a sound that was more like a groan than an ejaculation; but neither of them moved for some moments.

"What'll we do now?" said Dinny at last.

Bart did not speak, but he made a movement side wise, which his companion unconsciously imitated, and together they reverently laid the grisly remains in the case, which Bart covered, and then screwed down the lid, for he had come prepared.

"What'll the captain say?" whispered Dinny, as he held the lantern up for Bart to see the holes made ready for the screws.

Bart turned upon him fiercely.

"Don't say a word of it to him," he said harshly. "Poor lad, it would break his heart."

"Not tell him?"

"Dinny, lad, you'll keep your tongue about this night's work?"

"Not tell the boys?"

"Not tell a soul," said Bart. "We're friends, and it's our secret, lad. You'll hold your tongue?"

"Howlt my whisht? Yes," said Dinny, "I will. Bart, lad, d'ye feel freckened now?"

"No."

"Nor I, nayther. It was the thought that there was something else that freckened me. Phew, lad! it's very hot."

He wiped the great drops of sweat from his brow, and then, as Bart ended his task—

"Ye were scared, though, Bart," he said.

"Yes, I never felt so scared in my life."

"I shake hands, thin, lad, on that. Thin I needn't fale ashamed o' running away. Faix, but it's an ugly job! Oh! the divils. Sure, and whin I die I won't be buried here."

Dinny's observations were cut short by Bart placing the lantern on the deal case; and then together the two men bore their eerie load down to the boat and laid it across the bows, the lantern being hidden once more beneath the folds of the great cloak with which the rough coffin was solemnly draped.

"You'll be silent, Dinny," said Bart.

"Niver fear, my lad," said the Irishman.

Then the boat was run out as far as they could wade, the sail hoisted, and long before dawn they reached the schooner, over whose side hung a signal light.

As they reached the vessel, the captain's face appeared in the glow shed by the light. The coffin was lifted on board, and then down into the captain's cabin, after which the schooner's wide wings were spread, and she was speeding on over the calm waters to the shelter, far away, that formed the buccaneers' retreat and impregnable home, while Commodore Junk went down to his cabin, to kneel by the coffin side, and pray for strength to complete his vengeance against the world and those who had robbed him of the only one he loved.

Chapter Nineteen
The Pest of the West

The merchants of Bristol sent in a petition to His Majesty the King, saying that the trade of the port was being ruined, that their ships were taken, that the supplies of sugar and tobacco must run short, and that, while the ladies would suffer as to their coffee, there would soon be no snuff ground up for the titillation of the noses of the king's liege subjects.

Always the same story—Commodore Junk, in command of a long, low, fast-sailing schooner, was here, there, and everywhere. This sugar and coffee-laden ship was plundered and burnt off Kingston port, so near that the glow of the fire was seen. That brig, full of choice mahogany logs, was taken near Belize. A fine Bristol bark, just out of the great port of South Carolina, full of the choicest tobacco-leaf, was taken the next week. And so on, and so on. Ships from Caracas, from the Spanish, French, and Dutch settlements, heavily-laden, or from England outward bound, were seized. All was fish that came to the pirate's net, and if the vessels were foreign, so much the worse for them, the buccaneer captain dealing out his favours with fairly balanced hand till the shores of the great gulf and the islands that formed the eastern barrier rang with the news of his deeds.

Government heard what was said, and replied that five years before they had sent out a ship to capture Commodore Junk, that there was a severe engagement, and the captain was taken and hung, and afterwards gibbeted off the port where his deeds obtained most fame.

To which the Bristol merchants replied in a further petition that though it was as the Government stated, Commodore Junk's body had been taken down from the gibbet soon after it was hung up, that he had come to life again, and that his deeds were now ten times worse than before.

Moreover, that somewhere or another on the western shores of the great Mexican Gulf, he had a retreat where he lived in great luxury when ashore; that maidens, wives, and widows had been captured and taken there to live a life of terrible captivity; that many bloody deeds had been done after desperate fighting, men being compelled to walk the plank or sent adrift in small boats far from land; and that, though spies had been sent out, no one had been able to discover the mysterious retreat, even the Indians who had been bribed to go returning with their heads minus their ears, or else with strange tales that the buccaneer was under the protection of the great thunder gods, whose home was in the burning mountains, and that it was useless to try to destroy him and his crew.

Moreover, the men of Bristol said that it was a crying shame that their ships and cargoes should not have adequate protection, seeing what a deal they paid to the revenue for the goods they imported, and that one of His Majesty's ships ought to be more than a match for all the thunder gods in Central America, and His Majesty's petitioners would ever pray.

The king's minister of the time said that the men of Bristol were a set of old women, and that it was all nonsense about Commodore Junk; and for some months longer nothing was done. Then came such an angry clamour and such lengthy accounts of the crimes the buccaneer had committed that the Government concluded that they must do something, and gave their orders accordingly.

The result was that one day Captain Humphrey Armstrong walked along the Mall in his big boots, which creaked loudly over the gravel. The gold lace on his uniform glittered in the sunshine; and as he wore his cocked hat all on one side, and rested his left hand upon the hilt of his sword, which hung awkwardly across him, mixed up with the broad skirts of his coat, he looked as fine and gallant a specimen of humanity as was to be found in the king's service.

The officers of the king's guards, horse and foot, stared at him, and more than one pair of bright eyes rested with satisfaction on the handsome, manly face, as the captain went along smiling with satisfaction and apparently conceit.

It was with the former, not the latter, for the captain was on his way to Saint James's Square, to keep an appointment at Lord Loganstone's, and before long he was in earnest converse with Lady Jenny Wildersey, his lordship's youngest daughter, one of the most fashionable beauties of her day.

"Yes," said the captain, after nearly half an hour's preliminary conversation. "It is in the course of duty, and I must go."

"La!" said her ladyship, with a very sweet smile. "But couldn't you send someone else!"

"At the call of duty!" cried the captain. "No. Besides, you would not wish me to stay under such circumstances as those."

"La!" said her ladyship, as, after a show of resistance, she surrendered her lily-white hand, and suffered it to be kissed.

"And how long will it take you to capture this terrible buccaneer?"

"I shall be away for months," said the captain.

"La!" said the lady.

"But I shall fight like some knight-errant of old, and fly back."

"La!" said the lady.

"With the wings of my good ship," said the captain, "and hasten to lay the trophies of my victory at my darling's feet."

"You will be sure to bring him?" said the lady.

"I hope he will fall in the fight," said the captain.

"Then you are going to fight?"

"Yes, I am going out in command of a splendid ship with a crew of brave men, to attack and exterminate this horde of wasps, and I hope to do it like a man."

"But will anybody bleed?"

"I fear so."

"La! Will you be hurt?"

"I hope not. But I must run the risk; and if I come back wounded, it will be in your service, dearest, and then I shall claim my reward."

"No," said the lady, with one of her most winning looks. "I don't believe you. Sailors are worse than soldiers, and you will fall in love with one of the lovely Spanish ladies out there, and forget all about poor little me."

"Forget you!" cried the captain, passionately; "never! My love for you grows stronger every day; and as to beauty, was there ever a woman so beautiful as you?"

"La!"

Captain Humphrey was about to throw himself on his knees as well as his big boots would allow; but just then the door opened, and fresh visitors were announced, and though the topic of the captain's appointment to the sloop of war *Queen Jane*, for the extermination of the West Indian buccaneers, formed the staple of the conversation, he had to leave at last with nothing warmer than a smile, but full of a great deal of hope.

For love had blinded the eyes of the stout captain lately introduced to the fashionable beauty, and welcomed on account of the fact that he had lately succeeded to the Devonshire estates of the Armstrongs, consequent upon the death of his cousin James, who had been killed in a duel arising out of some affair of gallantry, the husband of the lady in question objecting to Captain James Armstrong's advances, and running him through the body.

So, deeply in love with as pretty a bit of artificiality as ever dressed, or rather believing himself deeply in love, Captain Humphrey joined his well-found ship at Falmouth, sailed for the far west and the land of the torrid sun; and the men of Bristol rubbed their hands, thought of their freights, and sat down to their ledgers, while they waited for the news of the hanging of Commodore Junk.

Chapter Twenty
The Pirate Chase

"It's like hunting a will-o'-the-wisp on Dartmoor," cried Captain Humphrey, as he sat in one of his ship's boats, wiping the perspiration from his sun-scorched face. "One day I'm ready to swear it is all a myth, the next that there are a dozen Commodore Junks."

For he had been out in the Mexican Gulf for six months, and was as far off finishing his task as on the day when he had reached Kingston harbour, and listened to the tales of the buccaneer's last deeds.

But it was no myth. Put in where he would, it was to hear fresh news of the pirates. Now some unfortunate captain would arrive in a small boat, with his crew, suffering from heat, thirst, and starvation. Now the half-burned hull of a goodly argosy would be encountered on the open sea. At another time news would come of a derelict that had been scuttled but not sunk, and seen in such and such latitude.

Wherever he went Captain Humphrey was met with news, and at last with reproaches and almost insult by the authorities at the various ports at which he touched, for the way in which his task was being done.

For there was he with a small, swift-sailing ship, full of stout seamen, bravely officered, well-armed, and with guns big enough to blow all the schooners in the west to matchwood, while from the captain to the smallest powder-monkey all were red-hot with desire to meet the Commodore and give him a foe who knew how to fight.

Six months of following out clues, of going here and there where the schooner had been seen, or where it was expected, but never even to see the tail-end of that huge main-sail that caught the wind, laid the long schooner over, and sent her rushing through the water in a way that made all attempts at escape childish. In gale or calm it was always the same, and the masters of the many traders knew from experience that if the buccaneer's schooner was in sight, they might as well heave-to as try to fly, for their capture was certain. Consequently, it was growing fast into a rule that when the long schooner fired a shot, it was the proper thing to lower sail or throw a vessel up in the wind, and wait, so as not to irritate the enemy by trying to escape.

Messages travelled slowly in those days, but all the same Captain Humphrey Armstrong had received a despatch hinting at a recall, and a friendly letter telling him that if he did not soon have something to show he would be superseded and in disgrace.

He was a rich man, and at the end of three months he did not scruple to offer rewards for information; he doubled his offer to the man who would bring him within reach of the Commodore's schooner; and beginning with ten guineas, he went on increasing, as the time went on, till he reached a hundred, and, at last, when six months had passed, it was known all round the coast that Captain Armstrong would give a thousand guineas to be brought alongside the schooner.

Captain Humphrey ground his teeth when he was alone in his cabin, and he swore as a Devon captain could swear in those days; but it did no good, and in spite of all his struggles, he could only look upon Commodore Junk as a will-o'-the-wisp.

"What will Lady Jenny think?" he groaned. "And I meant to do so much!"

At last what he dreaded arrived. He sailed into port one day, to find his recall; and he went back on board ship, ordered all sail to be made, and, ignoring the order, determined to find the Commodore or die.

Chapter Twenty One
The Black Schooner

Commodore Junk's schooner, with its enormous spars and sails, had been lying-to off the harbour of Saint Geronimo one afternoon, where she had taken in a good store of fresh fruit for her crew, while waiting the return of one of her officers who had been overland to Belize to pick up information that might be useful to the captain.

Bart Wrigley was silent that calm, still evening for a long time after the captain had spoken, and then—

"It's a mistake, my dear lad," he said angrily. "You do as you like, and I'll follow you through with it, and so will the men; but I say it's a mistake."

"And why!" asked the captain, coldly. "Are you afraid to meet the ship!"

"Nay, I don't know as I'm afraid," said Bart; "but where's the good? She's twice stronger than we, and we shall get nothing but hard knocks."

"Do you think I should be so mad as to attack such a ship as that on equal terms?"

"I dunno," growled Bart: "May be. Where's the good of fighting her at all?"

"Why do I pursue so many vessels, and take such revenge as I do!" said the captain. "Do you think I've forgotten mine and my brother's wrongs!"

"No; you wouldn't forget them," said Bart, slowly; "but you're going to run too much risk."

"Not too much to gain such sweet revenge, Bart," said the captain, excitedly; and the dark eyes which gazed at the rough, Devon man seemed to burn. "Do you know who commands this ship that has been hunting us these six mouths?"

"Yes; a brave officer in the king's service."

"A brave officer!" cried the captain, contemptuously.

"Well, that's what they say; and that he has sworn to die or take us."

"He—sworn!" cried the captain. "A brave captain! Did you and poor Abel find him so brave when you met him that night on the road to Slapton Lea?"

"What!" cried Bart. "No; 'tisn't him!"

"That ship is commanded by Captain Armstrong," said the captain, hoarsely; "by the man, Bart, who blasted my life; who sent my brother to his death out here, for it was through him poor Abel died."

"No! Never!" cried Bart, incredulously.

"It's true, Bart. I have just learned that it is he by Dinny, who has returned from Belize. She is commanded by the man I once thought I loved."

"But you don't love him now?"

"Love! Bart Wrigley, can you believe in a person's nature being changed by cruelty and wrong."

"No. Not yours," growled Bart.

"Then you may believe it, Bart; and now the time has come, and I am going to have my revenge. Do you know what I am going to do?"

"You told me," said Bart, roughly. "Fight."

"Yes; but so as to spare my men, and to spare myself. Bart, I am going to teach the king's grand officer what it is to trifle, and to treat those he holds beneath him as if they were meant for his pleasure, and made for that alone. I am going to destroy the ship of this grand officer, to scatter his men, and to take him prisoner if I can."

"No!" said Bart, hoarsely. "Don't do that."

"Why!" cried the captain, mockingly. "Are you afraid that I shall be weak once more? Don't be afraid, Bart. Mary Dell is dead, and it is the soul of her brother who moves this body, and he it is who will take a bitter revenge upon Captain Armstrong for slaying Mary Dell; for in spirit it is this he did."

"You won't kill him?" whispered Bart.

"Why not? Was Mary Dell spared? Was Abel, her brother, treated so tenderly that I should hold my hand?"

"But—" began Bart.

"Leave that to me, Bart Wrigley. Help me to get him into my power, and then he shall learn a truth which will make the traitor—the coward—wince. Brave officer of his Majesty the King! How brave you shall see. Now, do you understand why I mean to fight?"

"Yes," said Bart, sadly; "I see. But think twice, my lad."

"Bart!" cried the captain, passionately, "I've thought a hundred times; and if I were ashore, and could go there—"

"I know," said Bart, gloomily. "You'd come out more and more savage and determined, as you always have been. Think twice, my lad. You're rich; and you're safe. Once more, why not throw it up now and let's go home. I asks no more, captain. I've lived long enough to know all that; but come home now. There's a life o' peace yonder, and you can take it now; to-morrow it may be too late."

"Let it be so then, Bart."

"And you'll come home—to old Devon once again?"

"No! I'm going to meet the captain face to face, Bart, and plant my heel upon his neck."

Chapter Twenty Two
News at Last

Humphrey Armstrong sat in his cabin listening to the whirr of a beetle which had been attracted by the lights, and flown in through the open window, to make a bass to the treble hum of the mosquitoes which haunted the mouth of the river where the ship had anchored for the night.

The day had been intensely hot, and the cabin seemed ovenlike, as its occupant sat listening to the insect hum; and then to the strange croakings and rustling noises which came from the primeval forest on either side. Now and then a deep roar announced the presence of some huge creature of the cat tribe prowling in search of prey, and this would be followed by a distant answering call.

He walked to the window and looked out, to see the stars reflected in a blurred manner in the rushing waters of the river; while on either side he could see the bushes which fringed the muddy banks scintillating with the lamps of the fireflies. Now they died out, and there would be only a faint twinkle here and there; then, as if something had disturbed or agitated the wondrous insects, they would flash out into soft, lambent sparks of light which played about and darted and circled, and then once more died out, as if to give place to some other creature of their kind, which flashed out so broad a light that the leaves of the trees around could be plainly seen.

He had been away five days since the orders had come out for his return, in the vain hope that perhaps now he might at last encounter the buccaneer; but, so far, he had seen or heard nothing; and the pirate captain might have dropped out of sight, or never existed, on the evening when the captain searched creek after creek along the coast, till nightfall, when, for safety's sake, he had anchored at the mouth of the muddy stream.

He was lost in thought, and was puzzling out an answer to the question: How was it that the buccaneer schooner contrived to avoid him?—when his trained ears detected the sound of a paddle, and he gazed keenly over the dark waters, wondering whether his watch on deck had heard it, and how long they would be ere they challenged the approaching party in their boat?

The question had hardly been mentally asked when he heard the challenge from on deck, and the paddling ceased. Then came a certain amount of shouting, and a conversation, muffled by the distance, followed, and the boat was allowed to approach.

A minute later the officer of the watch came down to announce the arrival of a couple of Indians bearing news.

"It's the old story, sir, vamped up to get a bottle of rum; but I thought I'd better report it to you. Shall I kick them, and let them go!"

"No," said the captain, shortly, for he was ready now to snatch at straws. "What does the man say?"

"There are two of them, sir; and they say the pirate vessel is to be found a day's journey to the south, and that they have seen it lying at anchor."

"Do they seem honest!"

"Honest as Indians, sir. I think it's all made up."

"I'll come and see them."

The captain rose and went on deck, where he found a couple of soft, brown, plump-looking Indians, with large, dreamy eyes and languid manner, seated upon their heels near the gangway, where they could give a glance from time to time at their canoe swinging by a frail-looking bark rope.

The men did not stir as the captain came up, but crouched in their old position, gazing up at him furtively.

"Now," he said, sharply, "where is this pirate ship?"

The men looked at him vacantly.

"Commodore Junk!" said Humphrey.

"El Commodore Yunk; yes. Ship there."

One of the Indians had caught his meaning, and pointed southward.

"Have you seen the ship?"

The men nodded quickly and pointed again.

"Why have you come here to tell us?"

The Indian stared, then looked at his companion, with whom he rapidly exchanged a few words, ending by turning back, holding out his hands, and exclaiming—

"El Commodore Yunk. Money. Rum."

"There's a frankness about this fellow that makes me disposed to believe him," said Humphrey, grimly, as he smiled at the officer. "'Commodore

Yunk. Money. Rum.' And the pointing seems to me as effective as the longest speech. Look here, can you understand? Show us—"

"Show—show—way—El Commodore Yunk."

"Yes, that will do," said the captain. "But mind this; if you play us false—here, show him!"

"Show—El Commodore Yunk," cried the Indian, catching the last words. "Money—powd—rum."

"You shall have plenty," said Humphrey; "but make him understand that if he plays us false he shall be hung at the yard-arm."

The officer of the watch, quite a young man, seemed to enjoy his task; for, catching up the signal halyards, he rapidly made a noose, threw it over the Indian's head, and drew it tight. Then, pointing upward, he said slowly—

"If you cheat!"

"Hang um?" said the Indian, sharply.

"Yes. We shall hang you if you don't show Commodore Junk."

"Show El Commodore Yunk," said the Indian, composedly.

"I think he understands us," said the officer of the watch.

"Very well, then," cried Humphrey. "Let's start, then, at once. Now, then, south!" he cried to the man.

"South?" said the Indian.

"Yes, south!" cried the captain, pointing. "Show us the way."

"Show. El Commodore Yunk. No."

He shook his head, and pointed around him, and then to the lanterns, which shed a dim light over the scene.

"No. Dark," he said.

"He means it is too dark to go," said the second officer. "Look here, old brownskin. Light? sun?"

"Light—sun!" cried the Indian, eagerly, pointing to the east, and then seizing the thin rope which had been twisted round his neck, he ran to the gangway, slid down into his boat, made the cord fast, and came scrambling up again to secure the signal-line.

This done, he said a few words to his companion, and, going to the side, threw himself down under the bulwarks, and seemed to go to sleep at once.

"Yes; that's plain enough," said Humphrey. "He means to wait till daylight. Keep a strict watch. We may have found the right man at last."

He need have been under no anxiety as to the two informers, for they lay motionless till daybreak, and then rose suddenly, looked sharply round, and, going forward, pointed to the rope which moored them in mid-stream.

Half an hour later the sloop was gliding slowly out of the mouth of the river; the lowered sails caught the cool, moist morning breeze, and, in obedience to the Indian's directions which were embraced in the pointing of a brown hand southward, the king's ship sailed steadily along the coast a few miles from the shore, which, with its sandy beach alternating with bold headlands that ran down from regularly-formed volcanic-looking peaks, and creeks, and river estuaries, fringed with palm and mud-loving growth, showed plenty of spots where a vessel might find a hiding-place, and which it would have taken a fleet of boats to adequately explore.

The Indian's conduct increased the confidence of Humphrey; and as the day wore on the officers and crew, who had been for months chasing myths, began to look forward hopefully to an encounter with the pirates, and to believe that the preparations for action might not this time prove to have been in vain.

It was within two hours of sundown, as the men were at their drowsiest moment—many being fast asleep—when, as they were rounding a rocky point feathered with glorious palms, beyond which the country ran up toward the mountains in a glorious chaos of piled-up rock, deep ravine, and fire-scathed chine, the principal Indian suddenly seized the captain's arm and pointed straight before him to where, a couple of miles away, and looking as if she had just glided out of some hidden channel running into the land, there was a long, low, black-hulled schooner, spreading an enormous amount of canvas for so small a vessel; and as he saw the rake of the masts and the disproportioned size of her spars, Humphrey Armstrong felt a thrill of exultation run through him even as his whole crew was now galvanised into life, and he mentally repeated the words of the Indian—

"El Commodore Yunk."

Yes; there could be no doubt of it. The shape and size of the vessel answered the description exactly, and no trader or pleasure vessel, foreign or British, would sail with so dangerously an overweighting rig as that.

"At last, then!" cried Humphrey, excitedly, as he stood gazing at the long, suspicious-looking craft; and his heart beat heavily, his face flushed, and the hands which held his glass trembled with eagerness.

The men made way to right and left as their captain strode aft and exclaimed—

"Bring the poor fellows here. They shall have their reward and go."

"Was it treachery, or fear of the enemy?"

Humphrey asked himself this question as a shout came from the steersman, who, like the rest, had been gazing at the schooner, but who was the first to see and draw attention to a canoe being paddled rapidly for the shore.

No one had been attending to the two Indians, who had waited until the attention of all was bent upon the buccaneer, and then silently slipped over the side, glided down the rope, and cast off, to paddle shorewards.

There was good discipline on board ship even then, and at the call to quarters every man fell into place. The long gun was run in, loaded, run out, and directly after there was a puff of smoke, a loud report which went echoing among the mountains and through the densely-wooded ravines, as a round shot skipped over the water right in front of the schooner.

"Hurrah!" shouted the men, as they saw the long vessel alter her course a little.

"She surrenders," said Humphrey to himself; and in the brief moments that followed he saw himself returning to England in triumph, his task done, and beautiful, fashionable Lady Jenny Wildersey welcoming him with open arms.

It was a puff of fancy, dissipated like the puff of smoke which came from the schooner's bows; while, in company with the report that rumbled heavily away, came a round shot skipping over the calm surface of the sea, not forward like the summons to heave-to of the king's ship, but straight at her hull, and so well-aimed that it tore through the starboard bulwark amidships and passed just in front of the mainmast, which it almost grazed.

"The insolent!" exclaimed Humphrey, turning purple with rage. "How dare he!"

As he spoke he raised his spy-glass to his eye, for something could be seen fluttering up the side of the great main-sail, and directly after a large black flag was wafted out by the breeze in defiance of a ship-of-war double the schooner's size, and heavily armed, as well as manned by a picked and disciplined crew.

"Very good, Commodore!" cried Humphrey, with a smile. "You can't escape us now. Gentlemen, the ball has opened. Down with her spars, my lads. Never mind her hull; we want that to take back to Falmouth, from whence she shall sail next time with a different rig."

The men cheered and the firing commenced, when, to the annoyance of the captain, the wind dropped entirely, a dead calm ensued; night was coming on rapidly, as it descends in the tropic lands, and he had either to try and silence the schooner at long range, or man the boats and take her by boarding, a plan from which he shrank, knowing, as he did, that it could only be successful at a terrible cost of life, and this he dreaded for the sake of his men.

The sloop crept a little nearer in one of the puffs of wind that came from time to time, and the firing went on, Humphrey and his officers being astounded at the ability with which the schooner's guns were served and the accuracy of their aim.

"No wonder that they've carried all before them among the merchantmen," muttered Humphrey, as a shot came crashing into them, and three men were carried below disabled by splinters.

As he spoke he looked anxiously round, to make sure that the schooner would not be able to pass them in the approaching darkness, and then, feeling more and more that men who could serve their guns so well would be terrible adversaries in a case of boarding, and determined to spare his men till the schooner was disabled, he kept up the artillery duel till the only guide for laying their guns was the flash of the enemy's pieces when some shot was fired.

By this time the fire of the buccaneers had proved so effective that the sloop's bulwarks were shattered and her decks were slippery with blood, while her captain was fuming with rage at the unfortunate aim of his men; for, though the schooner had evidently been hit again and again, she seemed to have escaped the vital injury that a shot would have produced in one of her spars.

All at once, just as the darkness had become complete, the firing of the schooner ceased; and to have continued that on board of the sloop would have been wasting shot.

"Man the launch and jolly-boat!" said the captain sharply, and their crews waited with intense excitement the orders to go and board the schooner, a faint groan of disappointment arising as the men heard the instructions given to the two lieutenants to patrol on either side of the sloop, and be ready to attack and board only if the buccaneer should attempt to steal off in the darkness and escape.

The night wore on, with every one on the *qui vive*. Two more boats were ready waiting to push off and help in the attack on whichever side the schooner should attempt to escape; while, in the event, of an attack, the other patrolling boat was to come back to the sloop.

But hour after hour passed and no rushing of water was heard, no dip of long sweep, or creak of the great oar in the rowlock was heard; neither was a light seen; and the silence observed by the schooner was so profound that Humphrey, as he paced the deck, felt certain at last that she must have escaped; and, now that it was too late, he bitterly repented not attempting to capture the dangerous foe by a bold attack.

"She's gone," he groaned, "and I've lost my chance!"

He paced the deck in bitter disappointment, as he felt that he had let a prize slip through his fingers; and, as he waited, the night glided slowly by, till, slowly and tardily, the first signs of day appeared, and with a cry of joy Humphrey Armstrong ordered the signal of recall to be run up, for there, just as she had been last seen when night fell, lay the long, dark schooner, but without a man visible on board.

In a few minutes the two boats were alongside, and Humphrey gazed longingly at the prize he felt ready to give half his life to reach.

What should he do? Attempt to board her now that his four boats lay armed and ready for the fray?

The temptation was too great, and the order was given: the four boats to attack at once, the men receiving the command with a tremendous cheer, and their oars took the water at once; while, compelled by his position to remain on board, the captain feverishly watched the progress of his boats in the growing light, and frowned and stamped the deck in his anger as he saw the crews were exhausting themselves in a race to see which should first reach the silent, forbidding looking schooner.

He shouted to them to keep together, but they were beyond the reach of his voice, and matters seemed hopeless from the way in which they struggled, when a combined attack was requisite for success.

Then all at once the launch remained steady, and the smaller boats went off to right and left. Another minute and all were advancing together, so as to board in four different parts of the ship at once.

Humphrey Armstrong's eyes flashed, his lips parted, and his breast heaved as he watched his men dash on with a faintly heard cheer; but there was no response, not a moving figure could be seen on board the schooner, and it was plain that she had been deserted during the night.

"Curse him for an eel!" cried the captain, fiercely, as he felt that he was about to capture a vessel and leave her cunning commander to man another, and carry on his marauding as of old; but he had hardly uttered his angry denunciation when his four boats raced up to the schooner, and in a moment she seemed alive with men.

Almost before the English captain could realise the fact, great pieces of iron, probably the schooner's ballast, were thrown over into the boats, two of which were crushed through like so much paper, and the men as they sank left struggling in the water.

All that could be done was to rescue the drowning men; and as the two remaining boats were being overladen, and then made a desperate attack so as not to go back in disgrace, a furious fire of small-arms was poured from every port hole and from the schooner's deck, till, unable to penetrate the stout boarding-netting triced up all around the vessel, cut at, shot at, and thrust back into their boats with boarding-pikes, the sloop's two boats fell off, and began to slowly retrace their course.

The moment the way was clear Humphrey, who was almost beside himself with disappointment, begun pounding away at the buccaneer with his heavy guns; but instead of exciting a response he found that sails were being unfurled, and that, instead of the schooner being shut in, the bottom of the bay formed a kind of strait, and she was not in a *cul de sac*.

"She'll escape us after all!" groaned Humphrey, as he ordered sail to be made, and the sloop began to forge ahead, firing rapidly the while, as the schooner began to leave her behind.

She was sailing right in, and before the sloop could follow there were the two boats to be picked up.

This was done, the removal of the wounded being deferred till the buccaneer was captured, and all the time a furious fire was kept up without effect, for the schooner seemed to sail right inland, and disappeared round a headland, the last they saw of the heavily-rigged vessel being when she careened over at right angles to the sloop and her shot-torn sails passed slowly behind the rocky bluff.

"Only into shelter!" cried Humphrey Armstrong, excitedly; and giving rapid orders, fresh sail was made, and men placed in the chains with leads to keep up communications as to the soundings, but always to announce deep water, the land seeming to rise up sheer from an enormous depth in the channel-like gulf they entered.

"She's gone right through, sir, and will get away on the other side."

The sloop sailed on, with the water deep as ever, and before long she rounded the head, to find the narrow channel had opened out into a beautiful lake-like bay with the dense primeval forest running right down to its shores.

But the greatest beauty of the scene to Humphrey Armstrong was the sight of the schooner lying right across his course a quarter of a mile away, and ready to concentrate her fire and rake the sloop from stem to stern.

"Curse him! no wonder he has had so long a career!" said Humphrey, stamping with rage as he watched the execution of his orders, and a well-directed fire was once more made to answer that of the buccaneer. "With such a ship, crew, and place of retreat, he might have gone on for years."

The firing grew hotter than ever, and the schooner became enveloped in a cloud of smoke which elicited a burst of cheers from the sloop.

"She's afire! she's afire!" roared the men.

Humphrey's triumph was now at hand. The scourge of the western seas was at his mercy, and shrinking from attempting to board so desperate an adversary for the sake of his crew, he gave orders to lay the sloop right alongside of the schooner, where he could cast grappling-irons, and then pour his fire down upon her deck.

The orders were rapidly executed, and the sloop bore down right for the smoke-enveloped schooner with little fear of being raked now, for the pirates had ceased firing, and could be dimly-seen through the reek hurrying to and fro.

"Shall we give her one more salvo, sir?" asked the first officer, coming up to where Humphrey stood, trying to pierce the smoke with his glass.

"No, poor wretches! they're getting fire enough. I hope she will not blow up, for I'd give anything to take her home unhurt."

There was a perfect rush of flame and smoke now from the schooner, and once more Humphrey's men cheered and shook hands together, even the wounded in the excitement of their triumph taking up the cry, when, just in the height of the excitement, and when the sloop was within a hundred yards of the enemy, the men in the chains among the rest gazing hard at the rising smoke, the war vessel careened over in answer to her helm in the evolution which was to lay her side by side with the burning schooner, and then there was a tremendous jerk which threw nearly every one off his feet.

Then, shivering from head to heel, the sloop slowly surged back us if to gather force like a wave, and in obedience to the pressure upon her sails, struck again, literally leaping this time upon the keen-edged barrier of rocks under whose invisible shelter the schooner lay; and then, as a yell of horror rose from the men, the unfortunate ship remained fixed, her masts, sail laden, went over the side with a hideous crashing noise, and all was confusion, ruin, and despair.

The moments required to turn a stately, sail-crowded ship into a state of chaos are very few, and to Humphrey Armstrong's agony, as well aided by his officers, he was trying to do something to ameliorate their position, he saw how thoroughly he had been led into a cunningly-designed trap. The schooner had been artfully manoeuvred to place her behind the dangerous rocks, and, what was more, a glance at her now showed her sailing away from a couple of boats moored beyond them; and in each of which were barrels of burning pitch sending up volumes of blackened smoke.

"A trap! a trap!" he cried, grinding his teeth. "Let her be, my lads," he roared. "Prepare for boarders!"

The men sprang to their pikes and swords, while a couple of guns were freed from the wreck of cordage, and sail which the shock had brought down.

These guns had hardly been trained to bear upon the schooner from the deck of the helpless sloop when a deadly fire was opened by the former—a fire of so furious a character that the confusion was increased, and in spite of the efforts of captain and officers, the men shrank from working at the guns.

What followed was one terrible scene of despairing men striving for their lives against a foe of overpowering strength. The fierce fire of the schooner, as she came nearer and nearer, was feebly responded to, and in a short time the deck streamed with blood, as the shot came crashing through the bulwarks, sending showers of splinters to do deadly work with the hail of grape. There was no thought of capture now; no need of bidding the men attack: following the example of their officers, and one and all doggedly determined to sell their lives dearly, the men dragged gun after gun round as those they worked were disabled, and sent a shot in reply as often as they could.

With uniform torn and bedabbled with blood, face blackened with powder, and the red light of battle in his eyes, Humphrey Armstrong saw plainly enough that his case was hopeless, and that, with all her pomp of war and pride of discipline and strength, his sloop was prostrate before the buccaneer's snaky craft, and in his agony of spirit and rage he determined to wait till the pirates boarded, as he could see they would before long, and then blow up the magazine and send them to eternity in their triumph over the British ship.

But it was to destroy his men as well, and he felt that this should be the pirates' work when all was over.

"No," he muttered between his teeth, "it would be a coward's act, and they shall die like men."

The schooner's sides were vomiting smoke and flame, and she was close alongside now. She had been so manoeuvred as to sail right round the end of the reef, whose position seemed to be exactly known, so that from firing upon the sloop's bows, and raking from stem to stern, the firing had been continued as she passed along the larboard side round to the poop, which had been raked in turn, and here it was evident that the final attack was to be made.

It was not long in coming. Hardly had Humphrey seen the enemy's intentions and gathered his men together, than the schooner's side ground up against the shattered stern of the sloop. Heavy grappling-irons were thrown on board, and with a furious yelling a horde of blackened, savage-looking men poured on to the bloody splinter-strewn deck, and coming comparatively fresh upon the sloop's exhausted crew, bore down all opposition. Men were driven below, cut down, stunned, and driven to ask for quarter; and so furious was the onslaught that the sloop's crew were divided into two half helpless bodies, one of which threw down their arms, while the other, which included the captain and officers, backed slowly toward the bows, halting at every spot where they could make a stand, but forced to yield foot by foot, till their fate, it was plain to all, was to surrender or be driven through the shattered bulwarks into the sea.

It was a matter of minutes. The fight was desperate, but useless—Humphrey Armstrong and those around him seeming determined to sell their lives dearly, for no quarter was asked. They had given way step by step till there was nothing behind them but the shattered bulwarks, and then the sea, when, headed by their leader, the buccaneers made a desperate rush; there was the clashing of sword and pike; and, as sailor and officer fell, or were disarmed, Humphrey stepped in a half-congealed pool of blood, slipped, and went heavily backwards, the buccaneer's lieutenant leaping forward to brain him with a heavy axe.

There was a rush, a fierce shout, Black Mazzard was thrust aside, and the Commodore sprang past him to plant his foot upon the fallen officer's chest, while, the fight being over, the rest held their hands—the conquerors and conquered—to see what would be the captain's fate.

"Now, Captain Armstrong," cried the buccaneer leader, "beg for your wretched life, you cowardly dog!"

"Coward!" roared Humphrey, raising himself slightly on one hand, as with the other he swept the blood from his ensanguined face. "You cursed hound! you lie!"

The buccaneer shrank back as if from some blow; his foot was withdrawn from the wounded officer's chest, he lowered the point of his sword, and stood gazing at his prostrate enemy wildly.

"The captain shirks the job, lads," cried a coarse voice. "Here, let me come."

It was Black Mazzard who spoke, and, drunken with rum and the spirit of the furious fight, he pressed forward, axe in hand.

Humphrey raised himself a little higher, with his white teeth bared in fierce defiance as he prepared to meet the deathblow he saw about to fall.

But at that moment the buccaneer caught his lieutenant's uplifted arm.

"Enough!" he cried, fiercely; "no more blood. He is no coward. Bart— Dinny, take this gentleman ashore."

Humphrey Armstrong did not hear the words, for his defiant act exhausted his failing strength, and he fell back insensible to all that happened for many hours to come.

Chapter Twenty Three
Captain Humphrey comes to

Captain Humphrey lay upon his back staring at his conscience. He was weak from loss of blood, weaker from fever; and he would have fared better if he had had proper medical treatment instead of the rough but kindly doctoring and nursing of Bart the surgeon, and Dinny the hospital nurse.

This was after three weeks' doubtful journey, wherein Dinny said "the obstinate divil had tried all he knew to die." And it was so ungrateful, Dinny said, after the captain had saved his life, and that of all the prisoners who had not also been obstinate and died.

Humphrey's conscience was a great stone god full twelve feet high—an object that looked like a mummy-case set on end, as far as shape was concerned, but carved all over in the most wonderful way, the grotesque and weird bas-reliefs almost destroying the face, hands, and feet of the figure, flowing over them as they were, so that at first sight he looked upon a great mass of sculpture, out of which by degrees the features appeared.

The old artist who designed the idol had strange ideas of decorative effect. He had cut in the hard stone a fine contemplative face; but over it he had placed a gigantic headdress, whereon were stony plumes of feathers, wreaths, and strange symbols, while pendent in every possible direction about the body were writhing creatures and snakes, with variations of the human form, engaged in strange struggles, and amongst them human heads turned into bosses or decorations of the giant robe.

Humphrey Armstrong came partly to himself to see the cold, implacable face of this idol staring down at him from the gloom, ten feet from where he lay; and it seemed to him, by slow degrees, that this was his conscience sternly and silently upbraiding him for the loss of his ship and the lives of his men, destroyed by his want of skill as a commander.

Day after day, through his semi-delirium, did that great idol torture him, and seem, with its reproachful eyes, to burn into his brain.

Days passed, and by degrees he began to be aware that he was lying on a bed of comfortable rugs and skins, stretched in a curious room, whose walls were covered with hieroglyphics—thick, clumsy-looking hieroglyphics—

not like those of Egypt, but carved with a skill peculiar to another race. Here and there were medallions of heads of gods or rulers of the land. Flowers of a peculiar conventional type formed part of the decorations or surrounded panels, in which were panthers, alligators, or human figures. In the centre of the wall to his right was a recess in which, clearly cut and hardly touched by time, were the figures of a king seated upon a leopard-supported throne — seated cross-legged, as in the East, and in a wondrous costume — while another figure presented to him what seemed to be the spoil of a number of dead and living figures who were trampled under foot.

The room was evidently a palace chamber, or a portion of a temple of great antiquity; and by degrees Humphrey realised that the ceiling was not arched or supported by beams, but by the great stones of which it was composed being piled one above the other, like a flight of steps, from the walls on either side till they met in the middle.

The floor was of stone, and there was a large opening on his left, facing the recess where the carving of the king ornamented the wall; and this opening, once a window, looked out upon the forest, whose dull, green, subdued twilight stole into the place.

It was a weird look-out — upon tree-trunks strangled by serpent-like creepers, which seemed to be contending with them for the life-giving light which filtered down from above through clouds of verdure; while other trees and other serpent-like creepers seemed in friendly co-operation to have joined hands against the walls of the building, which they were striving to destroy. Huge roots were thrust between the joints of stones and shifted them out of place. One liana waved a trailing stem through the window-opening as if in triumph, and to call attention to the feat of another creeper which had twisted itself completely round a great block, lifted it from one side, and held it suspended like a vegetable feat of strength.

For nature was asserting herself on every hand, the growth of the forest penetrating the chamber like an invading army of leaves and stems, and mingling with the works of man to their steady overthrow; while, facing it all, stern, implacable, and calmly watching the progress of destruction going on, stood the stone idol, the work of a race passed from the face of the earth, and waiting, as it had waited for hundreds of years, till the potent forest growth should lay it low!

For a time it was all a nightmare-like confusion to Humphrey; but with returning strength came order in his intellect, and he questioned Bart, who brought him food, and from time to time added carpets and various little luxuries of cabin furniture, which seemed strangely incongruous in that place.

"Who told you to bring those things here?" he said one day.

"Commodore Junk."

"Why? Am I a prisoner?"

"Yes."

"Am I to be shot?"

"Don't know."

"Where am I?"

"Here."

"But what place is this?"

"Don't know."

"But—"

"Want any more wine or fruit?"

"No; I want my liberty."

"Belongs to the captain."

"Tell the captain I wish to see him."

Bart said no more, but took his departure.

The prisoner was more fortunate with Dinny, who could be communicative.

"That's it, captain, darlin'," he said one day. "Don't ye fale like a little boy again, and that I'm your mother washing your poor face!"

"Don't fool, my good fellow, but talk to me."

"Talk to you, is it?"

"Yes; you can talk to me."

"Talk to ye—can I talk to ye! Hark at him, mate!" he cried, appealing to the great idol. "Why, I'm a divil at it."

"Well, then, tell me how I came here."

"Faix, didn't I carry ye on my back?"

"Yes, but after the fight?"

"Afther the foight—oh! is it afther the foight ye mane? Sure, and it was the skipper's ordhers, and I carried ye here, and Bart—you know the tother one—he brought in the bed and the rugs and things to make ye dacent. It's a bit damp, and the threes have a bad habit of putting in their noses like the pigs at home; but it's an illigant bed-room for a gintleman afther all."

"It was the captain's orders, you say?"

"Sure, an' it was."

"And where are we?"

"Why, here we are."

"Yes, yes; but what place is this?"

"Sure, an' it's the skipper's palace."

"Commodore Junk's?"

"Yis."

"And what place is it—where are we?"

"Faix, and they say that sick payple is hard to deal wid. It's what I'm telling you sure. It's the skipper's palace, and here it is."

"My good fellow, you told me all that; but I want to know whereabouts it is."

"Oh-h! Whereabouts it is, you mane!"

"Yes, yes."

"Why, right away in the woods."

"Far from the shore!"

"Ah, would ye!" cried Dinny, with a grin full of cunning. "Ye'd be getting all the information out of me, and then as soon as ye get well be running away."

"Yes," said Humphrey, "If I can."

"Well, that's honest," cried Dinny. "And it's meself would do it if I got a chance."

"No," said Humphrey, sadly; "I could not do that and leave my men."

"Faix, and they'd leave ye if they got a chance, sor."

"How are they all!"

"Oh, they're getting right enough," said Dinny. "Ye've been the worst of 'em all yerself, and if ye don't make haste ye'll be last."

"But tell me, my lad, why am I kept in prison!"

"Tell ye why you're kept in prison?"

"Yes."

"An' ye want to know! Well, divil a wan of us can tell, unless it's the skipper's took a fancy to ye bekase ye're such a divil to fight, and he wants ye to jyne the rigiment."

"Regiment! Why, you've been a soldier!"

"And is it me a sodjer! Why, ye'll be wanting to make out next that I was a desarther when was only a prishner of war." Humphrey sighed.

"Sure, and ye're wanting something, sor. What'll I get ye! The skipper said ye were to have iverything you wanted."

"Then give me my liberty, my man, and let me go back to England — and disgrace."

"Sure, and I wouldn't go back to England to get that, sor. I'd sooner shtop here. The skipper's always telling Bart to look afther ye well."

"Why?" said Humphrey, sharply.

"Why?" said Dinny, scratching his head; "perhaps he wants to get ye in good condition before ye're hung."

"Hung?"

"Yis, sor. That's what Black Mazzard says."

"Is that the man who tried to cut me down with a boarding-axe?"

"That's the gintleman, sor; and now let me put ye tidy, and lay yer bed shtraight. Sure, and ye've got an illigant cabin here, as is good enough for a juke. Look at the ornaments on the walls."

"Are there any more places like this?"

"Anny more! Sure, the wood's full of 'em."

"But about here?"

"About here! Oh, this is only a little place. Sure, we all live here always when we ar'n't aboard the schooner."

"Ah, yes! The schooner. She was quite destroyed, was she not?"

"Divil a bit, sor. Your boys didn't shoot straight enough. The ship ye came in was, afther we'd got all we wanted out of her. She was burnt to the wather's edge, and then she sank off the reef."

Humphrey groaned.

"Ye needn't do that, sor, for she was a very owld boat, and not safe for a journey home. Mak' yer mind aisy, and mak' this yer home. There's plinty of room for ye, and — whisht! here's the captain coming. What'll he be doing here?"

"The captain!" cried Humphrey. "Then that man took my message."

"What message, sor?"

At that moment the steps which had been heard coming as it were down some long stone corridor halted at the doorway of the prisoner's chamber, someone drew aside a heavy rug, and the buccaneer, wearing a broad-leafed hat which shaded his face, entered the place.

"You can go, Dinny."

"Yis, sor, I'm going," said Dinny, obsequiously; and, after a glance at the prisoner, he hurriedly obeyed.

There was only a gloomy greenish twilight in the old chamber, such light as there was striking in through the forest-shaded window, and with his back to this, and retaining his hat, the captain seated himself upon a rug covered chest.

"You sent for me," he said, in a deep, abrupt tone.

Humphrey looked at him intently, the dark eyes meeting his, and the thick black brows contracted as the gaze was prolonged.

"You sent for me," he repeated, abruptly; "what more do you want?"

"I will tell you after a while," said Humphrey; "but first of all let me thank you for the kind treatment I have received at your hands."

"You need not thank me," was the short reply. "Better treatment than you would have given me."

"Well, yes," said Humphrey. "I am afraid it is."

"Your cousin would have hung me."

"My cousin! What do you know of my cousin!"

"England is little. Every Englishman of mark is known."

Humphrey looked at him curiously, and for the moment it seemed to him that he had heard that voice before, but his memory did not help him.

"My cousin would have done his duty," he said, gravely.

"His duty!" cried the captain, bitterly. "Your country has lost a treasure in the death of that man, sir."

"Good heavens, man! What do you know—"

"Enough, sir. Let Captain James Armstrong rest. The name is well represented now by a gentleman, and it is to that fact that Captain Humphrey owes his life."

The latter stared at the speaker wonderingly.

"Well, sir, why have you sent for me!"

"To thank you, Commodore Junk, and to ask you a question or two."

"Go on, sir. Perhaps I shall not answer you."

"I will risk it," said Humphrey, watching him narrowly, "You spared my life. Why?"

"I told you."

"Then you will give me my liberty?"

"What for?—to go away and return with another and better-manned ship to take us and serve the captain of the schooner as I have served you?"

"No. I wish to return home."

"What for?"

"Surely you cannot expect me to wish to stay here!"

"Why do you wish to go home to meet disgrace?"

Humphrey started at having his own words repeated.

"To be tried by court martial for the loss of your ship! Stay where you are, sir, and grow strong and well."

"If I stay here, sir, when I have full liberty to go, shall I not be playing the part of the coward you called me when I was beaten down?"

"You will not have full liberty to go, Captain Armstrong," said his captor, quietly. "You forget that you are a prisoner."

"You do not intend to kill me and my men?"

"We are not butchers, sir," was the cold reply.

"Then what is your object in detaining us. Is it ransom?"

"Possibly."

"Name the sum, then, sir, and if it is in my power it shall be paid."

"It is too soon to talk of ransom, Captain Armstrong," said his visitor, "you are weak and ill yet. Be patient, and grow well and strong. Some day I will talk over this matter with you again. But let me, before I go, warn you to be careful not to attempt to escape, or to encourage either of your men to make the attempt. Even I could not save you then, for the first man you met would shoot you down. Besides that risk, escape is impossible by land; and we shall take care that you do not get away by sea. Now, sir, have I listened to all you have to say?"

"One word, sir. I am growing stronger every day. Will you grant me some freedom?"

"Captain Armstrong is a gentleman," said his visitor; "if he will give his word that he will not attempt to escape, he shall be free to go anywhere within the bounds of our little settlement."

Humphrey sat thinking, with his brow knit and his teeth compressed.

"No," he said; "that would be debarring myself from escaping."

"You could not escape."

"I should like to try," said Humphrey, smiling.

"It would be utter madness, sir. Give me your word of honour that you will not attempt to leave this old palace, and you shall come and go as you please."

"No, sir, I will remain a prisoner with the chances open."

"As you will," said the buccaneer, coldly; and he rose and left the chamber, looking thoughtful and absent, while Humphrey lay back on his couch, gazing hard at the great stone idol, as if he expected to gain information from its stern mysterious countenance.

"Where have I seen him before?" he said, thoughtfully; and after gazing at the carven effigy for some time he closed his eyes and tried to think, but their last meeting on the deck of the sloop was all that would suggest itself, and he turned wearily upon his side.

"He seemed to have heard of our family, and his manner was strange; but I can't think now," he said, "I am hot and weak, and this place seems to stifle me."

Almost as he spoke he dropped asleep—the slumber of weakness and exhaustion—to be plunged in a heavy stupor for hours, perfectly unconscious of the fact that from time to time the great curtain was drawn aside and a big head thrust into the dim chamber, the owner gazing frowningly at the helpless prisoner, and then entering on tiptoe, to cross to the window and cautiously look out before returning to the couch, with the frown deepening as the man thought of how narrow the step was which led from life to death.

He had advanced close to the couch with a savage gleam of hatred in his eyes when Humphrey Armstrong moved uneasily, tossed his hands apart, and then, as if warned instinctively of danger, he opened his eyes, sprang up, and seized a piece of stone close by his side, the only weapon, within grasp.

"Well," said Bart, without stirring, and with a grim look of contempt, "heave it. I don't mind."

"Oh, it's you!" said the prisoner, setting down the stone and letting himself sink back. "I was dreaming, I suppose, and thought there was danger."

He laid his feverish cheek upon his hand, and seemed to fall asleep at once, his eyes closing and his breath coming easily.

"Trusts me," muttered Bart. "Poor lad! it ar'n't his fault. Man can't kill one as trusts him like that. I shall have to fight for him, I suppose. Always my way—always my way."

He seated himself at the foot of the couch with his features distorted as if by pain, and for hour after hour watched the sleeper, telling himself that he could not do him harm, though all the time a jealous hatred approaching fury was burning in his breast.

Chapter Twenty Four
The Prison Life

"Not dying, Bart?"

"No, not exactly dying," said that worthy in a low growl; "but s'pose you shoots at and wings a gull, picks it up, and takes it, and puts it in a cage; the wound heals up, and the bird seems sound; but after a time it don't peck, and don't preen its plumes, and if it don't beat itself again' the bars o' the cage, it sits and looks at the sea."

"What do you mean?"

"What I says, captain; and, after a time, if you don't let it go, that gull dies."

"Then you mean that Captain Armstrong is pining away?"

"That's it."

"Has he any suspicion of who we are?"

"Not a bit."

"And you think he's suffering for want of change?"

"Course I do. Anyone would—shut up in that dark place."

"Has he complyned?"

"Not he. Too brave a lad. Why not give him and his lads a boat, and let them go!"

"To come back with a strong force and destroy us."

"Ah, I never thought of that! Make him swear he wouldn't. He'd keep his word."

"But his men would not, Bart. No; he will have to stay."

"Let him loose, then, to run about the place. He can't get away."

"I am afraid."

"What of?"

"Some trouble arising. Mazzard does not like him."

"Ah! I never thought o' that neither," returned Bart, gloomily. "Black Mazzard's always grumbling about his being kept."

The buccaneer took a turn or two up and down the quarters he occupied in the vast range of buildings buried in the forest, a mile back from the head of the harbour where his schooner lay; and Bart watched him curiously till he stopped, with his face twitching, and the frown deepening upon his brow.

"He will not give his word of honour not to attempt to escape, Bart," said the captain, pausing at last before his follower.

"'Tar'n't likely," said Bart. "Who would? He'd get away if he could."

"The prisoners cannot escape through the forest; there is no way but the sea, and that must be properly watched. Due notice must be given to all that any attempt to escape will be followed by the punishment of death."

"I hear," said Bart. "Am I to tell the captain that?"

"No. He must know it; but I give him into your charge. You must watch over him, and protect him from himself and from anyone else."

"Black Mazzard!"

"From any one likely to do him harm," said the captain, sternly. "You understand?"

"Yes. I'm going," replied Bart, in a low growl, as he gazed in his leader's eyes; and then, with a curious, thoughtful look in his own, he went out of the captain's quarters and in the direction of the prison of the king's officer.

Bart had to go down the broad steps of an extensive, open amphitheatre, whose stones were dislodged by the redundant growth of the forest; and, after crossing the vast court-yard at the bottom, to mount the steps on the other side toward where, dominating a broad terrace overshadowed by trees, stood a small, square temple, over whose doorway was carved a huge, demoniacal head, defaced by the action of time, but with the features still clearly marked.

As Bart neared the building a figure appeared in the doorway for a moment, and then passed out into the sunshine.

"Hullo, my lad!" it exclaimed. "You there?"

Bart nodded.

"Been putting in the last six barr'ls of the sloop's powder, and some of these days you'll see the sun'll set it all alight, and blow the whole place to smithereens! Where are ye going?"

"Yonder, to the prisoners."

"Poor divils!" said Dinny. "Hadn't ye better kill the lot and put 'em out of their misery? They must be tired of it, and so am I. Faix, and it's a dirthy life for a man to lead!"

"Don't let the skipper hear you say that, my lad," growled Bart, "or it may be awkward for you!"

"I'll let annybody hear me!" cried Dinny. "Sure, an' it's the life of a baste to lead, and a man like that Black Mazzard bullying and finding fault. I'd have sent one of the powdher-kegs at his head this morning for the binifit of everybody here, only I might have blown myself up as well."

"Has he been swearing at you again!"

"Swearing! Bedad, Bart, he said things to me this morning as scorched the leaves of the threes yonder. If you go and look you can see 'em all crickled up. He can swear!"

Bart slouched away.

"It's a divil of a place!" muttered Dinny; "and it would make a wondherful stone-quarry; but I'm getting sick of it, and feeling as if I should like to desart. Black Mazzard again!" he muttered, drawing in his breath sharply. "I wish his greatest inimy would break his neck!"

Dinny walked sharply away, for the lieutenant seemed to have been gathering authority since the taking of the sloop, and lost no opportunity of showing it to all the crew.

Meanwhile, Bart had continued his way between the two piles of ruins, his path leading from the dazzling glow of the tropic sunshine into the subdued green twilight of the forest.

Here, at the end of some fifty paces, he came to the external portion of the building which formed Captain Humphrey's prison, and entering by a fairly well-preserved doorway, he raised a curtain, half-way down a corridor, passed through, and then came abreast of a recess, at the end of which was another broad hanging, which he drew aside, and entered the temple-chamber, where Humphrey lay sleeping on a couch.

As Bart approached he became aware of a faint rustling sound, as of someone retreating from the window among the trees, and starting forward, he looked out. But all was still; not a long rope-like liana quivering, no leaf crushed.

"Some monkey," muttered Bart, and turning back, he gazed down with a heavy frown at the frank, handsome face of the young officer, till he saw the features twitch, the eyes open and stare wonderingly into his; and once more the prisoner, roused by the presence of another gazing upon his sleeping face, suddenly sprang up.

"You here?"

"Yes, sir, I'm here," said Bart.

"What for? Why?"

"Nothing much, sir; only to tell you that you can go."

"Go?" cried the captain, excitedly.

"Yes, sir. Captain Junk's orders—where you like, so long as you don't try to escape."

"But I must escape!" cried Humphrey, angrily. "Tell the captain I will not give my parole."

"He don't want it, sir. You can go where you like, only if you try to escape you will be shot."

Humphrey Armstrong rose from where he had been lying, and made as if to go to the door, his face full of excitement, his eyes flashing, and his hands all of a tremble.

"Go!" he said, sharply. "Send that man who has acted as my servant."

"Servant!" muttered Bart, as he passed the curtain; "and him a prisoner! Dinny called hisself his turnkey, but said as there was no door to lock. Here! hoi! Dinny!"

"What do you want with him?" said a fierce voice; and he turned, to find the lieutenant coming out of one of the ruined buildings.

"Prisoner wants him," said Bart, sturdily. "Here, Dinny, Captain Armstrong wants you."

"Ay, ay," cried Dinny, who seemed to divine that Mazzard was about to stop him, and ran hastily on; while the lieutenant, who was half-drunk, stood muttering, and then walked slowly away.

"Not so well, sor!"

"Wine—water!" panted Humphrey, hoarsely. "I tried to walk to the door and fell back here."

"Sure, an ye're out of practice, sir," said Dinny, hastening to hold a vessel of water to the prisoner's lips. "That's better. Ye've tuk no exercise since ye've been betther."

"Ah!" sighed Humphrey; "the deadly sickness has gone. This place is so lonely."

"Ay, 'tis, sor. One always feels like an outside cock bird who wants a mate."

"Sit down and talk to me."

"Sure an' I will, wid pleasure, sor," said Dinny, eagerly. "There's so few gintlemen to talk to here."

"Tell me about your commander."

"An' what'll I tell you about him?"

"What kind of a man is he?"

"Sure, and he's as handsome as such a little chap can be."

"Has he a wife here?"

"Woife, sor? Not he!"

"A troop of mistresses, then, or a harem?"

"Divil a bit, sor. He's riddy to shoot the boys whiniver they take a new wife—Ingin or white. I belave he hates the whole sex, and thinks women is divils, sor. Why, he hit Black Mazzard once, sor, for asking him why he didn't choose a pretty gyurl, and not live like a monk."

"Is he brave?"

"Yes, sor; and I wouldn't anger him if I were you."

"Not I," said Humphrey. "There, the sickness has passed off. Now, help me out into the sunshine."

"Help ye out?" said Dinny, looking puzzled.

"Yes; into the bright sunshine. I seem to be decaying away here, man, and the warm light will give me strength."

"Shure, an' if I do, Black Mazzard will pison me wid a pishtol-ball."

"I have the captain's consent," said Humphrey.

"Sure, and ye're not deludhering a boy, are ye, sor?" said Dinny.

"No, no, my man, it is right. Help me; I did not know I was so weak."

"An' is it wake?" said Dinny, drawing the prisoner's arm well through his own. "Sure, and didn't I see gallons o' blood run out of ye? Faix, and there was quarts and quarts of it; and I belave ye'd have died if I hadn't nursed ye so tenderly as I did."

"My good fellow, you've been like a good angel to me," said Humphrey, feebly. "Hah! how glorious!" he sighed, closing his eyes as they stepped out of the long corridor into the opening cut through the forest, and then between the two piles of ruins into the glorious tropic sunshine.

"Will it be too warrum?" said Dinny.

"Warm! No, man, my heart has been chilled with lying there in the darkness. Take me farther out into the bright light."

"Sure, and it's the sun bating ye down ye'll be havin'," said Dinny. "Look at that, now!"

Dinny was gazing back at the pile of ancient buildings, and caught sight of a face in the shadow.

"Yes, I am trying to look," said Humphrey, with a sigh; "but my eyes are not used to the light."

"Sure, an' it's the captin, and he's kaping his oi on us," said Dinny to himself. "Well, all right, captain, darlin'! I'm not going to run away."

"What place is this?"

"Sure, an' it's meself don't know, sor. Mebbe it's the palace that the American good payple built for Christyphy Columbus. Mebbe," continued Dinny, "it's much owlder. Sure, and it shutes the captin, and we all live here whin we don't live somewhere else."

"Somewhere else?" said Humphrey, looking at Dinny wonderingly as he grasped his arm and signed to him to wait and give him breath.

"Well, I mane at say, sor, doing a bit o' business amongst the ships. Ah, look at her, thin, the darlin'!" he muttered, as a woman appeared for a moment among the lianas, held up her hand quickly to Dinny, and turned away.

"What woman was that!" said Humphrey, hastily.

"Woman, sor!"

"Yes; that woman who kissed her hand to you."

"An' did she kiss her hand to me, sor!"

"Yes, man, you must have seen."

"Sure, an' it must have been Misthress Greenheys, sor."

"Mistress Greenheys!"

"A widow lady, sor, whose husband had an accident one day wid his ship and got killed."

"And you know her!"

"We've been getting a little friendly lately," said Dinny, demurely. "There, sor, you're getting wake. Sit down on that owld stone in the shade. Bedad, it isn't illigant, the cutting upon it, for it's like a shkull, but it's moighty convanient under that three. That's better; and I'll go and ask Bart to bring ye a cigar."

"No, stop," said Humphrey. "I want to talk to you, man. That woman's husband was murdered, then?"

"Murdered! Faix, and that's thrue. Sure, an' someone hit him a bit too hard, sor, and he doied."

"Murdered by these buccaneers!" said Humphrey, excitedly, and he looked wildly around him, when his eye lighted on the trim, picturesque figure of the little woman, who was intently watching them, and he saw her exchange a sign with his companion.

"The key of life—the great motive which moves the world," said Humphrey to himself; and he turned suddenly on Dinny, who had his hand to his mouth and looked sheepish.

"You love that woman," he said, sharply.

"Whisht, captin, dear!" said Dinny, softly; and then in a whisper, with a roguish leer, "sure, it isn't me, sor; it's the darlin's took a bit of a fancy to me."

"Yes, and you love her," said Humphrey.

"Och, what a way ye have of putting it, sor! Sure, and the poor crittur lost her husband, and she's been living here iver since, and she isn't happy, and what could a boy do but thry to comfort her!"

"Are you going to marry her, Dinny?" said Humphrey, after a pause.

"Faix, an' I would if I had a chance, sor; but there's two obshticles in the way, and one of 'em's Black Mazzard."

"Then, why not take her, Dinny!"

"Tak' her, sor?"

"Yes; from this wretched place. Escape."

"Whisht! Don't say that word aloud again, darlin', or maybe the captin'll get to hear. Sure, and I belave that the great big sthone gods shticking up all over the place gets to hear what's said and whishpers it again to the captin, who always knows everything that goes on."

"Take her, and help me to escape," whispered Humphrey, earnestly.

"Whisht, man! Howld your tongue. Is it wanting to see me hanging on one of the trees! Eshcape?"

"Yes. I am a rich man, and if you can get me away I'll reward you handsomely."

"Hark at him!" said Dinny, scornfully. "Why, I should have to give up my share of what we've got shtored up here. Why, sor, I daresay I'm a richer man than yourself. Eshcape! and after all I've shworn."

Dinny turned away and began cutting a stick.

"Tell me," said Humphrey, "are there many of my men here?"

"Jist twenty, sor."

"And how many are there of the pirates!"

Dinny laughed with his eyes half shut.

"Shure, sor, what d'ye tak' me for? Ye don't think I'm going to tell ye that!"

Humphrey sighed, and was silent for a time; but an intense desire to know more about the place was burning within him, and he began to question his companion again.

"Are the prisoners in one of these old temples!"

"Yes. On the other side of the big pyrymid yonder, sor; but ye can't get to them widout going a long way round."

"Are there many women here besides that Mistress Greenheys?"

"Sure, yis, there is a dozen of 'em, sor. Not half enough, but just enough to kape the min quarrelling; and there's been no end of bother about the women being kept in the place."

Chapter Twenty Five
Plans of Escape

Humphrey Armstrong was weaker from his wounds than he believed; but the change from being shut up in the dim temple-chamber with the great stone idol for company to the comparatively free open air of the forest clearing rapidly restored the elasticity of his nature, and gave him ample opportunities for studying the state of affairs.

He found that the buccaneers went out but seldom, and that when expeditions were made they would be fairly divided. At one time the captain would be in command, at another the lieutenant, so that their settlement was never left unprotected.

As far as he could judge, they were about a hundred in number, and great dilapidated chambers in the range of temples and palaces formed admirable barracks and means of defence, such as in time of need could easily be held against attack.

But Humphrey's great idea was escape; and to accomplish this it seemed to him that his first need was to open up communication with his men.

This he determined to accomplish, for with the liberty given it seemed to be a very easy thing to walk to some heap of stones at the edge of the forest and there seat himself till he was unobserved, when he could quietly step into the dense thicket, and make his way to where his followers were imprisoned.

He had not long to wait, for it seemed that, after being closely watched for the first few days, the latitude allowed to him was greater. He had but to walk to the edge of the forest and wait, for the opportunity was sure to come.

Easy as it appeared though in theory, it proved less so in performance, and it was not till after several attempts that he felt one day sure of success.

It was soon after mid-day, when the great amphitheatre and the grotesquely ornamented ruins with their huge heads and shadowy trees were baking in the sun. The men who were often idling about had sought places where they could indulge in their siesta, and a silence as of the grave had fallen upon the place.

Humphrey Armstrong had walked to a pile of ruins beneath one of the trees, and seated himself upon a huge stone sculptured round with figures writhing in impossible attitudes, and one and all wearing highly ornamental head-dresses of feathers.

He lay back there as if half drowsy with the heat, and with half-closed eyes looked watchfully round to see whether he was observed. But as far as he could see the place was utterly deserted. Bart, who was often here and there giving a kind of supervision to the buccaneers' settlement, and seeing that people from the barracks did not collect near the captain's quarters, seemed to be absent. Dinny, who had been to him an hour before, had gone off on some duty with Dick Dullock, and everything pointed to the fact that this was the opportunity so long sought.

He hesitated no longer; but after casting another glance round at the dark, shadowy nooks among the trees and ruins, all of which seemed purply-black in contrast with the blazing glare of sunshine, he softly slid himself back from the stone and dropped down among the undergrowth, and raised his head to peer among the leaves.

He obtained a good view of the great amphitheatre and the surrounding ruins, but all was still. No one had seen him move, and not a leaf was stirring.

Trifles seemed magnified at those moments into great matters, and with his nerves strung up to the highest pitch of tension he started, for all at once something moved away by the edge of the forest on his left. But it was only a great butterfly which fluttered over the baking stones, above which the air seemed to quiver, and then, with its brightly-painted wings casting a broad shadow, it crossed the ruined amphitheatre and was gone.

Humphrey Armstrong crept from behind his resting-place right to the shelter of the trees at the edge of the forest, and his spirits rose as he found how easy an evasion seemed to be. He had only to secure the co-operation of half a dozen of his men, take advantage of the listlessness of the buccaneers some such hot day as this, make their way down to the shore, seize a boat, and then coast along till a settlement was reached or a ship seen to take them aboard.

It was very simple, and it seemed easier and easier as he got farther away from the ruins and his prison. On his right the forest was dense, but the buccaneers had cut down and burned numbers of trees so as to keep them back from encroaching farther on the old buildings; and along here among the mossy stumps Humphrey Armstrong crept.

But it was easy—nothing seemed more simple. Already he saw himself round on the other side of the ruins, holding communication with his fellow-prisoners and making plans, when, to his great delight, he found that he had hit upon what was evidently a way to the other side of the ancient ruins; for he suddenly came upon a narrow passage through the dense forest growth, literally a doorway cut in the tangle of creepers and vines that were matted among the trees. It must have been an arduous task, but it had been thoroughly done—the vines having been hewn through, or in places half divided and bent back, to go on interlacing at the sides, with the result that a maze-like path ran in and out among the trees.

The moment he was in this path the glare of the sunny day was exchanged for a dim greenish-hued twilight, which darkened with every step he took. Overhead a pencil of sunshine could be seen from time to time, but rarely, for the mighty forest trees interlaced their branches a hundred and fifty feet above his head, and the air was heavy with the moist odour of vegetable decay.

The forest path had evidently been rarely used of late, for the soft earth showed no imprints, the tender sickly growth of these deep shades had not been crushed; and as Humphrey realised these facts, he glanced back, to see how easily his trail could be followed—each step he had taken being either impressed in the vegetable soil or marked by the crushing down of moss or herb.

The sight of this impelled him to additional effort, so that he might gain some definite information about his people, and perhaps seek them by night, when once he had found the means of communication. In this spirit he was hurrying on when he came suddenly, in one of the darkest paths, upon a figure which barred his way, and it was with the addition of a rage-wrung savage exclamation that he uttered his captor's name.

There was a dead silence in the dark forest as these two stood face to face, buried, as it were, in a gloomy tunnel. After Humphrey's impatient ejaculation, drawn from him in his surprise, quite a minute elapsed; and then, half-mockingly, came in a deep, low voice—

"Yes! Commodore Junk!"

Humphrey stood glaring down at the obstacle in his path. He was tall and athletic, and, in spite of his weakness and the tales he had heard of the other's powers, he felt that he could seize this man, hurl him down, and plant his foot upon his chest; for the buccaneer captain was without weapons, and stood looking up at him with one hand resting upon his hips, the other raised to his beardless face, with a well-shaped, small index finger slightly impressing his rounded cheek.

"Yes," he said again, mockingly, "Commodore Junk! Well, Humphrey Armstrong, what mad fit is this?"

"Mad fit!" cried Humphrey, quickly recovering himself. "You allowed me to be at liberty, and I am exploring the place."

The buccaneer looked in his eyes, with the mocking smile growing more marked.

"Is this Captain Humphrey Armstrong, the brave commander sent to exterminate me and mine, stooping to make a miserable excuse—to tell a lie!"

"A lie!" cried Humphrey, fiercely, as he took a step in advance.

"Yes, a lie!" said the buccaneer, without moving a muscle. "You were trying to find some way by which you could escape."

"Well," cried Humphrey, passionately, "I am a prisoner. I have refused to give my parole; I was trying to find some way of escape."

"That is more like you," said the buccaneer, quietly. "Why? What do you require? Are you not well treated by my men?"

"You ask me why," cried Humphrey—"me, whom you have defeated—disgraced, and whom you hold here a prisoner. You ask me why!"

"Yes. I whom you would have taken, and, if I had not died sword in hand, have hung at your yard-arm, and then gibbeted at the nearest port as a scarecrow."

He was silent, and the buccaneer went on—

"I have looked back, and I cannot see you placing a cabin at my disposal, seeing me nursed back from the brink of death, treated as a man would treat his wounded brother."

"No," cried Humphrey, quickly; "and why have you done all this when it would have been kinder to have slain me on that wretched day?"

"Why have I done this!" said the buccaneer, with the colour deepening in his swarthy face. "Ah, why have I done this! Perhaps," he continued bitterly, "because I said to myself: 'This is a brave, true, English gentleman;' and I find instead a man who does not hesitate to lie to screen his paltry effort to escape."

Humphrey made a menacing gesture; but the buccaneer did not stir.

"Look here, sir," he continued. "I am in this place more powerful among my people than the king you serve. You smile; but you will find that it is true."

"If I am not killed, sir, trying to make some effort to escape."

"Escape!" cried the buccaneer, with his face lighting up. "Man, you have been warned before that you cannot escape. The forest beyond where we stand is one dense thicket through which no man can pass unless he cut his way inch by inch. It is one vast solitude, standing as it has stood since the world was made."

"Bah!" cried Humphrey, scornfully. "A determined man could make his way."

"How far!" cried the buccaneer. "A mile—two miles—and then, what is there?—starvation, fever, and death—lest in that vast wilderness. Even the Indians cannot penetrate those woods and mountains. Will you not take my word!"

"Would you take mine," said Humphrey, scornfully, "if our places were changed! I shall escape."

The buccaneer smiled.

"You have an easy master, captain," he said, quietly; "but I would like to see you wear your chains more easily. Humphrey Armstrong, you cannot escape. There is only one way from this place, and that is by the sea, and there is no need to guard that. Look here," he cried, laying his hand upon the prisoner's arm, "you have been planning this for days and days. You have lain out yonder upon that stone by the old palace, calculating how you could creep away; and you found your opportunity to-day, when you said to yourself, 'These people are all asleep now, and I will find my way round to where my men are prisoners.'"

As he spoke Humphrey changed colour and winced, for the buccaneer seemed to have read his every thought.

"And then you came upon this path through the forest, and you felt that this was the way to freedom."

"Are you a devil?" cried Humphrey, excitedly.

"Perhaps," was the mocking reply. "Perhaps only the great butterfly you watched before you started, as it lazily winged its way among the broken stones."

Humphrey uttered an exclamation, and gazed wildly in the dark, mocking eyes.

"Never mind what I am, captain, but pray understand this—you cannot escape from here. When you think you are most alone, there are eyes upon you which see your every act, and your movements are all known."

"I will not believe it," cried Humphrey, angrily.

"Then disbelieve it; but it is true. I tell you there is no escape, man. You may get away a few miles perhaps, but every step you take bristles with the threatenings of death. So be warned, and bear your fate patiently. Wait! Grow strong once more."

"And then!" cried Humphrey, excitedly. "What then?"

"Ah, yes," said the buccaneer, who assumed not to have heard his words, "you are still weak. That flush in your face is the flush of fever, and you are low and excited."

"Dog! You are mocking me!" cried Humphrey, furiously, for he felt the truth of every word that had been said, and his impotence maddened him.

"Dog!" cried the buccaneer as furiously.

"Yes; wretched cut-throat—murderer," cried Humphrey—"miserable wretch, whom I could strangle where you stand!"

The buccaneer turned of a sallow pallor, his brow knit, his eyes flashed, and his chest heaved, as he stood glaring at Humphrey; but the sudden storm of passion passed away, and with a smile of pity he said softly—

"You call names like a petulant boy. Come, I am not angry with you, let us go back to your room. The heat of this place is too much for you, and to-morrow you will be down with fever."

"Humph!" ejaculated Humphrey, angrily.

"It is true," said the buccaneer. "Come."

"There's something behind all this," cried the young man, excitedly. "We are alone here. I am the stronger; and, in spite of your boasting, there is no one here to help. You shall speak out, and tell me what this means."

His gesture was threatening now; but the buccaneer did not stir.

"I am not alone," he said, quietly. "I never am without someone to protect me. But there, you shall be answered. Why have I had you tended as I have? Well, suppose I have said to myself, 'Here is a brave man who should be one of us.'"

"One of you!" cried Humphrey, with a scornful laugh.

"Suppose," continued the buccaneer, with his nether lip quivering slightly, "I had said to myself, 'You are alone here. Your men obey you, but you have no friends among them—no companions whom you can trust. Why not make this man your friend?'"

Humphrey smiled, and the buccaneer's lip twitched slightly as he continued—

"You are fevered and disappointed now, and I shall not heed your words. I tell you once for all that you must accept your fate here as others have accepted theirs. I need not tell you that for one to escape from here would be to bring ruin upon all. Hence every one is his brother's guardian; and the Indians for hundreds of miles around, at first our enemies till they felt my power, are now my faithful friends."

Humphrey laughed mockingly.

"You laugh, sir. Well it is the laugh of ignorance, as you will find. It is no idle boast when I say that I am king here over my people, and the tribes to north and south."

"The Indians too?" said Humphrey.

"Yes, the Indians too, as you found to your cost."

"To my cost?"

"To your cost. Your ship was in my way. You troubled me; and your people had to be removed. Well, they were removed."

"The treacherous hounds!" cried Humphrey, grinding his teeth as he recalled the action of the two Indians, and their escape.

"Treacherous! No. You would have employed men to betray me; it was but fighting you with your own weapons, sir; and these you call treacherous hounds were true, brave fellows who risked their lives to save me and mine."

Humphrey was silent.

"Come, Captain Armstrong; you will suffer bitterly for this. There are chills and fevers in the depths of this forest which seize upon strangers like you, especially upon those weakened by their wounds, and I do not want to lose the officer and gentleman who is to be my friend and help here, where I am, as it were, alone."

"Your friend and help!" said Humphrey, haughtily. "I am your prisoner, sir; but you forget to whom you are speaking. How dare you ask me to link my fate with that of your cut-throat band—to share with you a life of plunder and disgrace, with the noose at the yard-arm of every ship in His Majesty's Navy waiting to end your miserable career? I tell you—I tell you—"

He made a clutch at the nearest branch to save himself, for his head swam, black spots veiled in mist and strangely blurred seemed to be descending from above to form a blinding veil before his eyes. He recovered himself for a moment, long enough to resent the hand stretched out to save him, and then all was blank, and with a hoarse sigh he would have fallen heavily but for the strong arms that caught him, held him firmly for a few moments, and then a faint catching sigh was heard in the stillness of the forest, as Humphrey Armstrong was lowered slowly upon the moss and a soft brown hand laid upon his forehead, as the buccaneer bent down upon one knee by his side.

"Want me?" said a deep low voice; and the buccaneer started as if from a dream, with his face hardening, and the wrinkles which had been smoothed reappearing deeply in the broad forehead.

"You here, Bart?"

"Ay, I'm here."

"Watching me?"

"Ay, watching of you."

The buccaneer rose and gave the interloper an angry look.

"Well, why not!" said Bart. "How did I know what he'd do?"

"And you've seen and heard all?"

"Everything," said Bart, coolly.

"When I told you to be within hearing only if I whistled or called."

"What's the use of that when a blow or a stab would stop them both?"

"Bart, I—"

"Go on, I don't mind," said Bart, quietly, "I want to live, and if you was to come to harm that would be the end of me."

The buccaneer gave an impatient stamp, but Bart paid no heed.

"Give me a lift up and I'll carry him back," he said quietly.

All this was done, and Dinny summoned, so that when, an hour later, Humphrey unclosed his eyes, it was with his head throbbing with fever, a wild half-delirious dreaminess troubling his brain, and the great stone image glaring down at him through the dim green twilight of the prison room.

It was a bitter experience for the prisoner to find that he had overrated his powers. The effort, the excitement, and the malaria of the forest prostrated him for a fortnight, and at the end of that time he found that he was in no condition to make a further attempt at securing the means of escape.

He lay in his gloomy chamber thinking over the buccaneer's insolent proposal, and fully expected that he would resent the way in which it had been received; but to his surprise he received the greatest of attention, and wine, fruit, and various delicacies that had evidently come from the stores of some well-found ship were placed before him to tempt his appetite.

Dinny was his regular attendant, and always cheery and ready to help him in every way; but no more was said for a time respecting an evasion, though Humphrey was waiting his time; for after lying for hours, day after day, debating his position, he came to the conclusion that if he did escape it must be through this light-spirited Irishman.

His captor did not come to him as far as he knew; but he had a suspicion that more than once the buccaneer had been watching from some point or another unknown to him. But one day a message was brought by Bart, who entered the gloomy chamber and in his short, half-surly way thus delivered himself—

"Orders from the skipper, sir."

"Orders from your captain!" said Humphrey, flushing.

"To say that he is waiting for your answer, sir."

"My answer, man? I gave him my answer."

"And that he can wait any time; but a message from you that you want to see him will bring him here."

"There is no other answer," said Humphrey, coldly.

"Better not say that," said Bart, after standing gazing at the prisoner for some time.

"What do you mean?" cried Humphrey, haughtily.

"Don't know. What am I to say to the captain?"

"I have told you. There is no answer," said Humphrey, coldly, and he turned away, but lay listening intently, for it struck him that he had heard a rustle in the great stone corridor without, as if someone had been listening; but the thick carpet-like curtain fell, and he heard no more, only lay watching the faint rays of light which descended through the dense foliage of the trees, as some breeze waved them softly, far on high, and slightly relieved the prevailing gloom.

Bart's visit had started a current of thought which was once more running strongly when Dinny entered with a basket of the delicious little grapes which grew wild in the sunny open parts of the mountain slopes.

"There, sor," he said, "and all me own picking, except about half of them which Misthress Greenheys sint for ye. Will ye take a few bunches now?"

"Dinny," said Humphrey in a low earnest voice, "have you thought of what I said to you?"

"Faix, and which? what is it ye mane, sor?"

"You know what I mean, man: about helping me to escape from here?"

"About helping ye to eshcape, sor? Oh, it's that ye mane!"

"Yes, man; will you help me?"

"Will I help ye, sor? D'ye see these threes outside the windy yonder, which isn't a windy bekase it has no glass in it?"

"Yes, yes, I see," cried Humphrey with all a sick man's petulance.

"Well, they've got no fruit upon 'em, sor."

"No, of course not. They are not of a fruit-bearing kind. What of that!"

"Faix, an' if I helped ye to eshcape, captain, darlin', sure and one of 'em would be having fruit hanging to it before the day was out, and a moighty foine kind of pear it would be."

Chapter Twenty Six
Under Another Rule

"You're to keep to your prison till further orders," said Bart one day as he entered the place.

"Who says so!" cried Humphrey, angrily.

"Lufftenant."

"What! Mazzard?"

"Yes, sir. His orders."

"Curse Lieutenant Mazzard!" cried Humphrey. "Where is the captain!"

No answer.

"Is this so-called lieutenant master here!"

"Tries to be," grumbled Bart.

"The captain is away, then?"

"Orders are, not to answer questions," said Bart, abruptly; and he left the chamber.

Humphrey was better. The whims and caprices of a sick man were giving way to the return of health, and with this he began to chafe angrily.

He laughed bitterly and seated himself by the window to gaze out at the dim arcade of forest, and wait till such time as he felt disposed to go out, and then have a good wander about the ruins, and perhaps go down that path where he had been arrested by the appearance of the captain.

He had no hope of encountering any of his crew, for, from what he could gather, fully half the survivors, sick of the prisoner's life, had joined the buccaneer crew, while the rest had been taken to some place farther along the coast—where, he could not gather from Dinny, who had been letting his tongue run and then suddenly stopped short. But all the same he clung to the hope that in the captain's absence he might discover something which would help him in his efforts to escape and come back, if not as commander, at all events as guide to an expedition that should root out this hornets'-nest.

Mid-day arrived, and he was looking forward to the coming of Dinny with his meal, an important matter to a man with nothing to do, and only his bitter thoughts for companions. The Irishman lightened his weary hours too, and every time he came the captive felt some little hope of winning him over to help him to escape.

"Ah, Dinny, my lad!" he said as he heard a step, and the hanging curtain was drawn aside, "what is it to-day?"

"Fish, eggs, and fruit," said Bart, gruffly.

"Oh! it's you!" said Humphrey, bitterly. "Dinny away with that cursed schooner!"

"Schooner's as fine a craft as ever sailed," growled Bart. "Orders to answer no questions."

"You need not answer, my good fellow," said the prisoner, haughtily. "That scoundrel of a buccaneer is away—I know that, and Dinny is with him, or you would not be doing this."

Bart's heavy face lightened as he saw the bitterness of the prisoner's manner when he spoke of the captain; but it grew sombre directly after, as if he resented it; and spreading the meal upon a broad stone, covered with a white cloth—a stone in front of the great idol, and probably once used for human sacrifice—he sullenly left the place.

The prisoner sat for a few minutes by the window wondering whether Lady Jenny was thinking about him, and sighed as he told himself that she was pining for him as he pined for her. Then turning to the mid-day meal he began with capital appetite, and not at all after the fashion of a man in love, to discuss some very excellent fish, which was made more enjoyable by a flask of fine wine.

"Yes," he said, half aloud, "I shall go just where I please."

He stopped and listened, for a voice certainly whispered from somewhere close at hand the word "Kelly!"

"Yes! what is it? Who called?" said the prisoner, aloud.

There was a momentary silence, and then a peculiar whispering voice said—

"Don't be frightened."

"I'm not," said Humphrey, trying to make out whence the voice came, and only able to surmise that it was from somewhere over the dark corner where he slept.

"I want Dennis Kelly," said the voice.

"He's not here. Away with the schooner," continued Humphrey.

"Oh!"

The ejaculation came like a moan of disappointment.

"Here, who are you?" cried Humphrey.

"No; he cannot be away, sir. But hist! hush, for heaven's sake! You will be heard," said the voice. "Speak low."

"Well, I'll speak in a whisper if you like," said Humphrey. "But where are you?"

"Up above your chamber," was the reply. "There is a place where the stones are broken away."

"Then I am watched," thought Humphrey, as the announcement recalled the captain.

"Can you see me?" he asked.

"I cannot see you where you are now, but I could if you went and lay down upon your couch."

"Then I'll go there," said Humphrey, crossing the great chamber to throw himself on the blankets and skins. "Now, then, what do you want with Dinny?"

"I knew the captain had gone to sea," said the voice, evasively; "but I did not know Kelly had been taken too. He cannot be, without letting me know."

"Can you come down and talk to me!"

"No; you are too well watched."

"Then how did you get here?"

"I crept through the forest and climbed up," was the reply. "I can see you now."

"But how did you know you could see me there?"

"I thought I could. I was watching for someone a little while ago, and saw the captain looking down through here."

"I thought as much," said Humphrey, half aloud; and he was about to speak again when Bart entered suddenly, looked sharply round, and showed the wisdom of his new visitor by going straight to the window and looking out.

"Who were you talking to?" he said, gruffly, as he came back, still looking suspiciously round.

"To myself," said Humphrey, quite truthfully, for his last remark had been so addressed.

Bart uttered a grunt, and glanced at the dinner.

"Done?" he said.

"No. Surely I may spend as long as I like over my meals here."

Bart nodded and went out, the heavy curtain falling behind him; while Humphrey slowly rose and went back to the stone altar, where he filled a silver cup from the flask and drank, and then began humming an air. After this he walked to the curtain and peered cautiously through into the dark corridor, to see the heavy figure of the buccaneer's henchman go slowly along past the patches of dull green light streaming through the openings which occurred some thirty feet apart.

"Gone!" said Humphrey, returning quickly. "Are you there?"

"Yes. I could hear everything."

"Listen!" said Humphrey, quickly. "You are Mistress Greenheys?"

"Yes."

"And you love Dennis Kelly?"

There was silence.

"You need not fear me. I know your history," continued Humphrey. "You are, like myself, a prisoner and in the power of that black-looking lieutenant."

There was a piteous sigh here, and then came with a sob—

"I am a miserable slave, sir."

"Yes, yes, I know. Then look here, can we not all escape together?"

"Escape, sir! How?"

"Through Dinny's help."

"He would not give it, sir. It would be impossible. I—I—there! I will speak out, sir—I can bear this horrible life no longer! I have asked him to take me away."

"Well, will he not?"

"He is afraid, sir."

"And yet he loves you?"

"He says so."

"And you believe it, or you would not run risks by coming here?"

"Risks!" said the woman, with a sigh. "If Mazzard knew I came here he would kill me!"

"The wretch!" muttered Humphrey. Then aloud, "Dinny must help us. Woman, surely.you can win him to our side! You will try!"

"Try, sir! I will do anything!"

"Work upon his feelings, and I will try and do the same."

"He fears the risk of the escape, and also what may happen to him when he gets back to England. He has been a buccaneer, and, he tells me, a soldier. He will be charged with desertion."

"I will answer for his safety," said Humphrey, hastily. And then running to the curtain he made sure that Bart was not listening.

"Be cautious," he said, as he went back and began to pace up and down, with his eyes fixed upon the ground. "Tell me, could we get a boat?"

"I don't know, sir; I think so. Would it not be better to take to the forest?"

"That we must consider. First of all, Dinny must be won over."

"I will try."

"How could I communicate with you?"

"You could not, sir. I came to-day to warn Dinny to be cautious, for Mazzard suspects something. He has gone to the men's place, or I could not be here."

"But you can come sometimes and speak to me. You will be able to know whether anyone is here."

"If I can come, sir," said the woman; "but it is very difficult. The Commodore is always about; nothing escapes him."

"A scoundrel!"

"I don't think he is such a very bad man," said the woman.

"Indeed! Ah, women always find an excuse for a good-looking scoundrel!"

"I don't think a man who is faithful to the woman he loved can be very bad," said the voice, softly.

"Faithful! why, I suppose he has a dozen wives here?"

"He! Oh, no! I don't know, sir, exactly, but I have seen him go to the old chamber in one of these ruinous places, and he goes there to pray by the side of a coffin."

"What!" cried Humphrey.

"Yes, a coffin; and it contains the body of the woman he loved, or else of his sister. No one here knows but Dinny and Bart, and—"

"Hist!" whispered Humphrey, catching up a bunch of grapes and beginning to eat them.

He had heard the distant step of his guardian, and then there was silence, for Bart seemed to creep up and listen before entering, which he did at last, to find the prisoner muttering to himself and eating the grapes.

"Done?"

"Yes. You can clear away."

Bart obeyed and turned to go, but as he reached the curtain —

"You have plenty of cigars?" he said.

"I?"

"Ah, well, I've got some there," growled Bart, and he handed the prisoner half a dozen roughly-made rolls of the tobacco-leaf. "Now, you understand," he continued, as he made to go once more, "you're to keep here till the skipper comes back."

"Are you afraid I shall escape?" said Humphrey, contemptuously.

"Not a bit, captain; but when one man's life depends on another's, it makes him careful."

The curtain dropped behind him, and Humphrey stood listening and thinking.

Bart's step could be faintly heard now, and, feeling safe, the prisoner went back to his couch, and gazed up in the direction from whence the voice had come.

"Are you still there?" he said, softly.

There was no reply; and a repetition of the question was followed by the same silence.

"It's strange," he said, gazing up in the gloom overhead to where, in the midst of a good deal of rough carving, there seemed to be a small opening, though he could not be sure. "Why should he come and watch me, and take this interest in my well-being? I am not like an ordinary prisoner, and his friendly way, his submission to the rough contempt with which I treated him — it's strange, very strange! What can it mean?"

He threw himself upon the couch, to lie for some time thinking and trying to interpret the meaning; but all was black and confused as the dark mass of carving from which the woman's voice had seemed to come; and, giving it up at last, he rose, and without any hesitation walked straight out through the opening, and made his way along the corridor to where the sun blazed forth and made him stand and shade his eyes, as he remained considering which way he should go.

The prisoner made a bold dash in a fresh direction, going straight toward where he believed the men's quarters to be; and, as before, the moment he had passed behind the ruins he found himself face to face with a dense wall of verdure, so matted together that, save to a bird or a small animal, farther progress was impossible.

Defeated here, he tried another and another place, till his perseverance was rewarded by the finding of one of the dark, maze-like paths formed by cutting away the smaller growth and zig-zagging through the trees.

Into this dark pathway he plunged, to find that at the end of five minutes he had lost all idea, through its abrupt turns, of the direction in which he was going; while before he had penetrated much farther the pathway forked, and, unable to decide which would lead him in the required direction, he took the path to the right.

It was plain enough that these green tunnels through the forest had been cut by the buccaneers for purposes of defence in case of an enemy carrying their outer works, so that he was in no way surprised to find the path he had taken led right to a huge crumbling stone building, whose mossy walls rose up among the trees sombre and forbidding, and completely barring his way.

It was a spot where a few resolute men might keep quite an army at bay, for the walls were of enormous extent, the windows mere stone lattices, and the doorway in front so low that a stooping attitude was necessary for him who would enter. This was consequent upon the falling of stones from above, and the blocking partially of the way.

There was a strange, mysterious aspect in the place, overgrown as it was with the redundant growth, which fascinated the explorer, and feeling impelled to go on he gave one glance sound, and was about to enter, when out of the utter stillness he heard a low sound as if someone had been watching him and given vent to a low exhalation of the breath.

Humphrey started and looked sharply round, unable to restrain a shudder: but no one was visible, and he was about to go on, feeling ashamed of his nervousness, when the sound was repeated, this time from above his head; and glancing up, he leaped back, for twenty feet above his head in the green gloom there was a curious, impish face gazing down at him; and as he made out more and more of the object, it seemed as if some strange goblin were suspended in mid-air and about to drop down upon his head.

"It's the darkness, I suppose," exclaimed Humphrey, angrily, as he uttered a loud hiss, whose effect was to make the strange object give itself a swing and reveal the fact that it was hanging by its tail alone from the end of a rope-like vine which depended from the vast ceiling of interlacing leaves.

With apparently not the slightest effort the goblin-like creature caught a loop of the same vine, clung there for a moment to gaze back at the intruder into this weird domain, displaying its curiously human countenance, and then sped upwards, when there was a rush as of a wave high above the visible portion of the interlacing boughs, and Humphrey knew that he had startled quite a flock of the little forest imps, who sped rapidly away.

"I must be very weak still," he muttered as he went now right up to the entrance, and after peering cautiously in for a moment or two he entered.

It was dim outside in the forest; here, after picking his way cautiously for a stop or two, it was nearly black. The place had probably been fairly lit when it was first constructed, far back in the dim past before the forest invaded the district and hid away these works of man; but now the greatest caution was needed to avoid the fallen blocks of masonry, and the explorer took step after step with the care of one who dreaded some chasm in his way.

He stopped and listened, for suddenly from his left there was a faint echoing splash so small and fine that it must have been caused by the drip of a bead of water from the roof, but it had fallen deep down into some dark hollow half filled with water, and a shiver ran through Humphrey's frame as he thought of the consequences of a slip into such a place, far from help, and doomed to struggle for a few minutes grasping at the dripping stony walls, seeking a means of climbing out, and then falling back into the darkness of the great unknown.

He felt as if he must turn back, but his eyes were now growing accustomed to the obscurity, and he made out that just in front there was, faintly marked out, the opening of a doorway leading into a chamber into which some faint light penetrated.

Going cautiously forward, he entered, to find to his astonishment that he was in a fair sized room whose stone walls were elaborately carved, as were the dark recesses or niches all around, before each of which sat, cross-legged, a well-carved image which seemed to be richly ornamented in imitation of its old highly-decorated dress. For a moment in the obscurity it seemed as if he had penetrated into the abode of the ancient people who had built the ruined city, and that here they were seated around in solemn conclave to discuss some matter connected with the long low form lying upon the skin spread floor, while to make the scene the more incongruous, these strangely-carved figures were looking down upon the object, which was carefully draped with a large Union Jack.

Humphrey paused just inside the threshold and removed his cap, for Sarah Greenheys' words recurred to him, and it seemed that he must have strayed into one of the many old temples of the place which had been turned by Commodore Junk into a mausoleum for the remains of the woman he was said to have loved, the draped object being without doubt the coffin which held her remains.

He stood gazing down at the coloured flag for a time; then with a glance round at the olden idols or effigies of the departed great of the place, and the dark niches at the mouths of which they sat, he went softly out, glanced to his right, and saw an opening which evidently gave, upon the chasm where he had heard the water drip, and stepped out once more into the comparative daylight of the forest.

The place might be used as a retreat, he thought, but its present use was plain enough, and he walked quickly back to where the path had branched, and took the other fork.

This narrow tunnel through the forest suddenly debouched upon another going across it at right, angles, and after a moment's hesitation the prisoner turned to the left, and to his great delight found that he had solved one of the topographical problems of the place, for this led towards what was evidently the outer part of the buccaneers' settlement, and of this he had proof by hearing the smothered sound of voices, which became clear as he proceeded, and at last were plainly to be made out as coming from a ruined building standing upon a terrace whose stones were lifted in all directions by the growth around.

This place had been made open by the liberal use of the axe and fire, half-burned trunks and charred roots of trees lying in all directions, the consequence being that Humphrey had to stop short at the mouth of the forest path unless he wanted to be seen. For, to judge from the eager talking, it was evident that a number of men were gathered in the great building at whose doorless opening the back of one of the buccaneers could be seen as he leaned against the stone, listening to someone who, in a hoarse voice which the listener seemed to recognise, was haranguing the rest.

Humphrey could not hear all that was said, but a word fell upon his ear from time to time, and as he pieced these words together it seemed as if the speaker were declaiming against tyranny and oppression, and calling upon his hearers to help him to put an end to the state of affairs existing.

Then came an excited outburst, as the speaker must have turned his face toward the door, for these words came plainly:

"The end of it will be that they'll escape, and bring a man-of-war down upon us, and all through his fooling." A murmur arose.

"He's gone mad, I tell you all; and if you like to choose a captain for yourselves, choose one, and I'll follow him like a man; but it's time something was done if we want to live." Another burst of murmurs rose here.

"He's mad, I tell you, or he wouldn't keep him like that. So what's it to be, my lads, a new captain or the yard-arm?"

Chapter Twenty Seven
Dinny Consents

The time glided on, and Humphrey always knew when his captor was at sea, for the severity of his imprisonment was then most felt. The lieutenant, Mazzard, was always left in charge of the place, but Bart remained behind by the captain's orders, and at these times Humphrey was sternly ordered to keep to his prison.

Dinny came and went, but, try him how he would, Humphrey could get nothing from him for days and days.

The tide turned at last.

"Well, sor," said Dinny one morning, "I've been thinking it over a great dale. I don't like desarting the captain, who has been like a brother to me; but there's Misthress Greenheys, and love's a wonderful excuse for a manny things."

"Yes," said Humphrey, eagerly, "go on."

"Sure, sor, she's compelled to be married like to a man she hates, and it hurts her falings as much as it does mine, and she wants me to get her away and make a rale marriage of it, such as a respectable woman likes; for ye see, all against her will, she's obliged to be Misthress Mazzard now, and there hasn't been any praste."

"I understand," said Humphrey. "The scoundrel!"

"Well, yes, sir, that's what he is; but by the same token I don't wonder at it, for if a man stood bechuckst good and avil and Misthress Greenheys was on the avil side, faix, he'd be sure to go toward the avil—at laste, he would if he was an Oirishman."

"Then you will!"

"Yis, sor, for the lady's sake; but I shall have to give up my share of the good things here, and behave very badly to the captain."

"My good fellow, I will provide you for life."

"That's moighty kind of you, sor, and I thank ye. Yis, I'll do it, for, ye see, though I don't want to behave badly to the captain, Black Mazzard's too much for me; and besides, I kape thinking that if, some day or another, I do mate wid an accident and get dancing on the toight-rope, I sha'n't have a chance of wedding the widdy Greenheys, and that would be a terrible disappointment to the poor darlin'."

"Yes, yes," cried Humphrey, impatiently. "Then tell me. You will help me by getting a boat ready, and we can all go down together and put to sea!"

"Hark at him!" said Dinny, with a laugh, after going to the great curtain and peering into the corridor. "Ye spake, sor, like a gintleman coming out of his house and calling for a kyar. Lave that all to me."

"I will, Dinny; but what do you propose doing, and when!"

"What do I propose doing, sor? Oh! it's all settled. The darlin' put an idee in my head, and it's tuk root like a seed."

"Trust a woman for ingenuity!" cried Humphrey, speaking with the authority of one who knew, though as to women's ways he was a child.

"Ah, an' she's a cliver one, sor!"

"Well, what is it, Dinny?" cried Humphrey, excitedly.

"Be aisy, sor, and lave it to us. The darlin' has set her moind on getting away from Black Mazzard, and she's too gintle a crature to go to extremities and tuk his head off some night like the lady did in the tint, or to handle a hammer and a nail and fix his head to the ground. She don't like to be too hard upon him, sor, so she proposed a plan to me, and it will be all right."

"But, Dinny—"

"Be aisy, sor, or ye'll spoil all. Jist wait quite riddy, like, till some avening I shall come to ye all in a hurry, hold up me little finger to ye, which will mane come, and ye'll foind it all cut and dhried for ye."

"But, my good fellow—"

"Faix, sor, don't go on like that before I've done. I want to say that ye must be at home here riddy. If the skipper asks ye to dinner, don't go; and if ye hear a big, powerful noise, don't git running out to see what it is, but go on aisy like, saying to yerself, 'Dinny's getting riddy for me, and he may come at anny time.'"

"And are you going to keep me in the dark?"

"An' he calls it kaping him in the dark! Ah, well, sor, I won't do that! I'll jist tell ye, thin. Ye know the owld chapel place?"

"Chapel!"

"Well, church, thin, sor. That's what they say it was. The little wan wid the stone picture of the owld gintleman sitting over the door."

"That square temple?"

"Yis, sor. It's all the same. The haythens who lived out here didn't know any betther, and the prastes were a bad lot, so they used to worship the owld gintleman, and give him a prisoner ivery now and then cut up aloive."

"Nonsense! How do you know that?"

"Faix, it's written on the stones so; and we found them althers wid places for the blood to run, and knives made out of flint-glass. It's thrue enough."

"But what about the temple?"

"Sure, it is the divil's temple, sor," said Dinny, with a twinkle of the eye; "and the skipper said it was just the place for it, so he fills it full of our divil's dust."

"Money?"

"An' is it money? That's all safe in another place, wid silver and gowld bars from the mines, as we tuk in ships, and gowld cups, sor. That's put away safe, for it's no use here, where there isn't a whisky-shop to go and spend it. No, sor; divil's dust, the black gunpowther."

"Oh, the magazine! Well, what of that?"

"Sure, sor, the darlin' put her pretty little lips close to my ear. 'Och, darlin', and loight of my ois,' I says. 'Sure, it's so dark in the wood here that ye've made a mistake. That's me ear, darlin', and not me mouth. Let me show ye'—"

"'No, Dinny,' she says, 'I'm like being another man's wife now, and I can foind me way to yer lips whether it's dark or light when it's proper and dacent to do so, and we've been to church.'"

"Dinny, you'll drive me mad!" cried Humphrey, impatiently.

"An' is it dhrive ye mad, when I'm thrying to set ye right? Then I'd better not tell ye, sor."

"Yes, yes! For goodness' sake, man, go on."

"Ah, well, thin, an' I will! She jist puts her lips to my ear and she says, 'Dinny, if ye lay a thrain from the powdher-magazine'—think of that now, the darlin'!—'lay a thrain,' she says, Dinny, 'and put a slow-match, same as ye have riddy for firing the big guns, and then be sure,' she says, 'and get out of the way'—as if I'd want to shtay, sor, and be sent to hiven in a hurry—'thin,' she says, 'the whole place will be blown up, and iverybody will be running to see what's the matther and put out the fire, and they'll be so busy wid that, they'll forget all about the prishner, and we can go down to the say and get away.'"

"Yes," said Humphrey, thoughtfully. "Is there much powder stored there!"

"Yis, sor, a dale. Ivery time a ship's been tuk all the powdher has been brought ashore and put there. It's a foin plan, sor, and all made out of the darlin's own head."

"Yes, Dinny, we ought to get away then."

"Sure, an' we will, sor. I'll have a boat wid plenty of wather and sun-dhried mate in her, and some fruit and fishing-lines. We shall do; but the plan isn't perfect yet."

"Why?"

"Sure, an' there's no arrangement for getting Black Mazzard to come that time to count over the powdher-barrels."

"What! and blow the scoundrel up!"

"Sure, sor, and it would be a kindness to him. He's the wickedest divil that ever breathed, and he gets worse ivery day, so wouldn't it be a kindness to try and send him to heaven before he gets too bad to go! But whist! I've stopped too long, sor. Ye understand?"

"Dinny, get me away from here, and you're a made man!"

"Faix, I dunno, sor. Mebbe there'll be one lot'll want to shoot me for a desarter—though I desarted by force—and another lot'll want to hang me for a pirate. I don't fale at all safe; but I know I shall be tuk and done for some day if I shtop, and as the darlin' says she'll niver make a mistake the right way wid her lips till I've taken her from Black Mazzard, why, I'll do the thrick."

More days passed, and every stroll outside his prison had to be taken by Humphrey with Bart as close to him as his shadow.

Dinny kept away again, and the plan to escape might as well have never been uttered.

Bart always went well-armed with his prisoner, and seemed unusually suspicious, as if fearing an attempt at escape.

Dinny's little widow came no more, and the hours grew so irksome with the confinement consequent upon the captains absence that Humphrey longed for his return.

He debated again and again all he had heard, and came to the conclusion that if he said anything it must be to the captain himself.

One morning Bart's manner showed that something had occurred. His sour face wore a smile, and he was evidently greatly relieved of his responsibility as he said to the prisoner:

"There, you can go out."

"Has the captain returned?"

Bart delivered himself of a short nod.

"Tell him I wish to see him. Bid him come here."

"What! the skipper? You mean, ask him if I may take you to him, and he'll see you."

"I said, Tell your skipper to come here!" said Humphrey, drawing himself up and speaking as if he were on the quarterdeck. "Tell him I wish to see him at once."

Bart drew a long breath, and wrinkled up his forehead so that it seemed as if he had an enormous weight upon his head. Then, smiling grimly, he slowly left the place.

The buccaneer, who looked anxious and dispirited, was listening to some complaint made by his lieutenant, and angry words were passing which made Bart as he heard them hasten his steps, and look sharply from one to the other as he entered.

Black Mazzard did what was a work of supererogation as he encountered Bart's eye—he scowled, his face being villainous enough without.

"Well," he said aloud, "I've warned you!" and he strode out of the old temple-chamber which formed the captain's quarters, his heavy boots thrust down about his ankles sounding dull on the thick rugs spread over the worn stones, and then clattering loudly as he stepped outside.

"You two been quarrelling?" said Bart, sharply.

"The dog's insolence is worse than ever!" cried the captain with flashing eyes. "Bart, I don't want to shed the blood of the man who has been my officer, but—"

"Let someone else bleed him," growled Bart. "Dick would; Dinny would give anything to do it. We're 'bout tired of him. I should like the job myself."

"Silence!" said the captain, sternly. "No, speak: tell me, what has been going on since I've been away?"

"Black Mazzard?"

The captain nodded.

"Half the time—well, no: say three-quarters—he's been drunk, t'other quarter he's spent in the south ruins preaching to the men."

"Preaching?"

"Yes, with you for text. Just in his old way; but I've been too busy with the prisoner."

"Yes, and he?"

"It's him who is master here. Here, get up!" The buccaneer started, threw back his head, and the dark eyes flashed as he exclaimed—

"What's this, sir? Have you been taking a lesson from Mazzard?"

"I? No; I'm only giving you your orders!"

"What orders?"

"Master Captain Humphrey Armstrong's. You're to get up and go to him directly. He wants you!"

The buccaneer sprang to his feet.

"He wants me—he has sent for me?" he cried, eagerly.

"Ay! You're to go to him. He's master here!"

A dull lurid flush came over the captain's swarthy face as his eyes encountered those of his henchman, and he frowned heavily.

"Of course you'll go!" said Bart, bitterly. "I should give up everything to him now, and let him do as he likes!"

"Bart!"

"Oh, all right! Say what you like, I don't mind. Only, if it's to be so, let him hang me out of my misery, and have done with it."

The buccaneer turned upon him fiercely, and his lips parted to speak; but as he saw the misery and despair in Bart's face his own softened.

"Is this my old friend and help speaking?" he said, softly. "I did not expect it, Bart, from you. Why do you speak to me like this?"

"Because you are going wrong. Because I can see how things are going to be, and it's natural for me to speak. Think I'm blind?"

"No, Bart, old friend. I only think you exaggerate and form ideas that are not true. I know what you mean; but you forget that I am Commodore Junk, and so I shall be to the end. Now, tell me," he continued, calmly; "this captain of the sloop asks to see me?"

"Orders you to come to him!"

"Well, he is accustomed to order, and illness has made him petulant. I will go."

"You'll go?"

"Yes. Perhaps he has something to say in answer to an offer I made."

"An offer?"

"Yes, Bart, to join us, and be one of my lieutenants."

"Join us, and be your lufftenant?" cried Bart.

"Yes, and my friend. I like him for the sake of his old generous ways, and I like him for his present manliness."

"You—like him?"

"Yes. It is not impossible, is it, that I should like to have a friend?"

"Friend?"

"Yes!" said the captain, sternly; "another friend! Don't stare, man, and think of the past. Mary Dell died, and lies yonder in the old temple, covered by the Union Jack, and Abel Dell still lives—Commodore Junk, seeking to take vengeance upon those who cut that young life short."

"Look here!" said Bart, who gasped as he listened to his companion's wild utterances; "are you going mad?"

"No, Bart, I am as sane as you."

"But you said—"

"What I chose to say, man. Let me believe all that if I like. Do you suppose I do not want some shield against the stings of my own thoughts? I choose to think all that, and it shall be so. You shall think it too. I am Commodore Junk, and if I wish this man to be my friend, and he consents, it shall be so!"

"And suppose some day natur says, 'I'm stronger than you, and I'll have my way,' what then?"

"I'll prove to nature, Bart, that she lies, for she shall not have her way. If at any time I feel myself the weaker, there are my pistols; there is the sea; there is the great tank with its black waters deep down below the temple."

"And you are going there—to him!"

"I am going there to him. Can you not trust me, Bart?"

The poor fellow made a weary gesture with his hands, and then, as the captain drew himself up, looking supremely handsome in his picturesque garb, and with his face flushed and brightened eyes, Bart followed him towards Humphrey's prison, walking at a distance, and with something of the manner of a faithful watch-dog who had been beaten heavily, but who had his duties to fulfil, and would do them till he died.

Chapter Twenty Eight
Another Duel

"Is that his step? No; its that miserable gaoler's," said Humphrey, as he lay back on his soft skin-covered couch with his arms beneath his head in a careless, indolent attitude.

Humphrey was beginning to feel the thrill of returning strength in his veins, and it brought with it his old independence of spirit and the memory that he had been trained to rule. His little episode with Bart that morning had roused him a little, and prepared him for his encounter with the buccaneer captain, upon whom he felt he was about to confer a favour.

A smile played about his lips as the step drew nearer, the difference between it and that of Bart being more and more marked as he listened, and then quite closed his eyes, while the heavy curtain was drawn aside, and the buccaneer entered the chamber. He took a step or two forward, which placed him in front of the stone idol, and there he stood gazing down at the handsome, manly figure of his prisoner, whose unstudied attitude formed a picture in that weird, picturesque place, which made the captain's breath come and go a little more quickly, and a faint sensation of vertigo tempt him to turn and hurry away.

The sensation was momentary. A frown puckered his brow, and he said quietly —

"Asleep?"

"No," said Humphrey, opening his eyes slowly; "no, my good fellow. I was only thinking."

The buccaneer frowned a little more heavily as he listened to his prisoner's cool, careless words, and felt the contemptuous tone in which he was addressed.

"You sent for me," he said, harshly, and his voice sounded coarse and rough.

"Well," said Humphrey, with insolent contempt, "how many ships have you plundered—how many throats have you cut this voyage?"

The buccaneer's eyes seemed to flash as he took a step forward, and made an angry gesture. But he checked himself on the instant, and, with a faint smile, replied—

"Captain Armstrong is disposed to be merry. Why have you sent for me?"

"Merry!" said Humphrey, still ignoring the question; "one need be, shut up in this tomb. Well, you are back again?"

"Yes; I am back again," said the buccaneer, smoothing his brow, and declining to be angry with his prisoner for his insulting way as he still lay back on the couch. "It is but the pecking of a prisoned bird," he said to himself.

"And not been caught and hanged yet? I was in hope that I had seen the last of you."

"I have heard tell before of prisoners reviling their captors," said the buccaneer, quietly.

"Revile! Well, is it not your portion!"

"For treating you with the consideration due to a gentleman?" said the buccaneer, whose features grew more calm and whose eyes brightened as if from satisfaction at finding the prisoner so cool and daring, and in how little account he was held. "I have given orders that the prisoner should be treated well. Is there anything more I can do?"

The harsh grating voice had grown soft, deep, rich, and mellow, while the dark, flashing eyes seemed to have become dreamy as they rested upon the prisoner's handsome, defiant face.

"Yes," said Humphrey, bitterly; "give me my liberty."

The buccaneer shook his head.

"Curse you! No; you profess to serve me—to treat me well—and you keep me here barred up like some wild beast whom you have caged."

"Barred—caged!" said the buccaneer, raising his eyebrows. "You have freedom to wander where you will."

"Bah! freedom!" cried Humphrey, springing up. "Curse you! why don't I strangle you where you stand?"

At that moment there was a rustling among the leaves outside the window, and Humphrey burst into a mocking laugh.

"How brave!" he cried. "The buccaneer captain comes to see his unarmed prisoner, and his guards wait outside the doorway, while another party stop by the window, ready to spring in."

The buccaneer's face turned of a deep dull red—the glow of annoyance, as he strode to the window and exclaimed fiercely—

"Why are you here? Go!"

"But—"

"Go, Bart," said the buccaneer, more quietly. "Captain Armstrong will not injure me."

There was a heavy rustling sound among the leaves and the buccaneer made as if to go to the great curtain; but he checked himself, turned, and smiling sadly—

"Captain Armstrong will believe me when I tell him that there is no one out there. Come, sir, you have sent for me. You have thought well upon all I said. All this has been so much angry petulance, and you are ready to take me by the hand—to become my friend. No, no; hear me. You do not think of what your life here may be."

"That of a pirate—a murderer!" cried Humphrey, scornfully.

"No," said the buccaneer, flushing once more. "I am rich. All that can be a something of the past. This land is mine, and here we can raise up a new nation, for my followers are devoted to me. Come! are we to be friends?"

"Friends!" cried Humphrey, scornfully—"a new nation—your people devoted!—why man, I sent for you to warn you!"

"You—to warn me?"

"Yes. One of your followers is plotting against you. He has been addressing your men; and if you don't take care, my good sir, you will be elevated over your people in a way more lofty than pleasant to the king of a new nation."

"I understand your sneers, sir," said the buccaneer, quietly; and there was more sadness than anger in his tone. "They are unworthy of the brave man who has warned me of a coming danger, and they are from your lips, sir, not from the heart of the brave adversary I have vowed to make my friend."

Humphrey winced, for the calm reproachful tone roused him, and he stood there frowning as the buccaneer went on.

"As to the plotting against me, I am always prepared for that. A man in my position makes many enemies. Even you have yours."

"Yes—you," cried Humphrey.

"No; I am a friend. There, I thank you for your warning. It is a proof, though you do not know it, that the gap between us grows less. Some day, Captain Armstrong, you will take my hand. We shall be friends."

Humphrey remained silent as the buccaneer left the chamber, and, once more alone, the prisoner asked himself if this was true—that he had bidden farewell to civilisation for ever, and this was to be his home, this strange compound of savage fierceness and gentle friendliness his companion to the end?

Chapter Twenty Nine
The Assassins

Humphrey Armstrong walked on blindly farther and farther into the forest, for he was moved more deeply than ever he had been moved before. The presence of this man was hateful to him, and yet he seemed to possess an influence that was inexplicable; and his soft deep tones, which alternated with his harsher utterances, rang in his ears now he was away.

"Good heavens!" he cried at last, as he nearly struck against one of the stone images which stood out almost as grey and green as the trees around, "what an end to an officer's career—the lieutenant of a wretched pirate king! New nation! Bah! what madness!"

"Captivity has unmanned me," he said to himself, as he sat down upon a mossy fragment of stone in the silent forest path, and the utter silence and calm seemed refreshing.

He sat thus for some time, with his head resting upon his hand, gazing back along the narrow path, when, to his horror, just coming into view, he saw the figure of the buccaneer approaching, with head bent and arms crossed over his chest, evidently deep in thought.

Humphrey started up and backed away round a curve before turning, and walked swiftly along the path, looking eagerly for a track by which he could avoid another encounter, when for the first time he became aware of the fact that he was in the way leading to the old temple which had been formed into a mausoleum, and, unless he should be able to find another path, bound for the ancient structure.

He almost ran along the meandering path, feeling annoyed with himself the while, till the gloomy pile loomed before him, and he climbed up the doorway and looked back.

All was silent and dim as he stooped and entered, stepping cautiously on, and then, as soon as well sheltered, turning to gaze back and see if the buccaneer came in sight.

The place struck chill and damp; there was a mysterious feeling of awe to oppress him as he recalled the chamber behind him, or rather, as he stood, upon his left; and its use, and the strange figures he had seen seated about, all added to the sense of awe and mystery by which he was surrounded; while the feeling of annoyance that he should have shrunk from meeting this man increased.

Just then there was the faint drip of water as he had heard it before, followed by the whispering echoes; and, moved by the desire to know how near he was to what must be a deep well-like chasm, he stooped, felt about him, and his hand encountered a good-sized fragment of the stone carving which had mouldered and been thrust by the root of some growing plant from the roof.

He did not pause to think, but threw it from him, to hear it strike against stone.

It had evidently missed what he intended, and he had turned to gaze again at the path, when he found that it had struck somewhere and rebounded, to fall with a hideous hollow echoing plash far below.

Humphrey's brow grew damp as he listened to the strange whispers of the water; and then he looked once more at the path, wondering whether the horrible noise had been heard, for just then the buccaneer came into sight and walked slowly toward the old temple.

But the echoes of that plash were too much shut up in the vast hollow below, and the buccaneer, still with his arms folded and chin resting upon his chest, walked on, evidently to enter the old building.

Humphrey hesitated for a moment, half intending to boldly meet his captor; but he shrank from the encounter, and weakly backed away farther into the darkness, till he was in the dim chamber where the coffin lay draped as before, and the strange figures of the old idols sat around.

There was no time for further hesitation. He must either boldly meet the buccaneer or hide.

He chose the latter course, glancing round for a moment, and then stepping cautiously into one of the recesses behind a sitting figure, where he could stand in complete darkness and wait till the buccaneer had gone.

The latter entered the next moment, and Humphrey felt half mad with himself at his spy-like conduct, for as he saw dimly the figure enter, he heard a low piteous moan, and saw him throw himself upon his knees beside the draped coffin, his hands clasped, and his frame bending with emotion, as in a broken voice he prayed aloud.

His words were incoherent, and but few of the utterances reached the listening man's ears, as he bit his lips with anger, and then listened with wonder at what seemed a strange revelation of character.

"Oh, give me strength!" he murmured. "I swore revenge—on all—for the wrongs for the death—loved—strength to fight down the weakness—to be—self—for strength—for strength—to live—revenge—death."

The last word of these agonised utterances was still quivering upon the air as if it had been torn from the speaker's breast, when the dimly-seen doorway was suddenly darkened, and there was a quick movement.

Humphrey Armstrong's position was one which enabled him, faint as was the light, to see everything—the draped coffin, the kneeling figure bent over it prostrate in agony of spirit, and a great crouching form stealing softly behind as if gathering for a spring.

Was it Bart? No; and the doorway was again darkened, and he saw that two more men were there.

Friends? Attendants? No. There was the dull gleam of steel uplifted by the figure bending over the buccaneer.

Assassination without doubt. The moment of peril had come, lightly as it had been treated, and, stirred to the heart by the treachery and horror of the deed intended, Humphrey sprang from his place of concealment, struck the buccaneer's assailant full in the chest, and they rolled out together on the temple floor.

"Quick, lads, help!" shouted the man whom Humphrey had seized, and his companions rushed in, for a general mêlée to ensue at terrible disadvantage, for the assailants were armed with knives, and those they assailed defenceless as to weapons other than those nature had supplied.

Humphrey knew this to his cost in the quick struggle which ensued. He had writhed round as he struggled with the would-be murderer, and contrived to get uppermost, when a keen sense of pain, as of a red-hot wire passing through one of his arms, made him loosen his hold for a moment, and the next he was dashed back.

He sprang up, though, to seize his assailant, stung by the pain into a fit of savage rage, when, as he clasped an enemy, he found that it was not his first antagonist, but a lesser man, with whom he closed fiercely just as the fellow was striving to get out of the doorway—a purpose he effected, dragging Humphrey with him.

The passage was darker than the inner temple, where hoarse panting and the sounds of contention were still going on, oaths, curses, and commands uttered in a savage voice to "Give it him now!"—"Now strike, you fool!"—"Curse him, he's like an eel!"—and the like came confusedly through the doorway, as, smarting with pain and grinding his teeth with rage, Humphrey struggled on in the passage, savagely determined to retain this one a prisoner, as he fought to get the mastery of the knife.

How it all occurred was more than he could afterwards clearly arrange in his own mind; what he could recall was that the pain weakened him, and the man with whom he struggled wrenched his left arm free, snatched the knife he held from his right hand, and would have plunged it into Humphrey's breast had not the latter struck him a sharp blow upwards in the face so vigorously, that the knife fell tinkling on the ground, and the struggle was resumed upon more equal terms.

It was a matter of less than a minute, during which Humphrey in his rage and pain fought less for life than to master his assailant and keep him prisoner. They had been down twice, tripping over the stone-strewn pavement, and once Humphrey had been forced against the wall, but by a sudden spring he had driven his opponent backwards, and they were struggling in the middle of the opening, when a wild shriek rang out from the inner temple—a cry which seemed to curdle the young officer's blood — and this was followed by a rush of someone escaping.

His retreat was only witnessed by one, for the struggle was continued on the floor. The two adversaries, locked in a tight embrace, strove to reach the feet, and, panting and weak, Humphrey had nearly succeeded in so doing, when his foe forced him backwards, and he fell to cling to the rugged stonework.

For as he was driven back the flooring seemed to crumble away beneath his feet; there was a terrible jerk, and he found himself hanging by his hands, his enemy clinging to him still, and the weight upon his muscles seeming as if it would tear them apart. In the hurry and excitement Humphrey could hardly comprehend his position for the moment. The next he understood it too well, for the stone which had given way fell with a hideous echoing noise, which came from a terrible distance below.

Almost in total darkness, his hands cramped into the interval between two masses of broken stone which formed part of the *débris* of the roof above, hanging over a hideous gulf at the full stretch of his arms, and with his adversary's hands fixed, talon-like, in garb and dress as he strove to clamber up him to the floor above.

At every throe, as the man strove to grip Humphrey with his knees and climb up, some fragment of stone rushed down, to fall far beneath, splashing and echoing with a repetition of sounds that robbed him of such strength as remained to him, and a dreamy sensation came on apace.

"It is the end," thought Humphrey, for his fingers felt as if they were yielding, the chilling sensation of paralysis increased, and in another minute he knew that he must fall, when the grip upon him increased, and the man who clung uttered a hoarse yell for help.

"Quick, for God's sake! Quick!" he shrieked. "I'm letting go!"

But at that instant something dark seemed to come between him and the gleaming wet stone away above him in the roof, and then there was quite an avalanche of small stones gliding by.

It was the scoundrel's companion come at the call for help, thought Humphrey; and he clung still in silence, wondering whether it was too late as his strained eye-balls glared upward.

"Where are you?" came in a husky voice.

It was to save his life; but though Humphrey recognised the voice, he could not speak, for his tongue and throat were dry.

"Are you here? Hold on!" cried the voice again; and then there was the sound of someone feeling about, but dislodging stones, which kept rattling down and splashing below.

"Where are you!" cried the voice above Humphrey; but still he could not reply. His hands were giving way, and he felt that his whole energy must be devoted to the one effort of clinging to the last ere he was plunged down into that awful gulf.

But the man who clung to him heard the hoarsely-whispered question, and broke out into a wild series of appeals for help—for mercy—for pity.

"For God's sake, captain!" he yelled, "save me—save me! It was Black Mazzard! He made me come! Do you hear! Help! I can't hold no longer! I'm falling! Help! Curse you—help!"

As these cries thrilled him through and through, Humphrey was conscious in the darkness that the hands he heard rustling above him and dislodging stones, every fall of which brought forth a shriek from the wretch below, suddenly touched his, and then, as if spasmodically, leaped to his wrists, round which they fastened with a grip like steel.

To Humphrey Armstrong it was all now like one hideous nightmare, during which he suffered, but could do nothing to free himself. The wretch's shrieks were growing fainter, and he clung in an inert way now, while someone seemed to be muttering above—

"I can do nothing more—I can do nothing more!" but the grip about Humphrey's wrists tightened, and two arms rested upon his hands and seemed to press them closer to the stones to which they clung.

"Captain—captain! Are you there?"

"Yes," came from close to Humphrey's face.

"Forgive me, skipper, and help me up! I'll be faithful to you! I'll kill Black Mazzard!"

"I can do nothing," said the buccaneer, hoarsely. "You are beyond my reach."

"Then go and fetch the lads and a rope. Don't let me fall into this cursed, watery hell!"

"If I quit my hold here, man, you will both go down; unless help comes, nothing can be done."

"Then, call help! Call help now, captain, and I'll be your slave! Curse him for leaving me here! Where's Joe Thorpe?"

"He was killed by Mazzard with a blow meant for me," said the buccaneer, slowly.

"Curse him! Curse him!" shrieked the man. "Oh, captain, save me, and I'll kill him for you! He wants to be skipper; and I'll kill him for you if you'll only—Ah!"

He uttered a despairing shriek, for as he spoke a sharp tearing sound was heard; the cloth he clung to gave way, and before he could get a fresh hold he was hanging suspended by the half-torn-off garb. He swung to and fro as he uttered one cry, and then there was an awful silence, followed by a plunge far below.

The water seemed to hiss and whisper and echo in all directions, and the silence, for what seemed quite a long space, was awful. It was, however, but a few instants, and then there was a terrific splashing as if a number of horrible creatures had rushed to prey upon the fallen man, whose shrieks for help began once more.

Appeals, curses, yells, piteous wails, followed each other in rapid succession as the water was beaten heavily. Then the cries were smothered, there was a gurgling sound, and the water whispered and lapped and echoed as it seemed to play against the stony walls of the place.

A few moments and the cries recommenced, and between every cry there was the hoarse panting of a swimmer fighting hard for his life as he struck out.

The buccaneer's eyes stared wildly down into the great cenote, or water-tank, whose vast proportions were hidden in the gloom. He could see nothing; but his imagination supplied the vacancy, and pictured before him the head and shoulders of his treacherous follower as he swam along the sides of the great gulf, striving to find a place to climb up; and this he did, for the hoarse panting and the cries ceased, and from the dripping and splashing it was evident that he had found some inequality in the wall, by means of which he climbed, with the water streaming from him.

The task was laborious, but he drew himself up and up, climbing slowly, and then he suddenly ceased, uttered a terrible cry, and once more there was a splash, the lapping and whispering of the water, and silence.

He was at the surface again, swimming hard in the darkness and striving once more to reach the place where he had climbed; but in the darkness he swam in quite a different direction, and his hoarse panting rose again, quick and agitated now, the strokes were taken more rapidly, and like a rat drowning in a tub of water, the miserable wretch toiled on, swimming more and more rapidly and clutching at the wall.

Once an inequality gave him a few moments' rest, and he clung desperately, uttering the most harrowing cries, but only to fall back with a heavy splash. Then he was up once more fighting for life, and the vast tank echoed with his gurgling appeals for help.

Again they were silenced, and the water whispered and lapped and echoed.

There was a splash, a hoarse gurgle, a beating of the water as a dog beats it before it sinks.

Again silence and the whispering and lapping against the sides more faint; then a gurgling sound, the water beat once or twice, a fainter echo or two, and then what sounded like a sigh of relief, and a silence that was indeed the silence of death.

Suddenly the silence in that darkness was broken, for a hoarse voice said—

"Climb up!"

"Climb!" exclaimed Humphrey, who seemed to have recovered his voice, while his frozen energies appeared to expand.

"Yes. Climb. I can hold you thus, but no more. Try and obtain a foothold."

Humphrey obeyed as one obeys who feels a stronger will acting upon him.

"Can you keep my hands fast?" he said. "They are numbed."

"Yes. You shall not slip now. Climb!"

Humphrey obeyed, and placed his feet upon a projection; but it gave way, and a great stone forced from the wall by his weight fell down with a splash which roused the echoes once more.

Humphrey felt half-paralysed again; but the voice above was once more raised.

"Now," it said, "there must be foothold in that spot where the stone fell. Try."

The young officer obeyed, and rousing himself for a supreme effort as his last before complete inaction set in, he strove hard. The hands seemed like steel bands about his wrists, and his struggle sent the blood coursing once more through his nerveless arms. Then, with a perfect avalanche of stones falling from the crumbling side, he strove and strained, and, how he knew not, found foothold, drew himself up, and half crawling, half dragged by the buccaneer as he backed up the slope, reached the level part of the passage between the entrance and the doorway of the inner temple, where he subsided on the stones, panting, exhausted, and with an icy feeling running through his nerves.

"Commodore Junk," he whispered hoarsely as he lay in the semi-darkness, "you have saved my life."

"As you saved mine."

Those two lay there in the gloomy passage listening to the solemn whisperings and lappings of the water, which seemed to be continued for an almost interminable time before they died out, and once more all was silent. But the expectancy remained. It seemed to both that at any moment the miserable would-be assassin might rise to the surface and shriek for help, or that perhaps he was still above water, clinging to the side of the cenote, paralysed with fear, and that as soon as he recovered himself he would make the hideous gulf echo with his appeals.

By degrees, though, as the heavy laboured panting of their breasts ceased, and their hearts ceased beating so tumultuously, a more matter-of-fact way of looking at their position came over them.

"Try if you can walk now," said the buccaneer in a low voice. "You will be better in your own place."

"Yes—soon," replied Humphrey, abruptly; and once more there was silence, a silence broken at last by the buccaneer.

"Captain Armstrong," he said softly, at last, "surely we can now be friends!"

"Friends? No! Why can we?" cried Humphrey, angrily.

"Because I claim your life, the life that I saved, as mine—because I owe you mine!"

"No, no! I tell you it is impossible! Enemies, sir, enemies to the bitter end. You forget why I came out here!"

"No," said the buccaneer, sadly. "You came to take my life—to destroy my people—but Fate said otherwise, and you became my prisoner—your life forfeited to me!"

"A life you dare not take!" cried Humphrey, sternly. "I am one of the king's officers—your king's men."

"I have no king!"

"Nonsense, man! You are a subject of His Majesty King George."

"No!" cried the buccaneer. "When that monarch ceased to give his people the protection they asked, and cruelly and unjustly banished them across the seas for no greater crime than defending a sister's honour from a villain, that king deserved no more obedience from those he wronged."

"The king—did this?" said Humphrey, wonderingly, as he gazed full in the speaker's face, struggling the while to grasp the clues of something misty in his mind—a something which he felt he ought to know, and which escaped him all the while.

"The king! Well, no; but his people whom he entrusts with the care of his laws."

"Stop!" cried Humphrey, raising himself upon one arm and gazing eagerly in the buccaneer's face; "a sister's honour—defended—punished—sent away for that! No; it is impossible! Yes—ah! I know you now! Abel Dell!"

The buccaneer shrank back, gazing at him wildly.

"That is what always seemed struggling in my brain," cried Humphrey, excitedly. "Of course, I know you now. And you were sent over here—a convict, and escaped."

The buccaneer hesitated for a few moments, with the deep colour going and coming in his face.

"Yes," he said, at last. "Abel Dell escaped from the dreary plantation where he laboured."

"And his sister!"

"You remember her story!"

"Remember! Yes," cried Humphrey. "She disappeared from near Dartmouth years ago."

"Yes."

"What became of her—poor girl?" said Humphrey, earnestly; and the buccaneer's cheeks coloured as the words of pity fell.

"She joined her brother out here."

"But he was a convict."

"She helped him to escape."

"I see it all," cried Humphrey, eagerly; "and he became the pirate—and you became the pirate—the buccaneer, Commodore Junk."

"Yes."

"Good heavens!" ejaculated Humphrey. "And the sister—your sister, man the handsome, dark girl whom my cousin—Oh, hang cousin James! What a scoundrel he could be!"

It was the sturdy, outspoken exclamation of an honest English gentleman, and as the buccaneer heard it, Humphrey felt his hand seized in a firm grip, to be held for a few moments and then dropped.

"But he's dead," continued Humphrey. "Let him rest. But tell me—the sister—Oh!"

A long look of apology and pity followed the ejaculation, as Humphrey recalled the scene in the temple, where the long coffin lay draped with the Union Jack—the anguish of the figure on its knees, and the passionate words of adjuration and prayer. It was as if a veil which hid his companion's character from him had been suddenly torn aside, and a look of sympathy beamed from his eyes as he stretched out his hand in a frank, manly fashion.

"I beg your pardon," he cried, softly. "I did not know all this. I am sorry I have been so abrupt in what I said."

"I have nothing to forgive," said the buccaneer, warmly, and his swarthy cheeks glowed as Humphrey gazed earnestly in his eyes.

"And for the sake of brave old Devon and home you spared my life and treated me as you have?"

"Not for the sake of brave old Devon," said the buccaneer, gravely, "but for your own. Now, Captain Humphrey Armstrong, can we be friends?"

"Yes!" exclaimed Humphrey, eagerly, as he stretched out his hand. "No!" he cried, letting it fall. "It is impossible, sir. I have my duty to do to my king and those I've left at home. I am your prisoner; do with me as you please, for, as a gentleman, I tell you that what you ask is impossible. We are enemies, and I must escape. When I do escape my task begins again—to root out your nest of hornets. So for heaven's sake, for the sake of what is past, the day I escape provide for your own safety; for my duty I must do!"

"Then you refuse me your friendship?"

"Yes. I am your enemy, sworn to do a certain duty; but I shall escape when the time has come, I can say no more."

Chapter Thirty
Dinny's History

"No, sor," said Dinny, one morning, "the captain thought that as two of 'em had got their doses there ought to be no more killing. Faix, he behaved like a lion when he came up that day. There was Black Mazzard and five-and-twenty more of 'em as had been over-persuaded by him, all shut up with plenty of firearms in the powder magazine. 'Don't go nigh 'em—it's madness,' says the captain; but he goes into his place and comes out again with a couple of pishtles shtuck in his belt, and his best sword on—the one wid an edge as you could show to your beard and it would all come off at wanst, knowing as it was no use to make a foight of it again' such a blade, as a strong beard will against a bad rashier. And then he sings out: 'Now, my lads, who's for me?'"

"And they all rushed to his aid!" said Humphrey.

"Well, you see, sor," said Dinny, "it wasn't quite a rush. Lads don't go rushing into a powdher-magazine when there's an ugly black divil aside as swears if annybody comes anigh, he'll blow the whole place up into smithereens."

"They never let him go alone?" cried Humphrey.

"Well, no, sor," said Dinny; "it wasn't exackly alone, bekase old Bart run up, and then two more walked up, and another one wint up to him in a slow crawl that made me want to take him by the scruff o' the neck and the sate of his breeches, and pitch him down into that great hole yander, where that blagguard was drowned. 'Oh, ye cowardly cur!' I says to him, quite red-hot like, sor—'Oh, ye cowardly cur! I says, you as was always boasting and bragging about and playing at Hector an' Archillus, and bouncing as if ye were a big ancient foighting man, and ye goo crawling up to yer captain that way!' And then he whispers to me confidential-like, he does: 'Och, Dinny, owld lad!' he says, 'it isn't the foighting I mind; but I'm thinking of my poor mother,' he says. 'Ah, get out, ye coward!' I says; 'ye're thinking of yerself.' 'Divil a bit!' he says; 'it's the powdher I'm thinking of. I'd foight anny man, or anny two men in the camp; but I can't fale to care about an encounter wid tin tons o' divil's dust!' Oh, I did give it him, sor!"

"You had better have gone yourself than stood preaching to another," said Humphrey, indignantly.

"That's jist what I said to meself, sor," cried Dinny; "but the baste wouldn't listen. 'Och!' he says, 'what would my mother's falings be if she was to hear that instead of dying properly of a broken head she heard that I was blown all into smithereens, widout a dacent-sized pace left for the praste to say a blessing over?' 'Ah, Dinny Kelly!' I says, 'that's a mane dirthy excuse, because ye're afraid; for the divil a bit wid your mother care what became of such an ill-looking, black buccaneer of a blagguard as ye are!'"

"Why, you're talking about yourself!" cried Humphrey.

"For sartin, sir. Sure, there isn't another boy in the whole crew that I dare to spake to in such an onrespectful way."

"Why, Dinny, man, you did go?"

"Yes, sor, I wint, but in a way that I'm quite ashamed of. I didn't think I was such a coward. But there! I niver turned back from a shtick in me loife, and I faced the powdher afther all; but oh, it's ashamed of meself intirely I am! A Kelly wouldn't have felt like that if it hadn't been for the climate. It's the hot weather takes it out of ye, sor. Why I felt over that job as a man couldn't fale in me own counthry."

"Well, go on."

"That's what I did, sor. I stuck close to the captain's tail as he wint sthraight up to the door—ye know the door, sor, where the owld gintleman's sitting over the porch, looking down at ye wid a plisant smile of his own."

"Yes, yes, I know. Go on."

"Well, sor, I did go on; and there stood Black Mazzard wid the two biggest pishtols we have on the primises, wan in each hand and the other shtuck in his belt. 'Kim another shtep,' he says, 'and I'll blow the place about your heads!' Och, and I looked up thin to ask a blessing on meself before I wint up in such a hurry that I hadn't time to confess; and bedad there was the owld gintleman expanding his mouth into the widest grin I iver saw in me life!"

"And the Commodore, what did he do?" cried Humphrey, impatiently.

"What did he do?"

"Yes—draw his men off?"

"Faix, he drew Black Mazzard's blood off, for he wint shtraight at him, knocking one pishtol up in the air wid his hand as he did so. I niver saw annything so nate in me life, sor. I told ye he'd got his best sword on—the sharp one."

"Yes, yes!"

"Well, sor, he seemed just to lift it up and howld it forninst him, as I'm howlding this knife—so; and it wint right through Black Mazzard; just bechuckst his shoulder and his neck; and as he pulls it out he takes him by the collar and drags him down upon his knees.

"'Come out, ye mad-brained idiots!' he shouts at the lads inside—'come out, or I'll fire the powdher meself!'

"Bedad, sor, ye might have heard a pin dhrop if there'd bin wan there, but there wasn't; and we heard Black Mazzard's pishtol dhrop instead—the big one being on the pavemint, where it went off bang and shot a corner off a big shtone. But nobody came from inside the magazine, and the owld gintleman grinned more and more, and seemed to rowl his oies; and I belave he wanted to hear the owld place go up. And there you could hear thim inside buzzing about like my mother's bees in the sthraw hive, when ye give it a larrup on the top wid a shtick."

Dinny gave his head a nod, and went on. "That roused up the Captain, and he roars out—'Here, Dinny—Dick—Bart,' he says, 'go in and fetch out these idiots.' And I shpat in me fist, and ran in wid the other two. 'Now, Dinny, my lad,' I says to meself, 'if ye're blown up it'll be bad for ye, but ye'll be blown up towards heaven, and that's a dale better than being blown down.' And avore I knew where I was, I was right in among the lads, about foive-and-twenty of them; and then talk about a foight, sor! Ah, musha, it was awful!"

"Did they make such a desperate defence!"

"Deshperate, sor! Oh, that don't describe it! Bedad, I nivver saw anything like it in me loife!"

"Were there many killed? Were you wounded!"

"Killed! Wounded! Did ye iver see a flock o' sheep when a big dog goes at 'em, sor?"

"Often, in Devon."

"Ah, then it's the same as it would be in Oireland. Bedad, sor, the name of the captain, and seeing Black Mazzard tuk, was enough. They all walked out and pitched their swords and pishtols down, in a hape before the shkipper and then stands in a row like sodgers; sure and it's meself that had some of the drilling of them.

"'Come here, Bart,' says the shkipper then; and as Bart goes up, the captain gives Black Mazzard a shove like and throws him down. 'Here,' he says, 'put your foot on this dog's throat.' Bart had it there before ye knew where ye were, and thin if the skipper didn't go right up to the row of min and walks slowly along 'em, looking 'em wan by wan in the face wid his dark oi, sor. And he made 'em turn white and shiver, he did, sor, till he'd looked 'em all down, and then he shteps out, little shtiff fellow as he is, and he says:

"'You fools, to be led away by a thing like that! How shall I punish 'em, Dinny?' he says, turning to me.

"'Sure, captain,' I says, 'they are all shtanding nate and handy, and if ye give me word, I'll shtand at wan ind and send a bullet through the lot, and there'll be no waste.'

"'Pah!' he says, 'I don't make war on the lads who've fought by my side. Go back to your quarthers,' he says, 'and if ye turn again me once more I'll give ye such a punishment as ye disarve. You shall have your Captain Mazzard.'

"'D'ye hear that, ye divils?' I says, for I couldn't stop meself, sor; and they give three cheers for the captain and wint off to quarthers; and that was all."

"But Mazzard—what of him!"

"Oh, he's putt away in as nice and plisant a place as a gintleman could wish to have, sor. It's cool, and undherground, and the only way to it is down through a hole in a stone like Father O'Grady's well, and Bart fades him wid food at the ind of a long shtick. He's safe enough now. But sure and the best thing for everyone would be for him to doi by accident through Bart forgetting to take him his mate."

"Starve him to death?" cried Humphrey.

"Faix, no, not a bit of it, sor. He's a bad one anny way, and if he died like a sparrow in a cage, sure it would be a blessing for all of us."

"And the widow Greenheys, Dinny!"

"Whisht! be aisy, sor, wid a lady's name."

"Dinny," cried Humphrey sternly, "how long are you going to play fast and loose with me!"

"'An' is it me ye mane?' Sure I couldn't do it, sor."

"Dinny, now is the time to escape, now that Mistress Greenheys is safe from the persecution of that scoundrel."

"Oh, whisht, sor! whisht! Sure and I've grown shtrong again, and ye want to timpt me from the ways of vartue."

"Nonsense, man! Your plan—the explosion!"

"Oh, faix! It was only me fun. I couldn't do such a thing."

"Do you want that man to escape or be set free, and lay claim again to that poor little woman?"

"Oh, the poor little crathur! no."

"Then help me to escape."

"Sure and ye're good friends wid the shkipper and don't want to go, sor."

"I must and will escape, Dinny, and you shall help me for Mistress Greenheys' sake."

"Ah, and it's touching me on me soft place ye are," said Dinny pitifully.

"For her sake, I tell you, and you shall be happy with her at home."

"Sure an' I haven't got an 'at home,'" said Dinny.

"Then, as I promised you, I'll make you one. Come, save her from that scoundrel."

"Faix, an' he is a blagguard anny way."

"Who is?" said a deep voice.

"Yerself for wan," said Dinny. "Sure, and Black Mazzard another; and I'm telling the captain here that he needn't grumble and call himself a prishner, for he's rowling in comfort; while as to Black Mazzard, ah, he should see his cell!"

Bart scowled and stopped till Dinny had finished and gone, leaving the prisoner alone with his thoughts, which were of liberty.

Chapter Thirty One
The Plan of Escape

Humphrey Armstrong sat gazing through the opening of his prison at the dark forest vistas and dreamed of England and its verdant fields and gold-cupped meadows.

The whole business connected with the Dells came back to him, and with it the figure of the handsome rustic fisher-girl standing as it were vividly before him, and with her his cousin, the cause of all the suffering.

"How strange it is," he thought again, "that I should be brought into contact with her brother like this! Poor fellow! more sinned against than sinning; and as for her—"

"Poor girl!"

There was a slight sound as of someone breathing hard, and the buccaneer stood before him.

He smiled gravely, and held out his hand; but Humphrey did not take it, and they remained gazing at each other for some few minutes in silence.

"Have you thought better of my proposals, Captain Armstrong?" said the buccaneer at last. "Are we to be friends?"

"It is impossible, sir," replied Humphrey, quietly. "After what has passed I grieve to have to reject your advances; but you must see that it can never be."

"I can wait," said the buccaneer, patiently. "The time will come."

Humphrey shook his head.

"Is there anything you want?"

"Yes," said Humphrey, sharply. "Liberty."

"Take it. It is in my hand."

"Liberty chained to you, sir! No. There, place me under no further obligations, sir. I will not fight against you; but pray understand that what you ask can never be."

"I can wait," said the buccaneer again, quietly, as he let his eyes rest for a few moments upon his prisoner's face, and then left the room.

Humphrey sprang up impatiently, and was about to pace the chamber like a wild beast in a cage when he heard voices in the corridor, and directly after Dinny entered. The man looked troubled and stood listening, then he stole to the curtain and went down the corridor, to stay away for quite a quarter of an hour before he returned.

"He's gone, sor, safe enough. Faix, captain, dear, I fale as if I ought to be hung."

"Hung, Dinny?"

"Yis, sor, for threachery to as good a friend as I iver had."

"What do you mean, Dinny?" cried Humphrey, eagerly.

"Mane, sor! Why, that all the grate min in the world, from Caesar down to Pater Donovan, have had their wake side. I've got mine, and I'm a fallen man."

"Speak out plainly," cried Humphrey, flushing.

"That's just what I'm doing, sor," said Dinny, with a soft smile. "It's Nature, sor. She was bad enough, and thin you helped her. Oh, there's no foighting agen it! It used to be so in Oireland. She says to the little birds in the spring—choose your partners, darlin's, she says, and they chose 'em; and she said the same to human man, and he chooses his."

"Oh, Dinny, if you hadn't quite such a long tongue!" cried Humphrey.

"Faix, it's a regular sarpint, sor, for length, and just as desaving; but as I was saying, what Nature says in owld Oireland in the spring she says out here in this baste of a counthry where there's nayther spring, summer, autumn, nor winther—nothing but a sort of moshposh of sunshine and howling thunderstorms."

"And—"

"Yis, sor, that's I'm a fallen man."

"And will you really help me to escape!"

"Whisht, sor! What are ye thinking about? Spaking aloud in a counthry where the parrots can talk like Christians and the threes is full of ugly little chaps, who sit and watch ye and say nothing, but howld toight wid their tails, and thin go and whishper their saycrets to one another, and look as knowing as Barny Higgins's pig."

"Dinny, will you speak sensibly?"

"Sinsibly! Why, what d'ye call this? Ar'n't I tellin' ye that it's been too much for me wid Black Mazzard shut up in his cage and the purty widow free to do as she plases; and sure and she plases me, sor, and I'm a fallen man."

"You'll help me?"

"Yis, sor, if ye'll go down on your bended knees and take an oath."

"Oath! What oath?"

"Niver to bethray or take part in annything agen Commodore Junk, the thruest, bravest boy that iver stepped."

"You are right, Dinny. He is a brave man, and I swear that I will not betray or attack him, come what may. Get me my liberty and the liberty of my men, and I'll be content. Stop! I cannot go so far as that; there are my men. I swear that I will not attack your captain without giving him due notice, that he may escape; but this nest of hornets must be burned out, and my men freed."

"Ah, well, we won't haggle about thrifles, sor. Swear this, sor:—Ye'll behave to the captain like a gintleman."

"I'll swear I will."

"Bedad, then, I'm wid ye; and there's one more favour I'll be asking ye, sor."

"What is it!"

"Whin we get safe home ye'll come and give Misthress Greenheys away."

"Yes, yes, Dinny. And now, tell me, what will you do?"

"Sure an' there's no betther way than I said before. I'll have an oi on a boat, and see that there's some wather and bishkits and a gun in her; and thin, sor, I'll set light to the magazine, for it'll be a rale plisure to blow up that owld gintleman as is always leering and grinning at me as much as to say, 'Och, Dinny, ye divil, I know all about the widdy, and first time ye go to see her I'll tell Black Mazzard, and then, 'ware, hawk!'"

"But when shall you do this?"

"First toime it seems aisy, sor."

"In the night?"

"Av coorse, sor."

"And how shall I know?"

"Hark at that, now! Faix, ar'n't I telling ye, sor, that I'll blow up the magazine! Sure an' ye don't pay so much attention to it when ye go to shleep that ye won't hear that?"

"Of course I shall hear it," said Humphrey, excitedly.

"Thin, that's the signal, sor; and when it goes fizz, lie riddy and wait till I kim to ye, and thin good bye to the rover's loife, and Black Mazzard will see the darlin' no more. Whisht!"

Chapter Thirty Two
The Explosion

A fortnight passed, during which the buccaneer visited his prisoner twice, as if to give him an opportunity to speak, but each time in company with Bart.

Both were very quiet and stern, and but few words were said. Everything was done to make the prisoner's condition more endurable, but the attentions now were irksome; and though Humphrey Armstrong lay listening for footsteps with the greatest anxiety, those which came down the corridor were not those he wished to hear.

At last, in the continuous absence of Dinny, he began to dread that the last conversation had been heard, and after fighting down the desire for a fortnight, he determined to risk exciting suspicion and ask Bart what had become of the Irishman.

Bart entered the place soon after he had come to the determination, bringing an Indian basket of fruit—the pleasant little grapes that grew wild in the sunny parts, and the succulent banana. These he placed upon the stone table in company with a bunch of flowers, where they looked like some offering made to the idol upon whose altar they had been placed.

Humphrey hesitated with the words upon his lips, and checked himself. If Dinny had been overheard and were imprisoned or watched, what good would he do? Better wait and bear the suspense.

"Your gift?" he said, aloud, taking up the flowers and smelling them, for the soft delicate blooms of the forest orchids suggested a room in Saint James's Square and a daintily-dressed lady who was bemoaning his absence.

"Mine? No. The captain picked them himself," said Bart, bitterly.

Humphrey laid them down and took up one of the long, yellow-skinned fruits, Bart watching his action, regarding the fruit with jealous eyes.

Humphrey turned sharply round to hide his face from his jailer, for he had changed colour. A spasm shot through him, and for the moment he felt as if he must betray himself, for as he turned over the banana in his fingers, they touched a roughening of the under part, and the next instant he saw that the fruit he held had been partly cut away with the point of a knife, so that a figure had been carved in the soft rind, and this could only have been the work of one hand, and intended as a signal to him that he was not forgotten. For the figure cut in the rind was that of a shamrock—a trefoil with its stalk.

He hastily tore off the rind in tiny strips and ate the fruit, but the soft, creamy pulp seemed like ashes, and his throat was dry, as he completely destroyed all trace of the cutting on the rind and threw it aside.

Noting that Bart was watching him narrowly, he hurriedly picked up one of the little bunches of grapes and began eating them as if suffering from thirst. Then forcing himself to appear calm he lay down upon the couch till Bart had finished his customary attentions and gone.

Night at last—a moonless night—that would have been dusk on the open shore, but there in the forest beneath the interlacing trees it was absolutely black; and after watching at his window for hours, with every sense upon the strain, he reluctantly came to the conclusion that no attempt would be made, Dinny either not being prepared—though his signal seemed to be to indicate readiness for the night though suitable for concealment, being too obscure for his purpose.

"One of them might have managed to come and give me a word," he said, fretfully, as at last, weary of watching the scintillations of the fireflies in a distant opening, he threw himself upon his couch to try and sleep, feeling that he would be wakeful all night, when all at once, just as he felt most troubled, his eyes closed, and he was deep in a dreamless sleep, lost to everything but the terrific roar which suddenly burst forth, following a vivid flash as of lightning, and as, confused and half-stunned, Humphrey started up, all idea of the proposed escape seemed to have passed away, and he sat watching for the next flash, listening for the next peal, thinking that this was a most terrific storm.

No flash—no peal—but a confused buzz of voices and the distant pattering of feet, while a dense, dank odour of exploded gunpowder penetrated the forest, and entered the window close to which the prisoner sat.

"Dinny—the escape!" he cried, excitedly, as he sprang from his bed, for now a flash did come with almost blinding force; but it was a mental flash, which left him quivering with excitement, as he sprang to the curtained corridor and listened there.

A step!—Dinny's! Yes, he knew it well! It was coming along the great stone passage!

"Quick! we shall easily get away, for they'll all crowd about the captain, asking him what to do."

Dinny led on rapidly till they reached the turning in the direction of the old temple which contained the cenote. Here they struck off to the left, and found, as they cleared the narrow forest path, that the odour of the exploded gunpowder was almost overpowering.

Not a hundred yards away voices were heard speaking rapidly, and directly after they were silent, and the captain's words rang out plainly as he gave orders to his people, though their import was not clear from the distance where the fugitives crept along by the edge of the ruins.

"Are you sure you are right?" whispered Humphrey.

"Roight, sor; I niver was more so. Whisht! Are ye there?"

"Yes, yes," came from down by the side of a great wall. "Oh, Dinny, I was afraid you were killed!"

"Kilt! Nay, my darling, there's a dale o' loife in me yet. Tak' howlt o' me hand, one on each side, and walk quick and shteady, and I'll have ye down by the say shore, where the boat is waiting, before ye know where ye are."

They started off at a sharp walk, pausing at times to listen to the jargon of excited voices behind, but rapidly advancing, on the whole, toward their goal.

"Do—do you think we can escape?" said the woman, panting with fear.

"An' is it eshcape, whin the boat's waiting, and everything riddy?" said Dinny scornfully. "Dyer hear her, sor? What a woman it is!"

The woman sighed as if not hopeful, and Dinny added an encouraging word:

"Sure an' the captain says he'll tak' care of us, darlin', and avore long we'll be sailing away over the salt say. It's a white sail I've got in the boat, and—"

"Hist, Dinny, you're talking too loudly, my man!" whispered Humphrey.

"Bedad and I am, sor. It's that owld sarpint of a tongue o' mine. Bad luck to it for being given me wrong. Faix and it belonged to some woman by rights."

They pressed on, and at the end of what seemed to be an interminably long time, Humphrey whispered:

"Are we near the sea?"

"Close to it now, sor. If it was Oireland ye'd hear the bating of the waves upon the shore; but they're too hot and wake in this counthry to do more than give a bit of a lap on the sands."

Another weary length of time passed, and still the sea-shore was not reached, but they were evidently near now, for the dull murmur of the billows in the sheltered gulf was plainly to be heard; and Mistress Greenheys, who, in spite of her bravery and decision, had begun to utter a low hysterical sob from time to time and hang more heavily upon her companions' arms, took courage at the thought of the safety the sea offered, and pressed sturdily forward for another few hundred yards and then stopped short.

"What is it, darlin'?" whispered Dinny.

"Voices!" she replied softly.

"Yes; our own," said Dinny. "There can't be anny others here."

"Hist!" ejaculated Humphrey. "Is there any other way down to the beach?"

"Divil a bit, sor, that we could foind, and the boat's yander, close inshore."

He took a step or two in advance, and listened.

"I am sure I heard whispering," said Humphrey; but all was still now, and feeling satisfied at last that it was the murmur of the waves, they crept on in utter silence, and were about to leave the shelter of the path by which they had come and make for the open sand when Dinny checked his companions, and they all stood listening, for a voice that was familiar said:

"The skipper's full of fancies. He hasn't been right since this captain was made prisoner, and he has been worse since the other prisoners escaped."

"Other prisoners! What prisoners?" thought Humphrey.

"You hold your tongue!" growled the familiar voice of Bart. "Do you want to scare them off?"

"Scare whom off?"

"Those who try to escape. Silence!"

Mistress Greenheys reeled up against Humphrey and would have fallen but for his strong arm which encircled her, lifted her from the ground and held her firmly as he stepped softly back, followed by Dinny, who did not speak till they had reached the shelter of some trees.

"Look at that, now!" he whispered out of the black darkness. "Have ye got the darling safe?"

"Yes, safe enough; but what does this mean?"

"Mane, sor? Sure and it's Bart yander wid two min."

"Take us down to the sea by some other path."

"Shure an' don't I tell ye there is no other path, sor. It's the only way. Murther, look at that!"

For at that moment a light flashed out and shimmered on the sea, sank, rose, and became brilliant, shining forth so that they could see that the three men down upon the shore had lit a pile of some inflammable material, beyond which, floating easily upon the surface of the sea and apparently close inshore, was a boat—the boat that was to bear them safely away.

They were sheltered by the trees, and besides, too far off to be seen by the men, whose acts, however, were plain enough to them, as one of them was seen to wade out to the boat, get hold of her mooring rope, and drag her ashore.

"The murtherin' villains!" muttered Dinny. "They're takkin' out the shtores. Look at that now! There's the barl o' wather and the bishkit, and now there's the sail. What'll I do intoirely? My heart's bruk wid 'em."

"Hush, my lad! You'll be heard," whispered Humphrey. "Is there no other boat we can get?"

"Divil a wan, sor, and if we shtay here we shall be tuk. What'll we do now?"

"Make a bold fight for it, and take them by surprise."

"Wid a woman as wan of our min, sor! Sure an' it would be a mad thrick. Wan of us would be sure to go down, you or me, even if we bate the divils. Look at 'em, the fire's going down, and they're coming back!"

Humphrey gave an angry stamp, for in her agony of dread Mistress Greenheys gave herself a wrest from his arm, and hurried back.

"What's that?" whispered Dinny.

"Mistress Greenheys."

"What? gone back, sor? Whisht! darlin'. Stop!"

If the woman heard his words they only added to her alarm, for she hurried on, apparently as well acquainted with the way back as Dinny, who immediately started in pursuit.

"What are you going to do?" whispered Humphrey.

"Do, sor! Go afther her."

"No, no; we must escape now we've got so far."

"Shure an' we will, sor; but to go forward's to go into prishn for you and to be dancing on nothing for me. Come on, sor. Let's catch up to me poor freckened darlin', and then tak' to the woods."

They hurried back in pursuit of their companion, but fear had made her fleet of foot, and in spite of their efforts they did not overtake her.

"She'll have gone back to her quarthers," said Dinny dismally. "Shall we go back to ours?"

"No!" cried Humphrey imperiously. "Good heavens, man! our absence has been found out before now. Let's take to the woods or hide in one of the ruins till we can get away."

"Shure an' ye're roight, sor. They've been afther ye, av coorse, and I've been missed and can't show meself now widout being thrated as a thraitor. Will ye thrust to me, and I'll find a place!"

"Trust you? yes," said Humphrey; "but what do you propose doing?"

"Doing, sor? Hoiding till we can find a chansh of getting away."

"Where will you hide?"

"Ye said ye'd thrust me, sor," whispered Dinny. "Come on."

Chapter Thirty Three
On the Qui Vive

The buccaneer had sought the ruined temple that evening in lowness of spirit and utter despondency. The old daring spirit seemed to be departing, and supremacy over the men passing rapidly away, and he knew how they talked among themselves, consequent upon Mazzard's teaching, of the growing weakness of their commander.

"And they're right," he said, bitterly. "I am losing power and strength, and growing more and more into the pitiful, weak creature they say. And yet how I have tried!"

He sprang to his feet, for at that moment there was the reflection of a flash which lit up the interior of the old temple, showing the weird figures sitting round as if watching him in his despondent mood.

It was but momentary, and then came a crash as if heaven and earth had come together, followed by a long, muttering roar as the thunder of the explosion died away.

The minute before the buccaneer had been inert, despondent and hopeless. The knowledge of what must have taken place brought back his flagging energies, and with a great dread seeming to compress his heart that evil might have befallen his prisoner, he tore out of the dark temple, and as fast as the gloom of the winding path would allow him toward the old amphitheatre.

Haste and the excitement made his breathing laboured as he strove to get on more rapidly, but only to be kept back by the maze-like paths, where he passed Humphrey and Dinny, and, gaining the open ground, dashed on to where his men were gathered.

"Bart! quick!" he cried, as soon as he was convinced that no harm could have befallen his prisoner. "Take men, and down the path to the shore. There will be an attempt to escape in the confusion, and they'll make for the sea."

Bart grasped the urgency of the case, called two men, and set off at a run, while Dinny was next summoned.

"Hah!" ejaculated the captain, drawing his breath between his teeth; "a traitor in the camp!"

He called for lights, and went straight to the corridor, entered and walked down it to the chamber, tenanted now by the grim idol alone, and stood for a few moments looking round.

"Well," he muttered, "he will learn the truth of what I said. The firing of the powder must have been planned."

He went back to where his men were waiting outside and walked through to the terrace above the old amphitheatre, to find that the magazine was completely swept away; but the darkness hid the shattered stones lying in all directions and the trees blasted and whitened and stripped of leaf and bark.

"My prisoner has escaped," he said aloud. "I think with the man who was his attendant, the Irishman, Dennis Kelly. Capture both; but no violence to either, on your lives."

There was a low murmur either of assent or objection, and he was turning away when Dick, the sailor, came up.

"Gone!" he said, laconically.

"Mazzard? Gone!" cried the buccaneer, excitedly.

"Yes; and the man who was on guard lying dead, crushed with a stone."

"From the explosion?" cried the buccaneer.

"From Black Mazzard's hands," replied Dick, stolidly.

"Well," said the captain, drawing in his breath hard as he thought of the possibility of the escaped prisoners coming in contact, "there will be two to capture when the day breaks. No one can get away."

In an hour a messenger came from the sea in the shape of Bart, and he made his way to the captain's side.

"Well?"

"You were right; they intended the sea;" and he explained about the boat.

"And yet you have come away?"

"Two men are watching," said Bart, stolidly.

"Bah! you must be mad."

"And two planks are rifted out of the boat. It will take a carpenter to make her float."

"Bart, forgive me."

"Forgive you! Ah, yes! I forgive."

"I have need of all your aid. Captain Armstrong has escaped."

"Not far."

"No; but there is worse news. Mazzard has brained his keeper, and is at liberty."

"Hah!" ejaculated Bart.

"And those two may meet."

"Always of him," muttered Bart, sadly. "Well, skipper, what is it to be now, when he is captured?"

"Death."

"To Captain Armstrong?"

"Man, are you mad? Let Mazzard be taken, and that Irishman, too."

"And—"

"Silence, man! Let them be taken. I rule here."

Bart drew a long breath.

"Nothing can be done till daylight, except wait."

Chapter Thirty Four
The Safest Place

"No, no, man; make for the forest," whispered Humphrey, just at daybreak, as Dinny began to take advantage of the coming light to seek a safe place of concealment.

"What for, sor? To get buried in threes that don't so much as grow a cabbage, where there's no wather and no company but monkeys and the shpotted tigers. Lave it to me, sor, and I'll tak' ye to a place where ye can lay shnug in hiding, and where maybe I can get spache of the darling as the bastes freckened away."

"Where shall you go, then? Why not to that old temple where Mazzard made his attempt to kill the captain?"

"There, sor! Why, the captain would find us directly. You lave it to me."

Humphrey would have taken to the forest without hesitation, but, worn-out and suffering keenly from disappointment, he was in no humour to oppose, and, signifying his willingness, he followed the Irishman by devious ways in and out of the ruins for some time, till Dinny crouched down, and motioned to Humphrey to do the same.

The place was such a chaos, and so changed by the terrific force of the explosion that Humphrey had felt as if he were journeying along quite a new portion of the forest outskirts, till, as he obeyed his companion and they crouched down among some dense herbage, he stared with astonishment at the sight before him, a couple of hundred yards away.

For there, beyond one of the piles of crumbling ruins, was a perfectly familiar pathway, out of which he saw step into the broad sunshine the picturesque figure of the buccaneer captain, who strode toward a group of waiting men.

A discussion seemed to take place, there were some sharp orders, and then the whole party disappeared.

"Why, Dinny, man, are you mad?" whispered Humphrey. "I trusted to you to take me to some place of hiding, and you've brought me right into the lion's den."

"Well, sor, and a moighty purty place too, so long as the lion's not at home. Sure and ye just saw him go out."

"But, Dinny—"

"Whisht! Don't spake so loud, sor. Sure, now, if a cannon-ball made a hole in the side of a ship, isn't that the safest place to put your head so as not to be hurt. They niver hit the same place twice."

"Then your hiding-place is my old lodging—my prison?"

"Av coorse it is! The skipper has been there to mak' sure that ye really are gone; and now he knows, he'll say to himself that this is the last place ye'd go and hide in; and troth, he's quite roight, isn't he?"

Humphrey hesitated for a few moments, and then, feeling how true the man's words were, he gave way.

"Sure, sor, and it's all roight," whispered Dinny. "Aren't I thrying to keep my head out of a noose, and d'ye think I'd be for coming here if it wasn't the safest place. Come along; sure, it is a lion's den, as ye call it, and the best spot I know."

He whispered to Humphrey to follow cautiously, and crept on all-fours among the dense growth, and in and out among the loose stones at the very edge of the forest, till the tunnel-like pathway was reached in safety, when, after crawling a few yards out of the blinding sunshine into the shadowy gloom, Dinny rose to his feet.

"There, sor," he said, "we can walk like Christians, now, and not like animal bastes. There isn't a sound."

As he spoke, there was a peculiar cry, and a gorgeously-plumaged bird flitted into sight, and perched on a piece of stone in the sunny opening of the tunnel, where its scarlet breast and dazzling golden-green plumage glittered in the sun.

"Sure and ye're a purty fowl, and I'm much obliged to ye for the information," said Dinny, as the bird erected its brilliant crest, stared wildly, and then flew off with its long green tail-feathers streaming out behind. "He says there's nobody about, sor, or he wouldn't be here. Come along."

It seemed like a dream to Humphrey after his sleepless night, to find himself once more in the gloomy corridor with the faint light streaming in at the side-openings, instead of in a boat, dancing over the blue waters and leaving the buccaneer's nest behind. But it was the bare reality, as Dinny went forward, drew the great curtain aside, and he passed in and on from behind the great idol to throw himself, worn-out and exhausted, upon his couch of skins.

"Sure and I wouldn't trate it like that, sor," cried Dinny, cheerfully. "We have eshcaped, sor, though we haven't got away, and been obliged to come back again."

"Don't talk folly, man."

"An' is it folly ye call it! Sure an' we have eshcaped, or else why are they all in purshuit of us? We've got away, and they fale it, and all that's happened is that we did rache the boat, but had to come back here for a rest till we were riddy to go on. Sure, sor, ye're hungry. Ate some of the tortillas and drink some of the wine, and thin, if ye won't think it presumption, I'll say—afther you."

"Eat and drink, man. You must be faint. I have no appetite."

"Ah!" ejaculated Dinny, after a pause of about a quarter of an hour, which he had bravely employed, "there's nothing like food and dhrink, if it's only potaties and butthermilk. Sure I'm ready for annything now, and so will ye be, sor, as soon as the wine begins to work."

"Dinny, I'm ready for anything, now; but we cannot stay here."

"Git up, sor, if ye wouldn't moind," said Dinny.

Humphrey obeyed dejectedly as the man advanced.

"Sure, sor, and it's a wondherful owld place this, and there must have been some strange games carried on. Now, sor, in all the months ye've been here, did ye iver look under the bed?"

"Under the bed, man?" cried Humphrey. "Why, it is a huge block of stone."

"Is it, now, sor? Sure and didn't I help fit up the place for ye when ye first came, an' by the captain's orders? Sure and I know all about it. 'Dinny, me boy,' me mother used to say to me, 'ye haven't got a watch and ye've got no money, but ye may have both some day, so beware of thayves and robbers; and whiniver ye go to slape in a sthrange place, be sure ye look under the bed.' An' yer mother niver gave you that advice, sor?"

He walked to the couch and threw up the skins which covered it, revealing what seemed to be a low, square bench of stone, whose top was one enormous slab.

"Now, sor," said Dinny, "would ye moind thrying to lift that?"

Humphrey stepped quickly to his side, bent down, seized the projecting slab, tried to raise it, and then straightened himself and shook his head.

"A dozen men could not raise it, Dinny," he said.

"No, sor, but a Kelly can. Look here."

He bent down, placed his shoulder to one corner, gave a thrust, and the whole top glided round as if on a pivot, and revealed an opening dimly lit apparently from below.

"There, sor," he said, "I dishcovered that by accident when I was here alone wan day. I pushed a big stone against that corner and it gave way, and when I pushed the whole place opened, and down there's as good a hiding-place as a man need have."

"Dinny," cried Humphrey, excitedly, "and doesn't the captain know of this?"

"Sure and I think the last man who knew of it died before the flood, sor, and it hasn't been opened since."

"And these rough stairs—where do they lead?"

"Down into the cabin, sor, where there's a little door out into the forest. Sure and the artful baste who made it little thought he was going to find us as purty a hiding-place as was ever made. There it is, sor, all ready for us if we hear annyone coming. If we do, down we go and twirl the lid of the pot back over our heads, and then we can either go or shtay."

"Can you move the cover when you are down?"

"Aisily, sor. I've thried it. Now, then, what do ye say to that?"

Humphrey's answer was to hold out his hand and wring that of his companion.

There was an ample supply of food in the place for a week, and water and wine. Dinny's ideas respecting their safety seemed to be quite correct, for though voices were heard at a distance, no one approached the place. They had the hidden subterranean tomb-like chamber into which they could retreat; and on the second night, while Dinny was watching and Humphrey, utterly worn-out, was sleeping feverishly and trying to forget the troubles and disappointments of his failure, there was a faint rustling noise heard, and directly after his name was whispered softly from above.

"Murther!" cried Dinny, unable to contain himself as he sprang up.

His exclamation and the noise he made brought Humphrey from his couch, alert, and ready for any struggle.

"What is it?" he said.

"Sure, sor, something freckened me. A mouse, I think."

"Dinny!" came in a reproachful voice from above.

"Mistress Greenheys!" cried Humphrey. "You there?"

"Yes. I cam' to try and learn tidings of you. I did not know you were both prisoners."

"Sure an' we're not, darlin'," said Dinny. "We only tuk refuge here, so as to be near you. An' where have you been?"

"I crept back to my place," said the woman, "and reached it without having been missed."

"Then ye're quite free to come and go?"

"Yes—quite."

"*Erin-go-bragh!*" cried Dinny, excitedly. "Then what ye've got to do, darling, is to go back and come again as soon as ye can wid something to ate, for we shall soon be starved."

"Yes, Dinny; I'll come again to-night."

"There's a darlin' for ye, sor. But tell us. What are they doing?"

"Searching for you far and wide; and the captain is furious. He says he will have you found."

"And ye've been quite well, darlin'?"

"Yes, Dinny. No, Dinny. I've been fretting to death to know what had become of you."

"Sure and I've been quite right, only I wanted to know about you. Nobody's middled wid ye, then?"

"No, Dinny—not yet."

"Arrah, shpake out now, and say what ye mane wid your 'not yet,'" cried Dinny, angrily.

"Black Mazzard."

"Well, he's shut up."

"He escaped the same time that you did."

"Eshcaped! Holy Moses!"

"That wretch free!" cried Humphrey.

"Yes, sir."

"Where is he?"

"No one knows, sir; but they have parties out searching for him and for you."

"Oh! murther! murther!" groaned Dinny. "My heart's bruk entirely. What'll I do at all? Shtop, darlin'; ye must come here."

"Stop here, Dinny! Oh, no, I couldn't!" said the woman, piteously.

"Sure no, and ye couldn't," said Dinny. "It wouldn't be dacent, darlin', for ye've got a characther to lose. Captain, dear, what'll I do?"

"We must wait, Dinny, and try to-night if we cannot find a boat."

"And lave that poor darlin' to be freckened to death by that great black baste? Oh, captain, dear, I'll have to go wid her and purtect her; and if I'm hung for it, why, I can't help it. I should have behaved like a man."

"Wait, Dinny," said the woman, cheerily. "You keep in hiding for a day or two, dear. If Black Mazzard does come and try to get me away, I can but die."

"Sure, an' what good'll that do me?" cried Dinny. "D'ye want to make me a widow, too!"

"Hush! You're talking too loudly," whispered the woman. "Good-bye! Next time I come I'll bring food. Perhaps good news."

"No, no; don't go yet, darlin'," cried Dinny. "She's gone. Oh, murther, sor! What'll I do! Can't ye put me out of me misery at wanst?"

Dinny calmed down at last, and Humphrey resumed his place upon the couch, which was arranged so that at any moment they might secure their retreat. But the night had not passed before the faithful little woman was back again with such provisions as she could bring and lower down to them, for she would not hear of Dinny coming out, threatening to keep away if he ran any risk.

This went on for two nights, during which time they had no alarm. Not a soul beside approached the place; and the same report was brought them that their hiding-place baffled all, but the captain was fiercely determined that the prisoners should be found.

"Then why not try to escape inland, Dinny!" said Humphrey, at last. "Surely, it cannot be impossible."

"Haven't we all thried it again and again wid the captain, sor!" said Dinny, in remonstrance. "He sot us all to work, so as to make sure that we couldn't be attacked from the land; and ye can't get in a mile annywhere, for thick forest worked together like a powerful big hurdle that's all solid, and beyant that's mountains—and burning mountains—and the divil knows what! Sure, and ye can't get that way at all widout an army of wood-cutters, and a life a hundred years long!"

A week went by, food was wanting, the prisoners were in despair, and they had both crept out again and again to the end of the corridor and listened to try and make out something; but all outside was solemnly still, and the place might have been once more the abode of death, had not a couple of sentries always been visible keeping watch, so that it was impossible to stir.

"I can't shtand this anny longer, sor," said Dinny one evening. "I'm going to see if I can't find her, sor. I must have news of the darlin', or I shall die!"

"It's madness, Dinny!" said Humphrey, excitedly.

"Sure, and I know it is, sor. I am mad."

"But you will injure her and yourself too."

"I can't help it, sor. I've a faling upon me that Black Mazzard has got her again, and I'm going to fetch her away."

"You are going to your death; and it will be through me, man!"

"Make your moind aisy, sor, about that. It would be all the same if ye were not here. Sure, and I'd be a poor sort of a boy if I towld a woman I loved her, and thin, when the darlin' was in difficulties, jist sat down quietly here, and left her in the lurch."

"She would not have you stir, Dinny, if she knew."

"What of that, sor! Let 'em hang me if they catch me; and if they do, sor, Oi'll doie like a Kelly. And not a word will I shpake of where ye are; and I wish ye safe away to your swateheart—for ye've got wan, I'm thinking, or ye wouldn't be so aiger to get away."

"Well, promise me this, Dinny—you'll wait a few hours and see if we have news."

"Faix, and for your sake, sor, I'll do that same," said Dinny.

He went to the window-opening and leaned there, listening; while Humphrey seated himself upon the edge of the couch to watch the opening above his head, in the expectancy that Mistress Greenheys might arrive and put an end to the terrible suspense as to her silence.

The still, sultry heat was terrible, not a leaf moved outside, and the darkness came on more obscure than usual; for as Humphrey looked out of the window from time to time, to gaze along the forest arcade, there was not a firefly visible, and the heavy, oppressive state of the air seamed to announce a coming storm.

Dinny's figure had long been invisible, but he made his presence known by crooning over snatches of the most depressing minor-keyed Irish melody he could recall; but after a time that ceased, and the silence grew heavy as the heat.

"How long have I been asleep?" he muttered, starting up and listening. "Dinny!"

No answer.

"Dinny! Hist! Are you asleep?"

He dare call no louder, but rose from the couch.

"Dennis Kelly, the traitor, has gone, Humphrey Armstrong!" cried a hoarse voice, and he felt himself driven back into the great tomb-like place.

"Commodore Junk!" cried Humphrey in his surprise.

"Yes, Commodore Junk. Hah! I have you. My prisoner once again."

"Your prisoner! No, not if I die for it!" cried Humphrey, passionately; and he struggled to free himself from the tightening grasp.

"I tell you it is madness. You have proved it yourself, and, weary with your folly, you have returned."

"Returned!" cried Humphrey, fiercely; "yes, but only to be free."

The captain tried to utter some angry appeal, but a fierce struggle had commenced, and the great stony place seemed to be full of whispers, of hoarse sighs, the catching of breath, harsh expirations as the contending pair swayed here and there—the captain, lithe and active as a panther, baffling again and again Humphrey's superior weight and strength. Twice over the latter tripped and nearly fell, but he recovered himself and struggled on, seeking to wind his arms round the buccaneer and lift and throw him with a west country wrestling trick. But try how he would, his adversary seemed to twist like an eel and recover himself, till suddenly, as they swayed here and there, with the thick rugs kicked on one side, there was a low, jangling noise as a sword escaped from its scabbard and fell upon the stony floor.

It was a trifling incident, but it attracted the buccaneer's attention for a moment—just long enough to put him off his guard—the result being that he was thrown heavily, Humphrey planting his knee upon his breast, and as he thrust out a hand it encountered the fallen sword, which he snatched up with a shout of triumph, shortened in his hand, and held to the buccaneer's throat.

"Now," he cried, fiercely, "I have the upper-hand, my lad. You are my prisoner. Make but one sound, and it is your last."

The buccaneer uttered a low moan, and snatched at the blade, but the intervening hand was thrust away, and the point pressed upon the heaving flesh.

"Do you give in?"

"No!" cried the buccaneer, fiercely. "Strike, Humphrey Armstrong; strike, and end my miserable life! Then go and say, I have slain the woman who loved me with all her heart!"

"What!" cried Humphrey, starting back, as the sword fell from his nerveless hand, and a flash, as of a revelation, enlightened him as to the meaning of much that had before seemed strange.

"Well, why do you not strike? Did I not speak plainly? I am Mary Dell!"

Chapter Thirty Five
A Fresh Alarm

"Yes; who called?" cried Humphrey, starting up.

"Hist! Be careful. It is me."

Humphrey sprang front his couch, and was about to speak, when the curtain was thrown roughly aside, and Bart entered quickly.

"What's the matter!" he said, roughly.

"Matter!" said Humphrey. "I—I—must have been dreaming."

Bart looked at him sourly, and then gave a suspicious look round.

"What time is it?" said Humphrey, hastily.

"Time! What do we know about time here? 'Bout four bells."

Humphrey gazed excitedly at the dimly-seen figure, visible by a faint light which streamed in beside the curtain, and then as the curtain fell he advanced slowly till he could peer through and see that Bart had gone right to the far end of the corridor, where he had a lantern set in a stone recess, beside which he ensconced himself, and played sentry once again.

"Escape is impossible unless I choose the gates of death," muttered Humphrey, as he stole back cautiously, and then in a low voice said—

"Hist! Did anyone call?"

"Yes. Is it safe to whisper?" came from above.

"Mistress Greenheys!" cried Humphrey, joyfully. "Speak low, don't whisper; it penetrates too far. How I have longed to hear from you!"

"Oh, sir, pray, pray, save him!"

"Dinny!" said Humphrey, starting.

"Yes. He is to be killed, and it was for your sake he ran that risk. Pray, try and save him."

"What can I do?"

"Implore the captain. He may listen to you. I cannot bear it, sir; it makes me feel half mad!"

"Have you seen him?"

"Seen him? No, sir. He's kept closely shut up in one of the stone chambers by the captain's quarters, and two men watch him night and day."

"As I am watched," said Humphrey, bitterly.

"Yes, sir; but you have not been untrue to your captain. You are not sentenced to death, and every man eager to see you hung. My poor Dennis! It is my fault, too. Why did we ever meet?"

Humphrey was silent.

"You will see the captain, sir, and ask him to spare his life?"

Humphrey ground his teeth. To ask Dinny's life was to ask a favour of Mary Dell, and to place himself under greater obligations still.

"That is not all the trouble," said the woman, who was evidently sobbing bitterly. "That wretch Mazzard is still at liberty."

"Not escaped?" cried Humphrey.

"Not escaped!—not taken!" said the woman. "He is in hiding about the place, and I have seen him."

She seemed to shudder, and her sobs grew more frequent.

"He has not dared to come to you?"

"No, sir; but he came near enough to speak to and threaten me. He will come some night and drag me away, and it would be better to die. Ah!"

She uttered a low cry; and as Humphrey listened he heard low, quick talking, a faint rustling overhead, and then the sound of the voices died away.

"Discovered!" said Humphrey, bitterly. "Fate is working against me now. Better, as she said, to die."

A quarter of an hour's silence ensued, and conscious that at any moment he might be watched, as far as the deep gloom would allow, Humphrey seated himself upon the edge of the old stone altar, and folded his arms, to see what would be the next buffet of fate he was to bear.

He had not long to wait.

There was the sound of a challenge at the end of the corridor, and a quick reply, followed by an angry muttering, and Humphrey laughed mockingly.

"Master and dog!" he said, bitterly. "Mistress and dog, I ought to say."

He drew himself up, for he heard a well-known step coming quickly along the passage. The curtain was snatched aside, and the buccaneer took a dozen strides into the place and stopped, looking round.

"Where are you?" cried the buccaneer, in a harsh, imperious voice, deep almost as that of a man.

There was no reply.

"Where are you, I say?" was repeated imperiously. "Are you ashamed to speak?"

"No! What do you want?"

The buccaneer started in surprise, and faced round.

"Are you there? Coward! Traitor! This explains all. This is the meaning of the haughty contempt—the miserable coldness. And for a woman like that— the mistress of the vilest slave among the men. Humphrey Armstrong— you, the brave officer, to stoop to this! Shame upon you! Shame!"

"Woman, are you mad!"

"Yes! Mad!" cried the buccaneer, fiercely. "I scorn myself for my weak, pitiful fancy for so despicable a creature as you. So this is the brave captain, holding nightly meetings with a woman like that!"

"As I would with anyone who could help me to escape from this vile bondage," said Humphrey.

"Vile! Who has made it vile?"

"You," said Humphrey, sternly; "and as if I were not degraded low enough by your base passion and declaration, you come here in the night to insult me by such an insinuation as that."

There was utter silence for a few moments, and then a quick step forward; and before Humphrey Armstrong could realise the fact, Mary Dell had cast herself down, thrown her arms around him, and laid her cheek against his feet.

"Trample on me and crush me, or kill me," she moaned. "I *am*, mad. I did not think it. Humphrey, have pity on me. You do not knew."

He trembled as she spoke, and clenched his fists tightly; but making an effort over himself, he said coldly—

"You have imprisoned the woman's lover, and she says he is to die. She came there, as she has come many times before, to plan escape with me and the man I persuaded to be the partner of my flight. For this he is to die."

"It is the men's will," groaned the prostrate woman.

"She has been praying to me to save her lover. I felt I could not ask you; but I do ask. Spare the poor fellow's life, and set him free."

"Do you wish it?"

"Yes."

"He shall be set free. You see, I can be merciful, while you alone are stern and cold. How long am I to suffer this?"

"How long will you keep me here a prisoner?"

"How long will you keep yourself a prisoner, you should say. It is for you to be master here; for me to be your slave. How can I humble myself— degrade myself—more?"

Humphrey drew his breath in an angry, impatient hiss.

"For Heaven's sake, rise!" he cried. "You lower yourself. You humble me. Come: let us talk sensibly. I do not want to be hard upon you. I will not say bitter things. Give me your hand."

He took the hand nearest to him as he bent down, and raised the prostrate woman.

"Be seated," he said, gravely. "Let me talk to you as I would to some one who can listen in an unprejudiced spirit."

There was no reply.

"In your character of the captain of these buccaneers you asked me, an English officer, to be your friend and companion—to share with you this command. Is that all?"

Still no reply.

"Let us tear away the veil," he continued; "for surely I am no egotist when I say to you that from the beginning it was more than this."

"No; I did not know then. I thought that you might be my friend; that I should keep up this disguise until the end," was faltered piteously.

"Impossible!" cried Humphrey, sternly. "Let me be plain with you. Let me tell you that I have sat here alone thinking, reading your character, pitying you for all that is past."

"Pity!" came in a deep, low voice.

"Yes," he said, gently, "pity. Let me try, too, and be grateful. For you spared my life at first; you saved it afterwards."

"Go on. You torture me."

"I must torture you, for I have words to speak that must be uttered."

He paused for a few moments; and then went on, speaking now quickly and agitatedly, as if the words he uttered gave him pain at the same time that they inflicted it upon another.

"When I was chosen to command this expedition, against one who had made the name of Commodore Junk a terror all round the gulf and amid the isles, I knew not what my fate might be. There were disease and death to combat, and I might never return."

He paused again. Then more hurriedly—

"There was one to whom—"

"Stop!" came in a quick, angry voice. "I know what you would say; but you do not love another. It is not true."

Humphrey Armstrong paused again, and then in a low, husky voice—

"I bade farewell to one whom I hoped on my return to make my wife. It pains me to say these words, but you force them from me."

"Have I not degraded myself enough? Have I not suffered till I am nearly mad that you tell me this?" came in piteous tones.

"Was I to blame!"

"You? No. It was our fate. What a triumph was mine, to find that I, the master who had lived so long with my secret known but to poor Bart, was now beaten, humbled—to find that day by day I was less powerful of will—that my men were beginning to lose confidence in me, and were ready to listen to the plots and plans of one whom I had spared, for him to become a more deadly enemy day by day. Humphrey Armstrong, have you no return to offer me for all I have suffered—all I have lost? Tell me this is false. You do not—you cannot—love this woman."

He was silent.

"Is she so beautiful? Is she so true? Will she give you wealth and power? Would she lay down her life for you? Would she degrade herself for you as I have done, and kneel before you, saying, 'Have pity on me—I love you'?"

"Hush, woman!" cried Humphrey, hoarsely; "and for pity's sake—the pity of which you speak—let us part and meet no more. I cannot, I will not listen to your words. Give me my liberty, and let me go."

"To denounce me and mine?"

"Am I such a coward, such a wretch, that I should do this?" he cried, passionately.

"Then stay. Listen: I will give you love such as woman never gave man before. I loved your cousin as a weak, foolish girl loves the first man who whispers compliments and sings her praises. It is to her all new and strange, the realisation of something of which she had dreamed. But as the veil fell from my eyes, and I saw how cowardly and base he was, that love withered away, and I thought that love was dead. But when you came my heart leaped, and I trembled and wondered. I shrank from you, telling myself that it was a momentary fancy; and I lied, for it was the first strong love of a lonely woman, thirsting for the sympathy of one who could love her in return."

"Oh! hush—hush!" cried Humphrey. "I have told you that it can never be."

"And she will never love you as I would—as I do," came in a low, imploring whisper.

"Yes, yes, a thousand times yes!" cried Humphrey.

"Even if it were not so I could not—No, I will not speak. I only say, for pity's sake let us part."

He paused, for there was no reply.

"You do not answer," he said, gently. "Think of what I say. I cannot give you love. I should be unworthy of yours if I could. My friendship I can give, and it shall be devoted to saving you from this life."

Still no reply; and the silence and darkness seemed deeper than before.

"You do not take my hand!" he said, bitterly. "You do not listen to my words! Come, for heaven's sake be just to me. Say that I have spoken well."

Still no reply, and he listened as he leaned forward; but there was nothing to be heard but the beating of his own heart.

He leaned forward with outstretched hand, and bending down it touched the cold stone of the altar.

He swept his hand to left and right, listening intently; but there was no sound.

"Why do you not speak?" he said, sternly, as he realised the folly of his first surmise.

His words seemed to murmur in the roof and die away, but there was no reply.

He took a few steps in different directions, suddenly and quickly, listening intently the while, feeling certain that he would hear her try to avoid him; but all was silent, and at last he made for the entrance, drew aside the curtain, and stood listening there.

Feeling sure that his visitor could not have gone that way he turned back, and with outstretched hands paced the great chamber to and fro till at each crossing he touched the stone wall.

Satisfied at length that he was alone, and that the great stone which formed his couch had not been moved, he went once more to the great curtain, pulled it aside, and passed through so as to go along the corridor, for now that his visitor had left him the desire to speak again came strongly.

Half-way down the passage he suddenly became aware of an advancing light, and directly after he saw that it was gleaming from the brown face of Bart.

"Hallo! What now?" he growled. "Where are you going?"

"The captain! Did you meet the captain?" said Humphrey hastily.

"Meet him! No. He came to me and sent me back," said Bart, grimly.

"Where is he, then?"

"At his quarters, of course."

Humphrey Armstrong turned upon his heel frowning, as he felt that a great deal of what he had been saying must have been addressed to vacancy.

He did not turn his head as he paced the corridor, but he was aware that he was followed by Bart, whose lantern shed its faint yellow gleam upon the great curtain till he had passed through, and all was in darkness as he crossed the great chamber and threw himself upon the couch. But the place was feebly illuminated directly after, as Bart drew the drapery aside and peered in, holding the lantern well above his head to satisfy himself that his prisoner was there.

Then he drew back, the great curtain fell into its place, and Humphrey's jailer went slowly to his niche, where he set down his light, seated himself, and with arms folded and chin resting upon his breast, moodily brooded over the position.

"A curse!" he muttered more than once—"a curse! If he were dead there would be peace once more, for she would forget him."

"Suppose," he thought, after a while—"suppose he was to be gone next time she came. Well, he might have escaped, and after a time she'd be at rest. It would be so easy, and it would be for her. And yet he's so brave and so handsome, such a man for her! Better see her happy and kill myself. Not that I need!" he said, bitterly; "for she said she'd do that if aught happened to him."

"It's hard work," he muttered, after a while, "seeing the woman you love care for some one else, and him lying there, and as good us asking you to put him out of the way."

Bart's head sank lower as he crouched there, struggling with the great temptation of his life, till at last he slowly rose, and, shading the lantern within his breast, stepped cautiously toward the curtain which draped the door. Stretching out his hand, he was in the act of drawing it softly aside when there was a firm clutch at his shoulder, and a low voice whispered in his ear—

"What are you going to do?"

Bart drew back, let fall the certain, and faced his leader.

"Nothing!" he said, abruptly.

"You villain!" whispered the buccaneer. "I read murder in your eye!"

"I'm tired of it," growled Bart. "I give it up. I know what I am. I hopes for nothing; but when I see you go mad for one who hates you, and who will bring ruin on us all, as well as make you unhappy, it makes me mad too. He's an enemy, and I could kill anybody as gives you pain!"

"As I could, and would, slay you if you hurt a hair of the head of the man I love!"

"The man you love!" muttered Bart, bitterly. "Time back it was the other Captain Armstrong. Now it's him. Anybody but a poor fellow like me!"

"You have told me again and again you were content to be my friend. Go back to the quarters, and I'll watch myself. I have no one here I can trust!"

Bart's face worked as they slowly returned along the corridor, and rage and pain were marked in turn upon his features.

As they reached the place where he set down his lantern, he stood in a bent attitude, as if pondering upon the words which had been said.

"Why are you waiting?" said the captain, imperiously.

"Them words o' yours," said Bart. "You said you could kill me."

"As I would have done," was the fierce reply, "if harm had befallen him!"

"Better it had!" said Bart, bitterly. "Better it had, and you'd killed me. Saved you from pain, and me from a life of misery. Am I to go?"

"Yes," said the captain, less firmly, as the man's tones betrayed the agony of his spirit. "Go; I have no one now whom I can trust!"

"Don't say that to me," said the poor fellow, hoarsely, as he fell upon his knees and clasped his hands. "Kill me if you like, captain, but don't doubt me. All these years I've done nothing but try and serve you faithful and well."

"And you would have slain the man I love!"

"Something tempted me, and it said that it was for your good, and when it was like that I felt I could do anything."

"You would have betrayed me!"

"I would have killed him as give you pain, him who has changed you, and broken you down to what you are. I knew as I now know, that it's ruin to you!"

"Silence, man, and go!"

"What has he done for you!" cried Bart. "Nought but give you hard words, and curse you ever since he has been here, and yet you go on loving him!"

"What have I ever done for you, Bart, but give you hard words and cold looks, and yet you have gone on loving me!"

"True," said Bart, hoarsely; "and so I shall till I die!"

"And so shall I, Bart, till I die!"

"Don't talk like that," he groaned. "It's better to live and suffer than to talk of death. I give in—once more I give in!"

"Then go; I will watch!"

"No, captain; don't send me away! Trust me this once. I am faithful to you!"

"Ay; but not to him."

There was a pause, and Bart seemed to be struggling hard with himself, till he had won some terrible victory.

"Tell me," he said at last, "tell me to swear. I'll be as true to him as I've been to you, and I'll swear it. I'll die for him, if you say I am!"

"Then swear, Bart. Swear that I may depend on you as I would on myself! That, for my sake, you will defend him from all evil, come when it may!"

"Because you love him?" said Bart, slowly.

"Because I love him, man!"

There was a painful silence for a few minutes, and then, as he knelt there, on the time-worn stones, the simple-hearted single-natured man said, in a low husky voice—

"I swear it: so help me God!"

Bart rose slowly, with his breath coming and going as if after some terrible struggle, and, as he stood there trembling, he felt his hand seized and held tightly between two warm, moist palms.

He let it rest there for a few moments, and then snatched it away.

"What are you going to do?" whispered the buccaneer.

"Obey orders," said Bart relapsing, as it were, to his former manner.

"No; stay. I have only you to trust."

"And you'll leave me now along of him?"

"Without a feeling of dread, Bart; because the temptation would come in vain."

"Are we all mad!" said Bart, softly, as he stood listening to the retiring footsteps; and then he sank down upon the stones, with his back to the wall, and the light shining upon his rugged head.

Chapter Thirty Six
One Prisoner Free

"Dinny! You here!"

"Yes, sor—it's me."

"But at liberty?"

"Yes, sor; and I'm to attend on ye as I did avore."

"But—"

"Oh, it's all right, sor! The captain's a bit busy, and I'm not to be hung at present. I'm to be kept till there's a big holiday, and be strung up then. It's the fashion out in this part of the counthry."

"My poor fellow," cried Humphrey, "I am glad to see you safe again!"

"Safe, sir! and d'ye call it safe, whin the first time, perhaps, as the skipper gets in a passion I shall be hung up in all me youth and beauty, like one o' the big drooping flowers on a tree!"

"Nonsense, man!"

"Oh, it's sinse, sor; and I shall droop, too, wid all my moight!"

"No, no," said Humphrey, as he pondered upon the past, and saw in Dinny's reprieve a desire to gratify him. "No, my lad. I appealed to the captain to spare your life, and this is the result."

"Did ye, now, sor! Sure, an' I thought that the pretty little darlin' had been down on her knees to him; and, knowing what a timpting little beauty she is, it made me shiver till I began to consider what sort of a man the captain is, and how, when the boys have been capturing the women, and sharing 'em out all round, the skipper niver wance took a fancy to a single sowl. Faix, and he's always seemed to take to you, sor, more than to annyone else. Some men's of a marrying sort, and some ar'n't. The skipper's one of the ar'n'ts."

Humphrey looked at the man curiously, but it was evident that he had no hidden meaning.

"Sure, sor," continued Dinny, "when I think about you two, it has always seemed to me as if the captain wanted to be David to your Jonathan, only the other way on, for the skipper isn't a bit like King David."

"Have you suffered much!"

"Suffered, sor!"

"I mean in prison."

"Divil a bit, sor! I've lived like a foighting-cock. They always fade a man up well in this part of the counthry before they finish him off."

"You may make your mind easy, Dinny," said Humphrey, thoughtfully; "the captain will not take your life unless he takes mine too."

"An' is it mak me moind aisy, sor, when I can't get spache of the darlin', and that Black Mazzard in hiding somewhere and freckening the poor sowl to death!"

"Surely, there is nothing to fear from him now?"

"Faix, and I don't know that same. I shall always be freckened about him till a dacent praste has tied us two together toightly, and then I sha'n't be happy till I know that Black Mazzard's nailed up bechuckst four boards; and if I've annything to do wid it they shall be as thick as trees and nailed wid screws."

"He has made his escape somewhere?"

"Not he, sor; and I don't like the look o' things. I've been too much shut up to see annything, being more like a cockroach in a whishky bottle and the cork tied down than annything else. But I'm skeart, captain darlin'; and if annything happens—whisht! have ye kept my saycret?"

He put his lips close to the prisoner's ears, and whispered as he gave a knowing look at the couch.

"It is a secret still, Dinny."

"Good luck to ye, sor! Thin, if annything happens, just you go there and lie shnug till I come to ye; and if ye'll tak' my advice ye'll keep on putting a dhrop o' wine in the cellar and shtoring up a bit o' food; and if it isn't wanted, why ye're no worse off."

"Explain yourself, my lad," said the prisoner, for the lively chatter of the Irishman relieved the tedium of his confinement.

"Hist!"

"Murther!" ejaculated Dinny, as a faint signal came from overhead. "Sure an' I was niver cut out for a prophet afther all."

"Dinny!—Captain Armstrong!" came from above.

"Good luck to ye, darlin'! kape on shpaking," whispered Dinny, excitedly. "It does me good to hear ye; but niver mind the captain, darlin'. Shpake to me."

"I came here—at great risk," came down, as if the speaker was panting heavily. "There's something wrong—I want to put you on your guard. Tell the captain. Quick! I dare not stay."

"But, darlin', what's wrong? Whisht! shpake out, and let's hear ye. Look at that, now! Why, she's gone!"

For there was a faint rustling overhead, and then all was silence once again.

"Sure, sor, would ye look at me," cried Dinny, with a most perplexed expression of countenance, "and tell me if I'm awake or it's only a dhrame."

"Dinny," said Humphrey, "she would not have come in such haste if there had not been good cause. Go and warn the captain. Quick!"

The day passed without news, and, weary with his tedious pacing of his great cell, Humphrey Armstrong threw himself upon his couch, where he lay, with the great solemn face of the old stone idol seeming to loom down mysteriously from above.

It was not until the next morning that he saw Dinny again. The night had passed quietly, and the day found Humphrey still watching. He, however, dropped into a pleasant slumber as the sun rose, in which sleep he was still plunged when Dinny came.

"Jist nawthing at all, sor," he said. "The darlin' must have got a craze in her head, for when I told the captain he trated me wid scorn, and Bart asked me if I was playing the fool."

"Then there is no danger!"

"Divil a bit, sor, that I can think out," said Dinny.

"But Mistress Greenheys."

"What about her, sor?"

"What did she say?"

"Sure an' you heard it all, sor. I couldn't repate it now if I thried."

"But you have seen her since?"

"Sin her! Bedad I'd only like to—if it was only to shpake wan word to her wid me oi. No, sor, I can't get spache of her."

"But is all quiet in the place?"

"An' is it quiet? Why, a tomb in Aygypt is a lively place to it. The schooner's getting rotting for want o' work, and the men do nothing but dhrink and shlape, and the captain's shut up all alone whin he isn't down in the forest saying his prayers."

"Is it the calm that comes before the storm, Dinny?" said Humphrey.

"Sure an' I don't know, sor; but I'll kape watch if I can, and give ye word if there's annything wrong; but me poor head's in a mix, and since I've been out of prishn I seem to see nothing but Black Mazzard shwarming all over the place and takkin' me darling away. Did ye intersade wid the captain, sor?"

"Dinny, I have not seen him again," said Humphrey, frowning.

"Not seen him, sor! Why, he has been here half a dozen toimes."

"Been here? No."

"Sure and I saw him wid me own ois, sor. Twice he came to the windy there and four toimes along by the big passage. Sure I thought ye'd been colloguing."

"I was not aware of it," said Humphrey, calmly; but his words did not express the feelings that were raging within his breast, and as soon as he was alone he tried to analyse them.

He must flee. He could do nothing else, and growing momentarily more excited, he tried to force himself to act and think.

The old temple. He would flee there for the present, he said. It would remove him from Mary's pursuit, for she would never dream of his seeking refuge there, and from that place he might perhaps be able to open up communication with Dinny.

He had no weapon, so he caught up a large table-knife and stuck it in his waistband. It was not much, but something, and at that moment he recalled Mary Dell's history—how she had told him that they had begun with a canoe; through that captured a larger boat; that larger boat had enabled them to take a vessel; and so on till the swift schooner had been obtained.

In the same way that knife should grow into a sword, he said to himself; and then he felt a sensation of half-blind rage at himself for making the comparison.

"What is this hateful unsexed creature to me!" he said, angrily, as he stood thinking as to his next step.

Food! He must have food. In his excitement and the fury of the haste that was upon him, the trouble of taking it angered him; but he knew that he must have it, and gathering together what he could, he paused once more to think and listen.

All was silent, and the drawing aside of the great curtain proved that Bart was not on guard, for there was no dull, yellow gleam of his lantern at the end of the corridor, and once more it came over the prisoner as a feeling of wonder that he should not again and again have taken such steps as these. Almost unguarded, his prison doors and windows always open, and freedom given him to wander about the ruins, and yet like a pinioned bird he had stayed.

"They know that the sea before, the forest and mountain behind, are stronger than bolt and bar," something seemed to whisper to him as he stood hesitating.

"But not to a determined man, ready to do or die!" he cried, as if forced to answer aloud; and he set his teeth as he still hesitated and paused before hurrying out of the great dark place.

He stopped. What would she do when she found that he had gone? What would she say of the man whom, with all her faults, she evidently dearly loved, and would sacrifice all to win?

Humphrey Armstrong stamped fiercely upon the old stone flooring, making the vaulted roof echo as he thrust his fingers into his ears in a child-like attempt to shut out and deafen himself to the silent whisperings which assailed him.

He gave one glance round, trying to penetrate the darkness, and hesitated no longer, but strode away, passing out of the long corridor out among the ruins, and, well accustomed to the place now, making straight for the pathway which, at its division, turned toward the old temple.

All was still; but it seemed lighter away to his left than he could quite account for, and he was starting again when a distant shout as of many voices came through the silence of the night and died away.

"Carousing," he muttered, and he hesitated again.

If the men were carousing the watch kept would be less strict, and there might be some chance of obtaining a boat.

"To start alone on a cruise," he said, half aloud. "What madness!" Then passionately: "It all seems madness, and I can do nothing but drift with fate."

Fighting down the strange hesitancy which kept assailing in various forms, especially now in that of conjuring up difficulties in the way of escape, he plunged sturdily into the forest path, and, as fast as the darkness allowed, went on straight for the old temple, a grim place of refuge, with its ghastly relics; of Abel Dell lying, as it were, in state; and the horrible, haunting recollections of the huge cavernous cenote where the would-be assassin had met his fate, and the other had been consigned as to his tomb.

It was painful work. Every now and then some thorny creeper of rapid growth hung across and tore his skin; at some sudden turn he came in contact with tree-trunk or mouldering stone; but the greater the difficulties in the darkness, the greater the rest seemed to Humphrey Armstrong's brain, and he kept on till a sudden turn brought him close to the fork, where one path went winding to the left toward the men's and the captain's quarters, the other to the temple.

As he approached he became conscious of a rustling sound, as of a wild creature passing through the forest, and he snatched his knife from his waist, ready to strike for life if attacked; but, firmly convinced that there were no denizens of the wild there but such as were more likely to avoid him, he kept on again, to reach the dividing path just as he became aware that it was no creature passing through the wilderness of trees, but someone, like himself, hurrying along the track from the men's quarters so rapidly, that they came in contact, and a hand seized him by the throat, and the point of some weapon seemed to be pressed against his breast, as a voice exclaimed in a hoarse whisper—

"Make the slightest sound and it is your last."

And as these words seemed to be hissed into his face, a shout arose from some distance along the path, and the tramping of feet and rustling of branches intimated that people were rapidly coming in pursuit.

"You!" exclaimed Humphrey, hoarsely, as he stood with hand uplifted to strike, but suspended in the act as if every muscle had suddenly become stone.

"Humphrey Armstrong!"

The hand that had grasped his throat dropped nerveless, and the weapon fell from his breast as the shouting of men increased.

"Well," said Humphrey, bitterly, as if he were forcing himself to say words that he did not mean, "why do you not strike? I was escaping. Call up your gang of cut-throats and end it all."

"Hush! For Heaven's sake, hush! You will be heard."

"Well," said Humphrey, aloud, and as if in defiance; but a warm soft hand was placed over his lips, and its owner whispered—

"You were trying to escape, or did you know?"

"Know!" said Humphrey, involuntarily speaking lower. "Know what? I was escaping."

"To the old temple! No, no, they are going there."

"Your hounds!"

"Silence, man, for your life!" was whispered close to his ear, and the hand once more sought his lips.

"Come on, my lads!" came out of the darkness ahead. "I know where to find him, snivelling yonder among the old images. Come on!"

There was a shout, and it seemed as if the leader of a body of men, beneath whose feet the rotten branches that bestrewed the path crackled, had suddenly halted for his companions to close up before saying a few final words of encouragement.

"Now then," the voice said in thick, husky tones, "stand by me, my lads. He's gone on there, and there's no getting back. One good, bold blow and we'll scotch him like a snake. Then fair share and share alike of all there is hidden away, and start straight. He's no good now, and the others'll join in when he's gone. Ready?"

"Ay, ay!" came in hoarse, drunken tones; and as Humphrey felt himself pressed back into the pathway by which he had come, there was a staggering of feet, and a dull trampling, as about a dozen men passed on, leaving behind them the thick reek of hot, spirit-laden breath.

"Now!" as the steps passed on. "Now," was whispered in Humphrey's ear; "this way."

"Ah!" arose in a fierce growl, as some one of the party who had not gone on with the rest made a dash at and seized the buccaneer captain. "Prisoner! Who is it? Here, hi mates, I've—"

He said no more. Without pause or thought why he did this—why he sought to save his companion—Humphrey Armstrong made a spring in the direction of the voice, his hands came in contact with a coarse bull throat, and its owner was driven backwards, to fall with his head striking a projecting piece of stone, dragging the buccaneer in the fall.

The man was stunned, and lay perfectly inert as Humphrey and his companion struggled to their feet, panting with exertion, and listening for the return of the party who had gone on.

But they had not heard the noise of the struggle, the maze-like turnings of the path had shut it out, and their voices came now muffled and soft, as if from a distance.

Then Humphrey felt his hand gripped firmly.

"This way."

"What! Are you going to take me back to prison?" said Humphrey mockingly.

"Do you wish to go straight to death?"

"I am going straight to liberty!" cried Humphrey.

"This way, then," whispered his companion; and without a word Humphrey allowed himself to be led back along the dark arcade, listening to the heavy panting of his guide, who seemed to be breathing heavily, and as if in pain.

For some time no word was spoken. Then, as he became aware of his companion's purpose, Humphrey stopped short.

"You are leading me back to that cursed prison," he said fiercely. "Loose my hand."

"I am leading you to the only place where you will be safe," was whispered back. "Have I not suffered enough, man? Do you think I wish to die with the knowledge that, these dogs will seize and rend you in their drunken frenzy?"

"Rend me!"

"Yes. They have risen. That wretch, whom I have spared so long in my weak folly, is at their head. Humphrey Armstrong, believe me, I am trying to save your life!"

"Then why not make for the shore? A boat! Give me a boat and let me go!"

"Half the men who were faithful to me are dead, treacherously burned to death in their quarters. I cannot explain; but the doorway was blocked by those fiends. The landing-place is guarded by a portion of his bloodthirsty gang. To go to the shore is to seek your death. Will you not trust me now?"

"It is to keep me here!" he cried fiercely.

"To keep you here when I would gladly say go! Trust me. Give me time to think. I was coming to save you when we met. Will you not believe?"

"Yes!" cried Humphrey, hoarsely. "I will trust you!"

"Hah!"

That was all. His hand was gripped more tightly; and, as he yielded it to his companion, he felt himself led with unerring decision in and out among the mouldering ruins of the edge of the clearing to the side of the old amphitheatre, a faint metallic clink from time to time indicating that a sword was being struck upon the stones to make sure of the way.

"You are going back there?" said Humphrey.

"Yes," came back hoarsely. "Do not speak. We may be heard."

Humphrey was conscious that his guide had led him to the old altar and sunk upon it with a moan; but she still tightly clung to his hand.

There they remained in silence as if listening for pursuit; and the deep, hoarse breathing of both sounded painfully loud in the utter darkness.

Humphrey essayed to speak again and again, but he felt that he could not trust himself to utter words.

It was his companion who broke the painful silence as she still clung to his hand.

"I ought to have acted sooner," she said bitterly. "I might have known it would come to this; but in my cruel selfishness I could not speak—I could not let you go. Do not blame me—do not reproach me. It was my madness; and now the punishment has come."

"I do not understand you," he said huskily.

"You do," she said gently. "But it is no time to think of this. Listen! These men will search every spot to find and slay me—and you; but you shall escape. Now, listen? Below this old place there is a rock chamber, known only to me and Bart—who lies wounded yonder and helpless; but he will not betray the secret, even if he thinks that you are there. You will go to the end of your couch, press heavily with your shoulder against the corner, forcing it in this direction, and then the great stone will move upon a pivot. There is a way down—"

"You need not tell me," said Humphrey at this point. "I know."

"Thank Heaven!" she ejaculated. "Keep in hiding there till the wretches are off their guard; and then cautiously make your way by night down to the landing-place, and by some means seize a boat. There will be no guard kept when I am gone."

"And my people—my poor fellows?"

"Gone," she said quietly. "They seized a boat and escaped long ago. All has been confusion here since—since I have been mad," she added piteously.

"Escaped!"

"Yes; and you will escape. And in the future, when you are away—and happy—don't curse me—think of me as a poor lost woman, driven by fate—to what I am—but who saw and loved you, Humphrey Armstrong, as woman has seldom loved before."

"Oh, hush!" he said huskily. "For Heaven's sake don't speak like that!"

"No," she said gently, after listening for a few moments; but all was still. "I will not speak. It is nearly over now. You will forgive me?"

"Forgive you—yes!"

She uttered a low sigh, full of thankfulness, as she still clung to his hand.

"It is enough," she said. "Now, go! You know the way. Be cautious, be patient, and bide your time; and then Heaven speed you safely home!—He has forgiven me," she sighed to herself, and the pressure upon his hand seemed to increase.

"Well," she said after a few moments' pause, "why do you stay?"

Her voice startled him in its intensity, for it seemed to echo through the place; and his hand had, as it had been for many minutes past, grasped hers with crushing force as the tide rose to its fullest height and bore him on.

"And you!" he said. "What will you do?"

"I!" she said with a faint laugh; "I shall wait here until they come."

"Wait here!" cried Humphrey. "They will kill you!"

"Yes," she said softly.

"Then why not share my flight? Come with me now while there is time. I will protect you and take you where you will. I cannot leave you like this!"

"Not leave me?" she said with a sob.

"No. Do you think me such a cur that I could leave you to the mercy of these wretches?"

"It is too late," she said. "Go!"

"Go?"

"Yer, while there is time."

"But you can hide as well as I!" he cried excitedly. "Come!"

"It is too late," she said, and he felt her hand tremble in his grasp.

"And leave you?" he cried. "I would sooner die!"

"Then you do love me?" she cried wildly, as she half rose from the altar, but sank back.

"Love you!" he cried passionately. "I have fought with it, I have battled with it till I have been nearly mad! Love you, Mary, my brave, true heroine! I love you with all my heart!"

She uttered a wild cry of joy as he threw himself upon his knees and clasped her to his heart, his face buried in her breast and her two arms clung tightly round his neck, as she uttered a low moan of mingled joy and pain.

"Love you!" he whispered, as he raised his face, and his lips sought hers; "my darling! words will not tell my love! Come, what is the world to us? You are my world, my own, my love! Come!"

She clung to him passionately for a few moments.

"At last!" she said softly, as if to herself; "the love of one true noble man! Ah!"

A low deep sigh escaped her, and then, as if roused to a sense of her position, she thrust him back and listened.

"Hark!" she said, as a low shout arose. "They are coming back—they will be here soon! Quick! lose no time! You must escape!"

"And you?" he said, wildly.

She took his hand and laid it slowly upon her bosom, to press it there, so that he could fool the heavy dull throb of her heart.

For a moment even then he did not realise what she meant. Then, with a wild cry he leaped to his feet, for his hand was wet with the warm blood which welled from a terrible wound.

"You are hurt?" he cried.

"To the death, Humphrey. Oh, my love, my love! Take me in your arms once more and hold me to your heart. Tell me that you will remember me, and then lay me here, upon this old stone, with your kiss wet upon my lips. Death will be easy then!"

"Death easy! I leave you! If you must die it shall be together!" he panted, as he once more enfolded her in his arms.

"This is madness," she whispered, as she struggled feebly in his embrace. "Go, for pity's sake—go!"

"My place is here!" he said in a low fierce voice, as he took up the sword she had let fall upon the pavement. "We shall not die alone. Whose cowardly hand inflicted that wound?"

"You need not ask," she said feebly. "He missed before—the blow was true this time."

"The fiend! The devil!" groaned Humphrey, as the sword quivered in his grasp. "Well, we shall want a slave to open the gates of death. His shall be the task!"

She clung to him with failing strength, and drew herself up by him till she could once more rest upon his breast, with her arms tightly clasped about his neck.

"You told me at last you loved me," she panted. "You said the words I have so hungered to hear—words I thought that I should have died and never heard pass your lips. Now that I know it, and that it is true, do not embitter my last moments by showing me that I have tried in vain."

"I could not live without you now!" he cried passionately, as he held her to him more tightly still.

"They are coming. It is too late for me. Let me die in peace, knowing that you are saved."

He raised her in his arms and bore her to the great stone, and, as he laid her gently down, the noise of the coming gang could be heard.

There was not a moment to lose, and any slip in his instructions would have resulted in destruction; but as he pressed against the stone it easily revolved, and he stooped once more and raised the fainting woman in his arms, to bear her down into the tomb-like structure and place her at the foot of the broad stone stairs which led into the vault.

As he loosened her arms from about his neck and passed quickly up again, there were heavy steps in the long corridor, and lights flashed through the openings of the great curtain. So close were the men that Humphrey saw their faces as he stood on the upper step, and dragged at the slab by two great hollows underneath, made, apparently, by the olden masons for the mover's hands.

For the moment Humphrey, as he bent down there beneath the place on which he had so often slept or lain to think, felt certain that he must have been seen; but the muffled voices came close up, the steps trampled here and there, sounding dull and hollow, and there was no seizing of the great stone, no smiting upon its sides.

He held his breath as he stood bending down and listening for some indication of danger; but it seemed as if the men had coursed all over the place, searching in all directions, and were about to go, when, all at once, there was a shout close to the place where he had raised Mary from the altar.

The shout was followed by a muffled sound of many voices, and he listened, wondering what it meant. Some discovery had evidently been made, but what?

He shuddered, and a chill of horror shot through him, for he knew directly after.

It was blood.

Chapter Thirty Seven
In the Vault

With the deathly silence which ensued as the heavy echoing steps of the searchers passed away, the men being completely at fault as to why certain drops of blood should be lying near the couch, Humphrey descended the steps once more.

"They are gone," he whispered, but there was no reply; and, feeling softly about, his hand came in contact with Mary's arm, to find that she lay back in a corner of the vault, with a kerchief pressed tightly against her breast.

He hastily bandaged the wound, firmly binding the handkerchief which she held there with his own and the broad scarf he wore, and, after placing her in a more comfortable position, began to search in the darkness for the food and water which were there.

The water was soon found—a deep, cool cistern in the middle of the floor.

The food lay close at hand, and with it one of the silver cups he had had in use above. With this he bore some of the cool refreshing liquid to the wounded woman, holding some to her lips and bathing her brow, till she uttered a sigh and returned to consciousness, her first act being to stretch out her hand and lay it upon Humphrey's shoulder to draw him nearer to her.

"Don't leave me!" she said feebly. "It is very dark!"

"But we are safe," he whispered. "They are gone."

"Yes," she sighed; "I heard them. How long is it to day?"

"It cannot be long now," he said, as he took her hand.

She sighed as she felt the unwonted tenderness and rested her head against his shoulder.

"No," she said, softly, "it cannot be long now. It will come too soon!"

There was so much meaning in her voice that he felt a cold chill, as if the hand of death had passed between to separate these two so strangely brought together.

"Are you in pain!" he said.

"Pain! No. Happy—so happy!" she whispered. "For you do love me!"

"Love you!" he cried.

"And she—at home?"

"That was not love," he said, wildly. "But now tell me about this place—shall we see the day when it comes?"

"You will," she said, softly. "I shall—perhaps."

"Perhaps! No, you shall!" he whispered, as he pressed his arm gently around her, forgetting everything now of the past, save that this woman loved him, and that there was a future before them of hope and joy. "Tell me what I can do—to help you."

"Hold me like that," she whispered, with a sigh of content. "It is better so. It could never have been—only my wild dream—a woman's thirst for the love of one in whom she could believe. A woman's love!"

Little more than an hour could have passed, during which Humphrey had twice heard sounds of voices, and once a heavy step overhead—this last making him steal his right hand softly toward the sword that lay by his side—when a faint light seemed to gleam on the surface of the water in the centre of the vault; and soon after he found that this served to shed a softened dawn through the place—a dawn which grow stronger, but was never more than a subdued twilight. It was enough, though, to show him the proportions of the place, its quaint carving, and the fact that beside the long shaft which opened out far above his head there was what seemed to be a stone grille, beyond which was the tangled growth of the forest, much of which, in root and long, prickly shoot, penetrated nearly to where they sat.

As the light grew stronger he saw that his companion seemed to have lost the old masculine look given by her attire; for coat and vest had been cast aside, and the loose shirt, open at the neck, had more the aspect of a robe. Her dark hair curled closely about her temples; and as Humphrey Armstrong gazed down at the face, with its parted lips and long lashes lying upon the creamy dark cheeks, his heart throbbed, for he felt that he had won the love of as handsome a woman as any upon whom his eyes had ever lit.

He forgot the wound, the bandaging kerchief seeming in the semi-darkness like some scarf; and as he sat and gazed he bent down lower and softly touched the moist forehead with his lips.

Mary awoke up with a frightened start and gazed at him wildly, but as consciousness came her look softened and she nestled to him.

"I did not mean to wake you," he said.

She started again and looked at him wildly, as if she fancied she had detected a chilliness in his manner; but his eyes undeceived her, and as he raised her hand to his lips, she let it rest there for a few moments, and then stole it round his neck.

"Tell me," he said gently, "your wound?"

She shook her head softly.

"No," she whispered; "let it rest. Talk of yourself. You will wait here two days, and then steal out at night and make your way down to the shore. You know the way!"

"If I do not you will guide me," he said.

She looked at him keenly to see if he meant what he said, and then, reading the sincerity of his words in his frank eyes, she shook her head again.

"No," she whispered. "You asked me of my wound. It is home. Humphrey Armstrong, this is to be my tomb!"

"What!" he cried. "Oh, no! no! no! You must live to bless me with your love!"

"Live to disgrace you with my love!"

"Mary!"

There was such a depth of love, such intensity in the tone in which he uttered her name, that she moaned aloud.

"Ah, you are in pain!" he cried.

"In pain for you," she whispered, "for you suffer for my sake. Hist! Do you hear?"

She clung to him tightly.

"No," he said, "there is nothing."

"Yes," she said, softly. "Steps. I can hear them—they are coming back."

He listened once more, but his ears were wanting in the preternatural keenness brought on by his companion's exalted nerves. He heard nothing for a few moments, and then with a start he seized the sword, for steps were faintly heard now to grow plainer and plainer till they were close overhead.

Mary signed to him to listen; and at that moment the stone slab moved gently a few inches, for someone had seated himself upon the edge, and the buzz of talking was heard.

"Now, my lad," cried a hoarse, drink-engendered voice, which came plainly to where they crouched, "you know all about it, and I'm captain now. Where's that prisoner?"

"Sure, and how could I know anny way, Black Mazzard?"

"Captain Mazzard!" roared the first speaker.

"Oh! Murther! Put them pishtols away, and I'll call ye captain, or adhmiral if ye like!"

"No fooling! Where is that prisoner?"

"Which one, sor?"

"No fooling, Paddy! Captain Armstrong?"

"Faix, an' he must have run away, skeart loike, whin he heerd you were coming."

"You know where he is?"

"Faix, and that's thrue," said Dinny.

"Where is he, then? Tell me the truth, and I'll let you live this time. Tell me a lie, and I'll hang you."

"Och, don't, captain! Ye'd waken yer crew horribly if ye were to hang me."

"I'll hang you, as sure as you stand there, if you don't confess."

"Murther! Don't, now, captain, for I shouldn't die dacently if ye did hang me. It isn't a way I've been accustomed to. Ah, moind! That pishtol might go off."

"It will go off if you don't speak. He's hidden somewhere here, and you know where. Speak out!"

"Shpake out! And is it shpake out?" said Dinny, slowly as with advanced blade Humphrey stood ready to plunge it into the breast of the first man who attempted to descend. "Oh, well, I'll shpake out then."

"The traitor!" mattered Humphrey. "False to one, false to all."

"Where is he, then?" roared Mazzard.

"Faix, he's in his skin, captain."

"You dog!" roared Mazzard. And there was the report of a pistol, followed by a wild shriek.

"Don't—don't kill!" cried a piteous woman's voice. "Don't kill him!"

"Not kill him!" snarled Mazzard.

"No—no! Spare him, and I'll tell you."

"Bedad, an' if ye do, I'll niver forgive ye," cried Dinny, fiercely. "Ye don't know nawthing. He's eshcaped."

"Where is he!" roared Mazzard. "Speak out, woman, or I'll blow his head off!"

Humphrey sprang up a couple of steps to defend Dinny; but Mary Dell lay there, and to show himself was to betray her—the woman whom he knew he passionately loved. Of himself he thought nothing.

But the task of betrayal to save her lover was spared to Mistress Greenheys, for, as Black Mazzard stood with one hand on Dinny's shoulder, and his second pistol pointed close to his ear, so that his second shot should not fail, one of his men exclaimed aloud—

"Why, he's there! Look at the blood!"

Mazzard turned and glanced down at the floor upon which he stood, then at the stained stone which formed the cover of the vault. He uttered a harsh laugh, for the stone had been slightly moved.

"Here, half a dozen of you!" he roared. "Lay hold!"

His men seized the stone; and after one or two trials to raise it up, it was thrust sideways, and the hiding-place revealed.

With a yell of savage delight Black Mazzard began to descend, followed by his crew. There was the clash of swords, two men fell, wallowing in their blood, and then Humphrey drew back into the corner before Mary Dell, determined to defend her to the last.

Two more men went down; and there was a brief pause, followed by a savage rush and a *mêlée*, in which Humphrey's sword snapped off at the hilt, and the next minute he was above in the great chamber, pinioned between two of Mazzard's men; and Mary Dell was borne up to lie at her conqueror's feet.

"You savage!" roared Humphrey, as he sank panting on a stone.

"Savage!" retorted Mazzard, with a brutal grin. "Stand up, you dog!"

"Stand yourself—in the presence of your king's officer!" shouted Humphrey in his rage.

"King!" cried Mazzard, mockingly. "I'm king here. Now then, you!" he cried to his men, who enjoyed seeing him bearded. "Quick!—two ropes!"

He turned sharply upon his men, who hurried off to obey the command.

Humphrey gazed at Mazzard aghast. The threat implied in the order seemed too horrible to be believed, and for the moment he looked round in doubt.

But Mazzard was in power; and in a few minutes the ropes were forthcoming.

Humphrey glanced from the men who approached and then at Mary Dell, with the intention of proclaiming her sex; but a horrible feeling of dread thrilled through him at the thought of making such a revelation to the monsters who had gained the upper-hand, and, gathering himself up, he waited his time, and then wrested himself free, sending the men who held him right and left, and leaped to where—unable to stand upright—his fellow prisoner was held.

Before they could recover from their surprise he had torn a sword from one of them, and, whirling it round his head, he drove them back, and clasping Mary Dell's waist, stood with flashing eyes, ready for the first who would attack.

"Is there no man here who will help?" he shouted.

"Bedad there is!" cried Dinny, leaping upon the nearest, and in a moment tearing his weapon from his hand. "If I die for it, captain, it shall be like a man."

Black Mazzard stood for a moment aghast at the daring displayed. Then a grim look of savagery crossed his evil countenance, and he drew his sword.

"Now, my lads," he said, fiercely, "it's three ropes we want, I see. Come on."

He made a rush forward, followed by his men; but at this moment a solitary shot flashed from the folds of the curtain, and as the report reverberated through the great stone chamber, Black Mazzard span round as if upon a pivot, and fell with a heavy thud upon the floor.

His men paused in their onslaught, appalled by the suddenness of their leader's fall; but as they saw Bart come forward, piece in hand, their hesitation turned to rage, and they advanced once more to the attack.

"Good-bye!" whispered Humphrey, bending for a moment over Mary, who clung to him, her eyes fixed on his with a longing, despairing gaze, and then, as he thrust her back, the attack began.

The odds were about eight to one, and the issue could not for a moment be in doubt; but hardly had sword met sword, and blow been exchanged, when a ringing cheer arose, and with a rush a couple of dozen well-armed sailors dashed in by corridor and window, and the tables were completely turned.

There was a rush made for the door, but those who tried in that direction were driven back; while half a dozen who backed into a corner of the great chamber, as if desperately determined to sell their lives dearly, were boldly attacked and beaten down, the whole party being reduced from the savage band of followers of the dead ruffian at their feet to a herd of helpless prisoners, abject to a degree.

Humphrey saw nothing of this, only that they were saved; for, dropping his sword, he sank on his knees by the side of her who lay back with her eyes fixed upon him, full of a longing, imploring look, whose import he read too well.

He bent down closely to her to take her hand in his, and started to find that it was cold; but there was vitality in it enough for the fingers to close upon his hand tightly, while the lips he kissed moved slightly, and he heard as faintly as if just breathed—

"It is better so."

"No, no!" he panted. "We are saved! Mary—dearest—"

He said no more, for the longing look in those eyes seemed intensified, and the pupils dilated slowly to remain fixed and stern.

It was the buccaneer's last look on earth.

Chapter Thirty Eight
Last Words

The officer who led the strong boat's crew to the rescue, guided by some of Captain Armstrong's men who had escaped weeks before and after terrible privations at last found help, drew back and signed to his followers.

It was enough. Hats were doffed, and a strange silence reigned in the gloomy chamber as Humphrey knelt there holding the dead hand in his till he was touched upon the shoulder, and looking up slowly, half-stunned by the event, it was to meet the pale, drawn face of Bart.

"Do they know, captain?" he whispered, meaningly.

For a few moments Humphrey did not realise the import of his question, till he turned and gazed down once more upon the stern, handsome face fixing rigidly in death.

"No," he said quickly, as he drew a handkerchief from his breast and softly spread it over the face of the dead. "It is our secret—ours alone."

"Hah!" sighed Bart, and he drew back for a moment, and then gave Humphrey an imploring look before advancing once more, going down upon his knee, and taking and kissing the cold hand lying across the motionless breast.

"Captain Humphrey Armstrong, I think!" said the officer of the rescue party.

"Yes," said Humphrey, in a dreamy way.

"We were just in time, it seems."

"Yes," said Humphrey, with a dazed look.

"I'm glad you are safe, sir; and this is—"

He had not finished his sentence when one of Black Mazzard's men yelled out—

"The Commodore—our captain—sir!"

"Once," said Humphrey, roused by the ruffian's words, and gazing sharply round; "but one who spared my life, sir, and with this poor fellow here defended me from that dead scoundrel and his gang!"

As he spoke he spurned the body of Black Mazzard, who had hardly stirred since he received Bart's bullet.

"I am at your service, Captain Armstrong," said the officer, "and will take my instructions from you."

"For the wretches taken in arms, sir, I have nothing to say; but for this poor wounded fellow I ask proper help and protection. I will be answerable for him."

Bart looked at him quickly and reeled slightly as he limped to his side.

"Thank ye, captain," he said. "I ought to hate you, but she loved you, and that's enough for me. If I don't see you again, sir—God bless you and good-bye!"

"But we shall see each other again, Bart, and I hope—here, quick!" he cried, "help here; the poor fellow is fainting from loss of blood!"

Bart was borne off to be tended by the surgeon, and Humphrey Armstrong stood gazing down at the motionless form at his feet.

He did not speak for some minutes, and all around respected his sorrow by standing aloof; but he turned at last to the officer—

"I ask honourable burial, sir, for the dead—dead to save my life."

The officer bowed gravely, and then turned away to give a few short, sharp orders to his men, who signed to their prisoners.

These were rapidly marched down to the boats, two and two, till it came to the turn of Dinny, who stood with Mrs Greenheys clinging to him, trembling with dread.

"Now, my fine fellow," said the warrant officer who had the prisoners in charge; "this way."

"Sure, and ye'll let me have a wurrud wid the captain first?"

"No nonsense. Come along!"

"Sure, an' he'd like to shpake to me wan wurrud," said Dinny. "Wouldn't ye, sor!"

Humphrey, who was standing with his arms folded, wrapped in thought, looked up sharply on hearing the familiar tones of the Irishman's voice.

"There, what did I tell ye, sor?" he cried. "Sure, an' I'm not a buccaneer by trade—only a prishner."

Humphrey strode up, for Mrs Greenheys had run to him with clasped hands.

"I'd take it kindly of ye, sor, if ye'd explain me position to these gintlemen—that I'm not an inimy, but a friend."

"Yes," said Humphrey, turning to the officer in command; "a very good friend to me, sir, and one who would be glad to serve the king."

"Or anny wan else who behave dacently to him."

"Let him tend his companion," said Humphrey. "He is a good nurse for a wounded man."

Mistress Greenheys caught Humphrey's hand and kissed it.

"But she would have betrayed us," he said to himself, as he looked down into the little woman's tearful face; "still, it was for the sake of the man she loved."

That night, covered with the English flag, which she had so often defied, the so-called Commodore Junk was borne to the resting-place selected by Humphrey Armstrong.

It was a solemn scene as the roughly-made bier was borne by lantern-light through the dark arcade of the forest, and the sailors looked up wonderingly at the strange aspect of the mouldering old pile.

But their wonder increased as they entered the gloomy temple, and the yellow light of their lanterns fell upon the flag-draped coffin in the centre, and the weird-looking figures seated round.

Side by side with the remains of her brother, Mary Dell was laid and then draped with the same flag, spread by Humphrey Armstrong's hands, the picture exciting the wonder of the officer in command, to whom it all seemed mysterious and strange. Greater wonder than all, though, was that Humphrey Armstrong, lately a prisoner of the famous buccaneer who had been laid to rest, should display such deep emotion as he slowly left the spot.

As he stepped outside volleys were fired by the men, and as the reports of the pieces rumbled through the antique building, and echoed in the cavernous cenote, the reverberation loosened some portion of the roof over the vast reservoir; an avalanche of stone falling with a reverberating hollow splash, and a great bird flew out and disappeared in the darkness overhead.

Three days later, laden with the valuable plunder amassed by the buccaneers, and a vast amount consigned to the flames in pursuance of the orders to thoroughly destroy the hornets'-nest, the rescue ship set sail, in company with the buccaneer's fast schooner, the prize Humphrey Armstrong once longed to take into Dartmouth Harbour. But the sight of the warship's consort only gave him pain now as he lay in his berth or reclined helplessly on deck, suffering from the serious fever which supervened.

"It's a curious whim," said the captain of the ship to his lieutenant. "One would have thought he'd rather have had a couple of decent sailors to tend him, and not those two fellows, who must have been regular pirates in their time."

But it was so. Humphrey Armstrong was not content without Bart or Dinny at his side all through his severe illness, which lasted till they were nearing home.

During the voyage he learned by degrees the whole history of the escape of the relics of his crew, consequent upon the division in the camp and the chaotic state of discipline which obtained among the buccaneers during the latter days. He heard more, too, of their struggles to reach a port, and of the rescue which had been planned and successfully carried out.

One evening as Humphrey Armstrong sat on deck wondering to himself that he could be so changed as to look with distaste upon the western shores of England, gilded by the evening sun, he became conscious of another presence close behind, and looking sharply round it was to see the haggard, worn face of Bart as he stood there, bent and terribly changed by mental suffering, and his wounds.

As he saw Humphrey Armstrong gaze wonderingly at him he raised one hand and pointed to the dimly-seen cliff line, ruddy in the western glow.

"Home, sir," he cried, hoarsely.

"Yes, Bart, home," said Humphrey, gloomily. "What are you going to do!"

"You know best, sir. Prison, or the rope!"

Humphrey started sadly, and held out his hand, which the rough fellow, after a momentary hesitation, took.

"Bart, my lad," said Humphrey, "why not take the old cottage and settle down to your former life! I should like it if you'd do this thing. Will you!"

"Will I!" said the poor fellow in suffocating tones. "God bless you, sir! You've made me happier than I ever hoped to be again."

"Take it or buy it, Bart, as soon as you reach home. I wish it done, only it is to be kept unchanged, as we two keep her secret."

A fortnight had passed, during which period Humphrey Armstrong had kept himself quite in seclusion, when in obedience to a stern resolve he journeyed slowly up to town.

He had good excuse for his dilatory ways, being still far from strong; but now he was bound on the task of performing what he told himself was his duty—that of going straight to Lady Jenny Wildersey, confessing every thing in an open, manly way, and begging her to set him free from the engagement he had made.

"I could not marry such a woman now," he said to himself again and again; "she would drive me mad!"

It was a hard struggle, but he was determined to carry it through, and one morning he crossed the Park and the Mall, and made his way straight into Saint James's Square.

Everything looked the same, except himself, for he was bronzed and worn, and his countenance displayed a scar. But he was as brightly dressed as on the day he called to say fare well, for he had had to attend at the admiral's to give an account of his proceedings, and had found, to his surprise, that not only was the loss of his ship condoned by the complete rooting out of the buccaneers, but he had been promoted, and was shortly to engage in another expedition, this time to the East.

Saint James's Square looked just as of old, and the same servant opened to his hasty knock and met him with a smile.

He had come without sending notice, and he had made no inquiry since his landing, telling himself that it was better so; and now, strung up for his painful task, he strode into the great marble-paved hall.

"Ask Lady Jenny if she will see me—a private interview," he said to the ponderous old butler who came forward as the footman closed the door.

"Lady Jenny, sir? The countess is at the lakes with his lordship."

"The countess! I said Lady Jenny."

"Yes, sir," said the old butler with a smile. "We always speak of her young ladyship now as the countess."

"The countess! Why, you don't mean—"

"Yes, sir; she was married to the Earl of Winterleyton a year ago, sir. His lordship's town house is a hundred and ten Queen Square, and Hallybury, Bassenthwaite, sir."

"Oh!" said Humphrey, calmly; "I have been to the West Indies, and had not heard the news."

He nodded good-humouredly to the old butler, and went off across the square.

"Now, it's my belief," said the old butler, "that he's another on 'em as her young ladyship was always a-leading on!"

"Thank Heaven!" said Humphrey, with a sigh of relief; and he went and behaved like an Englishman, for he walked straight to his club, ordered his dinner, and for the first time for months thoroughly enjoyed it; while as he sat afterwards over the remains of his bottle of fine old Carbonell port—a wine that was likely to restore some of the lost blood to his veins—he filled his glass slowly, thought of his next expedition, and that it with its earnest work would be the best remedy for a mind diseased, and made up his mind that if he could persuade him to leave his newly-made wife he would have Dinny for one of his men.

"And old Bart, too, if he will serve," he said half aloud. Then two or three times over, as a pretty, powdered-and-painted image, all silk and gewgaws and flowers, filled his imagination, "What a release! Thank Heaven!"

At last there was but one glass left in the bottle, and raising the handled basket in which it reclined, he carefully poured it out, and held it up, seeming to see in the candle-lit, ruby rays a torrid land, a sun-browned face, and two dark, imploring eyes gazing into his till they grew dewy, and all around him seemed to be blurred and dim. He was almost alone in the great club-room, for the various diners had risen and gone, and for the time being the long, gloomy place seemed to be the old prison chamber, with its stone altar and great carven idol gazing stolidly down upon him as he said softly:

"Mary Dell! True woman! I shall never love again!"

He drained the glass to the memory of Commodore Junk, and, stubborn Englishman to the last, he kept his word.